THE STREET SEEMED DESERTED. Then he became aware that his own footsteps were being echoed, pace for pace. He looked back over his shoulder, nervously.

A small, neat man, dressed in city clothes, with a bowler hat and carrying an impeccably furled umbrella, came on behind him, perhaps ten yards away.

The man smiled cheerfully and nodded. Instinctively Willi half-raised a hand in greeting. He walked on.

Willi's mood had been so light he almost dismissed it. Instead he found himself wondering. He turned the corner past the deserted children's playground. Stealth returned. He slowed his pace fractionally, hoping to be overtaken. By half way down the long street the little man remained obstinately behind. Willi speeded up slightly.

Abruptly the footsteps behind stopped dead. The street was still empty. There was a pause of a second or two more. Then the man called out: "Reiter?"

THE GRUDGE

PAUL CHEVALIER

FAWCETT CREST • NEW YORK

THE GRUDGE

This book contains the complete text of the original hardcover edition.

Published by Fawcett Crest Books, CBS Educational and Professional Publishing, a division of CBS Inc., by arrangement with St. Martin's Press.

Copyright © 1980 by Paul Chevalier

ISBN: 0-449-24478-4

Printed in the United States of America

First Fawcett Crest Printing: January 1982

10 9 8 7 6 5 4 3 2 1

For
TONI
and for Leigh, Sylvia, Les,
Peg and John

1

The Reichsführer-SS was uneasy. He could take no pleasure in the bright August morning, or in the hushed peace of the large and superbly furnished suite at his Prinz Albrechtstrasse headquarters.

Barely a month ago, conspirators—many of whom still had to be rooted out—had attempted to cut down the Führer. Since then Himmler had been given new, extraordinary powers. In addition to his command of the powerful SS Empire and his office as Reichs Minister for the Interior, he had now become Commander in Chief of the Replacement Army. The Führer, recognising his devotion, had drawn him closer, had given him his trust and his confidence. Heinrich Himmler was proud, privileged and exalted. But this morning he was apprehensive.

He was powerful. He was entrusted with great work. But as always, there remained one obstacle to absolute confidence in himself and in his destiny under the Führer. And its name was Martin Bormann.

Himmler might have Hitler's trust and benediction, but Bormann had the Führer's ear. And as long as that situation endured there was little comfort and no lasting safety for the Reichsführer-SS.

Even had Himmler and Bormann liked each other—and they did not—it would have nettled that the sly, calculating, resourceful Party Secretary commanded a machine even more powerful than the SS with all its resources. Through its Gauleiters, the Party controlled political thought, political leadership and, of course, the Party funds. And to a man, the huge army of local and national office-holders loathed the SS. With Bormann's encouragement, even petty officials these days took pleasure in demonstrating openly their contempt for the Waffen-SS, the SD, the Gestapo and the entire complex which he, Himmler, controlled. And under Bormann's protection they were immune from its menace.

Himmler was tired. He had been overworked. The pursuit of the July 20th conspirators was proving a heavy additional burden. Now, this morning, he had a new worry: From SS informers in East Prussia he had separate and almost identical reports of a plan which would further extend Bormann's power and reach. The region's Gauleiter, Erich Koch, in his capacity as regional Defence Commissioner was proposing the formation locally of a Volkssturm, or Home Guard. Its recruits were to be the unfit, the pensioners and the teenagers. Its uniform and equipment were to come from East Prussian war factories commandeered by Koch and—worse— the suggestion was that the force should be controlled not by the Wehrmacht, not even by the Replacement Army, but by the Party. By Koch himself. Under Bormann.

Himmler looked up from the reports, his expression composed and shuttered. A worm of self-pity worked in him. There was always something ... He was loyal, he told himself. He worked like a dog, had struggled harder than most for the Reich, had deserved his honours. But always— always there was someone ready to claw him down. And almost always that someone was Bormann. He burned silently, already aware of the greater threat behind the Koch plan. He avoided the eyes of his personal assistant, Rudolf Brandt, and his masseur and confidant, Felix Kersten. Both had read the reports. Both were uneasy, fearing an outburst.

To break the uncomfortable silence, Kersten, voicing almost exactly Himmler's own immediate response, said very tentatively: "It is an affront, of course. If such an organisation is to come into being, then its recruitment, reporting—no, total control—should be the business of C-in-C Replacement Army. It must not happen."

For a moment he thought he had been too outspoken. Himmler stared at him impassively, his spectacles glittering. The splendid clock on the marble mantel ticked away a few fraught seconds. Himmler said mildly: "It is not to be borne. I am not concerned here solely with the misplaced zeal of a Party official. The wider issues are what we must be anxious about." He spoke with a soft, detached air, as he often did when he was unsure of himself. Himmler hoped it looked like only marginal concern. But it masked inner panic and both Kersten and Brandt knew it.

Kersten had served Himmler for years. His was a position unlike any other. Morell and Karl Brandt, the Führer's doctors, were simply that. They might hear an occasional unguarded exchange, might witness both the Fuhrer's command and his confusion. They might receive occasional confidences. But they were never consulted. But Kersten had a far greater role. He had been Himmler's confidant from the start. He had acted as the Reichsführer's emissary on matters both routine and dangerous, at home and abroad. It had been Kersten who, in October last year, had travelled to Stockholm to sound out British and American representatives on a peace that might, through Himmler and Schellenberg, have been made behind Hitler's back—or, if the Allies so demanded—over his dead body.

Kersten knew well enough what 'the wider issues' were. If this Home Guard of Koch's succeeded, or even if it sounded substantial enough, it would surely delight the Führer, further thrusting Bormann, as Koch's superior, into the warm spotlight of the Führer's gratitude and approval.

"The Führer will, of course, be delighted," he said aloud. He was careful to say it thoughtfully, as if testing one possible theory. "Which means that Bormann triumphs once again."

Himmler nodded. He sat back in his huge chair and completed the prognosis with a spurious air of thoughtfulness.

"It is a pity we didn't press the idea ourselves," he said. "Putting it into action, that is." He brought his fingertips together in schoolmasterish fashion. "The idea, the concept itself, has been around since the Great War. There is nothing new in it at all. However, that is not important now. What you miss, Felix, is the likelihood of a still wider result."

Kersten missed nothing, in fact. But he remained silent. He glanced at Brandt, Himmler's personal aide, who sat opposite him at exactly the same angle to the big desk. Brandt remained alert but silent. He was a simple man, able in his way, but without the stretch of imagination that could make him more than a listener in any matter beyond routine administration.

"The real danger," Himmler went on, "is that the Führer may be moved to authorise the raising of a fully national Volkssturm. And then where are we? I'll tell you. We then face a real challenge to my authority as head of the Replacement Army and yet another centre of power which would be in almost certain conflict with the Ministry of the Interior. Not to mention yet another area in which the Party Secretary would be entitled to meddle and to expand his influence."

The Reichsführer's spectacles glinted at Kersten reproachfully, "At the same time, Kersten, we must not forget that if the formation of a Volkssturm does anything to help the national war effort, or to inspire the Führer with the people's determination to wage total war and win, then it has a merit and a value which should be welcomed, regardless of personal feelings."

The rebuke was accepted. Kersten did not miss the swift switch to his surname, or the pious expression of fidelity to the Führer which since the Bomb Plot, had become such a regular part of Himmler's daily utterances. Himmler had said, publicly and privately, that Hitler's deliverance was an act of Providence; a sign to them all, the German people, that he *was* their deliverer, divinely inspired and protected. Well, almost that. Kersten cut in quickly now, sensing that Brandt might be about to echo this pious nonsense.

"I only meant, Reichsführer, that the interests of the German people and, indeed, of the Führer who has such a burden already, would not likely be best served by the Party Secretary. Now if the whole thing could be co-ordinated by yourself as C-in-C of the People's Army, what a chance there would be to make it work efficiently." He deliberately used the term 'People's Army' knowing it to be Himmler's own emotional preference.

"Yes, yes," said Himmler irritably. "But I fear it will not fall that way."

Kersten feigned thoughtfulness again and not really with anything specific in mind: "It is, of course, early days. These are reports from our own people on the spot. Nothing is announced. We have, perhaps, thirty days. There would still be time for a proposal of our own to go to the Führer. The idea is, as you say, an old one. It is not an original concept."

Himmler smiled thinly at him. Brandt smiled admiringly, too, and joined in: "Is it even possible that the proposals of the Reichsführer could arrive first at the Führer's HQ? Whatever is proposed in East Prussia may then be seen as only a spontaneous and local expression of what you had planned on a national scale."

Himmler thought about it. It was a matter of fine timing. If it fell right, it might, perhaps, be made to seem that the plan had been formed all along in the Interior Ministry. At best. At second best it might be possible, in the discussion that would naturally ensue, to cloud the matter of where exactly the plan had originated.

There were terrible risks. What if Bormann took a hand? He would be sure to see any proposal put before the Führer. He could not suppress such a proposal document; that would be too risky, even for him. But he could delay it, leapfrog the report of his own man. And even if he, Himmler, started work at once and hustled the thing to Rastenburg he might still fail to beat the Koch papers by a long stretch. Bormann was superbly placed then to represent anything arriving late from the Interior Ministry as last-minute opportunism. Worse, Bormann would be angered, and would find a way to wreak a revenge of some kind.

It was upon this thought that Himmler's resolve melted. He feared Bormann and would sooner concede the coup than arouse his rival's malice.

Pursing his lips, he said: "I think not. I cannot be seen to compete without dignity for the honour of proposing something of value. It is unseemly." He grew even more detached in tone. Leaning back in his chair, he closed his eyes and murmured: "Koch! If only we had received earlier warning. These reports suggest the plan is well advanced. It is clear that Koch will announce something, at least locally, before the end of next month. Once he has done that, there is nothing we can do."

Again the three fell silent. The clear implication was that Koch must not make any such announcement. If that were possible. Was it? Brandt gave it thought. Assassination? Too direct, too obvious; the man was a known nuisance to the SS and his death would stir up a hornet's nest. Bormann would retaliate. It was exactly the sort of thing the Führer didn't need, too.

But what, Himmler mused, if he could somehow buy time? He watched his aides, hoping for the suggestion he preferred to condone than originate.

Again Kersten knew what was expected of him. He was reluctant. Eliminating a Gauleiter of Koch's standing would be a risky business. With the treachery of July 20th still vividly in mind, with his own health still shattered, Hitler would react viciously to anything that smacked even faintly of conspiracy. It was hard to see how they could move.

Brandt said it suddenly: "An accident?"

The Reichsführer looked at them earnestly. "In these fateful times," he lectured, "none of us must shrink from any course of action which can realistically help the German people. We owe it to the Führer to grasp every means within our power to further the successful prosecution of the war and especially to take such steps as seem likely to make his sacrifice less. It follows that sometimes one will have to do

11

things which, under other circumstances, would seem improper if not downright immoral."

"Does that mean you approve?" Brandt said.

Himmler blinked. "It does, yes." He leaned forward in his chair and began spelling out, for immediate investigation, possible areas of Koch's vulnerability to fate and possible means of taking advantage of them.

But his fear of Bormann remained, and even while he spoke, his old stomach trouble seemed to return.

2

For twenty-four hours, Himmler brooded on the Koch affair. He had no real stomach for the idea of removing the man—unless it could be made absolutely foolproof. It was pleasant to contemplate, that was all. And these exercises were never entirely wasted. Ways and means . . . these days it was sensible to look into everything of the kind. Meanwhile, if Brandt had the time and patience to put together some sort of plan—well fine. Himmler alone could put it into motion: no dangerous step could be taken that might compromise him. This was his ambivalent mood as he awaited a new report.

It was Brandt who proposed the next steps the following morning. It came as something of an anti-climax to the morning's work. The search for the less obvious July 20th conspirators was now at white heat and spreading every hour. Friends, collaborators, sympathisers . . . much of Himmler's morning had already been taken up in meetings with Muller, head of the Gestapo, and Schellenberg of the SD.

Brandt, settling himself in his master's room, noted that treason and treachery seemed to have a tonic effect on Himmler. Each new root or branch of the central conspiracy uncovered by the investigators seemed to afford him some perverse pleasure and excitement. Himmler had also had his early massage from Kersten and looked relaxed, brisk and decisive.

Kersten reappeared now and Himmler indicated that he

should remain. But it was Brandt that he fixed with his impassive stare.

"You want to talk about the Koch thing," he said with the patient tone of one who permits a folly but will wash his hands of it if it should fail. "Before you begin . . . If the thing is possible, you have my backing. You alone will handle it and there will be no written orders and you will take no risks which can possibly compromise us. If you cannot offer complete success and safety—forget it. Is that understood?"

Brandt was confident so far at least. He referred to a single page of notes and began briskly: "Koch himself. Before he can make an announcement at all, he will have to come to Berlin. I think that is clear? He must check his plans with the people who would have to put them into effect?"

It was clear. Koch might have Bormann's sanction for his plan, but Bormann was currently sticking close to Hitler. And Hitler was at the Wolf's Lair in East Prussia, a long way from the central party machinery in Berlin.

"He must come to Berlin," Brandt repeated. "And it follows that he will fly. He always does. We have established . . ."

Himmler held up a hand. "Wait!" he said sharply. "No bombs. That's an amateur's game. It is unreliable. The man might even survive."

"No, Reichsführer," Brandt said. "No bombs. Koch's aircraft will crash though. Simply because the pilot will deliberately crash-land in open, difficult country.

"Once safely down, a small unit of SS will, by arrangement, be there to 'find' the wreckage, complete the picture of a tragic accident and ensure that the thing burns—along with Koch and any other passengers and the crew."

For once Himmler seemed startled. "Any other passengers?" he echoed. "Any?" He shuddered. Suppose Bormann himself were to return to Berlin, briefly, with Koch. He adjusted his expression. "Let's be clear about this. Koch would have to be the only passenger of such rank."

Brandt barely hesitated. "Koch alone, then, if opportunity offers. The pilot, alas, will have to be found in the wreckage, too. A missing pilot would hardly make the thing convincing. On the other hand, what more certain mark of authenticity could such an accident have than that the pilot, too, failed to escape?"

Himmler smiled sceptically. "And you have found a pilot willing to do away with himself?"

Brandt smiled, too, to show that he appreciated the little

joke. "No, Reichsführer. The pilot will be told that he is to be picked up by the SS unit and carried to safety and that his name will never appear on the flight plan. An authority trustworthy and acceptable to him will tell him this."

"Go on."

"It might have been thought preferable to have an SS pilot. But there are objections. If we simply substituted an SS pilot for the regular Luftwaffe pilot, there would be grave dangers if anything goes wrong. If for some reason, everyone survives, our man would be sure to be identified. Or they might discover him to be SS before he has a chance to crash. No, a Luftwaffe pilot is essential—just in case. We remain uninvolved.

"At the same time, we do need a man of considerable skill and experience—of both day and night flying. The best possible man, in fact. And I think I have the answer—a man of just such skills. And Luftwaffe. And whether he kills himself in the attempt or the SS unit deals with him . . ." Brandt shrugged.

Himmler had been shifting papers from one side of his desk to the other, seeming to be only half attending. He looked up now, doubt and disinterest evident in the pursing of his small mouth.

"The pilot we have," Brandt persisted, "is here in Berlin on leave. His mother was killed in Monday's air raid. For the moment he is free and does not have to report back to his station—"

"Which is?" Himmler cut in.

Brandt bobbed his head. Something like a giggle escaped him. "Rastenburg," he said smugly. "He is second in command there. Recommended especially by Reich Marshal Goering." On a rising note, he added: "He has even flown the Führer. He is acknowledged to be a thoroughly experienced pilot. And better still, he is a minor hero, a Knight's Cross holder, above suspicion."

Brandt had Himmler's attention now.

"There was no great work attached to this," Brandt went on modestly. "We simply started at the Rastenburg end and looked into the backgrounds of the people there. Right away, this Major Reiter's record showed that he was ideal for the job."

"Very nice," Himmler said acidly. "Now suppose you tell me why this man—Reiter, is it?—is not only going to do what is asked of him, but keep his mouth shut."

Again Brandt looked smug, sitting on the punch-line. He enjoyed the suspense as long as he dared. Then he said:

"It was good luck, really, just good luck. You see, Reiter has a brother. The brother is Standartenführer Reiter, one of our own, who is also here in Berlin on the same compassionate leave—I have put him discreetly on stand-by, incidentally. He will recruit his brother—on the certain understanding that his own career, not to say his own safety, depends upon his doing it, and doing it in total secrecy."

Himmler frowned. Brandt and Kersten watched him anxiously as he tested the logic of the proposal. After a moment or two, Himmler held out his hand without comment.

Brandt, perfectly prepared, as always, handed him the personal dossier of SS Standartenführer Eugen Reiter. Himmler studied the details and photographs briefly. "Do I know him?"

Brandt considered. "He was a guest at Wewelsburg once or twice and you probably spoke to him. But that was a long time ago, in the days of courses at Wewelsburg for Obersturmführers and ranks below. On the whole I'd have thought there's nothing there to have brought him to your notice. He's really an administrator under General Juttner rather than a fighting man."

Himmler grunted. "We all have to serve in different ways. Is he a good man?"

"Reliable," Brandt said judiciously. "Steady advancement to his present fairly senior rank. No blemish of any kind."

Himmler looked up, expressionless behind the glinting spectacles. "Unfortunate," he said thoughtfully, "to lose a good servant like this. Always assuming, that is, that we go ahead with this idea of yours. You understand?" Brandt hesitated only fractionally. He understood. Neither of the Reiters was to be allowed to live. "Perhaps the brother Eugen could be careless during the next raid on Berlin." Himmler squinted at Brandt to see if he was taking it in. "After all, some good men are, every time."

Himmler studied the papers a few moments more. He shook his head. "It isn't exactly without cost, is it? All this trouble . . ." He chewed the inside of his cheek. At last he conceded: "It has a certain value, Rudolf. The problems, though, are enormous. You will need total secrecy and perfect timing. Not the easiest of commodities." He turned to Kersten. "Lend a hand here, Felix, will you? You have a sure touch." He turned away and got up to stand looking down on the city below. The day was again warm and bright but the windows remained closed. Pneumatic drills were at work on the broad avenue, where gangs were urgently repairing a big water main ruptured during the last RAF raid.

The good weather remained the only crumb of comfort. The war news was bad. Both Brandt and Kersten were privately appalled. American troops were reportedly in Nantes and Angers and driving on towards the Loire. On the Eastern front the Russians had broken through the Marienburg Line, and the British and Canadians were racing towards Holland. There were even rumours that Turkey might repudiate their pact of friendship with Germany and change sides.

Outside, a ravaged Berlin sprawled dustily under skies of cloudless blue. On the surface it was calm enough. But there was scarcely anyone who did not shiver at the thought of what might happen before winter came again. At one time it had been possible to grumble, to express doubts even. In August 1944 no-one dared criticise anything at all. You kept your mouth shut and your head down. Anything else was suicidal. The cells were already packed with famous names: Generals, men of achievement and honourable service. Schellenberg's and Gestapo Muller's men were everywhere. The trials of their victims were being held in halls, classrooms, anywhere. Summary executions followed the trials around the clock.

Himmler seemed to come out of his reverie. He looked at Brandt directly. "All right," he said. "Take the next step. Carefully. And do nothing which is outside our own resources. See Reiter and report again. Don't fail me." He spoke softly, gently even. But the threat was clear. He motioned with his hand dismissively that Kersten should leave. To Brandt he signalled that he was ready for his next appointment.

3

In the early evening of that same August day, Harvey Marsh left his two-roomed flat in Temple Chambers and walked shirt-sleeved and reluctant up Bouverie Street to his night shift. He carried an old cricket pullover just in case.

This was the last of four twelve-hour shifts before his three days off. The dying day was marvellous; the river, behind him, infinitely appealing. And it was cooler down there. Ahead, on the *Evening News* corner, the long rows of yellow vans were quiet at last, but the buildings themselves still exhaled the familiar halitosis of warm machinery and printers' ink.

For once there was no raid in progress. That was something. There had been eight the day before, four of them between seven and nine in the evening. Well, they were alerts really, rather than raids. No manned German aircraft ventured as far as London at this stage of the war: just the incessant V1's—which were wearing everyone down. He was tired, edgy, stale. He longed to get away, was impatient to see something of the war at first hand before it ended. Weeks had gone by since McNair had tipped him that accreditation was only a matter of time.

It was something he couldn't hurry. McNair did what he could, but the War Office would move when it would. Forget it. There were some compensations while he waited. When his shift was over he would go up to the MOI, have breakfast there, wait while Ronnie got ready—perhaps napping in a chair—and then go home to her place. It had been a long summer, this. These mornings when they went home together had a golden, dreamlike quality about them that made up for almost everything else. The sirens, the guns and the heat made sleep impossible. But they would drink tea, smoke, make love, sleep a little, wake, make love—and so on until the cool of the evening and the time for their respective shifts.

On the steps of the office he stopped to look back at the wedge of river he could see; one more look before submerging. The barrage balloons were riding high in the pink sky over the south bank. He thought he heard a distant roll of thunder. Inside the building the air conditioning seemed to be off again. Going up in the lift sweat began to break out on the inside of his arms.

Bass was on the Desk. Harvey sighed. It always took Bass longer than anyone else to hand over. He was the kind who hung around, looking for compliments, building alibis or giving gratuitous advice.

His own deputies on the main Desk seemed to be Dixon and Banning. He checked that off on the rota pinned to the board. Dixon was a smoothie, reliable, but an unreachable personality. Banning was a sulky trainee who swung unpredictably between a word-perfect or hopeless re-write. Tyson was sitting at the Teleprinter Board. Coming or Going? He checked that off, too. Coming in. Good. Tyson was the best. None of the rest of his shift mattered much. With luck he'd get through the night without having to talk to any of them. And his relief at eight in the morning? . . . Sam Prentice. That was a bonus. Sam was always early.

Harvey waited, watching Bass pound his heavyweight Royal with bitten, ruined fingers. Finally, he got in: "Anything running?"

Bass smiled, detachedly, held up a restraining finger and thumped to the end of the paragraph. He pulled out the carbon-book with an old-timer's all-in-one flourish and yelled: "Copy!"

Tyson, behind him, unmoved, a dead half-inch of cigarette wobbling on his underlip, snatched it and had the first words on the wire without sitting down to the keys. Harvey smiled. It could have been Hitler's obituary or Errol Flynn on a rape charge; Tyson would have done it poker-faced, standing, cigarette end dangling.

Bass was fidgeting with the bunches of flimsies under the bridge of the Desk. That looked bad; stuff neither spiked nor used was another Bass fault. He hoarded cables, wanting to talk them out with his relief. In the end they were apt to come up in the copy of the next shift, and late. Harvey walked round behind him and riffled. One bunch was Wilson, with 7th Army, yards of it, all colour and no substance. That wanted stopping. Another bunch was scraps from MacArthur's HQ in the Pacific; there was nothing worth even a page now, but enough bits and pieces, perhaps, to hash together for a morning roundup story on the whole Pacific theatre. There was some other stuff he couldn't make sense of yet.

"Quiet," Bass announced.

"Thank Christ."

"Anything good is out. Flashed in full, then summaries. And it's all out on confirmation copy except what's outside with the lads now. Nothing else threatens." Bass nibbled the remains of a fingernail already well down the fleshline. "With any luck the midnight Russian Communique will be your worst. Christ, I hope I'm not on the night they link with the Americans."

Harvey grunted. "How's the book?" Bass was doing a book

on butterflies. It was one of the many hobbies he turned into books. He sat most of the night when it was quiet enough, feeding the juniors his copy and then splattering the results with black pencil.

"Great. Halfway at least." Bass nodded, looked at Harvey and got up. Harvey slid into the Night Editor's chair behind him. The Hot Seat. He lifted his chin at the youngsters. He began reading in.

Bass was about ready to leave next time he glanced up. "Sorry about all that garbage," Bass said. "I didn't have a chance to do it but perhaps you'd better put a stop on Wilson. He's overdoing it, costing us a fortune. The Old Man will go mad. There's nowhere we can use all that stuff about the French. He's sent five hundred already and he's still at it."

As if to confirm it, the nearest teleprinter bell rang. Tyson tucked a fresh cable flimsy from Wilson under Harvey's cigarettes. What got into war correspondents? You gave them a uniform and a portable typewriter, put them on a plane to the war and straight away every last one of them forgot reporting, economy and speed and became a writer of immortal, descriptive prose.

Harvey looked up, nodded a goodbye to Bass and scribbled a cable to Wilson: UNNEED FURTHER FRENCH COLOUR UNLESS SUBSTANTIAL GAINS.

By nine he'd read in, tidied up, had all the strings in hand, and nothing fresh had broken out anywhere in the world. The juniors had turned in some good re-writes. He resolved Bass's leftovers by ramming them firmly on the 'not' spike. He was ready to assume command.

"Let's have some tea," he said. He stabbed the Despatch bell and Phil, the most competent of the Despatch shift managers appeared, beaming. Phil was a hard little man from Hackney. He wore sleeve garters and trousers that came up almost to his armpits. Harvey was glad to see him. He was quick, clean and cheerful. "Thank God it's you," he said.

Phil nodded: "You've got the quality tonight."

"Get some tea put on, eh? And toast. Let's live while the war stands still."

The subs relaxed and smiled a little, even Banning. While they were waiting, Harvey took a look at Rommel's Obit, hanging ready on a hook. At ten-fifteen the early papers came up and he marked them all dutifully with the agency's scores.

The night slipped by in routine. He didn't even remember Ronnie until about three a.m. The Russian communique, as Bass had suggested, was a bastard. The usual tortured language, strings of place-names announced as taken, lists of tanks, guns and equipment either captured or destroyed—and the real substance buried in the verbiage so that only fevered work on the maps, re-drawing the whole profile of the Russian thrust, could reveal the real story. Finally it was done and out on the wire.

A card school began out in Despatch. Behind Harvey, Tyson was napping, awkwardly, his face flopped sideways on the copy-holder of his main teleprinter. The juniors stolidly began work on rehashing the news of the last twelve hours into Morning Roundups, to be taped and re-issued at six.

Harvey smoked quietly, unable to sleep. He amused himself by writing his favourite word into a piece of Banning's about Rabaul airfield. The last Japanese pockets of resistance were being winkled out . . . 'winkled' was a word Harvey had invented in 1942. It had superseded 'mopping up' in print everywhere these days. He thought of it as his contribution to the war.

At last he sat back, stunned by the heat. The windows were closed and the blackout in place. The room was thick with smoke. He felt ten years older than when he'd arrived. He lit a cigarette and felt himself to be withdrawing up a long tunnel. The din of typewriters and teleprinters receded.

Could he part with Ronnie? More than anything else he wanted to go home and lie in Ronnie's arms. What was so terrible about doing it Ronnie's way? No more of this. No more bitter tea and red-eyed nights. No more McNair and no more Bass. Just Ronnie and the kind of life her father would provide.

No, wait. He spelled it out to himself, for the thousandth time. He could not have Ronnie and persist with his bid to join Wilson and the others in the field. He could have accreditation. He could have a uniform, go out there, stay there, moving with the armies until it was all over. Then what? The Paris bureau? Berlin? The Big Time. He mocked himself with the words.

But he couldn't have that and Ronnie. She had made that very clear. There were other, simpler ways of earning a living. And Ronnie's idea of a living was not sitting at home in Surbiton or Sheen writing letters to a husband married to a different way of life. He was sure she loved him. But with the reservations and conditions of a young woman from another world entirely.

He jumped when the teleprinter behind him, under Tyson's head, came to life.

"Harve," Tyson warned.

Harvey got up and took a look. He came wide awake.

"Let it come and let's get the flash going," he said. "Three bells, right? Flash—"

"Wait, I haven't got them all in." Tyson's fingers flickered over his switches, checking the daily and evening papers were in, the specials and others out. He flushed through the imprint of his copyholder still clear on his cheek.

"Christ!" Harvey snapped. "Come on! 'Flash. British High Commissioner, two officers and two NCOs killed in Irgun terrorist attack in Jerusalem tonight. More. Ends Flash.' Okay?" He checked his watch. "Christ, we lost about five seconds there. If Reuter was faster, McNair will have my balls. Keep the sodding things switched in, ready for anything, will you?" Harvey beckoned. "Banning, put this out as a confirmation will you, and check if there's a hand delivery just about now. Dixon, watch this printer and feed the adds to that flash out as fast as the stuff comes in."

The room came alive again. Tyson, humbled, began putting the Morning Leads onto Creed tape for automatic running in an hour. Phil appeared with more tea. Light appeared round the edges of the blackout. Typewriters began to crash. The night and the calm were over.

At seven-forty-five, Sam Prentice, bearded, imperturbable and inscrutable, came in wearing a Poilu helmet and began to read himself in. Almost before he had realised it, Harvey was off the Desk, stretching, yawning, scratching. Red-eyed, with a terrible taste in his mouth, he went down two flights to clean his teeth and shave. By eight he was speeding in a cab through the morning chill to the Ministry of Information in Russell Square.

The modern wedding-cake edifice which had been Senate House of London University looked dormant and improbable at that time of day. A giant, white mausoleum, perhaps; a Bloomsbury oddity of arcane purpose—but never the swarming home of the world's free press. Its orginal interiors had been subdivided, boxed, partitioned and apportioned to a degree which made it impossible to recognise the interior from its pre-war grandeur.

The man in the front hall examined his Press pass carefully, though he knew Harvey well, saw him eight times a week, coming and going. Harvey privately thought he was one of Ronnie's many ageing admirers and he wondered now if the man disliked him because he was so patently The Mouth's lover and thus enjoying something that so many men in the building would have given a year's money for.

He hesitated before going up to the canteen. On impulse he walked instead to the ABP office, a partitioned cubbyhole that was exactly one third of a room looking out onto the Goodge Street frontage. Associated Press had the left-hand third and the *Chicago Sun* the other. P.A.-Reuter had the luxury of a whole room a few yards further along the corridor.

There was no-one in the agency's MOI hutch, but AP's door stood ajar and the ABP man was in there, sweet-talking Berenice, a very beautiful girl with the fastest shorthand and the saddest face Harvey had ever seen. She always looked pure, burnished and elegant, and her reputation was spotless, too, which in this place was something of an achievement. The old joke about the Press Section was that when a three-bell signal was given in the early hours for a read-out communique, what everyone rushed out quickly for was not to take down the communique but to see who was emerging in dressing gowns and disarray from which office.

"You look lovely, Berenice," he told her. He lifted a hand to Vic Hall, a mousy old gent who maintained the fiction that he liked the job because it gave him 'plenty of time for free-lance work'.

Berenice smiled. She was the only woman Harvey had ever known who could do that; just smile, and make it into a greeting, a thank-you and an equable comment that words would have destroyed.

"Anything, Vic?"

"Nothing you don't know about. One short Air Ministry and Ministry of Home Security bulletin last night: eleven dead, 31 injured. Another early this morning, roughly the same. I think one of the bloody things knocked a piece off Olympia last night. There were still heavy rescue rigs up there as I came past on the bus."

Upstairs in the canteen the first rush was over. The night shift people had breakfasted and gone home to sleep if they could. The day shift hadn't been in long enough to justify coffee. Only a few tables were occupied by late breakfasters who were either in no hurry to go home—or had already eaten this week's egg.

He couldn't see Ronnie at first. He took a tray and wondered dyspeptically if he really wanted to eat anything. But Gwen, a motherly 40-year-old in whom Ronnie trusted, produced a plate for him; bacon and egg. He took it guiltily.

"You've got to keep your strength up," she said, winking lewdly. She always said the same thing.

Then Ronnie came through from the kitchen. His gut lurched, as it always did when he first saw her.

Ronnie Croft was not a great beauty. Her face was too softly contoured for classic looks. Her eyes too widely, candidly open for chic. She was built a little too generously and could not have modelled her own dress size with style. But she had this mouth—was known throughout the building and parts of Fleet Street as just that: The Mouth. It was wide and full. The top lip arched outrageously, exposing a subtle margin of white teeth, and both lips presented almost vertically, rather than horizontally. It gave her mouth a look of exquisite delicacy. The lips seemed never to be set firmly, but always marginally, breathlessly open. It riveted the attention, turned heads, broke strong men, won all her battles for her easily.

And Ronnie shone. She had a radiance, an animation, a nervous intensity of appeal which was almost an aura. Her hair was dark and shoulder length, but coiled up in the wartime halo-band which was so popular now. She wore no rings or jewellery and her own clothes were all but covered by a white, regulation kitchen-coat. And yet she looked, as she always did, a rich man's child.

Ronnie smiled at him and the happiness she beamed at everyone was almost unbearable. Almost giddy with this effect, Harvey tried to sound offhand. "Nearly through?"

"Five minutes." She went on smiling until she shook it off with a movement of her head.

He was almost through with the egg and bacon when she came across to his table, carrying two coffees.

"I know what you want to do this morning," she said. "You want to walk all the way home, shower and lie in bed with me all day until six tonight. Isn't that right?"

Harvey wanted to say that he ought to go out to Eastcote sometime and see his father for an hour or two. He hadn't seen him for a month. It was Saturday and Frank Marsh was always at home on Saturday afternoons. In the morning he would go out and gather his fragmented one-person rations. At this time of the year he would work in the garden until it

23

was nearly dark. Only later would he change and walk round to his pub.

"Brilliant diagnosis, Miss Croft. Except a cab is quicker than walking. And it saves energy I can use in better ways."

Ronnie shook her head, wondering. "Six foot one, built like a storm trooper and can't be used in the Army, Navy, Air Force or Marines because you had rheumatic fever as a child. Incredible. If they could see your staying power in bed, love, the Medical Board would want to run a new check on you."

"I never performed for an audience," Harvey said thoughtfully. "Does it appeal?"

"You're a randy sod, Harvey Marsh. And you have egg on your lip. Come home with me, then. But tomorrow we'll go out and see your Dad. It's more than a month since you went, and you don't know if he's alive or dead."

Harvey drank his coffee and went silently through the private purgatory of his meeting-Ronnie routine. McNair could stick the war correspondent job. He would quit ABP and take anything that Ronnie's father offered. He would marry Ronnie after all and grow rich and sleek and have Ronnie every day of his life that he was able.

It was a reaction he experienced four times a week when he came off shift, sick of sordid newsrooms, tired and in need of the arms of a beautiful woman. He knew he would feel different later. Fervently he hoped he could keep his mouth shut until then.

4

SS Standartenführer Dr. Rudolf Brandt was enjoying himself. He had kept his visitor waiting for 90 minutes. For an SS Colonel, Reiter looked uncommonly nervous and impressionable. At 38 he was young for his rank, considering he had won no decorations, exhibited no bravery, and seen little action.

"Sit down," Brandt said. And turning, stood at the window for some moments in unconscious imitation of Himmler himself. Even more demoralising, he then paced the room, behind his visitor's back.

"You are something to do with Officers' Records, I think. Under General Juttner?"

Reiter, relieved at finding the interview on a tangible level, agreed. "Yes, I have overall care of—"

"Never mind," Brandt interrupted. "We have a change of pace for you. You are now required to do something for the SS, for your country even. Something considerably more adventurous." He paced a little more to let this sink in.

Reiter looked both irritated and uncomfortable. He was a tall man, but thin. His looks were a contradiction. Full face he was pleasant looking, handsome even. In profile the features appeared hawkish, drawn and covert; the eyes restive and fearful. He said nothing, inclining his head this way and that as Brandt passed. He tried to remember to smile.

"You have a brother," Brandt said abruptly. "A Luftwaffe officer." It was not a question.

"Correct, Dr Brandt."

"I know it is correct. I know everything about you. You are on leave here in Berlin. Your brother is also on leave. Your mother was killed in an air raid last week." He sat down now, behind his desk, and stared at Reiter.

"Now listen. The SS has need of your brother's services. His skills. It is a matter of the utmost secrecy. For various reasons, the Reichsführer does not wish to use an SS pilot. Your brother has immense flying skill. The job to be done demands those skills. It is as simple as that. You—" Brandt let his palm fall heavily on his blotter—"You are privileged to persuade your brother to undertake a simple task on behalf of the SS."

Eugen Reiter paled. He thought himself a good SS man. But this had the feel of something dangerous, he didn't know why. 'Utmost secrecy. For various reasons . . .' He licked his lips nervously.

"The Reichsführer wishes this?" he said. He didn't altogether recognise his own voice.

"He does," Brandt said. "It is not a long job. With any luck your brother might even continue his present leave. From the moment of commencement to the end of the task might be less than twenty-four hours. Once it is ready, that is, to begin. It is even possible that your brother's superiors will never need to know that he has left Berlin. If there is a delay, however, he will plead illness before returning."

Reiter, flustered, now considered. It didn't sound too bad after all.

"My task?" he said. "What must—what may I do in the Reichsführer's service?"

"Nothing more." Brandt said airily. "Recruit your brother for this one simple job. That is all."

Reiter began to look and feel more confident. "Then I will approach him immediately." He gave his knee a little slap with his glove and made to stand up.

"Sit down," Brandt said coldly. "There is a little more to it than that." He leaned back in his chair, gratified that Reiter's smile had vanished again. Poor stuff, some of the SS these days. It had been a different matter at the start. Still, Reiter was only an admin man, a glorified clerk.

"I must tell you," Brandt said, "that your brother will almost certainly not like the mission. The Luftwaffe has that tradition; in some arms of the Services they can afford to have scruples and ideals. No doubt your brother indulges himself in this way, too.

"To begin with, we are talking about one flight, almost certainly from Rastenburg to Berlin. By day or night, I couldn't say. Your brother will hold himself in twenty-four hour readiness from the moment you have spoken with him. I say from Rastenburg to Berlin, but in fact the aircraft will never reach Berlin. It will crash-land. And it will do this in a specific area to be detailed later; open, difficult country. Your brother will either force-land with the aircraft or jump. In either event he will be picked up by an SS unit and returned to Berlin. The fate of the aircraft and its passengers, if any, their identity—none of these things will concern him. The aircraft will almost certainly be a Junkers 52 transport from his own command." He watched Reiter digest this much.

Reiter was appalled. The airfield at Rastenburg was used regularly by both high-ranking officials from the East Prussian capital and by travellers to and from the Führer's HQ at Wolf's Lair. The Führer himself, though he had his own pilot, had sometimes been carried by his brother Willi's command. He knew now why he had felt uneasy about the proposition. Remembering the bomb plot of so short a time ago, he was seized by the sudden fear that he had stumbled into a fresh development of that conspiracy.

His mouth dry, he tried to sound controlled. He had to get away from here and think about his next move. He said anxiously, and a trifle irrelevantly: "From his own command? I think you said, Dr Brandt, that no-one would know of this. If he left his own field . . ."

Brandt was impatient. "Yes, yes. Let us say that he will have, uh, assistance, in quietly and discreetly exchanging places at the last moment with the pilot routinely detailed for the flight."

Reiter nodded judiciously, his mind in a whirl. "And the pilot who is displaced?"

"Will not live," Brandt said.

Reiter ran out of questions. It was mad. It sounded dangerous to the point of lunacy. What is more, he was perfectly sure Willi wouldn't listen to any of it. Even if he, Eugen, asked it, begged it even, on the grounds that it would harm his career if he could not perform the only thing that he had ever been asked by the Reichsführer-SS himself. Or his personal assistant, that is. A new and equally worrying thought hit him. What if the Reichsführer-SS was not asking it; was in fact in ignorance of the whole thing? He was out of his depth, and he trembled inwardly. His palms sweated. Cold sweat ran from under his arms and trickled down into his shirt at the waist.

"Doctor," he said, his voice unstable, "my brother Willi is a strong-minded man. As you say, the Luftwaffe does rather indulge itself in the matter of principles. I feel sure he would never agree to taking part in this mission. I don't, frankly, see how he can be involved. For myself, I know better than to ask the purpose of the undertaking. But I'm sure he would." He did his best to look earnest and sincere. "I am very much afraid that it simply wouldn't be possible to persuade him." He lifted his hand, inviting Brandt to see that his hands were tied in the matter.

Brandt studied him for a moment. What he'd seen of Reiter he didn't much like. That helped. He let his anger grow. He was suddenly furious with jumped-up, faithless bastards like this. Flash young bastards, keen enough to wear the uniform of the SS, they had been through all the training, taken the oaths of allegiance, but still had no idea of where their first loyalty lay. People like this Reiter had sat farting about in their offices all through the war, safe behind their planning boards and their routines. Their war had been merely the loss of luxuries and some small discomforts. That was all. Discomfort! He'd bring this one up to date—and swiftly.

He said, very quietly. "Standartenführer, you don't understand. The Reichsführer does not ask, he commands it. And you will not fail. You may tell your brother this—and it may stiffen his arrogant Luftwaffe backbone somewhat—if he does not perform this task, and satisfactorily at that, you will both live to regret it." He paused. But not for long.

"The same applies if one word of this conversation comes to the wrong ears—by any route." He smiled grotesquely at Reiter, enjoying the frozen astonishment, the indignation and naked fear that Reiter showed in quick succession.

Eugen Reiter struggled to speak. For a moment Brandt thought he was going to be violent. Finally, he managed, through teeth clamped together: "Threats, Dr Brandt? Threats? I am a senior officer, a good party member." His voice was a strangled squeak. "I cannot believe that General Juttner will approve this kind of treatment of one of his officers." The words were brave enough, but Reiter's jerky agitation suggested deep fear.

Brandt stood up. "I hope you will not speak of this to Obergruppenführer Juttner," he said mildly. "The Reichsführer would regard that as a very serious indiscretion. For the rest, you have your instructions. You will do as you are told." Then, as he saw Reiter's effort to regain his composure, Brandt erupted theatrically: "Where the hell have you been while this war was being fought? Here and now in Berlin you must know the cells are full of well-meaning idiots. Better men, more senior than you, my friend, disappear daily and never again see the light. It's your choice. You will recruit your brother and you will both keep your mouths shut, or you'll follow your mother to the family vault before the week is out."

Carried away with his performance, Brandt suddenly seized Reiter's cap from the edge of his desk and hurled it at the door. "You are dismissed! You will be sent for when I am ready."

He watched Reiter falter to the door and bend to pick up his cap, defeat and humiliation in every line of his back. Bravo, he told himself. Uncle Heinrich would have been pleased with all that.

But when the door closed he sat for a moment, wondering if he hadn't gone a bit over the top, gambled just a little too much. Himmler had said nothing about threats on the scale that he'd used against Reiter. It was a fairly serious matter. If Reiter blabbed everything to his superior, Juttner, for instance . . . Himmler would not welcome having to explain any part of the affair to a man of such high rank, albeit a subordinate.

Brandt endured an uncomfortable moment in which he

wondered if he wouldn't end up in a cell somewhere himself. It only needed one of these affairs—and there were many of them, these days—to go wrong, badly wrong. This week it was the Reiters. Last week someone else. Next week . . . ? He thrust the thought away. It wasn't likely this time, anyway, he told himself. Reiter would do as he was told. And if he couldn't for some reason perform it, he would be quietly eliminated anyway . . .

5

Reimund Reiter, portly and balding, was an emotional man, easily upset. At 58, his heart was not good; he had angina pains every time an air raid warning sounded. Now, at dinner with his nephews, Eugen and Willi, he felt the angina grip his chest. Nothing had been said, but that further trouble was about to fall on the house of Reiter he had no doubt. And he trembled.

One look at Eugen's face gave him enough to worry about. Eugen was the cocky one; arrogant, self-assured, ideal SS material. Tonight, as they sat down to eat, Eugen had somehow crumbled. Something had replaced his usual unlikeable mask of superiority with one of misery and fear. And nothing was so catching as fear. His brother Willi, always the quiet one, had seen it but evidently chose to ignore it. So they ate in stolid silence, fear like a guest at dinner.

Their uncle felt old and tired and he wished both of them a hundred miles away. This was his home and he had immediately opened it to them when their own home had been blasted into rubble. It had seemed a good idea at the time. He needed company, would have preferred Willi alone, but could not bring himself to make the gesture of excluding Eugen.

His wife had been killed in April 1943, running, too late, to the shelter. Their only son, Helmut, had died at Voronezh while performing battlefront surgery on the ravaged bodies left in the wake of a savage tank battle. What was left? He was a dentist, or had been. His practice, formerly the most fashionable in this once elegant suburb of Berlin, was now almost at a standstill. What work there was left gave him no interest or comfort. When the Russian Bear was at the back door, what need had sheep of teeth?

Reimund, a sentimental little man, also felt cheated. This might have been a pleasant evening. Frau Krause, his housekeeper, had made a fine stew from God knew what. For once there was enough for everyone. He himself had produced a bottle of fine Italian wine he had been saving for months. Even if the RAF came again, for a while at least it could have been a little like the old days, with one's own kin, *die Verwandte*, around. Worse days, the winter, he knew, would not be long in coming. Tonight could have been a little something to remember. He might even have found something in Eugen to like, which, God knew, was difficult enough.

He ate his stew, greedily, determined to enjoy that at least, and as he ate he looked anxiously from face to face. Eugen seemed to have difficulty eating at all. Willi, a sensitive young man, looked impassive. He could not have helped notice the change in his brother, but seemed determined not to acknowledge it. Reimund sighed, poured himself some more wine. He put their unbending silence down to the tragic loss of their mother—though he had not known a time, even as little boys, when Eugen and Willi had been close.

They got somehow to the end of the meal. Reimund pushed his plate away. Immediately, Eugen got half to his feet.

"Uncle, if you could excuse us, I must speak privately with Willi. It is a matter of urgency. Perhaps Frau Krause could clear later. This won't wait."

Fearful, the little dentist left the room. But outside the double doors of his dining room, he halted and remained there, straining to hear what was said. Eugen should not treat him in this way, he thought. In his own house! And yet he had the certain feeling that he did not, would not, want to know what had caused so remarkable a change in the demeanour of SS Standartenführer Eugen Reiter. When SS colonels were worried, for God's sake, what hope was there for anyone else?

The double doors were too thick. He could distinguish Eugen's voice, but not what he said. He spoke for several minutes in a low voice. Willi, so far as he could tell, had said nothing at all.

Inside the room, Willi listened incredulously to his brother's account of his extraordinary interview with Brandt. He sat very still, his chin in his cupped hands. While he looked calm enough his mind seethed. He caught his breath as

Brandt's mad plan was unfolded. With an immense effort of will, he continued to stare coldly. It was all ludicrous, of course. Perhaps just barely possible to carry out, even in terms that would suit Brandt. But dangerous even to contemplate. Dangerous if it succeeded, dangerous if it didn't. Dangerous to become involved even remotely in any kind of wild conspiracy, even if the target were not the Führer himself but someone who had simply become inconvenient to the SS. It was unthinkable. He watched Eugen's face, pinched and strained as he had never seen it in five years of war, wearing fear for the first time—and nakedly.

His attention slipped for a moment. He found himself thinking about his mother again. The wonderful woman. Gentle, self-sacrificing, as German in the end as any of them, though the family had given her a bad time when she had first come from England to marry his father. He remembered her with love; understanding now, for the very first time, something of what her life must have been here in Berlin all these years. She had been torn by the war with England; she had confessed it to him once, and then never again yielded to such unproductive, un-German emotions. At the outbreak of war in order to be truly patriotic she had given up speaking English, even to him, though she had taught him as a child (Eugen had no ear for languages) and conversations between them had always been in English. Willi missed her. He watched Eugen's mouth moving and he wondered what she would have made of this. He felt she had been betrayed somehow.

His brother stopped speaking. He was on his feet, gripping the back of his chair.

"For Christ's sake, say something," Eugen whispered.

Willi got up and moved steadily to the door. "You're mad," he said. He almost smiled. He had never much liked his brother. He felt almost glad of the betrayal; it left him free to indulge dislike fully for the first time. At the back of his mind a voice spoke one phrase: Eugen no longer exists. He shook the thought off. That was—theatrical, unnecessary.

As he reached the door, Eugen thrust him aside and got his back to it. Something like a flush was creeping into his pallor, and his breathing was ragged.

"This is very, very serious, Willi. You can't just walk away."

Willi looked at him coldly, making no attempt to pass. "I don't care how serious it is—for you. You're mad if you think

I'm going anywhere near that bunch of ghouls in the Prinz Albrechtstrasse."

Eugen put out a restraining hand. He softened his voice, keeping his tone urgent and insistent. "You're not listening, Willi. I didn't say this was a request, a thing lightly asked. It's an order, and one which has to be obeyed."

As Willi opened his mouth to speak, his brother cut in: "Listen. Please listen. I know—I know what you're going to say. That Himmler doesn't give orders to the Luftwaffe. But I've been told that we don't have any choice. Do you understand that? Either I successfully recruit you for this job, or they'll kill us both. Do you hear me?"

Willi sagged and stepped away from the door. "All right," he said. "I can see that you believe it. But you're letting your desire to please your masters run away with you. All right, they said it. I believe that much. You always were a humourless bastard, a bit literal minded. You wouldn't have been SS material if you weren't." He sat down wearily at the head of the table. "They wouldn't dare do anything of the sort. To you possibly. Just possibly." He looked at Eugen coldly. "That's your problem. It always has been. You're in a dirty trade. Don't tell me that in your Officers Records that you haven't closed the files a few times on people—friends even. People just like yourself: well-meaning, enjoying the uniform and the grubby glory one minute—and in someone's way the next. What did you think about the SS then? That it was all part of the risk? Well you were taking the same risk, brother, all these years. And now it's your turn. Your luck has run out. But don't involve me."

Eugen looked panic-stricken. "They'll kill you," he said. "You stupid bastard. Christ, that smug air force attitude makes me sick. This isn't one of your high-minded games. Brandt spelled it out to me and I'll do the same for you. The cells in Berlin are full of men of good conscience. The only temporary shortage is of walls and firing squads enough to stand them up against. Do you really think I'll get a rap over the knuckles and a black mark on my sheet? Listen, Willi, if I go back without you, you'll never see me again. Try that on your conscience." He came forward a few steps and pointed a trembling finger at Willi: "What would our mother think of you? That you had a chance to keep us both alive and couldn't quite bring yourself to it?"

Willi sat quietly at the table, staring into the soft gloss of the wood. Incredible. He found it all incredible. He remembered this same table, before the war, groaning with food, glistening in the candlelight, reflecting happy faces and good times. He had sat there as a child, listening to his father's voice, his mother's; how could things have changed so much? It was all gone. Only the table remained, and that, nowadays, Uncle Reimund normally kept under a blanket in the innermost corner of the room, against the danger of flying glass and debris.

He was aware that Eugen had stopped talking, was watching him closely. He tried hard to appear to be thinking things over. At last he roused himself to say: "Give me a little time. Your concern for me and my conscience is touching. Your own danger, frankly, leaves me cold. You've run with that pack all these years and enjoyed every minute of it. Now they've turned on you it's no fun any more. Well tough." He reached out and touched the lip of a silver bread bowl, one of the few treasures miraculously salvaged from their own home and brought here to Uncle Reimund for safe keeping. He looked up at Eugen. "For our parents' sake, I'll think about it. That's a big step. To give thought to murder, brother of mine. A bloody big step. So whether it's yes or no from me, that's it between you and me anyway. If I do it, I won't want you within a hundred miles of reminding me. If I don't, well you asked just the same, and it's something no-one asks even of his brother. Either way, I don't want you near me."

Something of Eugen's composure returned. He might not have heard anything except the promise of consideration. "How long will you want?" he asked.

Willi stood up. "Give me until morning," he said.

Eugen tried to manage a smile. "I think I know how you feel, Willi. But these are terrible times. Look what's happened in Germany. It's unbelievable that we could come to this. Things are bad. Desperate even. If it's for Germany, how can any of us hold out for clean hands?"

Willi's expression of disgust was undisguised.

"Piss off," he said.

Outside the room, Reimund Reiter stepped away from the door softly. His heart thumped painfully, and he had difficulty in getting his breath. When Willi emerged, Reimund appeared to be coming from the living room.

"All finished?" he asked Willi shakily.

Willi smiled and slipped an arm around his shoulders.

"All finished, uncle. Let's go and sit a while like old times.

33

Tell me about the songs we used to sing here. Does the piano still play?" He led the old man into the room across the hall.

For a while he sat smiling, listening to the little dentist's nostalgic stories of life in the great old times. He needed to listen. If Eugen was right, there would be precious little future for either of them. And that might just kill off this last, gentle, rather foolish old man, the last of the Reiters.

He had told Eugen he would sleep on it. But he knew that he wasn't going to do anything of the sort. He would have to go to Pelz or Milch or someone with this, whatever the consequence for Eugen of his doing so. He would have no regrets. Or if he did, he would smother them, the way for years now one had had to smother much else. Eugen was a lout, the perfect SS man except that it was doubtful he even had the physical courage that some of the kind had. He didn't feel anything toward Eugen. All that had begun to trickle away years ago.

He was impatient for the morning. There would be no rest until he had got this off his back. It was even possible that the story wasn't safe with Milch, Goering or anyone. Both he and Eugen had in one absurd stroke of fate become an embarrassment. Perhaps neither would be allowed to live.

Willi smiled. If that was the way of it . . . He shrugged it off in his mind. He was lucky, perhaps, to have survived thus far anyway.

6

Up in London's West End, despite the brilliant early evening sunshine, the night had begun for thousands seeking a few hours of release from the drudgery of war. For factory workers, bored wives whose husbands were away fighting the war, servicemen and women on leave and for the soldiers, sailors and airmen of a dozen different nationalities—wearing uniforms ranging from the starkly practical battledress to the comic-opera gaudy—there was a chance to forget separation, loneliness, bombs, rationing, shortages, long shift hours, and the very real possibility that tonight might be the last.

The theatres would be packed again. *Blithe Spirit* was in

its fourth year. Ralph Lynn was playing in *Is Your Honeymoon Really Necessary?* at the Duke of York's. And they were already queuing outside the Empire Leicester Square to see Irene Dunne in *The White Cliffs of Dover*.

For some it would be a night of destiny. For others a night of romance. There would be deaths, narrow escapes, partings, meetings, vows made and broken. In the pubs and clubs and bars there would be crowds. And more crowds in the dance halls. Light and music and life everywhere behind the blacked-out windows, once it grew dark.

But Frank Marsh sat alone in his office, smoking and thinking lewdly about Miss Bedell.

His office was simply the middle segment of a five-room row, brick-built in 1938, and the pride of its owners, Owens & Laycock, coal merchants. It looked out on a huge coal wharf, not far from where the Piccadilly Line trains rattled through non-stop to Acton Town. On the street side it showed a smart front to a semi-depressed parade of shops. Each of the five windows was painted with the names of different coal merchants and customers still had stubborn allegiance to one or the other, though Owens & Laycock had long since swallowed up all five. Each window had its own display: Coalite in green hyacinth bowls in one, massive slabs of Welsh steam coal in another, a pyramid of Ovoids in a third.

At one time the offices had been a row of huts. Frank Marsh could remember them. Moving into the new place had been the best thing that had happened to him in twelve years. It had made 'going to the office' a little conceit that even he could believe in. It had been better, even, than the sudden death of his wife, Edith, at the age of 51 in 1936.

He shared the middle room with Miss Bedell, who sat next to the window, screened from the street door and customers by a small counter and partition.

Miss Bedell was a plain woman, heavily boned, single, 38 years old and a virgin. Her mind, too, had been mostly virginal when she first came to Owens & Laycock. But without trying she excited all the men, except old Mr Spencer, who was 63, weighed 96 pounds and wore a clean wing collar every day. She wore her long toffee-coloured hair braided and coiled over her ears like unbecoming headphones. Her face was reddish and her spectacles owlish, but what excited the men were her massive breasts, neat waist and cornucopian hips. Philomena Bedell made her own clothes, frowning long into her lonely evenings over white and cream

35

linens spectacularly unsuitable for an office overlooking a coal wharf. Everything she wore had the same neckline: square and low enough to reveal a great deal of creamy flesh.

Year by year, the heat of the stares, allusions, jokes, suggestions had become a powerful drug to her. She did not want sex; or at least she didn't want the cruelly animal ingredient that was the common factor of the men's jokes. But she did enjoy fantasising it a little within the safety of her flat in Gunnersbury Park.

Frank Marsh sat now, on Miss Bedell's high swivel chair, breathing in the elusive remnant of her fragrance, doing his own wild fantasising. For months now, since he had been given the other desk in the room, he had dreamed through the seasons of somehow being with her here, alone, and of seizing her by force; of plunging both hands full of her white quivering flesh. He always thought of it in those terms, too, liking the sound of the words 'massive', 'creamy' and 'quivering'.

He wiped his forehead with the back of his hand. By Christ, he'd like to make her quiver! He tried now to cope with the thought of somehow stripping all the clothes from a creamy, quivering, massive Philomena Bedell. But his hands began to shake long before he could hold the final, gorgeously, breathtakingly indecent scene steady in his mind's eye. He sighed deeply and lit another Gold Flake. He loved Gold Flake. These days you had to take what you could get. But this morning, the kiosk at Eastcote Station had some in stock. Just like that. Only 20 per customer, though. Even so, it had made his day, almost.

He sensed, rather than saw, that the wharf had died for the day. Even though the windows had a fine glaze of coal dust, the late sun glinted brilliantly on the black dunes of coal. There were new miniature mountains in the Owens & Laycock bays. One that looked like Derby Brights. That was good. Some customers couldn't get it through their heads that in this year of the war they couldn't have their Derby Brights, Washed Kitchen Nuts or whatever. It was all nonsense anyway. Welsh Steam, though you couldn't tell them, was beautiful. Once you got it alight it was all tarry and gassy, a beautiful sight in a grate.

From a long way off, the heavy, repeating slam of shunting trucks roused him. He held his windy, heavy-smoker's breath to listen for a second or two. Then wished he hadn't. It was a melancholy sound. He was already depressed and lonely. He needed a woman, too. A whore even. Perhaps he'd go Up West one night and have one of the Piccadilly Commandos. He wasn't really the type; but if he went with someone else, perhaps . . . Someone like old Henry Gibbs, for instance; he was another randy old sod.

He blew an assertive cloud of smoke over Miss Bedell's smart new Smith-Corona, tidily covered for the night. But he smiled at himself. It was an old dream, that one. Here he was, at 56 and he'd never had a prostitute yet. He didn't have the confidence. Perhaps if he had the money. More money, not much, just more. With a little more money he might feel more confident. But he'd never had the money, either.

At 56, Frank Marsh looked a little over 60. He was a stooped figure, under average height, tending to portliness rather than fat. His sandy hair was thin and combed back over a lot of baldness. The sandy moustache was nicotine-dark in the middle; he liked to keep a cigarette dangling there while he did long, boring jobs, like his monthly statements. Statements on ruled and headed forms, with Owens & Laycock in copperplate above the neat, double red rule. And below, in his own copperplate, the endless accounts for anthracite nuts, large coke, small coke, boiler nuts. He could do them with his eyes shut.

Since Edith's death, he had enjoyed this time of day. There was nothing now to rush home for. There was no dinner waiting. No-one expected him. Harvey had been gone from the house since before his mother had died. He could get himself something cold, or not, as he pleased.

And it meant he could have this place to himself for a while like this. He didn't know why he enjoyed it, only that he did. He'd look in the other rooms, sniff and poke about, starting with the end room, the one with no street door, which belonged to District Manager, Sidney Dobbs, a huge, almost spherical man. Dobbs was baby-faced, snow-haired and had the ponderous authority of a senior policeman. His room smelled of cigars. Frank Marsh admired that; he smoked cigars only at Christmas. The next room was identical to his own and was inhabited by old Mr Spencer. The traveller, Watson, who had a Morris 10 and called on bulk customers, had a desk in the other corner, but like Dobbs, was often out. He was in some awe of Watson because the man was so well informed. Watson knew everything about the war, read *The Daily Telegraph* and the *Daily Mail* every day and had a theory about everything that might happen next. Some said

Watson drank too much. Others that he drank because of his job; a lot of orders could only be taken in pubs from Pinner to Parsons Green.

Frank Marsh always skipped his own room. Sitting where Philomena's generous behind had sat all day was the only attraction. In the next room Harry Townsend, the local manager, worked and ran the cash drawer, checked the receipts of the van men (one 5-ton lorry, four horse-drawn 3-ton 'vans' and two horse-drawn 'trolleys') and kept an eye on the lad, Alan Perry, a careless, carefree 16-year-old who wrote up all orders on the standard delivery notes and couldn't wait to be in the war.

The end room housed the big docket books and Arthur, the redheaded, angular, unemotional young despatch clerk who made up the loads, allocated assignments and received the complaints of the men through a sliding window onto the wharf.

He decided not to go out on the wharf. It looked hot and dirty. Some evenings he would take a walk round the coal heaps, picking his way over the rails and perhaps spotting some of their own incoming trucks, waiting for a shunt to the O & L bays for unloading. But not this evening. His cuffs already looked grey and felt tacky. In weather like this, too, his unsatisfied lust for Philomena was exhausting. What he really wanted now was to shed his shiny, blue-serge office suit, change into a pair of old flannels and old garden shoes and drop into the pub for a while. Sod the garden tonight. The beans probably wanted watering, but sod them, too. A couple of gins would help him to sleep. Double British Summertime might help the farmers and the factory workers, but sunlight at ten o'clock at night in August was unnatural, whatever anyone said.

He shrugged and locked up.

Outside the Underground station he bought an evening paper. The Germans seemed to be falling back steadily in France. Someone was predicting the liberation of Paris by the end of the month. But Frank was unmoved. Unfit for service in the 1914–18 affair, he had been 30 when it ended. He was armoured not only against the hardships of the Home Front but also against spurious optimism about the peace that would follow. He enjoyed listening to Watson's account of how everything was going to change, but he was afraid that it was already too late for him. Nothing much would ever really change. His boy Harvey, though—he was young enough. And doing well. Clever bugger, Harvey. Scholarships, single-minded about what he had wanted to do, and now there he was, night-editor in a big news agency at 28. It had seemed so easy for him. He might enjoy the 'new society'. For himself, he'd be satisfied with either a crack at Philomena or something very like her, or else dry up and blow away and be done with it all.

He hoped there wouldn't be any sirens tonight. At the beginning of the month there had been sirens all the bloody time. The first two days there had been raids lasting all night, then again at breakfast and lunch and again all night. Flying bombs, V1's, dropping all over the bloody place. Dozens of the things must have dropped on the night of the 1st alone. Fulham had been clobbered, and Chelsea, the West End, and all the way out to North London. The official word was that most fell on the way to the capital, but a damn lot had got through that night.

Not that it made much difference to his sleep. Sometimes he slept through, whatever was happening. He often ignored the Anderson shelter in the garden and lay, alternately scornful and petrified, between the sheets of his and Edith's old double bed until he dropped off. If anything fell near enough he would wake, sweating and listening to the throaty purr of the monsters as they came on over the city and the suburbs. As long as they purred you were all right. When the motor cut while it was still loud in your ears—that was when you stopped breathing and lay, heart thumping, waiting for the explosion, the shock wave, the rattle of debris and dust and the choking smell of old plaster. Every Londoner now associated that smell with bombed-out buildings and houses.

It was as he let himself in that he had the idea.

The walk from the station had taken longer than usual. His feet were hurting. The little house was hot and smelled stale. He could still distinguish the odour of a kipper that he had fried two nights ago. He sat down at the foot of the stairs and took his shoes off, wiggling his toes. He had another hole in both socks. He listened to the silence. It washed over him, filling his mind with memories of how it had been at the start. Edith had been attractive then, and he had loved her; well, wanted her. They had bought this house, when all the rest were still empty, for £5 down and £5 a month. Three rooms up and two down, semi-detached, a little donkey boiler in the kitchen to heat the water, the paving stones all pink and white alternately down the street, and trees already growing in the grass verges. Now it was a shell, not a home. He never used the downstairs rooms. He ate in the kitchen, slept in the smallest bedroom because it needed the least cleaning. What was it all for? It was wasted, empty. Full of melancholy.

Then it struck him. But why empty? Why not share it? Enough people were displaced, on the move, these days. There must be thousands who needed somewhere to stay, close to London and with easy access. People away from home on war jobs. Wives taking rooms to be near husbands. Parents, locking up their homes and moving closer to serving sons and daughters.

Why not let a room?

Why not? He moved slowly about, getting his supper, thinking it over. A little extra cash would make all the difference. Some new clothes. A little cash to splash out with. Up West. A girl. A woman. Perhaps—just perhaps—the money might make all the difference with massive, creamy, quivering Philomena.

By the time he sat down to eat he was determined to do it. He would get Harvey's advice on it. He felt elated. He put the wireless on, hummed along with a dance band. He decided he would water the beans. And he would go out, in a while, and have a couple of gins at the King's Head.

And sod the bombs. And sod the war.

7

He was kept waiting in an ante-room for an hour and it was already late in the morning before a harassed aide admitted to Willi Reiter that General Dietrich Pelz was not at Luftwaffe Headquarters. The commander of the now redundant bomber force was someone he knew. If he had to unload his story on someone of sufficiently high rank, Pelz had been a good bet. Impatient and anxious over the loss of time, Willi tried to see Milch, the Chief of Staff, instead. But it seemed that Milch was unavailable, too. And it was clear that Milch's aide was frankly sceptical about the urgency of any matter raised by a relatively junior officer.

His sense of urgency growing, Willi tried the office of General Karl Moller. His father had served with Moller and counted him as a friend. The name, Reiter, alone might get him a few minutes privately.

The orderly was back within five minutes. General Moller would see him.

"Reiter," Moller acknowledged Willi's smart salute and came round his desk with his hand outstretched. "I remember you well enough. It's Willi, isn't it? And your brother is . . . Eugen? You see I really do remember—just as well as I remember your dear father, my good friend." Moller settled himself again behind his desk, his hands folded across his stomach. "I gather you have something of importance to communicate and that failing Generals Pelz and Milch you are willing to unfold it to me. Is that right?" He smiled at Willi's expression. "Oh, there are precious few secrets in this headquarters, Major. Unless we mean to keep them that is. Anyway, what is it that is making you so anxious?"

Willi sat down in the offered chair. He had no clear opinion of Moller. Perhaps he couldn't afford to be choosy. The man had the rank and seemed friendly enough. It occurred to him that Moller had almost certainly known his mother, too, and it was on the tip of his tongue to explain about the raid, his mother's death and his own presence in Berlin. But no, all that was unimportant now. He drew a deep breath and began. "General," he said, "I apologise. I should, perhaps, have come to you first. I am sorry. With the kind of information I have, I hardly knew what to do. I asked for General Pelz only because I am known to him, served under him two years ago. But really any senior officer will know better than I what must be done about a matter which seems to involve political conspiracy."

Moller at once leaned forward across his desk. "Go on."

Willi had rehearsed the details of his talk with Eugen during his long wait in Pelz's ante-room. He delivered them now, bluntly and without guesswork or elaboration. When he stopped speaking there was a long silence. Moller stared at him steadily, as if trying to determine why the brothers Reiter should have been singled out for this approach by Himmler's staff.

"You were right to come here," he said at last. "You could not have done anything else. Let me say straight away that you have nothing with which to reproach yourself." He looked away, as if slightly embarrassed himself. "You say that Eugen, your own brother, was willing—no, anxious—that you should undertake this criminal mission?"

Willi flushed. A slight emphasis on the words 'your own brother', and the heavy reassurance that he had done the right thing, sounded very much like accusation. It was as though Moller thought that some men would have been slower to incriminate their own close kin.

He said with some edge: "My brother, yes. But with respect, General, not the little boy you used to know. Standartenführer Reiter has known very well for years now what kind of people he serves. You cannot, I think, achieve senior rank in the SS and a clear conscience at the same time. I will be frank. I do not like my brother. I have not liked him for many years. I could wish it had been otherwise. But when a man attempts to recruit you for murder—and clearly doesn't care that he puts your life in jeopardy, too, what then do you owe him? Is that the action of a brother?"

Moller held up a hand. It was a gesture that conceded the point. But Willi added coldly. "General, I believe that had it been I who was supposed to recruit Eugen, I would have refused and taken the consequences." He spoke with such evident bitterness that Moller got up and patted him on the shoulder. "All right, Willi. I do not doubt that you would. You are wholly right to bring this matter here, whatever the circumstances." Moller shook his head now, amazed. "I find this kind of thing as unpalatable as you. And as astonishing. But of course, one knows that there are plots and counterplots on all sides these days. We must decide what has to be done." He chewed his lip. "I think Goering should be told. We do not know who was to be the target of this affair, and it is better that the Reich Marshal is warned." He took a few strides to the door and back, thinking.

"Look," he said at last. "Don't go further away than this floor. The orderly will show you a lounge along the hall where you can get something to eat. I'm afraid you'll have to wait. You, too, may have to see Goering. I'll send for you as soon as something can be arranged." He led Willi to the door. Before it closed he could hear Moller bawling for his aide.

For three hours, Willi sat in an overheated lounge area. An orderly brought him sandwiches and coffee almost immediately. He was suddenly desperately tired. He had slept badly, tormented by the kind of doubts that had perhaps lay behind his outburst in front of Moller. Had there been some other way to handle it, without implicating Eugen? Could he have appealed to Eugen to face his own problem some other way? By coming here, had he really condemned Eugen? Had that been inescapable? Should he have told Eugen first? Given him the chance to run?

He sighed. Telling Moller about it had been a load off his shoulders. He calmed his other fears by telling himself that when Eugen realised that he wasn't coming back there might still be time, then, to run if he could and if he wanted to.

He woke, suddenly, from a warm and comfortable doze to find another orderly at his side. General Moller required him again at once.

He recognised Milch as soon as he came into the room and snapped to attention.

"Sit down," Milch said. Moller showed encouragement.

"The Reich Marshal may want to see you at some point," Milch said. "Meanwhile, you should know he has no intention of taking this story of yours to Himmler. It's a bad business, of course. But we do not want trouble with Himmler at this time. Meanwhile, if everything you have told General Moller is true—"

"If?" Willi cut in indignantly. "It is true."

Milch ignored the interruption. "That's what I said. If your story is true in every detail, then you are in some personal danger. The Reich Marshal is concerned about that and is anxious that we deal first only with that aspect of the matter."

An orderly came in with coffee and schnapps. He set it down in front of Milch, and Moller waved him from the room. Milch picked up the pot at once and began pouring three cups. "There is no question but that you must not return to your command," he said mildly.

"I'm not worried by SS threats," Willi said. It sounded brave enough, but he wondered whether he'd said it only because he was emboldened by having got the story through to Goering himself.

Milch eyed him coldly. "Shut up, Reiter," he said. "You may be surprised that the Reich Marshal does not plan to confront Himmler with this story. If so, it's something you'll have to bite on. Himmler is a devil. Who knows what he might do? You might still have a nasty accident somewhere, somehow. If the story's true—I'm sorry—if you have understood the nature of the threat to yourself and your brother correctly, then he's unlikely to forget you."

Willi said, hopefully: "The Führer? It wouldn't be possible to complain to him?"

"No!" Moller said emphatically. "That's out. Goering believes that Himmler is riding high at the moment while the fortunes of the Luftwaffe are in decline. He thinks that as Himmler would certainly deny the approach, it might automatically be seen as malicious Luftwaffe troublemaking. Anyway, whether or not the complaint succeeded, your brother would be likely to find himself on the Russian front and you might still be reached by one or more of Himmler's creatures."

He saw Willi's expression of scorn, and hurried on: "You are not married, I think?"

"No."

"And your parents are dead. You have my sympathy. I myself have suffered just such a loss recently. At this stage of the war, few Germans haven't. Anyway, that leaves you something of a free agent. You have no other ties?"

Willi was baffled. "No, no ties. Free agent for what?"

"That is up to the Reich Marshal."

Moller, Willi noticed, slipped very easily from the formal, 'the Reich Marshal' to plain 'Goering'.

"Meanwhile," Milch looked at his watch, "quarters will be found for you here. For your own sake," he got up and, preparing to leave, speeded up his delivery, "you will not be allowed to leave the building at any time. An effort will be made to make you comfortable. Understood?"

Uneasy, Willi looked from Milch to Moller. "Am I under arrest? I have done nothing."

"Of course not!" Moller took his arm and walked him to the door. "The Reich Marshal is adamant that no harm must come to you." He smiled and tapped the Knight's Cross at Willi's collar. "I think this has something to do with his concern. Goering is nothing if not a sentimental man."

They were at the door. An orderly waited for him. Willi wanted to protest. He wanted to ask more questions. He had thought the interview was only just beginning. He threw off Moller's pressure on his arm. His temper flared suddenly. "I would like to see the Reich Marshal," he said. He was only vaguely aware that he was on very thin ice.

But Moller only smiled.

"I will try to arrange it for you. Get some rest. You may need it."

The door closed. The orderly waited, looking at him, wonderingly.

"Lead on," Willi growled.

8

Willi woke suddenly to a sense of loss and disorientation. It was something he remembered vividly from his flying days; he had slept like that as a bomber pilot, dozing away the hours in the dispersal huts waiting for the weather to turn. It took time to remember who and what and where the hell you were. He had been dreaming deeply of the old days before the war, when his parents were alive and well and he and Eugen were students; when summers seemed to last forever and everything seemed so perfect and so set to stay that way. For a few moments he couldn't even remember which field this was. The orderly shaking him was a man he couldn't recognise. Then he clicked back into the present. It was no airfield at all. He was at Luftwaffe HQ. The orderly was not his. He remembered the rest of it . . .

"Please, Herr Major," the orderly insisted. "You are called to the Reich Marshal."

Willi knuckled his eyes, looked at his watch. It was 2 a.m. His mouth was dry and sour. The tiny room he had been put in had no windows. He felt queasy and his head ached. He said nothing, stepping into the tiny bathroom cubicle to comb his hair and rinse his mouth. The orderly watched him, agitatedly. He handed Willi his cap and stepped to the door, anxious to impart a sense of urgency. He set a smart pace down the corridors, Willi grumbling and the orderly looking back anxiously over his shoulder.

"In here, please, Major." The man let him into an ante-room. "An Officer will fetch you when the Reich Marshal is ready to receive you." He said it in the tones of long routine.

Willi had been decorated by Goering in 1942, but the great man had been in a hurry and had left immediately after the investiture. The residual impression was one of keen eyes, astonishing bulk and—oddly—perfume. Now he didn't really know what to expect. He knew that he wasn't nervous, and wondered about that. Perhaps it was because despite his rank and wealth, Goering needed friends just as badly. The controversy about the Reich Marshal still raged. After the failure of the long night-bombing of England, the fiasco of Eagle Day and the decisive defeat over the Channel and southeast England, it had become fashionable to disparage both Goering and the air force he had built, to suggest that he had promised everything and delivered nothing. But like many Luftwaffe officers, Willi knew that both they and Goering had done what they could. They had not deserved scorn and dismissive sneers. Goering himself was still full of fight and plans to rebuild the Luftwaffe and return to the offensive. He'd been overruled, Hitler insisting that priority should be given exclusively to the building of fighters as a defence against the ceaseless British and American bombing raids. Goering's idea had been to carry the war back to England, bombing Allied airfields and smashing the dreaded Fortresses and Lancasters on the ground. Now there were too few aircraft of any kind at all and only innocents believed that the Luftwaffe would ever again become a real power.

A youngish major with only one arm opened the same door and beckoned. They walked in silence the length of yet another long corridor. He was not announced. The major simply opened a door and motioned him inside. The door closed behind him.

Goering was sitting at a very small walnut kneehole desk at the back of the room. A bright lamp with a green shade threw bright light downward, leaving the huge head in the deep gloom of the rest of the room. The eyes seemed keen still, though sunk in dark circles. It was always alleged that Goering spent most of his time hunting, but he looked desperately tired now. He looked up, unsmiling.

"Major Reiter," he said. "Sit down, won't you." The voice, too, was tired. Soft, impersonal, almost remote.

Willi sat very still. His chair creaked. The room was warm, close, deathly quiet. He watched as Goering leafed through what was clearly Willi's personal file. Goering evidently had some trouble with his eyes. He wore no spectacles, but from time to time he peered closely at some detail. At length he closed the folder and put his elbow on it, then propped his massive chin with his hand.

"You seem to have run out of luck, Willi Reiter," the Reich

Marshal said. He looked at Willi thoughtfully. "You perform wonderful service. You are wounded, but not too seriously. You recover from your wounds, are taken from combat flying and seem all set to survive the war." He tapped the file gently with his other hand. "Then, poof! You run smack into Himmler. Too bad."

Willi smiled. He said nothing.

Goering lifted his great head. "You have flown as a bomber pilot, indeed as a bomber ace, over England, Poland and Russia. And won the Knight's Cross." He sucked at his teeth, shaking his head.

"And now," he said, "you must disappear."

Willi was stunned. "Disappear?"

Goering nodded. He might have been answering some routine question. "Think," he said gently. "You cannot remain in full view of the SS. You cannot obtain redress. General Moller has, I think, outlined some of the problems. Now, unless you want to become a slow-moving target, what else is there for you? I have to tell you that the Luftwaffe cannot sustain you in any other course."

Goering knitted his fingers together and rested his fat hands on the dossier. He sat very still, watching, his breathing shallow and noisy in the quiet of the dark room.

Willi was thinking desperately. It was clear that Goering was keen that he should do something. But what? What did he mean, disappear? How could he? He sat very still himself, saying nothing.

"On the other hand," Goering said, "if you decide to cooperate, we can do a great deal to help you—before we erase all traces of such help." He smiled grimly.

Willi was getting the idea. He was being led along gently. He told himself that he was a veteran officer, that he was owed something by this leader of men, that he would not too easily acquiesce in anything that didn't make some kind of immediate and long-term sense. Despite Moller's remark, he was sure that Goering, as a politician, dealt first in expediency rather than sentiment. When moments had ticked by without further clues, he decided to play along. "Where would I go?" he asked. "What should I do?"

He had said the right thing. Goering looked at him, as if pleased that Willi had picked up some vital clue in a very odd game. Goering creaked back in his chair and his face moved further into the darkness. "Well, Switzerland might seem sensible," he said. "Though Himmler's arm is long . . ." His left hand made a little despairing gesture.

Switzerland? Willi couldn't believe it, couldn't take it in. Was the man serious? Was this it, then? Was his war over? It seemed that he was being dismissed, sent into exile. He shook his head, bewildered.

Goering must have taken it as dissent. "I agree," he said. "But there is one other course of action." He stopped there. His tone was kindly, less remote. He seemed to suggest that he understood Willi's confusion and anxiety.

"What is that?" Willi heard himself ask.

"I've been looking at your file," Goering said. "And that suggests an alternative. You have flown over England. You speak English. You have visited England. You even have the advantage of an English mother . . ." Again he stopped and seemed to be waiting.

Willi hunched his shoulders. So? He was still in the dark.

Goering pursed his lips judiciously. "There is an element of risk, of course. But that's something you accepted years ago when you took up flying. You would be as safe there as anywhere."

Willi got it. He sat bolt upright. "In England?" He almost shouted it.

Unbelievably, Goering nodded, watching him closely.

Willi wanted to laugh. It was so bloody wild. Was the great Reich Marshal mad, after all? What the hell was he talking about? "And what the hell am I supposed to do there, for God's sake?" he demanded. Indignation rose in him, swiftly, scorchingly.

Goering's expression did not change. He tipped his head on one side. "Surprise and confusion I can understand, Major Reiter. But you forget yourself. I had been wondering why an officer with your record is still only Major, not *Oberst* Reiter. I think I see why." He smiled briefly to indicate that he had not really taken offence, and then went on: "Another solution is that you should be arrested for some misdemeanour, not yet decided, and held under Luftwaffe guard. That way you would be safe enough to satisfy my conscience. Your trial would be indefinitely postponed for one reason or another. Then, at the end of the war, your record would be cleared. There would be a promotion, perhaps, and a reference to 'special duties' which would explain all the mystery."

He looked at Willi foxily. "Of course," he said, "that wouldn't quite cover the matter if Himmler decided to twist the whole thing round and suggest that you, at the instigation of others as yet unidentified, approached your brother with some plot or other, or that the two of you evolved something together. That man could produce a whole range of permutations, all of them very much the sort of thing which he has powers to investigate and punish. The Reichsführer-SS excels at such things."

Willi's temper flared dangerously. "And when Himmler rants, the Luftwaffe trembles?" He choked the words out and sat defiantly glaring at the huge man behind the very small desk. For the moment he was without a fear. Let them do what the hell they liked . . .

Goering stared back at him, unmoved. One elbow back on the desk, he smoothed his bottom lip gently with the flat of his thumbnail. If he had never been spoken to in this way by any officer—far less one of such relatively junior rank—he gave no sign.

Little by little Willi's breathing returned to normal. He was suddenly struck with Goering's patience. The seconds limped by. He began to realise that the man was concerned for him. He had probably given him enough offence already to warrant execution. He slumped in his chair. All right, so Goering was trying to help. He didn't understand what the hell was supposed to happen next. He was trapped. The only clear thing was that they apparently had some idea of what to do with him.

Willi stirred. Goering's eyes were in the deep shadow cast by the lamp. He could tell nothing of the man's expression. "I want to apologise for my manner, Herr Reich Marshal," he said. "I understand now that an effort is being made to help me. I am grateful. Can you tell me why England is suggested?"

Goering was evidently pleased. He grinned. "For a man with all your gifts it is the safest place in Europe at the moment. You don't believe that? Even Uncle Heinrich couldn't get you there." He shifted his bulk in the chair and became more businesslike. "Right. Now—getting there. We can give you an aircraft. An FW190D. It will outrun most pursuit. There is some risk, of course, from fighters and anti-aircraft defences, but we think you would have the benefit of surprise." He put his head back suddenly and roared with laughter. "It isn't every day that a lone sheep takes a fast run into the middle of a pack of wolves. That will worry them a bit. And we think you would be able to put the FW down in any one of a dozen places which might give you time to fire it

49

and get clear before you're reached. You'd melt into the countryside. We can help with all the details there. Next— how to live. Again, we can help: the right clothes, money, an identity card, ration book—everything. Now think about it. You speak perfect English. You know the country. You could quite easily become English for a while. Until the war is over. It isn't anywhere near as desperate as it sounds. The only thing—the whole thing is: get down, get clear and submerge."

Willi's mind was racing. It was a breathtaking idea. But it was true. It was just possible. Just . . .

He must have looked dubious. Goering went on: "The British are all over their invasion scare now. Overconfident if anything. They no longer look for invaders or agents dropping out of the sky." He laughed, a short bitter sound. "It is one of the failures they can't level at the Luftwaffe, that. That the very idea of a German agent should be laughable to the British. However, it is so. Even their Home Guard will soon be disbanded, I'm told. In a few months—who knows? —the whole thing may be over."

Despite himself, Willi found he was reaching towards the idea. He said ruefully: "You make it sound almost like a holiday, Herr Reich Marshal."

Goering's smile died. "The next few months," he said heavily, "are going to be the hardest yet for all Germans. Even with the risks involved, you may find you'll be getting the best end of it. And don't worry about your career or your service record. As a Luftwaffe officer—at least in the foreseeable future—you have no career. None of us has."

Willi was silent. He knew it to be true, but he was still surprised at this kind of candour.

Goering pushed his chair back away from the desk. The interview was ending. "Think about it, Reiter. Consider carefully what you will need to make it work. Whatever it is, within reason, you'll get it. Meanwhile, I have asked that General Moller will arrange special quarters for you here . . . You are confined to this headquarters. No-one must know you are here. You understand?" Goering swivelled his chair away from the light so that his body was at right-angles to the desk. "An officer will be assigned to assist you if you decide to try this idea. Let him help you all he can."

Willie stood and came smartly to attention. "Thank you, Reich Marshal." He could think of nothing else to say.

"Good luck," Goering said. It was barely more than a

throaty whisper. He bent his body forward from the waist, easing the weight on his spine with a little grunt of pleasure. He did not turn to see Willi leave.

An orderly waited in the corridor outside. "Back to the room, I think," Willi told him. He followed the man blindly, going over and over the interview in his mind. It was bewildering, and yet . . . they were right! Christ! In a few minutes they had stood his world on end. An hour ago he was an officer with a brilliant record and an enviable decoration. Now? He was being shunted out, shot off into exile, a fugitive from his own kind. Safer with the enemy than with his own people!

He sat on the bed, his mind and emotions in turmoil. Rational thought was impossible. Over and over he told himself that the idea was absurd. But the next moment he found himself making mental lists. Had he, then, accepted the idea? Or if he hadn't was it the simple realisation that he had no real choice but to give it a try?

At one point he rang the bell by the head of the bed and when the orderly appeared, asked the man for paper and a pen. When they arrived, he sat down at the small table and looked at the blank sheets. How the hell was he to know what he would need?

Getting there shouldn't be difficult. A single aircraft always stood a good chance of getting through the coastal defences. And a fighter, moving high and fast, stood a better chance than a bomber. By the time he was seen—and he would be seen—he would perhaps be on the way down; and that they wouldn't expect.

His anger ebbed and he found himself intrigued and excited by the audacity of the idea itself, and by the hazards and how they might be reduced.

Money, identification, ration documents—all these things were obvious. It would be the less obvious things that might trip him up. If he could get hold of some recent British newspapers it would help. He knew that some came in daily from Lisbon. He would have to think himself into the plan. Begin to formulate a whole new personality and approach. As an Englishman, why wouldn't he be in the British Forces, for example? Exempt? Medically unfit? Discharged as wounded? He had only the haziest idea of what constituted grounds for exemption in England. He did have his leg wound, of course. It didn't trouble him much, but it looked ugly enough. Perhaps that would be best. A discharge certificate. Could the

Luftwaffe really produce such documentation? It seemed improbable.

A limp would forestall quite a lot of questions. And he did limp. The British were odd, though. Perhaps they wouldn't even ask such questions.

He sat on, trying to reach back to his stay in England. He'd gone to London in the spring of '38 to polish his English at a private language school. His mother had wanted to join him, had planned to at one point, and then decided that she should not leave his father. He couldn't remember why. She'd wanted Eugen to go, too, but Eugen was already involved with the SS and did nothing that was out of character for an SS junior officer. At the time, he remembered, Eugen had been obsessed by all that mystical SS claptrap about German culture and ethnology and had been indignant at the suggestion that he could spare the time. So he'd gone alone.

He'd made friends, learned a great deal about the English—at least those in the southern counties—won some girls. One of them, a pretty secretary from Dollis Hill had spent most of her summer ironing out the kinks in his accent. Willi learned ten times as much about colloquial English in bed in her cramped South Kensington flat as he'd learned in his daily stint at the Mayfield Language School. The Mayfield! The name came to him, suddenly. He hadn't thought of it for years. It was all in another age. That summer and autumn, until he was recalled in the spring of 1939, had been the best years of his adult life. Better than the years at university, better even than his flying training and the first heady months as a young pilot without problems or real responsibility. He could still, at moments like this, recall the glow of those days. And how they had ended, abruptly, with a summons from the German Embassy.

He was surprised to find that he could, fleetingly, recall the wrench it had been to return home. London, at that time, had been a kind of temporary Eden, a last escape before the real business of life claimed him.

He shook it off, as something uncomfortable, and found himself staring at the obligatory photograph of Hitler on the wall opposite the bed. What was it Goering had said? You have no career. None of us has. So it was all over. And even the top men were saying so. Not openly yet. But they believed that.

Willi felt a deep sadness for Germany. For the friends he'd had and lost. For poor old Father, who could not have stood this final stage of defeat. For his mother, who could have been torn in two all over again; happy that her England was to survive, saddened that it had to be Germany that went down as once before. And finally, for himself, because all the sweat and struggle of the last few years had come to this: a big nothing.

He gave Hitler the finger and was startled like a guilty schoolboy by a knock and the entrance of a huge Gefreiter, a man of well over six and a half feet tall.

"Excuse me, Herr Major," he said. "General Moller has ordered that I should show you to a more comfortable room and to tell you that you should take your meals in the Senior Officers Mess whenever you feel ready. Dinner is from seven." He grinned. "Raids permitting."

Willi was comforted by this concern for his comfort. It was clear that they were thinking about the problems of Willi Reiter. He got up and followed the Gefreiter. He made up his mind never to think about Eugen again. He was alive and whole, and that was a damn sight better off than many. Perhaps Goering was right. He might even be getting the best end of it all.

As he moved down the corridors he glanced curiously in at the occupants. Officers worked over maps, intelligence reports, requisitions, troop movements, personnel files. Some held urgent-sounding telephone conversations. Others lounged, waiting, waiting. He knew their feelings, their frustrations, their anxieties. He'd done most jobs himself. He was moved by sudden sympathy for their coming plight. However well they performed, their efforts would come to nothing. He wondered how long it would be before they knew it the way Goering knew it.

It was odd, after years of feeling kinship with men like this, that he should now feel apart. He had a sudden frisson of fear. It was something a little like the feeling of a first solo flight. Or that moment, as a bomber pilot, when you first crossed the enemy coast and the searchlights lit you up for the guns to knock down. It was terrible, but exhilarating and not altogether unpleasant.

9

On the night of August 13th, London got its third all-night alert in a row. The sirens sounded at 11.4 p.m. and there was no All-Clear until 6.5 a.m. next morning. Flying Bombs roared overhead through the summer night like so many monstrous, fire-tailed hornets. Londoners held their breath, exhaling only when they flew on past to drop on some other poor devils. The best endeavours of the Luftwaffe over four years of war had never rattled them as badly as Hitler's Victory Weapon No. 1.

That night, several fell in North London. One cut its engine and dived into a timber yard, blowing a crater big enough for two London buses, starting a blaze which melted the tarmac surfaces of the surrounding streets, and causing 40 families to evacuate their homes. Another dropped on a queue outside a cinema, killing 24 people who were never found. A third swooped on a No. 77 bus on Lavender Hill, leaving only four identifiable wheels and a cavernous tangle of gas and water mains.

It was so bad that night that Frank Marsh went down to his own shelter. He started the night in bed with a bottle of Guinness and his library book. But the room was too warm and airless behind the blackout curtains to read or sleep. He got up, switched off his bedlight and opened the curtains and windows. As if on cue, he heard first a faint drone, then the tell-tale engine cut-out. Seconds later, the window frames rattled and the explosion blossomed in red fury on the sky-line away to the east. It was near enough. He picked up his torch, book, dressing gown and beer and padded down to the back door. The night was clear and soft, the sky more purple than black. The night perfume of tobacco plants—he was trying to grow enough of the stuff to roll his own—hung heavy about the little garden. He heard the Gilchrists come out into their garden: Ted, Marie, young Peter and little Stella. He decided against calling out to them. He rather fancied Marie, with her jet black curls and heavy, bouncing breasts, and was afraid that Ted knew it.

Instead, he pushed open the door to his Anderson shelter, made a mental note to pick and cook some of the rhubarb that grew generously on its roof, and ducked down inside. He rather liked the damp earthy smells, and the chill of the little refuge was welcome after the heat of the house. He didn't bother to put a light on. It was pleasant just to lie on the chair-bed, drinking in the night, watching the stars in the narrow strip of sky he could see, and letting his mind run free.

Philomena Bedell surfaced quite quickly. He was used to that. She was hardly ever out of his thoughts now. How to get close to her, how to get her clothes off, how to avail himself of all that gorgeously rounded, infinitely soft and feminine flesh . . .

He smiled in the dark. "Silly old bugger," he rebuked himself.

His lust for Philomena had been given an extra twist today. For a few minutes at lunchtime he had been alone with her. Everyone else had disappeared into The Volunteer at 12.30. He'd wanted to go, too, but before he could get away, Harry Townsend had asked him to look after the cash drawer if he wasn't going out. So he was stuck. Then he discovered that Phil had brought sandwiches. So he combed his hair in the wash-house at the back, winked at himself in the spotted mirror and returned quickly—only to find that Watson had got there first.

Watson wasn't drunk, but he wasn't sober, either. "All down at the pub, eh?" he boomed. He smoothed his moustache. "Leaving the beautiful Miss Bedell. Suits me fine. I'll have you all to myself." His glazed, protuberant eye noted Frank's return, but seemed not to feel that Marsh counted. "I know," he shouted. "We'll have our own party." With some difficulty, he wrestled a large silver flask from his back pocket, uncovered the cap and held it under Philomena's nose.

She simpered. She coloured unbecomingly, and uttered a series of negative sounds which did not quite add up to a refusal.

Frank had returned to his sandwiches, defeated. He could not compete with Watson. The man had a car, a petrol ration, two or three different suits for work, and that air about him of being a man who Measured Up To Life, taking it as it came, unwaveringly.

For the next forty-five minutes, Frank burned. Watson,

emboldened by drink, first perched his fat arse on Philomena's desk, pushing aside her machine. Then, almost at once, began bending close, whispering in her ear, staring unashamedly down her dress, and even—he could swear—giving one of those majestic breasts an outrageous squeeze. He didn't see it, but he was sure it happened. Certainly Phil stood up, abruptly, causing Watson to wobble back off the end of the desk. Her face and neck were crimson. She gathered her bag and fled to the wash-house.

A rumble of gunfire not too far distant brought Frank back to the uncomfortable but more easily supportable present. He wouldn't think about today any more. He couldn't blame Watson. Grabbing Phil's breast was exactly the sort of fantasy he indulged in himself. The only difference was that Watson had the nerve. It was a bit pathetic of him to resent old Watson at all. For all his worldliness, the man was just another randy old devil like himself. And though they didn't know it down on the coal wharf, Watson hadn't even had the advantages that he, Frank Marsh, had started with. He'd kept that quiet, of course: it was one thing never to have started to run, and quite another to have started well and given up spinelessly . . . There had been the good school paid for by his hard-working, self-sacrificing parents; university; an English degree. He'd been a teacher, for God's sake—than which nothing was more respectable in these times. And then . . . he allowed himself to feel the twinges of guilt, to turn the pages of failure privately for a moment, before he made the effort of will to think about something else. It was an old, old story—and one which Edith had told every living soul she'd come into contact with: the little failures at first, like not getting promotion, not getting out to a better school when he'd had the chance; and, finally, after Edith's death, the shame and indignity of being left behind when his school, a London grammar, had been evacuated with the cream of the staff. He had been designated 'non-essential'. After that he'd half-heartedly tried the Civil Service, but much of it had vanished to places like Chester, Evesham, Droitwich and Worcester. He should have gone, if that's what it took. But he didn't. And many of the big London firms had gone to the country, too. He'd been lucky, in the end, to find anything at all which hadn't meant uprooting himself. Thank God, Edith had gone by the time he'd come to this. He'd never have heard the end of it.

Frank wondered how Harvey was doing. He hadn't been

over lately. He was a good son, though. He cared about his old man. Frank sometimes thought how odd it was that Harvey should be his son. He knew he looked like an old wreck. But inside he felt as young as he ever did; and it was disorienting to feel father to someone as large and solid and successful as Harvey.

Harvey now—he never seemed to have trouble finding women. That Ronnie of his was a cracker. He would willingly give his sugar ration for six months for a quick feel of that one. There he went again. He wasn't supposed to think unfatherly things like that.

Another rattle of anti-aircraft fire was repeated closer, only a mile or so away, seconds later. They'd locked onto one. He heard the V1 approaching and then flying on. Not here, then. Thank God for that. After a pause he heard the explosion, well to the north and west. Some poor sods somewhere had bought it.

He had his cigarettes and lighter beside him on an old kitchen chair. The last of his Gold Flake had gone. All he'd been able to get was Grand Fleet, a brand he'd never heard of before. They tasted terrible and burned away too fast. But he'd been lucky to get anything.

Several times he composed himself for sleep, but his mind remained stubbornly alert. Marie, now, she was a lovely piece. And Phil . . . Christ, he needed a woman! He lit another cigarette. The night remained peaceful. Perhaps he'd be better off in bed. He didn't move. An hour passed. Two hours. I'll get up and make some tea in a minute, he told himself. But it was too much trouble. Lying there in the dark he gradually developed an awareness of himself, of his life and state of mind. It was all most unusual. A night of reckoning. And he found it deeply troubling.

He thought about the house and the scruffy state it was in. He'd noticed that the last time Ronnie had been over with Harvey. He'd suddenly seen it as she might see it. It needed a lot of work. He hadn't bothered for much too long.

He needed to smarten himself up, too; his clothes needed a press. The suit he wore for the office was really only fit for the garden. He ought to give it up now, wear his best instead and buy another one. He could afford it, and he had the coupons. He hadn't bothered with last year's at all; he'd given them to Marie for the kids. Well, to see her smile and shake her breasts at him really.

The night wore on. And still sleep eluded him. He thought

57

about Edith and had no regrets. He'd done more than his share. He'd been unlucky and picked a first-class, cold, spiteful, bitch. He was glad she'd gone. It was she who had made him old before his time.

But now? He was lonely. No denying that. Any remedy? Well, he was not too old to need a woman, anyway; someone mature and not too demanding. As for the rest, if he could have endured Edith all those years and still smile, he had the makings of a husband, surely?

All likelihood of sleep vanished. He thumbed his lighter to look at his watch. Four-fifteen. Still no All-Clear. Stiffly, he got off the chair-bed and flexed his legs. His joints cracked loudly in the peace of the pre-dawn stillness. He felt oddly light-headed and reckless. One part of him wanted to do something about everything at once; another, somewhere at the front of his mind, watched himself cynically, reserving judgement, not believing it.

This Frank Marsh, he told himself, as he closed the back door quietly, is not the one that went out there five hours ago. He half believed that. And as if to underline it, he marched upstairs, emptied the pockets of his old office suit, double-checked them, came down with the suit rolled up in a ball, and put it in the dustbin outside the back door. It was time for a gesture.

In the kitchen, his eye fell on a dismal landscape in water-colour which hung on the wall over the donkey-boiler alcove. Edith had bought it for 1/6d at a jumble sale and had it re-framed at several times the cost, convinced that because it wasn't just a print it must be artistic. He lifted it down, put it in the centre of the kitchen floor and then, feeling a little silly, but also very pleased with himself, stepped on it with both feet. The glass crunched. He trod the shards in, stepped away and left it lying there.

"Up yours, Edith, wherever you are," he said aloud.

He moved quietly about the house, looking at the rooms with what he hoped was a stranger's eye, noting what had to be done, what might be done if he could afford it. His excitement mounted, but he distrusted it. He must be controlled about this.

"New suit tomorrow," he said softly. Noah looked at him blearily from his basket in the corner by the window. "There's going to be a change round here," he told his only witness. The old tom yawned and blinked in slow-motion, unimpressed.

His control slipped for a moment as he lay down on his bed

and set the alarm to ring in one hour. Quite loudly he announced to the ceiling: "I'm going to do this bloody place up like new. And while I'm at it, I'm going to have a go at me, too. I'm going to get a lodger, put the money in my pocket, live better and pull myself up by my bastard bootlaces."

He fell back on the pillows and was asleep almost at once. Just before he drifted away, he said, apropos of nothing at all: "And up yours, too, Watson."

10

At dinner Willi had spoken to no-one. The big room had been crowded with senior Luftwaffe officers and even one or two visiting Wehrmacht generals. The diners ate with the curious preoccupation of the enclosed working group, their conversations carried from desk and conference room to dining table and back without interruption.

Willi sat at the far end of one long table. Those who came after him tended to drift to the other end. He drew some curious glances. They saw him limp in. They noted the yellow collar patches, the pilot's badge, the black wound badge below, and they saw the Knight's Cross. He was an oddity in this company. No-one stared, but they noted his presence and he felt, rather than heard, the whispered questions. He did hear snatches of a conversation about General Christian, Goering's liaison officer at Hitler's headquarters, much of it uncomplimentary.

An orderly served his meal briskly. When he had finished he sat on for a few minutes with his ersatz coffee, glad enough to be alone with his thoughts, even after hours spent in his room. A rough plan was formulating in his mind. Already he had ticked off a list of things he would ask Moller to supply. He was worried about time. How much time did he have?

By now, Eugen would surely be under pressure from Himmler's office? If not worse. Once Eugen had admitted failure he could expect no breathing space himself. Yet Moller and Milch had seemed unconcerned. Why not?

It was a point he kept returning to, uneasily. One reason

could be that they really had no intention of getting him away at all. Oh, they would spare his feelings a bit. Make it look good. But would the Focke-Wulf they gave him really make it to England? Or was he intended to die a flyer's death in the Channel? Rigging any plane so that it just as easily became his coffin was simple enough. That could explain their apparent unconcern about time. And the idea had the advantage that it saved everyone else a lot of trouble. No messy ends. No further problems. It even looked better. If anything of it became known they could always say he stole the aircraft ... The line of thought chilled him and he couldn't quite dismiss it. His gut moved with sudden unease and he signalled the waiter, impatient with himself.

"Herr Major?"

"There is a Gefreiter, called Stiefel, in General Moller's office, I think. He is to show me a room for the night." It wasn't quite the truth. Willi knew his way back to the room well enough. The fact was that Stiefel had told him to summon him whenever he was ready. The implication was that he was not to be without escort. And that was chilling, too.

The waiter pointed across the room. The huge man was already in waiting, chatting to a cook in whites on the other side of the serving hatch. When the orderly touched his arm, Stiefel brought his heels together and waited for Willi to approach.

He followed the big Corporal into the lift, preoccupied by the man's size. Willi was six feet tall exactly. This man was more than a head taller and built like a wrestler. But he was no clod. He smiled at Willi now, transforming a brown, impassive face into one of winning geniality. "I think you'll find your room comfortable, Herr Major." His speech was soft and not uncultured, the accent Bavarian. Willi nodded warily and followed him to the room he had used for an hour before dinner. It led off a small lounge area with doors on three walls. The room reassured him. It was furnished in shades of green and grey to the standard of a good hotel. Bed, hanging space, dressing table, desk, small bathroom.

"Is there anything the major wishes?"

Willie was about to ask for more paper when he realised that the desk was fully equipped. There was even a portable Adler standing in the kneehole.

"Perhaps a drink later," Willi said.

"If you will ring when you are ready." Stiefel indicated the bellpush by the dressing table.

When the man was gone, Willie undressed and put on the dressing-gown lying folded at the end of the bed. The room was clearly intended for use by very senior officers unexpectedly detained at HQ overnight.

He sat down at the desk and began briskly committing the outline of his plan to paper. He did it in two columns; on the left the action, on the right the shopping list of everything he thought he would need. It took him two hours and even then he was still remembering important details to write in the margin. Exhausted, he finally lay down on the bed and fell into a deep sleep.

11

Goering was back again from Carin Hall. He had meant to spend two days tramping the Schorfheide forest, sitting and working by the lake, luxuriating in his private Eden. But the news that Montgomery had launched a new push, with an estimated 1,000-aircraft 'carpet-bombing' towards his objective, Falaise, had brought the Reich Marshal hurrying back to Luftwaffe Headquarters at Wildpark-Werder on the outskirts of Berlin. He was still wearing breeches and a favourite cashmere jacket.

The Russians, too, had begun a new offensive, striking out from their bridgeheads on the Vistula. And the Reich Marshal had the feeling that worse news was on the way. He spent two hours with Milch, Moller, Galland and others. The mood of the meeting was grim. When it broke up, Goering motioned for Moller to remain. He disagreed too often with Galland and had begun to disregard Milch altogether. With Moller he was more straightforward. For a few minutes they talked about the little that the Luftwaffe could do about anything.

As he turned to go, Moller brought up the subject of the brothers Reiter. He was anxious to have both matters settled and soon.

"I hope he has the sense to go," Goering said. "It would be sad if we had to make another arrangement."

Moller nodded. "I think he'll do as he's advised." He knew that Goering was sincere in wanting to help Willi Reiter. "But what of the brother?"

Goering chewed the inside of his lip. "You say you've taken him? Was that wise? How was it done? On whose authority?"

Moller looked prim. "It was done on my orders. It's not that I shirk the responsibility, it's just that I found it was a decision that had been taken. It's probably the right thing. You will recall that we agreed that we could not let the brother report back with his bad news until our man was clear away. We could not afford to have Himmler's people getting jumpy—and perhaps finding out that our Reiter was here at all, however briefly. But if you think on from there, Reich Marshal, you will see that if this much is logical, then it is also inescapable that we cannot let the brother go at all. Especially if you consider that it may take days before we are ready to put our man into the air."

Goering agreed. "You're right, of course, Karl. We can't let him go. Himmler would be on to it at once. Oh, nothing would be said. They might even get rid of him themselves—on the Russian front. But you can be sure that we should suffer sometime, some way. And if Himmler could document it and store it away, then one day for sure he would find a way of telling the Führer all about it. So what do you propose?"

Moller looked uncomfortable. "For the SS?" He made a short, sharp sibilant sound and drew his finger quickly across his throat.

Goering pulled at his underlip, thinking it over. "Yes. The only thing is, he ought to be found somewhere—after a raid. Anything else is too suspicious." He looked down at his clothes. "We'll speak again later. But no more of this. I've had enough of problems for today. The brothers Reiter are a very minor matter—as indeed they are for Uncle Heinrich."

He turned to leave and then looked back. A thought seemed to have struck him. "One last thing, Karl. I haven't given approval—finally—for our Reiter to go. I'll tell you when. Is that understood?"

Moller nodded amiably enough and watched his chief go. His private view was different. Useless to tell Goering that, Knight's Cross holder or not, son of an old friend or not, Willi Reiter was a dangerous embarrassment.

It wouldn't do, of course, to let Himmler win. But equally it wasn't going to help Goering or the Luftwaffe in general if Himmler ever discovered that he had certainly lost.

Reluctantly, Moller sought out Colonel Prelle, a man who was not only good at these things but didn't talk about them. First there was a matter of Eugen Reiter. After that—well, for Goering's sake the brother, Willi, must certainly be seen to take the air. But Moller shuddered at the naïveté implicit in the notion of Reiter being allowed to get as far as England. Suppose the man crashed, injuring himself, and was taken. Himmler would hear of it at once through the normal POW channels.

Better that Prelle should handle it, Moller reasoned. The war was problem enough without internecine struggle.

12

In a cell-like room in the basement of a nearby building, used primarily for the storage of files, reconnaissance film, map supplies and the like, Eugen Reiter sat on a cot bed. He wore full SS uniform, except for his cap which had been lost in the brief struggle.

By his watch it was 11.30 p.m. The building was silent. He had been thrown into the room two and a half hours earlier. He still could not believe what was happening to him. He raged silently. Though he had only three cigarettes left, and the room was almost airtight, he smoked continually. Smoke hung in thick coils in the room, stinging his eyes.

He wanted to shout and bang on the sturdy door. But so far he retained a great deal of dignity. He was a Standartenführer SS, for God's sake, and he would do nothing that a senior officer should not. He would not bluster. He would not show fear.

Nevertheless, he was afraid.

It had happened as he left his uncle's house. All day he had waited for word from Willi. He had been shocked to find him gone from the house at all. As the hours passed, he grew more and more uneasy that Willi had done the very thing that was guaranteed to get them both killed.

He had stayed close to the phone for hour after hour. But

the phone had not rung at all. In one way, that was a mercy. He had expected Brandt to be breathing down his neck by now, and he had invented a dozen lies to buy both Willi and himself time. Time, perhaps to talk again.

At last he'd been unable to stand the waiting and had stepped out into the darkening street for some sort of relief from his tension. The night was soft and cool. He breathed deeply, conscious of the beginnings of a headache.

He never saw his attackers. He assumed there was more than one. He heard no step behind him, had no sense of danger. There was only the explosion in his head as he was struck from behind. He stayed conscious just long enough to feel his legs going and to have the feeling of being lifted bodily.

About 30 minutes later at the outside—he'd checked that with his watch—he had opened his eyes painfully to find himself in this room. He made the immediate assumption that a minion of Brandt's had made the attack, though he couldn't understand why. He would not have been surprised at arrest, and after that almost anything. But this didn't ring right. Nothing about the room told him anything. It was a sort of storeroom. It might be anywhere.

He calmed his fears by telling himself that it wasn't as bad as it looked. Someone had taken an order of Brandt's too seriously, perhaps. He would tell Brandt frankly of Willi's refusal to co-operate despite the threat. Surely Brandt would accept that. "I remember what you said would be the price of failure," he would tell Brandt. "But what does it profit the SS to lose a good and loyal officer?"

His spirits rose with this piece of logic. It was nonsense, of course, to suppose that anything worse would happen other than that he would be in Himmler's bad books. The threat had been simply something said to impress upon him the importance and the urgency of the task he'd been given. He understood that. Unfortunately Willi hadn't, or if he had, had chosen to run the risk. No, what had happened here was that someone had been told to bring him in. The order had been given, perhaps, in tones that led someone to overdo things a little. He would not complain. A rueful shrug would cover the matter. He would tell Brandt—

The key turned in the heavy door. The door swung open. Eugen Reiter stood up, calming himself. A gust of fresh air came in from the corridor. Eugen relaxed a little. It was over. The mistake had been realised.

Hope died instantly. A huge man in Luftwaffe uniform stepped quickly into the room and pressed the door shut behind him. It closed with a sigh and a click, like a safe.

The big man smiled at Eugen, and though he wanted to be on his dignity, in his relief Eugen began to form a smile in return. The Luftwaffe uniform bothered him a little. He began to say something about it. The sound never came out.

Stiefel hit him in the throat with a huge fist, cutting off his air supply at once. The blow crushed Eugen's trachea and larynx and hurled him into a heap in a corner of the room. He lay there, making desperate noises as he struggled to draw breath through his smashed airway. His eyes began to bulge and his skin to change colour. He saw nothing, heard nothing. His brain threatened to explode. In seconds, consciousness began to slip away.

Stiefel lifted the SS man and laid him on the bed. He unbuttoned the black tunic and then the shirt. He sat back a moment, reached into his own tunic and brought out a steel hatpin about seven inches long. With the fingers of his left hand he felt, like a surgeon, for a point in Reiter's rib-cage. Then with his right hand he slid the pin directly into the heart. Eugen Reiter died without a sound and with scarcely a tremor.

The big man waited, then checked the pulse to be sure. Briskly humming under his breath *Humoreske*, a tune his mother had loved, he rebuttoned the jacket, turned off the light and left, re-locking the door.

13

Ronnie had been 19 when her mother, a youthful, elegant and bored 40, had left to live the haphazard camp-follower life as mistress of a Squadron-Leader she had met at a party and had known only three weeks.

It had been a heavy blow for her father, lately arrived as a new 'young' independent film distributor. Not simply because he loved Justine; his attachment to her had for years been compounded of two parts passion and one part responsibility of the kind a parent feels for a wayward child. But it also shattered his own image of his marriage in relation to his business career. Everyone in the trade knew Justine Croft. Over a period of years the trade papers had carried pictures of them together at premieres, gala openings, Variety Club events and Command performances. In future years it was going to be one of the sadnesses of Croft's life that his knighthood had failed to come in time for them to be featured in the trades as Sir David and Lady Croft. Meanwhile he was too busy to feel more than twinges of sadness and loss; mostly in those rare moments of the day when he found himself totally alone: in the bath, in the lavatory, before he dropped off to sleep at night on his side of the double bed.

But for Ronnie it had been a stunning, bewildering blow. It was one of the facets of life her education hadn't prepared her for. She knew about horses, clothes, style, how to behave with servants and, more or less, about sex. She had matriculated, could get by in French and German and had diplomas in domestic science, dietetics and first aid. But she had never ridden on public transport, never been inside a hospital or a bank and never walked entirely alone in a city.

Quite suddenly, when Justine left, she needed to know a great many things her expensive Sussex boarding school had not taught her.

The apparent ease with which her father took his loss and carried on with his life baffled her. He closed the big house near Newbury and moved himself and Ronnie into a capacious flat in Mount Street. Quite coincidentally, he became frantically busy; because of the war films which were first banned, then tolerated, and then seen as a valuable builder of morale. Everyone suddenly wanted films. The Forces, the Home Front, the government propagandists. Croft found himself a leader in a boom industry that was also nationally important. He had little time to lick his emotional wounds.

But Ronnie still pined for her mother, whom she loved. Briefly, she also had the child's selfish wound that her mother's love for a man had proved greater than her need to be with Ronnie. But that had quickly healed.

Simpler, more mundane trials intervened. The Mount Street flat came equipped with an elderly couple. They couldn't be driven out of London by the bombing, but they couldn't be persuaded, either, to live in. Feeling more secure against Hitler that way, they carried their valuables and blankets every night to a shelter in Balham. One day, when they were not in attendance, Ronnie needed a meal. She knew how, and had someone supplied the ingredients, as at school, she could have produced a Cordon Bleu meal for six. But what did you cook for one in a hurry? Where was the food kept? And where bought, and at what cost? How did ration books work? She realised now, too, that she knew London's West End theatres and restaurants very well, but little of the streets which connected them. She could not have been less fitted for London life in wartime than a nun who had renounced her vows and left an enclosed order in a foreign country.

She received letters from Justine, describing life in a cottage near an airfield at Bassingbourne in Cambridgeshire. It seemed that the elegant Justine braved an outdoor closet, wore gumboots and cooked meals for her lover on an oilstove. But the one time Ronnie had seen Justine for lunch, at the Dorchester, she'd looked as elegant as ever. It had been hard to reconcile the two images.

Little by little, the hurt eased. What remained was a tremendous admiration for her mother which subtracted nothing at all from her quite separate love for her father, and an indelible impression that love really was something that transcended matters of good sense, convenience and form.

Between times, she had learned fast. And grown up fast. Her father had found her a job in Wardour Street in the stills department of a major distributor. She left after a week or two and became a doctor's receptionist. Then a petrol pump attendant, a BBC typist at Bush House and still later, a disher out of meals at one of the new British Restaurants. Under the Direction of Labour order she had to do something useful. She had been offered better jobs, but nothing that afforded her either protection from call-up for the services or the munitions factories, or the sense of really helping.

The callow Ronnie who had begun 1940 helpless and abashed had, by the following year, made an exciting transformation. If she was stronger, more capable, infinitely more sophisticated, she was also more tense, more vulnerable, more tender-hearted. She had, at last, had a look at Life being beautiful and filthy, breakneck and boring, heart-filling and heart-breaking.

Still the separation between her father and Justine rankled somewhere in the back of her mind, leaving a residual tension which she projected as intensity; something that both flawed her and made her more lovely.

Six months ago she had wanted a commission in the WRNS. She had said so to her father, but David Croft had wisely deferred action though he promised to speak to some-one about it. Ronnie's speed over the last twelve months had astonished him and made him wary of her enthusiasms; he also wanted to keep her near him, or at least accessible somewhere in London. Having her with him preserved some-thing of his marriage, left him feeling free to cope with the new pressures. So that when he found himself sought after by the Films Division of the Ministry of Information—and with the ear of the Minister, Brendan Bracken, at the same moment that Ronnie cooled down sufficiently to recognise that she simply wanted to do something, anything useful, he was glad enough to act quickly. The job in the MOI canteen as night manageress was useful, was in London, and Ronnie did have some sort of qualifications.

She took the job and in less than a week had met Harvey and begun a careful affair with him. By the second week she had gone to bed with him, first at the Ritz and then at the Regent Palace. Later they began spending the time off shift together at Temple Chambers. By the time Ronnie had begun to look for a flat for herself, a further metamorphosis had taken place.

Her feeling for Harvey did several things for Ronnie. It helped her to understand Justine, who presumably had love. It intensified her feeling for her father, who did not. And it rounded out her knowledge of life in some startling ways.

She had, for instance, recognised almost at once that Har-vey was steeling himself for a break with her. She read the signs not in the impatience or irritability that sours a rela-tionship wearing thin; that wasn't Harvey at all. But it was clear enough just the same in his careful amiability and in a subtle lessening of the tensions between them after, say, the first month. There was no question of Harvey preparing to use a quarrel to force a break. That wasn't honest and Harvey wouldn't have done it. Ronnie knew it, admired it, but felt twinges of guilt.

The fact was that though Harvey pleased her in countless ways, she did not love him, had never said so, no matter how close they had been. So that while she was guiltless in those terms, she also knew perfectly well that Harvey believed something else again. His idea, she could see, was that she was simply nursing her love for him, holding back, until she received his own declaration. Despite his apparent sophisti-cation, she knew instinctively that Harvey simply hadn't experience enough of women to believe in one who was willing, anxious even, to share sex, companionship and the many other comforts of such an affair without ever needing to claim the man forever.

She found him attractive, uniquely companionable, dependable, honest, funny, sensitive and very special. It was a great deal. It was a long way towards love. But it wasn't love. She could not, as Justine had, leave her own comfortable background and set up house for Harvey in some suburb such as Richmond or Sheen and simply wait there, accepting second place in his life after his job.

It was complicated. She was aware that Harvey had also been careful not to speak of love, and she accepted that, in stepping carefully round the commitments of words, he had been, was being, rather less honest than he would have wanted. Now she not only absolved him from all blame, but tenderly regretted that he should have to feel guilt on her account.

Ronnie understood why he wanted the break. Harvey was ambitious. He sometimes grumbled about being kept out of the war by a medical technicality, and he meant it honestly enough. But the ambitious Harvey recognised that with a great many good journalists away in the services, he had a unique opportunity to push his own talents far and fast. Harvey was good. She'd heard that, and she'd heard about offers from Reuter and Ex-Tel—offers that, as yet, were not quite good enough. He wanted one of the big international wire services, preferably Associated Press or UPI, and more: he wanted not a desk job here in London, but command of an overseas bureau of his own. She had heard about it in their pillow talk. Paris would do him, when it was free. Or Berlin, after the surrender. And after that . . . New York and the top rungs of his own specialist trade.

In theory it was possible. Soon after the war, perhaps, things would change quickly. But for the moment the way was clear for just such a deal. And what he didn't want, didn't need, was a wife. He couldn't ask anyone like Ronnie to leave a protected, moneyed background and wait, somewhere in suburban London, for a call to a long series of globe-hopping moves towards the top. Harvey's unspoken idea was, Ronnie knew, that what they had now was time out of war: fun, wonderful, but not a sound base for a future like this.

Though it saddened her, Ronnie reasoned differently. Harvey's plan made sense only up to a point. She could see him bargaining for the Paris office and getting it. But she didn't see him pushing into the chauvinistic top echelons of AP or UPI. The Americans holding fast to the top rungs weren't likely to help Harvey, an outsider, up to a Vice-Presidency—even in due time. For the rest, she already knew enough about the newspaper game to know that it was an enclosed, demanding life, in which even the big names were forever at the mercy of a telephone or a cable; their lives interrupted and fragmented by the sudden eruption of events. They left their homes, their wives, children, holidays, anniversaries and hobbies suddenly to collect or direct the news. They left by air in the middle of the night, never knowing exactly when they could return to pick up the threads of their own lives. They were no more than well-paid gypsies with a fever which gave them no peace all their working lives.

Harvey deserved better. She would have preferred her father to find a place for Harvey in the film industry, where the rewards were greater and the wives travelled with the company, on the company. One hurdle there was already overcome. Croft liked him. But when she had said as much, Harvey's reaction had been dramatic, aloof, indignant, alarmed. She regretted it at once, knowing that it sounded as if she were setting him up for marriage, and never again ventured even close to the subject.

One way to cope with Harvey now was to tell him. But that wouldn't do, either. He would be astonished, dismayed even. Some part of his ego needed to believe that she loved him, would not be able to accept that, even after all they had shared, she was not won. Even if it made things easier for him, it would spoil everything else.

She determined to keep her guilt. What she did, instead, was to hold Harvey off a little herself. She made excuses not to see him too often.

His relief was touching. She could almost see the need for a break receding in his mind. If she wasn't getting intense, perhaps he need not. Perhaps, after all, they were just loving friends.

Ronnie could have wept for him.

Harvey threw himself into his work afresh. The war was hotting up. He had been on the night desk on what Hitler called 'The worst day of my life'. The assault on the South of France had begun, and in the Argentan-Falaise gap twenty-three German divisions were locked in a narrow pocket by Patton, Bradley and the French.

At ABP it had been a fevered exhausting night. When

Sam Prentice relieved him at eight, after 'reading in' to the night's events, background stories waiting to go out on Creed tape hung like yards of perforated pasta from the 'waiting' pins by the master printer, and every machine in the room had been hammering out history for several hours.

Prentice took one look at the pale juniors and at Harvey and almost pulled him out of the seat at the head of the horseshoe ring of tables.

"Go on," he said. "Get out. Piss off. Leave." He was already dabbling masterfully through the pile of cable flimsies barely 'tasted'.

Harvey walked stiffly down Whitefriars Street to Temple Chambers, blinking in the early sun. He wanted only sleep. He'd eaten toast, drunk tea through the night. He fell exhausted into his bed and slept at once.

The clamour of the phone woke him at five. It was McNair.

"I hate to do this to you, but Bass is off sick. Can you take his shift?"

"What about you taking it?" Harvey growled.

McNair said patiently: "I'll be there with you. The tide's coming in, son. Get here, will you?"

Harvey got there. And stayed there, snatching a few fretful hours of sleep in the cork-lined, sound-proof phone box, using a pile of old morgue papers for a pillow, eating only cheese rolls and the inevitable toast, drinking gallons of tea to keep his eyes open. He sent a copy-boy down to Temple Chambers for a clean shirt, and changed in the wash-room. Otherwise he was there for four days.

In that 96 hours, St. Malo and Falaise, Chartres and Orleans were abandoned by the Germans, and Field Marshal Von Kluge, replaced by Field Marshal Walther Model, committed suicide rather than risk the Führer's wrath or worse.

Just once on the Thursday night, Harvey reeled out of the building to escape for a few minutes the incessant, deafening clash of the banked teleprinters and the smell of carbon books, copy paper, heaped ashtrays and stewed tea. His neck ached, his eyes were red-rimmed, and his beard was silken down.

He stood, weaving and uncertain, on the corner of the street by the Black and White Milk Bar, his eyes unable to cope with the blackout's gloom. A raid was in progress. Anti-aircraft guns flashed and roared above Ludgate Hill. A monstrous fire-glow grew again in the sky behind St. Paul's. He wondered about Ronnie and couldn't place what she might be doing or thinking in the unreal world created by his fatigue. Who was Ronnie, exactly?

Shrapnel began to fall in a deadly clatter round him. A fearsome dagger-like shard of tortured steel six inches long struck the pavement in front of him, sparking on the kerb. He saw it by the feeble light from the Black and White as someone fumbled out into the night. He moved inside, ordered coffee and fell asleep before it came, his forehead resting on the defunct chromium taps for milk-shake flavours.

When it was all over it was Saturday. He went to bed and slept 24 hours without undressing; sticky, tacky-mouthed and uncaring.

Monday morning he bathed, shaved, changed, ate his bacon ration for the week, drank a pot full of coffee and rang Ronnie. Her voice, soft with sleep, was suddenly very dear to him.

"Dinner," he said. "And dancing."

"If we must." She sounded pleased to hear him.

They talked a long time. She laughed a lot and he listened to the cool, clear appeal of it. She had known, of course, about the four days out of his life. He'd rung her twice to forecast his release. Even so, he marvelled that there was no word of complaint from her, as there would have been with most. He was moved by her, even over the phone. But he felt safer still from involvement. Once or twice during the day, more confident now of his detachment, he wondered if marriage mightn't work after all. And didn't astonish himself.

Monday evening, he took Ronnie to the Piccadilly Hotel. The Food (Restrictions on Meals in Establishments) Order, 1941 made little difference to anyone hungry enough. Ronnie had been eating snacks only at the MOI. Since breakfast, Harvey had opened a tin of soup and fried some croutons for it. That was all. They ate eagerly now.

He particularly noticed her hair. When he'd first met Ronnie, she had her hair done regularly by Max of South Audley Street. Now she was wearing it, just as she did during the day, in the halo roll which every other girl seemed to have adopted.

An eight-piece band played for dancing. Uniforms jammed the dance floor: the blue and black oddity of the Dutch, the khaki smartness of the British, Poles and Free French, the glamorous olive drab of the Americans. The room bristled with belts, straps, shoulder patches, decorations and glinting buttons. Chagrined by the martial splendour, Harvey, wear-

72

ing the only dark grey suit on the dance floor, whispered: "You're much too nice for a man like me." He kissed her forehead. "No-one is good enough, but I'm the furthest away. Look at all this."

Ronnie looked up, her eyebrows simulating surprise: "Did I ask you to marry me?"

About four bars later, Harvey said tensely: "No, but you will."

"And you'd talk me out of it." She said it flatly, calmly, without any trace of resentment.

He felt very put down and tried to make light of it. "Look around," he said. "All this glamour. What about a dashing Pole? A hand-kissing Free Frenchman—an All-American hero, even? They'd love you in America." He didn't believe it himself, either, but it made him feel better to say it.

Ronnie lost the beat for a moment and Harvey thought he'd overdone it. She looked at him bleakly. "You've made your point, Harvey. I'm free to do what I want. Okay? Now you can sleep with me all next week and with a clear conscience."

Harvey winced. "I asked for that."

"You did rather." She looked up at him for a moment, then impulsively kissed him on the cheek. "But it doesn't mean you can't sleep with me this week. You can say it all again—at intervals."

Harvey stopped dead in the middle of the dance floor and kissed her fervently. Two or three couples saw it and fell back. There was a ripple of applause which reached the bandstand; the music stopped. Still the kiss went on. The leader signalled the clarinet; he came to the front of the stand and softly played the opening bars of *Concerto for Two*. When Harvey looked up, the whole floor was watching. They broke, embarrassed, and the laughter and applause followed them back to their table.

Ronnie beamed at him. Harvey grinned, too, but was faintly embarrassed. He flagged their waiter. "Your place or mine?" he asked Ronnie gruffly.

"Mine," she said. "Your cat watches."

It was well after midnight. Quiet. Nothing since the All-Clear at about nine-thirty. The very first cab he stopped had no objection to a run down to West Kensington.

Most of Ronnie's clothes and her cherished possessions were now at Mount Street, but she had also taken a tiny flat in Queen's Club Gardens. The whole Queen's Club area, with its squares and tennis courts, always an oasis in a desert of squalor, had somehow escaped damage, though five or six streets around it had been reduced to rubble.

The little flat, with its gleaming white paintwork and restful greens, had a welcoming look that Harvey's could never offer. They stood in the dark a long time, the door still wide open. "Make-up off," Ronnie muttered against his mouth.

"Not a chance," Harvey said. He unzipped her dress and she kicked it away. He couldn't see her face clearly. She stepped out of her shoes and her mouth dropped down to his neck. Harvey reached out, found the edge of the door and shut it with his back. He picked her up with his hands under her buttocks, tried to walk with her that way, lost his footing when he trod on a shoe. As they fell, Harvey rolled to take the impact of the floor.

They stayed down for some minutes.

"Put a side lamp on," Ronnie said. "I'll do the blackout. I want to see."

Harvey went into the bedroom, undressed and switched on the bedside lamp.

Ronnie appeared in the doorway, naked. "Now then," she said. "Without an audience . . ."

She was breathtaking. Harvey wanted her badly, but he was diverted by the sheer perfection of her. Again he felt moved to say the words he was sure she wanted to hear. He clamped his mouth shut and went to pick her up.

At about three he sat up, chilled. Ronnie, wearing a wide-awake scrubbed look, was watching him.

"There's a drink on the table." Ronnie pointed.

Harvey drank it. "I'd like some tea," he said. "Any chance?"

When she came back with it Harvey was dressing. He was uncomfortable in her flat. If she was disappointed she didn't show it. She thought she understood.

"I know I'm a bastard," Harvey said. "But not all bastard."

Ronnie said nothing.

"I wish," Harvey said, "that once in a while your calm would crack." It was unfair but he hadn't been able to avoid saying it. He looked at her. "For Christ's sake, Ronnie. Shout. Call me names . . ."

"You're just a bit old-fashioned," Ronnie said at last. "You keep thinking I've done you a favour. Somewhere you heard that nice ladies don't actually like sex and that all mistresses want to be wives." She held out a hand to him. "Such foolishness. Come to bed."

It was hard to refuse. He kissed her tenderly, held her close for a while. But when he broke to drink the tea, he put on his jacket. Then he sat on the edge of the bed for a while, stroking her hair. For a while she smiled, dreamily. Once, when he thought she was asleep she startled him by opening her eyes wide, suddenly, and grinning. At last she slept, her lips slightly apart. He let himself out and trod softly down the stairs to the street.

The cool night air hung heavy with the bombsite smell. It was so quiet he could hear the low voices of the wardens at the ARP post on the corner as they gossiped and sipped tea from tin mugs. He began to walk towards the main road.

He was attuned to the night, feeling the high tuning-fork hum of the London 'silence'.

Because he was alert, listening to the sound of his own muffled footfalls, he heard the sound before the wardens. The loud motor-cycle rasp, drawing nearer. He thought he was mistaken at first. There was no Alert on.

He stopped. The roar grew and became unmistakable. He shrugged and walked on, looking up. Suddenly, there it was, unbelievable, the flaming tail illuminating its head-on direction.

The motor cut.

For a second he stood, stupidly. The howl of its monstrous earthward dive filled the night. He threw himself flat and waited. He squirmed into the ground, tried to cover his ears.

The explosion blotted out everything. He felt the hot rush of the blast. He shouted obscenely as the earth heaved under him. It seemed to go on for minutes. He lay still, shocked, while rubble cascaded down on his back. For an interminable time it seemed to rain assorted solids. Then it was over. He got up, shakily. He heard shouts and sounds, but as if from afar. He shook his head, hoping to clear the deafness. It helped a little. He couldn't quite remember where he was. He stood, dusted himself off, already a little fearful for Ronnie.

He looked round. The street looked different. Perhaps he had walked further than he thought. This one was unrecognisable. The blast had come from his left. He walked back that way, moving faster when he realised that anywhere further back than the main road could mean that Queen's Club had been hit. He began to run. He heard other running feet, shouts, whistles.

At the corner there was a small grocer. He knew it. But was uncertain about the orientation of the four streets that met there. As he drew level, muttering to himself, he jumped, startled by two people locked in a clumsy embrace in the shop's darkened doorway.

"Jesus," he said aggrievedly. "No-one is that hard-up." He said it loudly, on the move, already past them. He now saw the back of the Queen's Club rooflines looming in the darkness against the purplish sky. It was equally clear that the V1 had fallen diagonally across the road from where he stood. There was the flicker of fire, urgent shouts, the flash of masked torches in the centre of the street. Then, as the smoke and dust cleared, he could see the ragged smoking gap in the row of little terraced houses. Even as he watched someone began to scream continuously.

Harvey stepped off the kerb, distressed. First he'd make sure of Ronnie, then he'd go and help. He looked back at the shop doorway. The dim figures seemed not to have changed position.

Something about the lack of movement or sound from them worried him. He took two steps back and peered into the deep shadows, feeling foolish.

"I'd go home if I were you," he said. "If home is still there." It sounded silly, but he felt he had to say something.

He waited. When there was no response he stepped closer. At first he had the notion that the couple were having intercourse, or had just had it and were arrested in a long moment of breath-stopping ecstasy. The girl, her eyes wide, her head back, mouth open, sagged back, almost prone but not quite. The man, with his back to him, held her round the waist, crouched over her. They were both motionless.

He sensed that they were dead before he touched them. But he needed to go on with the movement, needed to see them fall, before he yelped in an outcry of pity, anger, fright and revulsion.

The two bodies crumpled into the angle of shop doorway like dummies from which support is suddenly removed. They were untouched, unblemished. Just dead. Victims of the bizarre effects of blast.

Harvey backed away, then ran across the road. "Fine bloody war correspondent I'm going to make," he told himself aloud. He heard the sound of ambulances close at hand. A rescue truck drew up with a squeal of brakes and helmeted workers were throwing a barrier across pavements both sides of the street. Running blindly across the road to the crews beginning to gather round the mounds of rubble where six or seven homes had stood only five minutes before, he ran straight into the arms of a policeman. Hardly recognising his own voice, he took the man across the road to the shop and left him there examining the bodies.

Ronnie's block was on the other side of the bombed houses. He crunched through grit and broken brick in the square, pounded up the stairs, ignoring the almost hysterical porter. He put his key in the lock, threw open the door and called out.

He switched the hall light on, froze when he saw the splintered doorframes and felt, rather saw, that the living room was somehow open to the night.

"Christ!" he shouted pointlessly. "Ronnie."

He found her in the bedroom bruised and shaken. The bedroom door, blown off its hinges, lay across the bed. Ronnie was sitting on the edge, crying silently, sucking in huge breaths, holding her upper arm.

"I can't move it, can't feel it," she said shakily.

He found the torch in the bedside table, looked all over the arm. A welt was beginning to grow on the arm, just below the shoulder where the door had caught her.

"If it had caught you on the head you'd be dead," he said idiotically. "Sit here a minute." He pushed the door off onto the floor and wrapped her arm in the quilt. Glass crunched underfoot everywhere as he moved round the flat. The windows were gone from the living room. So were the frames. There were only splintered oblong holes in the walls, open to the night. The shredded curtains were wrapped around splintered spars of wood. He propped the broken living room door up behind the front door. The kitchen, he found, was more or less intact; it had been ajar, probably, and spared because of it. He first checked the blackout in there and then carried Ronnie through, sat her down and put a kettle on. When it boiled he made hot sweet tea, poured scotch into it and stood over her while she sipped it, shivering. He drank some himself.

The whole upper area of Ronnie's arm turned purple and black. He found a silk scarf in the bedroom chest, looped it over her head and made her carry the arm in a sling. But by first light she trembled violently when she had to move it and gritted her teeth with: "Not so much pain as a kind of fierce cramp."

Under her instruction he took what clothes she needed from the bedroom, helped her dress, painfully, and then went out to get a cab. It took a very long time. At last he captured an ancient Beardmore coming down from Hammersmith and bribed the driver to forget his breakfast.

By six they were at St Stephen's Hospital. After a long wait for X-ray a very young doctor told her: "Nothing very much to worry about. Hairline fracture of the humerus. If you want to wear the sling for a day or two until the bruise subsides a bit, then do. But you ought to have some physiotherapy. And you ought to work the arm normally."

Harvey took her home to Mount Street. The housekeeper, Mrs Beaney, enfolded her and hustled her off to bed. She gave Harvey a look that suggested criminal negligence on his part.

He waited until she was settled. He looked at himself in a hall mirror. His face was filthy. There was a dusting of plaster and dust on his hair. When he went in to see her, she looked strained and tired. He couldn't equate the Ronnie who smiled wanly at him now with the Ronnie who, only a few hours ago, had danced and been the centre of attraction.

"We both need a holiday," he said ruefully. It was meant to be a joke. If people took time off at all, they went to see relatives they were parted from. Or they sat at home, reading and sleeping, especially sleeping. They sat in the sun to simulate pre-war suntans. They dug gardens and walked for the exercise.

"I know," Ronnie said. "And I can arrange it." But she wouldn't say how, or where, or when.

Harvey went back to Temple Chambers. He hadn't fed his cat. He thought he looked forty, felt sixty. A holiday? The whole world needed a holiday.

14

Where had it all gone wrong? Both Reiters had disappeared and Brandt was faced with the necessity of telling Himmler. The idea had seemed sound enough. He could think of a score of small affairs of the kind which had been dealt with easily and without repercussions. But this one, through no fault of his, had not only misfired, but looked like becoming the sort of thing which would produce problems.

It was a failure at a bad time, too. Goebbels had gone prickly again. The pressures from Bormann were unceasing. The People's Courts were still busy hanging conspirators as fast as Himmler could unearth them. The Reichsführer was overworking. He was tired and testy. There was no telling how he would react to additional problems now. So Brandt rehearsed the manner of breaking the news over and over, couching it in such a way as to absolve himself from any blame and as though it was, in any case, only a temporary setback from which a solution might still be snatched.

The Gestapo had begun looking for the Reiters. They had frightened Reimund, the Uncle, but were satisfied that he knew nothing. The chances were, Brandt thought, that they had bolted together. He couldn't be sure that they were acting in concert and were unlikely to surface somewhere and talk. And because of that uncertainty the matter couldn't simply be closed. He sweated, knowing that only the death of both men would now satisfy Himmler.

He fretted for 24 hours, hoping for news, then chose a moment when the ante-room of Himmler's Prinz Albrecht-strasse office was full of visitors with a claim on the Reichsführer's time. He offered the news as a not-too-significant titbit, sandwiching its release between visitors. "One other thing, Reichsführer," he said as casually as he could. "The man Reiter has disappeared."

Himmler sat back and stared at him. In his nervousness Brandt for once found this disconcerting, though he knew the ploy well. There was a short silence.

"Disappeared." Himmler weighed the word. "Which one?"

Brandt was caught on one foot. This was not precisely how he had planned to deliver the details and it threw him. He reddened and his anxiety deepened.

"Uh—our man," Brandt said. He hurried on: "Of course the Gestapo has made thorough enquiries. He was staying with an uncle—"

"Dead? Alive? Run off?" Himmler interrupted.

"I'm not sure yet," Brandt confessed. He took a deep breath. "It seems, though that the brother, too, is missing. Of course the Luftwaffe may know more about that, but to find out what they know may take a little longer."

Himmler looked unmoved. He fidgeted with his papers. "We must know," he said finally. "We must have the facts."

"We shall," Brandt assured him earnestly.

"Meanwhile," Himmler went on, "there is Koch. I'm not

79

sure that we would be right to pursue that any longer. It always had its dangers. They will be much greater now." He looked at Brandt sorrowfully. "I may have to take a back seat after all when Koch's plan is announced. When it is enthusiastically endorsed by the Führer. When it results in my authority and my planning being eroded by that parasite Bormann." He took off his spectacles and began to polish them, then the bitterness of the moment made him throw them down. He shook his head sadly.

Brandt felt the back of his neck grow rigid. He braced himself for an outburst, or worse. He heard the clock ticking. The silence lengthened. The moment seemed to freeze into a weird tableau.

Himmler burned but at once adopted an expression of inscrutability while he considered the debacle. From this result it was clear that the Koch project had been unsound from the start. Only the fortuitous existence of the brothers Reiter, one a Luftwaffe pilot and the other a tool ready to hand, had tempted him to consider the matter beyond that first conversation. Now the whole thing appeared absurd. He had allowed Brandt to move him towards endorsing it and in the process had lost several days in which a more practical answer to Koch might have been found.

He toyed with the idea of revenge. Brandt deserved punishment. But there would be little satisfaction in that. If he ordered Brandt's death he would simply lose a good man. If he kept him but punished him in some other way he would, almost certainly, lose some of the value of the man. Good sense suggested that he should bite on the failure and make light of it. That way he would win renewed loyalty from Brandt and perhaps inspire in him a renewed fervour that could be directed towards wiping out the error.

At last he said, quietly: "Never mind, Rudolf. It seemed a good idea at the time, eh? And your solution did promise well. It's not your fault."

Brandt was staggered. This was so unlike Himmler that his surprise outweighed his relief. For a moment he couldn't trust himself to speak. When he recovered he said, feeling genuine gratitude towards his chief: "We will find out exactly where both men are. And when they're found they will both have to be eliminated. You agree, Reichsführer?"

"Quite," Himmler said. He put his spectacles back on, peered at his papers. "Is that Ohlendorf out there? If so, send him in."

Still dazed, Brandt hurried to obey, feeling better than he had for many hours. And even as he ushered in the head of the Inland SD, SS-Brigadeführer Ohlendorf, he made an iron vow to himself that he would find and eliminate the brothers Reiter. He had Himmler's approval. Nothing would save them.

15

By the third day Willi's close confinement was beginning to eat at his self-confidence. For twenty-four hours after his interview with Goering he had been buoyed up by the thought that the old fox wouldn't have bothered with all that charade if he had not intended to get him clear away. But his isolation brought on claustrophobia. He jumped whenever his door was approached. His fears fed on his nerves. In no time he found himself constantly in fear of an assassin. After all, he again reasoned feverishly, that was the easiest solution for everyone involved.

He paced endlessly up and down the tiny room, its plain paint and featureless utility turning his thoughts constantly inward. It even began to feel like a coffin. Twice the power had failed in the whole building and he lost not only the light but the air conditioning, so that if he smoked more than one cigarette the room filled with smoke.

He was not allowed to leave the room, even for exercise. Three times a day his huge escort, Stiefel, took him along the corridors to his meals and immediately back to his room. When he asked for clean linen, cigarettes, books and newspapers they were produced so quickly that he began to feel they were humouring a condemned man. On the second night there was a heavy raid on the inner city. Stiefel at once appeared to conduct him to a senior officers' shelter in the basement, then waited outside the shelter door for the duration of the RAF's 45-minute onslaught.

He continued to eat with the senior officers, too; on the basis, he assumed, that none of them would be likely to know him or even to be curious about him. Once he saw Milch in the dining room, and another time Bodenschatsch, but he knew none of the generals with which the headquarters seemed to be peppered.

Each time he left it for a meal, the room was cleaned and tidied. The oddity of this got on his nerves. It suggested a constant watch by some unseen authority, as on a caged animal.

He read the newspapers, could not concentrate on the books. Instead he went over and over his lists and plans, checking and re-checking, finding hope in the very idea of flight.

Then, after lunch on the third day, there was a knock and a young captain stepped into the room. He stood there nervously, smiling uncertainly.

Willi was speechless. He shook his head, astonished and overjoyed. He knew his visitor well. He was Dieter Bauer, a young pilot who had served in Willi's own staffel in 1941 until grounded by an unlucky wound; a near-miss from an anti-aircraft shell over the Kent coast had punched a hole in the side of his Dornier immediately behind Bauer's cockpit. The bomber had limped on home, but a shell splinter had sliced through the heavy deltoid muscle at front and back of Bauer's left shoulder.

He had liked Bauer enormously, remembered him as a shy, keen and rather impressionable young man who had hero-worshipped Willi in his day as a bomber ace with a coveted decoration.

This Bauer was thinner and without some of the ingenuous appeal he'd had then. But Willi was so delighted to see a friendly face from better days that he was suddenly filled with emotion. Here, surely, was someone he could talk to—and, more important, trust.

Willi leapt forward and embraced Bauer warmly, clapping him on the back. Absurdly, he still could not find words to express his elation.

Bauer seemed overwhelmed. His pleasure, too, was apparent.

"Dieter, you old bastard!"

"Willi!"

They laughed. Willi thought his own laughter sounded a little hysterical. He backed off, smiling. "Good to see you, my friend. What on earth are you doing here? And should you be here at all?"

"Oh yes," Bauer said shyly. "The Reich Marshal has sent me."

Willi looked him over. He still had the boyish face and the

tentative unassuming charm. He had been going to ask, "How's the shoulder?" when he suddenly took in what Bauer had said.

"You?" He looked incredulous. "You're the one who—"

"That's right," Bauer nodded happily. He looked at Willi very seriously. "Anything I can do." He spread his arms wide.

"That's wonderful," Willi breathed. "Just wonderful."

And again Bauer's face dissolved into embarrassment like a schoolboy who had been too roundly complimented.

Willi grabbed his good arm and sat him down urgently, demanding to know how he came to be on Goering's staff. "Old Hermann clearly thinks a lot of you," he said.

"It was luck, really," Bauer said surprisingly. "I mean, I can't use the arm too much. The surgery didn't entirely work. So they had to find something for me to do. And in a sort of way I've become a bit of a specialist." He grinned, then said very soberly: "The Reich Marshal trusts me with all sorts of things." He said it proudly, and then as if to make light of it: "I mean he finds me useful. And I've learned a lot more than I knew when I was with you." He was at once embarrassed again and began pulling at his right eyebrow. It was a mannerism which Willi remembered, suddenly, vividly, from briefings long ago. "I don't mean that. What I mean is . . ."

"I know what you mean," Willi punched him lightly on the chest. "But you actually like old Hermann?" He looked incredulous.

"In a way, yes." Bauer said seriously. He hesitated, framing the thought. "You know in a headquarters like this . . . there is so much laxity, apathy—cynicism even—among the top people." His expression urged Willi to believe it. "Oh, Moller's all right. But Milch!" He wrinkled his face in disgust. "The Reich Marshal, though, always has enthusiasm—and speed. Always. He's always trying at least." He stopped abruptly, conscious that a new veneration was perhaps too much in evidence. "Well anyway," he said apologetically, "all the rest have simply given up."

Willi was impressed. Despite himself he wondered if there wasn't something in what Bauer had said. "I'm sure you're right," he said. "Or anyway, I hope to God you're right." He sat back. "What are your orders now, then?"

Bauer nodded seriously. He produced the folder from under the stiff arm that he held against his body. "My instructions are that you will tell me what you need and that I am to produce it if it is humanly possible."

83

Willi's spirits soared again. So he was not just an embarrassment to the Luftwaffe high command. And not one that could much more easily be disposed of than by the involved plan he'd been invited to embrace. It was true, after all.

"I don't want you to tell me anything you shouldn't, but in order to judge what you need—uh, what exactly is the nature of the mission?" Bauer said.

Willi stared. "You mean you don't know?"

"No," Bauer shook his head, smiling.

Willi took a deep breath. "I'll try to keep it brief," he said. "No, don't write anything down yet, for God's sake." He lit a cigarette. "I am to fly to England, one way trip. I am to make some sort of landing, burn the aircraft and melt into the scenery until the war is over and it is safe for me to come out." He watched Bauer's face.

The young pilot swore. He looked stunned. After a few moments he refocused on Willi. "And this is not a joke?"

"Not my kind of joke," Willi said.

"Great God." He fidgeted with the edge of his pad. "Is it permitted to ask why?"

Willi said, carefully: "Let's say that quite inadvertently I have mortally offended the SS. I think probably that the less you know about it the better. But if it helps, I have not disgraced this uniform. Rather it's the case that I would not do so and thus have made an enemy of Himmler. I have been told by the Reich Marshal that Germany will not be safe for me, that the Luftwaffe cannot protect me, and that in all probability the only place in all Europe beyond the reach of the Gestapo is England itself."

Bauer gaped. He shook his head. "Bloody fantastic," he muttered at last. "Bloody fantastic."

"And ironic?" Willi said.

Bauer nodded. "The only place a German officer may hide . . . is among the enemy? Yes, that is ironic. God, Willi, how the hell can I help? Just tell me. I'll work my legs off on this one. Anything—anything at all, my friend."

Willi grinned. "Thanks. How about an aircraft? I was promised a Focke-Wulfe."

"You've got it," Bauer said promptly. "In good shape. Newish, even. No problems. Next?"

"Point of departure?"

Bauer did not even need his file. "That will have to be Rangsdorf. It doesn't matter why. Just let's say that's where some of my—jobs have been based. I know the people. They have special instructions to humour me."

"Can I go in daylight?"

"Yes." Bauer thought about it.

"When?"

"I'll let you know. It depends on what you ask from me. How long it takes to assemble it. What about fuel?"

"Nothing special," Willi said. "Full tanks, nothing more. But I do want some special equipment. First, I need a big explosive charge in the aircraft. Something stable—I don't want anything that's going to spread me all over the English countryside if I make a bad landing. So we're talking about electrical detonation and a good switch; something I can't trip by accident. On the other hand, when I do throw it, it must be reliable—must blow that aircraft apart after about 25 seconds. So much so that I want even the experts to be puzzling for days about whether or not I was in it when it blew up. Can you do that?"

"No problem," Bauer said. He grinned. "You see—I have learned a few useful things."

"And before that I need to be able to make smoke. Again, it must work."

Bauer looked puzzled. "Smoke?"

"As if I'd been hit," Willi explained. "I want to be able to pour it out of the tail." He saw Bauer's scepticism and waved away the objection he was forming. "I know it's improbable. But it may hold someone for a few seconds, just thinking about it. Can it be done?"

"Nothing simpler," Bauer said confidently. "Next?"

"A bicycle. It doesn't have to be English, but it would help if it was. Otherwise paint out, or machine out, any maker's name or badge." He paused while Bauer scribbled in his notebook. "And it's got to go behind the seat. I know there isn't a lot of room in an FW, but it should be possible . . . just. If necessary I could lose an inch or two in the cockpit if you want to shove the seat forward."

Bauer smiled. It made him look as young as Willi remembered him. "My lads will enjoy all this. Nothing too testing so far, though. And—"

"Clothes next. A sports jacket," Willi said. "Do we both understand what that means, in English terms?"

"We do," Bauer said. "And grey flannel slacks?"

Willi grinned, too. "And grey flannel slacks. You're obviously an expert. Two suitable shirts. Plain ties. Brown shoes,

English style—none of our civilian, strength-through-joy stuff, all cardboard lumps and bumps. Grey socks." He handed Bauer one of his sheets. "Here, I've written down all my sizes."

Bauer took the sheet and tucked it into the folder. "Listen," Willi warned. "All this stuff has to be passably British. If you're in doubt, show me. No labels, unless of course, you can manage the real thing. Even then, show me if you're in doubt." He returned to his lists. "A rucksack, a money belt, small change, handkerchiefs—and a bunch of keys—never mind to what. And don't bother with underwear. If I get searched down to my underwear I'm lost anyway. It's the surface that counts, that's what has to be good enough to keep me from being searched."

They worked for another half-hour. When Willi finally folded his lists, Bauer said: "One thing. About the money. No problems there. You can have plenty of it. But I have to tell you—it's not the real thing."

Willi stared. "Counterfeit? What sort of notes?"

"Five-pound notes," Bauer said. "It seems we have a surfeit. Don't trouble yourself too much about detection. The British aren't used to counterfeit money. It's not like America, where it happens all the time and they're constantly alert to it. And this stuff is good. Very good. It will take a very long time before it is noticed."

"How much?"

"How much do you want to risk?"

Willi thought about it.

"Three thousand?" he said finally.

Bauer thought about it, too. "It can be done," he said. "We'd better divide it between the money belt—for emergencies, say—and the rucksack which will have to take the rest."

He stood up. "I'll come and see you again tomorrow," he promised. He held out his hand.

At the door, Bauer looked back. He shook his head at Willi. "Don't worry about this lot," he said. "We'll do it right. Sooner you than me."

Willi smiled thinly. "Don't you believe it," he said. He liked Bauer. He was confident now that he was going to get what he needed, but saddened by the thought that Bauer and a good many like him needed luck more than he did.

16

"I'm worried about you," Goering told Hitler. "You should not remain here in Rastenburg through the winter." He looked out of the window of the Führer's hut at the gloomy woodland settlement. In the poor light filtering through the tall trees, the separate compounds ringed with wire, the gates, sentries and overgrown bunkers looked more like a concentration camp than a headquarters. "What have you done about your Swiss specialist?"

"I can't think of that at the moment," Hitler said irritably. "I'll send someone to Montreux to fetch him when I'm ready."

"I'd like to have your word on that," Goering said sternly. "I shan't hesitate to make a nuisance of myself on this subject."

"Yes, yes," Hitler said testily.

Goering sighed. The Wolf's Lair got on his nerves. It always did. All this rustic wooden furniture. And poor food. And no proper ventilation in the bedrooms. Most of all he hated the mosquitoes which were everywhere. The local joke was that the huge Rastenburg variety got that way by feeding on the blood of the SS guards. Goering silently cursed Morell, Hitler's doctor. The man ought long since to have insisted on a change and a rest. Hitler looked terrible. For a while after the July 20th business he had seemed buoyed up by his narrow escape. The idea that Providence had spared him, that it was His Destiny to go on directing the war, had excited him and seen him over the first few weeks. Now anti-climax seemed to have set in. The man twitched. He was pale. His eyes were red-rimmed with fatigue and his temper was even more uncertain than usual. The Reich Marshal glanced covertly at his watch. There was still a little time to go before the ritual preparation for the 6 p.m. Staff Conference. He changed the subject.

"I don't criticise you on this score," he said. "If everyone worked as you work, the war would take a sharp turn for the better at once." He could see that he had reclaimed Hitler's attention, and he went on earnestly: "The Luftwaffe, now, does what it can. You have set us a new role in this phase of the war, and with the men and machines we have we will do what flesh and blood may—no, more than that."

"Exactly." Hitler's eyes gleamed. "A superhuman effort. That is all that's needed. Total war. Total, merciless, unceasing war." He frowned suddenly. "You know there has been little else in my life for years now. No diversions, no amusements, no comforts. I only ask what I perform myself."

Goering nodded vigorously. "I understand that. We all understand that." But the Führer stood up and moved to the window, staring out; a sure sign that he was into his stride.

"I wonder sometimes if the German people do realise what sacrifices I have made. If they think that all they hear from me is war, war, war. There are those, you know, who believe that I love war." He turned abruptly and looked to Goering for denial.

"Never," Goering said fervently. "They do understand. They do."

For a moment Hitler seemed satisfied. Then he went on: "But there are those who think it of me. I know that. Cowards—"

"And shirkers," Goering suggested.

"Shirkers," Hitler agreed.

"It's a pity we don't all pull together," Goering sighed.

It was the wrong thing to say. Hitler sat down again and fixed him with a steady glare.

"Why do you say that?" he demanded. "Do you know of any who hold back? People of that kind must be punished. If they are among us, the leaders, the punishment must be even more severe."

Goering was suddenly flustered. For a moment the personal censorship which had to be imposed on anything at all which was said to Hitler had slipped. Without meaning to, he found himself saying, in a complaining tone: "No, I know of nothing concrete. Nothing I can put my finger on. And yet," he paused, reluctantly, and yet knowing there was no way out, now, added: "And yet sometimes I sense that even interdepartmentally there are unsatisfactory areas." He smiled dismissively, and lifting his tone, slapped his enormous thighs decisively. "We must never allow rivalries, things like that, to interfere with the prosecution of the war."

"But it happens?" Hitler insisted. "It has happened? You know of instances?" He was clearly in a mood to be petty.

Goering gestured widely, making light of it. "Oh, I know of instances, yes. I've just had an instance of it."

"Tell me," Hitler commanded.

Goering sniffed and pursed his lips. His tone suggested it was the sort of pinprick which had to be endured. "A veteran bomber pilot with a brother in the SS came to Luftwaffe HQ to report that an attempt had been made to recruit him into some absurd plot." Watching Hitler closely, he shivered a little. He made the rest of the story in two quick sentences, wondering if this was wise after all.

Hitler listened transfixed. His eyes glittered oddly as he considered what he'd been told. "You never knew the identity of the intended victim?"

Goering shook his head.

"Or what plane? From where?"

"No. He was to be told when he had agreed to undertake the affair."

"It could have been me," Hitler said.

"I don't think so," Goering said. "The affair was begun so stupidly, so overtly that I think the target was small fry." He wagged a fat finger at the Führer. "But you must always be on your guard. I'm very glad you have the SS to protect you now."

"What steps have you taken?" Hitler demanded. He was clearly not going to be side-tracked.

"What steps?" Goering's mind moved quickly. He'd come this far. Had been forced to in a way. There was nothing to be gained now by backing off again. If he played it carefully he could allow Hitler to suspect the SS if he wanted to, and at the same time he would have got in first with a clean breast of the affair if it ever came up again at a later date. If Himmler was equally worried he might some day twist the story round. He made up his mind.

"It would be easier to take steps," he said carefully, "if the officer concerned had not since disappeared."

"Disappeared?" Hitler's interest was fanned again.

"That's right," Goering said. "The Officer, a Knight's Cross holder and a very brave young man indeed was, of course, ordered to report on a daily basis while a statement was taken and his statement investigated to the full. No doubt I should have had to ensure that Himmler saw a transcript of the statement—as a courtesy and especially since the allegation was that the man's brother had approached him on behalf of Dr Brandt. But the officer never reappeared at HQ and all efforts to trace him have so far failed. We have, of course, sent a memo across to the Reichssicherheitshauptampt." He added slyly: "They're much better at that sort of thing than we are."

"God!" Hitler suddenly exclaimed. "If only we could get on with fighting the war."

"Exactly," Goering agreed. "That is what I was saying. As if we don't have enough problems—that there are people who will sabotage the war effort with all this sort of underhand plotting."

Hitler interrupted: "But you don't believe the story of SS involvement?"

"I do not!" Goering lied. "Some filthy little group, perhaps. Not the SS. I'm sure that both brothers were led to believe that there was SS involvement. But no. If I believed that, then I'd be ready to throw up my hands and cry 'We're done for!'"

The Führer looked at the Bavarian clock on a side table. It was time for the 6 p.m. Staff Conference. Punctually on the appointed time, Gerda Daranowski, one of Hitler's favourite secretaries, appeared in the doorway; slim, efficient-looking in a severe tailored suit and white blouse. She inclined her head. Hitler stood up at once. He put an arm round Goering's fat shoulders and walked with him. "You are right," he said. "Not to believe this lie. Heinrich has better control than that. But your own attitude does you credit. You are an example to others. Thank you for telling me, too. I know that you didn't want to. I sensed that, you know. You didn't want to tell me such things, knowing how the telling would upset me. Thank you, Hermann."

Goering couldn't believe his luck. He kept his face straight as they went towards the Conference Room together. He hoped Bormann would notice the special favour in which he was held. The Führer's arm was still round his shoulders.

He made a mental note that he could now safely give the order that Willi Reiter should be airborne as fast as possible, before Himmler's snoops switched their attention to Luftwaffe HQ. If he'd had to, he'd have taken the risk anyway. Now there was no risk. "Up yours, Heinrich," he thought. "Get yourself out of that one."

17

In Berlin it was one of those perfect late summer mornings. The sky was almost cloudless, the sun bright; but as yet there was no heat in it to cloy the day. It was ideal flying weather, with only cool light airs and maximum visibility.

Bauer found Willi sitting on his bed, dressed and ready. He looked up uncertainly. His right hand was ceaselessly clicking his old, leather-covered Thorens jerk-wheel lighter. Bauer remembered it from the old days. It had always been Willi's talisman.

Willi's breakfast tray, delivered by the quiet giant, Stiefel, at seven according to Bauer's instructions, sat on the desk. Bauer inspected it. Only the coffee cup had been used. "You may regret that before the day's out," he said. Willi only grunted.

There was an awkward pause. Willi looked at Bauer. He could think of nothing much to say. At one moment he thought he would give a hand or a foot to be out in the open air again, whatever the hazards; and as suddenly he would feel an odd attachment to his tiny prison. He had become used to it. He had slept, fed and been protected here in this centrally heated womb. The problems were outside and the sounds of war had reached him only faintly.

Bauer was weeding his right eyebrow again. He accurately diagnosed Willi's mood and lifted his tone to one of brisk enthusiasm. "Wait until you see what sort of a day I've arranged for you. You won't be sorry to be out of this hole."

Willi nodded. He stood up, pulled his uniform jacket down. He looked keenly at Bauer. "So this is it? I really am going?"

Bauer mimed astonishment. "Did you doubt it?" He looked round. "Anything you want here?"

Willi picked up the family photograph he had tucked into a groove in the pen tray on his first day. The smiling sepia faces looked out on another time, uncomprehending. He tucked it into his wallet. "Nothing," he said. "Let's go." At the door he dived back and rescued a roll of rough rye bread from his tray and pocketed that, too.

Once outside the cool morning air hit him like a cold shower. He stood for a moment on the top step, gulping clean air. His nose and throat were dry and tingling from days and nights in the stale, recirculated air. He squinted at the sky. Dieter was right. It was a perfect day. At once he felt a lot better. Bauer was enjoying himself. Like a magician who performs the unbelievable, he now waved Willi to a huge, if slightly elderly, Mercedes. "It used to belong to General Fromm. It seems the Luftwaffe was short of wheels and a whole batch like this were reissued." He scowled: "If we keep losing generals in the cells of the Prinz Albrechtstrasse we'll soon have one apiece."

Though they started the drive to Rangsdorf in quiet good humour, they were both soon depressed by mile after mile of bombed-out buildings. Once or twice Bauer indicated some particularly grisly ruin. In the outer suburbs of the city, Willi turned to stare back at a huge, fire-gutted factory surrounded by the still-fresh greens of summer. He reflected ruefully on the time when, caught up in the excitement and aggressions of the early days of the war, he would have been proud of producing just such an effect on the soil to which he was now escaping.

Bauer glanced at him anxiously. Partly because he wanted to lift Willi's mood and partly because he really believed it, he said with jubilant conviction: "You know—I think you're going to get away with this."

It had some effect. Willi forgot the scenery. "If I do," he said smiling, "it will be thanks to you entirely." He hadn't wanted to ask questions before, wanting Bauer to have his complete trust, but now he said, tentatively: "The stuff is at Rangsdorf? All of it?"

"Everything."

There it was. It brooked no questions. Willi took a big breath. Dieter Bauer was all right. And he could be right, too, with his prediction. Perhaps he would get away with it.

A repair gang of wretched-looking Todt labourers was working on a crater in the approach road to the airfield. They waited while the overseeing Luftwaffe men, stripped to the waist, hauled round two giant sheets of perforated metal alloy to bridge the hole, then drove gingerly across. Another gang was using a mechanical shovel to fill a crater behind the administration block. The control tower crawled with men replacing glass.

They pulled up behind the admin block. "Wait here,"

Bauer told him. He walked briskly away. Willi looked round curiously. He knew Rangsdorf only slightly. Most of the hangars looked empty. A JU52 transport stood out on its apron, but that was all. He wanted to get out and look round for the promised FW, but Bauer might be back. He looked at his watch. It was 9.30. He wondered how long it would be before he got away. He realised only now that he had given no thought at all to the physical details of the flight. Could Dieter provide all that, too? Dismayed, he got out and walked nervously round and round the car.

Bauer wouldn't have gone to all the trouble to collect the stuff they'd agreed upon and forgotten something as basic and important as this. He felt his spirits lift again. He could get away with it. He did a few tap steps he'd once learned at dancing class when he was 14. He'd held on to them, once in a while performing them in the mess; always with the modest implication that there was more if he cared to attempt it.

Bauer found him standing there grinning. "Come on," he said briskly. Willi got back into the car. Bauer roared round the patched perimeter road to a small hangar at the north end of the field. Now Willi saw the FW. It was a D12, not the fastest thing in the air, but good enough. He stared. As they got closer he saw it looked good, smart in its patchy camouflage of black, grey, white. Two fitters snapped to attention as they swept up. So did the guard on the door of the flimsy hangar-office. Bauer produced a key, unlocked the door and waved Willi inside.

Willi stared. It was all there. He broke into a huge grin, overwhelmed. Bauer had told him, but seeing it was different. He picked up the brown sports jacket, feeling the thick, soft tweed, turned over the shirts, socks . . .

"The money," Bauer said proudly. On the plank table were a new, stiff money belt and some thick packets in tough, blue bank paper. Watching Willi's astonishment and delight, Bauer's own smile was broad and happy. But he broke off to consult his watch. "Uh—can I ask you to get changed quickly. For one reason and another I have to get you away swiftly now." While Willi stripped, he began laying things out in the order Willi would need them, beginning with the money belt, which was already packed to its capacity.

When he was dressed, Willi held up his arms, staring at the sleeves of the sports jacket. It was a perfect fit. The money was a bit bulky round his waist. But he need not button the jacket. He shook his head dazedly.

Bauer held out a tiny automatic pistol.

Willi put up a hand. "I don't want that, thanks."

Bauer hesitated, almost withdrew it. Then he said: "Look, throw it out en route if you like. But just for now—take it, please." He held it out firmly.

Willi shrugged. He looked at the gun again. It was British; the Browning .22. He checked the safety catch, finally stuck it into his belt at the back, under the jacket. It was uncomfortable and he would throw it out, but . . .

"That's loaded, by the way," Bauer said. "Now. Map pack. Recommended flight pattern. No problems, really, if you stick to that. It's your sky until you're over the North Sea and turning in from the east. And even then, anything the Yanks have got up will be glad not to see you if you don't see them. Anything that isn't on a bomb run—and that'll be RAF at this time of day, they leave it to the Yanks in daylight, as you know—anything RAF you see will be in ground-support, low and preoccupied. You'll be well out of reach." He threw up his hands. "After that, well you know best. Now here's the met." He handed over the met flimsy and Willi glanced at it. He smiled to himself. "That's right," Bauer said happily. "Cloud over the east coast of Britain, elsewhere perfect. I said I'd fix everything." He checked his watch again. "Come," he said. He put an arm tentatively round Willi's shoulders. Their roles really were reversed, Willi thought. Dieter Bauer, the shy, deferential acolyte had become the boss. And bomber ace Reiter had become his protégé.

On the apron, Bauer nodded to the fitters. A moment later the FW's engine whined, caught, roared and fined down to the warm-up.

Willi turned to say something, but Bauer took him by the arm and hustled him forward. He motioned Willi up onto the wing root and followed him.

"Smoke," Bauer shouted. He reached in and indicated a switch on the left of the panel. It was marked only with a daub of grey paint. "Over there," Bauer couldn't reach it, "under the edge—a big fat rocker switch. You can't miss it and you can't flip it with your knee. It turns through about ninety degrees. Twenty-five seconds. That's what you wanted. That's your funeral if you don't get out fast enough. Okay?"

Bauer dropped back to the ground. Willi took his hand. "Dieter," he began. He wasn't sure what he wanted to say. He was grateful, but much more than that. Despite its purpose, planning this had been a little like the old days—before the cynicism, self-interest and defeatism had crept in. It had warmed him. He felt sure that Bauer recognised it, too, and he was unable to discuss it. He shook Bauer's hand again. "You know," he said, "I never really believed the FW would materialise." He realised that was wrong. "I don't mean that. Once you'd told me, I was sure, of course. But before that. I thought there'd be a bomb or something. I don't know—I just never really believed they wanted me to get away." He laughed.

Bauer looked at him. "And you were right," he said. "They didn't. Or, at least, some didn't."

He let Willi take it in, first, let the shock hit him. Then he nodded, unsmiling: "You're all right. There's nothing wrong with that FW. It'll get you there. You'll do it. Now, for Christ's sake, get on with it."

Bauer stepped forward, touched Willi briefly on the arm and turned away abruptly. The two men standing by looked at the little scene curiously. At Willi standing there, dazed. They watched Bauer climb into his opulent staff car, wave once and then drive off without a backward glance.

Willi straightened up. He nodded to the men. One of them gave him a hand up onto the step. He settled himself, tucked the map pack under his left thigh, and looked over the FW's controls. He checked the fuel, the flaps, the revs. It was all in order. Half his mind was still on what Bauer had said. No point in worrying about that now. He made an effort to concentrate. He slid the canopy shut, checked it, lifted a hand and began to roll the FW190 forward. He checked his watch. It was one minute to ten.

There would be time later to think about Dieter Bauer.

The FW lifted sweetly. It responded magnificently to every touch. Willi set himself into a first climb to 15,000 feet. There was an uncomfortable bulge in his left pocket. He took out the bread roll and bit into it. He was suddenly fiercely hungry.

18

Willi streaked in from the east over the Sussex coast at almost exactly noon. His D12's Junkers Jumo straight engine gave him range enough, a speed of well in excess of 450 mph and a useful ceiling of 37,000 feet. At his present altitude he hoped to be safe enough for the relatively short time he would be in the air over England. He was in trouble if he was pursued by Mustangs; but then he was in trouble if he was pursued too soon by anything—the D12 wasn't armed and anyway he wasn't a fighter pilot. His only immediate problem was the cold. He'd climbed high in the last few minutes to have the advantage of the long drop, but he'd been cold from the start in his 'English' clothes. His legs were numb, his teeth chattered and cold sweat ran down his sides.

He had Littlehampton below him, the sensitive Southampton and Solent areas away past his port wing. It was clear and bright below the cloud layer, with superb visibility. His rough course was due North to Guildford.

Observer Corps stations at Selsey and Shoreham picked him up immediately, despite his height, and leaped to their phones. Within five minutes a flight of three Mustangs was in the air and climbing to look for him. Their Leader, a Flight-Lieutenant Pendry, was told over the R/T: "Single Bandit 32,000 feet, Woking in two minutes." It sounded like a rare treat. With some undisciplined hallooing, the Mustangs swung to head him off. But they were already too late.

Willi had planned it carefully. When Guildford swam up ahead, like a planner's model in miniature, he changed course abruptly. For the benefit of plotters below, the FW banked steeply and dived into sparse cloud, now heading due West. Away to his left some ineffective puffs of smoke appeared a thousand feet below, possibly from nervous gunners, anxious to prove something, on the outskirts of Aldershot.

Willi hung on. For the moment there was nothing he could do if he was intercepted. He tried to relax. A strong sense of unreality gripped him. He had felt it at Rangsdorf, Bauer going off like that. He realised that it had been Bauer who had cleared the flight alone. Bauer who had fixed everything, done everything. And he was clearly well-known there. There would be no way out for him if he had, as he'd suggested, gone against his orders. But who gave those orders? Surely not Goering ... And if not Goering, then perhaps there was protection for poor old Dieter there. He fervently hoped so.

He had expected to feel something special, taking off from German soil for the very last time. But what lay ahead had driven out of his mind any sentimental twinges he might otherwise have suffered. He felt nothing now, except excitement alternating with fear.

Other than the things Bauer had assembled for him, he had nothing except the small, post-card sized family group, taken in a Berlin studio in 1936. He had left behind at his uncle's house everything else in the world he possessed—except his lighter. He grieved over his pilot's badge. He had thought never to part with that. It was still pinned to the uniform he had left in the hangar office. He was rueful, too, about the dress uniform he had worn only once or twice. That, too, was with his other kit at Uncle Reimund's. The Knight's Cross he had put in an envelope addressed to Goering and left it on the pillow in his room. He wondered briefly about his uncle's safety, and then about what his parents would have thought of all this. Then the urge to survive took over.

He'd managed it so far, but he wasn't yet ready to believe that his luck would hold all the way. He pushed the FW to the limit now and held on, counting the seconds, forcing himself to hold the course a little longer, knowing that the longer his heading stayed constant the greater was the chance that something would loom up and blow him out of the sky at any moment.

The seconds ticked on. The back of his neck prickled with fear. He glanced down at his knees and feet, saw the brown shoes and grey slacks and forced a grin.

Still nothing. The opposition were certainly up by now, and either right behind or already directly ahead. But just for this moment there was no sign of anything.

Had he really been able to take the defences by surprise? A lone fighter with limited range, apparently heading staight into trouble? That's how it must look. And that's how he'd planned it: that they would reason that by now he would have to turn if he wanted to get out in one piece. Had that made them over-confident? They could not know he had no such plans.

One more minute, he told himself. He counted it off, then at last put the nose of the FW down in a steep dive.

In clear view of barrage-balloon sites just south of Reading he let them see smoke pouring from his tail. It was the oldest trick in the book, but it might just work. Nothing so confuses the hunter who hasn't fired a shot as to see the hunted seemingly fall smoking from the sky. Watchers would have to assume he'd been hit by AA fire.

While the balloon commander was reporting the smoking FW, the confused and disappointed Mustang Leader was reporting: "Sweeping south to Sector Three. Bandit not seen. Repeat not seen. Any directions?"

A few moments later, barrage-balloons west of the Reading sprawl began hurriedly lofting their elephantine charges, then checked, wondering if it was worthwhile. Their commander reported the German hit and falling fast, smoking, towards Newbury.

Willi had no difficulty recognising the line of the Downs beyond Newbury. Satisfied, he came out of the dive and began climbing again, fast. He cut the smoke and disappeared into the thin cloud. He still had plenty of fuel. If he could stay out of trouble for another few minutes he would have cleared the first and most obvious hurdle—leaving just the really tricky part.

In the long hours of his confinement at Wildpark-Werder, Willi had had plenty of time to consider exactly how and where he might put the Focke-Wulf down on English soil.

What he needed was isolation, safety from surprise, for a few minutes in which to get clear of the aircraft. And a choice of escape routes. He'd considered the Norfolk coast, lonely and flat; the Essex marshes; Romney Marsh; and a dozen other places, some of which he even knew a little. But in every case there had been, along with the isolation, the danger of being surprised, of being seen getting clear.

He'd studied the maps and roads, gone through the pros and cons of every likely area in the south of England. But all the time, at the back of his mind, there had been one place which seemed so supremely suitable that he had to force himself to complete the exercise of considering the others at all.

In the year before the war, he'd joined a small party of students from Berlin—one or two of whom he'd known—and spent time with them tramping the British countryside. They had walked, in almost perfect weather, through the Chilterns and the Cotswolds. It had been superb, idyllic. The others went home after three weeks. Willi, staying on, glad to be on his own again and with a taste now for walking, had swung south. So it was by himself that he first explored the full length of that oldest of old roads, the Ridgeway. It marched, high and lonely, eighty miles from Avebury in Wiltshire to the Thames at Goring: Torn and scarred, baked and scoured under the dramatic skies for more than two thousand years, the rutted bald track had been used since the Iron Age by rich and poor, pilgrim and merchant. In the downland below, even the mediaeval knight with his armed escort had been an easy prey to ambush. On the Ridgeway that was impossible. You could see exactly what was coming and from where. And for centuries the traveller had preferred the rigours of the rugged track, the pitiless skies and the scant shelter of the old hill forts.

For all that time, the Ridgeway's appeal was the same as it was for Willi now. It was safe from surprises. Depending on what threatened, you could go forward, back, or escape down either side.

A quick study of a physical map had further suggested that the perfect point to put down was the Ridgeway's route across the White Horse Hills. At its highest it was 600 feet of hard climb away from any possible interception. And as to the top itself, he could overfly the track, even picking his field— simulating engine trouble and ready to put down the moment he saw a chance. One sweep should be enough. It would be a snap decision and he might still walk into trouble, but the odds were greatly against it. The Ridgeway was a lonely place in peacetime. In wartime it should be even more so. And though he would be watched from below until the moment he put down, it would take a time to reach up to him from the flatlands. All he needed was a very few minutes.

That was the only really dangerous part. Getting down ought to be easy enough. Safely putting distance between himself and the burning aircraft was something else. It was the high point of danger, even though it would last only a minute or two. If he was actually seen leaving the aircraft he was finished. Anyone climbing out of a German aircraft had to be a German; and not only that, but a German spy, a candidate for the firing squad. But if he could once put a hundred yards between himself and the FW—fifty yards, even—he would have achieved a convincing magician's trick.

There would be nothing at all to connect him with the burning aircraft in which the pilot, poor bastard, was presumably frying alive. And he need not fear being seen by anyone, except perhaps by the police or military. He would be just a walker, wheeling his bicycle along a spectacular feature of the countryside.

He felt sure it would work. There was some chance of other walkers, of course. But not too many in wartime, he thought. If there were, then he needed only half a mile between himself and them. Even if they ran towards the 'crash'—and running wasn't easy on the Ridgeway—he could be free and clear in time. Standing there, as much shocked and surprised by the intrusion into the peace of a summer afternoon as anyone else.

It was unlikely the Ridgeway was still patrolled. The Home Guard might do it after dark, perhaps, with diminishing enthusiasm. In 1940 and 1941 they might have had a post up there during the day, patrolled it regularly and anxiously. Willi's information was that no-one in Britain any longer believed in the possibility of a German invasion—from the sky or anywhere else. The old men and boys of under military age who mostly made up the force had long since anticipated the final order to Stand Down.

As to the rest, he'd faced worse problems many times before. Cornfields had flanked the old track when he'd last seen it. It was clear of trees, open to the sky. Some of the fields would be pretty rough, of course, but the FW was expendable. All he had to do was get down in one piece, still able to move fast . . .

There was more flak now coming up from a gunsite behind Newbury racecourse. He had levelled out at 10,000 feet and the gunners below were more accurate. A flurry of bursts flowered behind him, close enough for him to feel the concussion and the shaking. He banked again, let them see the black smoke again from the tail section, and veered sharply across the main road ribboning away to the west. It didn't take him out of sight of the gunners, but in another few seconds he'd be making his one sweep along the western end of the range of hills. He closed off the oxygen and got rid of his mask.

Almost at once he saw the huge chalk White Horse itself,

now under his port wing; the neck and head straining, as if at a wild gallop over the brow of the hill which bore his name.

That was it.

He dropped to a few hundred feet, banked steeply when he saw Swindon racing up, and flew back along the switchback line of the Ridgeway. He stared down anxiously. Sweat broke out in rivulets under his eyes, under the arms, down his back. His own smoke was still feathered out, obscuring his view a little. Bauer had done a good job on the smoke; perhaps too good.

A few people in one section; others toiling up the hill below. Then a clear stretch. Gloriously clear. Nothing to spoil it. The old track, bald and clear, lifted and fell away dramatically but you couldn't judge that too well from the air. A terrific burst of gunfire mushroomed ahead of him. They were homing in on him fast. He dropped lower still, losing speed, seeming to limp along above the road, no more than 150 feet above it.

He cursed. It was no good. He simply couldn't mark a spot that fast. He'd have to swing out over the North slopes and take one more run at it.

The FW would have done it like a bird if this had been an air display. Willi stood it agonisingly on one wing, at the same time dropping another 50 feet. "This time," he told himself. "This time."

He pointed the FW at a bright yellow field in which the hay had just been cut. The bales stood in regular rows, at this height like so many neat boxes on a suede, ochre background. It looked unreal in its perfection. The bales were a hazard, but there were wide aisles between them.

"Come on then, sweetheart," he muttered. "Now!" He had seconds to go. He blinked sweat away, braced himself.

The FW fell, howling, full flaps, the lot. The yellow ground of England rushed up. It looked even. Too late now anyway. Ten feet. The wheels touched, bounced, touched. Something hit the undercarriage a fearful blow. The FW's nose was pulled round to the right. Something, perhaps the whole wheel assembly, tore away with a loud crack. He hit the ground with a sickening crunch of metal, tortured engines, dust. His head struck the canopy, pulling his helmet half off. The crippled aircraft yawed away to the left, ploughing into the rise of the ground. He braced himself and gave up the effort to hold it straight. The port wing crumpled.

The sliding, hammering, slithering, buckling ride went on

for what seemed like ten seconds more, but was probably half that. He had a fleeting impression of the port wing tearing away and bowling away behind him like a mad kite. Dust and earth showered up round the canopy.

And then he was still.

Willi let out a triumphant yell. His voice seemed a long way off. He snatched off the helmet. His head was wet with sweat. He still couldn't hear anything. He felt as if he were watching a film with a faulty soundtrack. The silence made him nervous. He wondered if the blow on the head had affected his hearing.

He punched the canopy knob with the heel of his hand and slid it back. No trouble there. The cool air swept in instantly drying the film of sweat on his face. He got up on his seat, not daring to look around. He had one leg over the cockpit before he remembered the truncated wing. He had to perch on the cropped wing-root to push the canopy all the way back, pull the seat forward and feel for the bicycle. He hefted it clear, threw it down, followed by the rucksack.

Now he reached in under the control panel for the black plastic switch. He flipped it, felt and almost heard the rockers click click into place. He had twenty-five seconds. Move! He began counting under his breath. One more thing: close the canopy.

He jumped down, picked up the bicycle and the rucksack and began a heavy-footed run for the nearest cover, the thick hedgerow bordering the track. Ten seconds.

He almost launched himself at the thinnest patch; then he noticed a break, a gate, and changed course, stumbling, legs pumping furiously. Fifteen seconds.

He ran blindly, unaware that he was almost shouting the seconds. He put his feet down on the hard baked chalk, rutted and treacherous. Memory stirred. He was on the Ridgeway itself. Sweat poured from his forehead, blurring his vision. He put a foot in a deep rut, stumbled and pitched forward onto his face. And lay there, panting.

The explosion came like a benediction. He felt the shock wave, saw, from his ant's eye view, the far hedgerow flail and recover.

For a few seconds more he lay still, half-expecting a rifle butt on the back of his head, or a boot pinning him down.

There was nothing.

He moved sideways a little, like a crab, looked both ways up and down the track. Nothing. Getting up was still worrying for a moment. The blood roared in his head. He felt faint. Finally he made it.

Willi stood tall. There was a dull pain in his head; he was otherwise in good shape. He picked up the bicycle, perched the rucksack on the saddle and turned for a last look at the D12. It was burning furiously. As he watched, the black cross on the tail section began to fade magically in the heat.

He looked up. A lark sang overhead. He understood the initial silence at last. On the Ridgeway there was nothing else. It began to look as if he'd made it. Someone might have seen him, but it was doubtful. He began to grin. The tensions of the last few days began to ebb. He felt as he used to after a mission. When you were safely down you couldn't remember the fear, the cramp, the cold or climbing out of the aircraft, eating, talking, reporting. You were high on relief.

There was another small explosion from the D12 that he couldn't account for. He was reminded that he ought to be moving, and fast. He turned. And froze.

A man was watching him.

The shock drove the blood from his face. He couldn't catch his breath. His heart hammered against his ribcage. Disappointment hit him like a cold douche. He felt his legs tremble.

He forced a grin and at the same time tried to focus more clearly.

The man was young; a boy really, with fair hair and ruddy skin. Willi had a quick impression of rough working clothes, a thick belt, heavy boots. Had he just arrived, or had he seen anything?

They stood staring at each other. The boy's mouth was agape. Willi hoped it was more with astonishment than fear.

"Hello," he said. He didn't recognise the sound of his own voice. He cleared his throat and tried again. "Hello," he said. And then: "Did you see the crash?"

The boy's throat worked a little. His mouth moved. It was three or four seconds before he was able to make a sound which sounded like assent.

He was afraid. Willi had to know why. Had to know how much he had seen. He moved a step or two closer, at an angle, making much of the innocence of swinging the knapsack down to the road in front of him and leaning the bicycle against the hedgerow.

Willi nodded towards the D12. "Some blaze," he said cheerfully. Smoke now rose in an oily cloud, obscuring much of the field. The fire sounded as a muted roar. "Did you see if the pilot managed to get clear?" Willi asked. He watched the boy's face closely. When there was no reply, he moved a little closer still. He was becoming anxious. The field was farm-land. Farms meant farm hands. This was clearly one and there could be others close by.

Still the boy stood rooted, his eyes blinking rapidly.

"I said I wonder if you saw anyone get away from the crash," Willi persisted. And when there was still no answer he shrugged and bent to pick up the knapsack as if to go. He sensed, rather than saw the movement.

He looked up in time enough to deflect the first rush. He took a heavy blow intended for his head on the shoulder and staggered back, startled. The boy's face was distorted with fear and hostility. It was clear now that he had seen Willi run from the aircraft and knew himself to be alone with an enemy. He came on again in a rush, using fists and knees, too frightened to be clear-headed about it. Willi hurled him off. The boy sprawled on his back and for a moment Willi stood breathing hard and adapting.

The boy took the breathing space to be lack of aggression and, scrambling up, came in again at a run. This time Willi side-stepped like a matador and chopped him savagely be-hind the ear. He fell headlong with an animal moan of pain.

Willi took a moment more to consider. He could not let the boy go. He remembered something that Bauer had said during the hours they had spent together planning the flight. "One thing you may have to be prepared for, Willi, if you want to stay at liberty: Killing. Somewhere, sometime, it may be a choice between your life and someone else's. In those clothes, don't fool yourself you'll go into the cage like any other POW. And killing calls for quite a different sort of nerve than it did when you bombed from twenty thousand feet."

The boy moved suddenly. On his knees, scrabbling, then bent double like a sprinter's start, then running heavily, stumbling and sliding over the deeply-scored chalk.

Willi now saw that a small Fordson tractor stood at the bend of the track, half out of sight. He breathed raggedly, horrified and reluctant. He heard the tractor start up and began to run.

The tractor jolted out of the side of the track to sit astride the central ruts, the boy in the saddle, his back defenceless. Willi came up behind him on the run. He swung the knap-sack wildly, holding on by one strap. It clouted the boy on the side of the head and toppled him out of his seat in slow motion. The tractor ran ahead a little distance, nosed into the hedgerow and stalled there.

As the boy struggled to his feet, whimpering, Willi kicked him in the temple. He stiffened, collapsed and lay still. Willi bent and turned him on his side. He was uncomfortably aware that he, too, had been making some kind of primitive noise. He straightened to look both ways up the track. There was nothing in sight.

Willi took a deep breath. If he stopped to think about what he was going to do, he'd never do it. Now, while he was angry enough! For perhaps twenty seconds he hesitated, trembling. Then he bent and tilted the boy's head forward into his chest. He took a step back, poised himself and slammed the toe of his heavy walking shoe into the nape of the boy's neck. He almost heard the snap of the spinal column.

He stood back shaking violently. When he had his breathing under control he bent and picked the boy up in a fireman's lift. He was young, but burly, something close to 170 pounds. Willi carried him back along the track and set him down gently inside the field, just behind the hedgerow. Casual walkers would miss him, but anyone who really looked for him would find him soon enough.

The boy's eyes were only partly closed, giving him an oddly furtive look. Willi closed them. He saw that the kid was very young and vulnerable. There was a tattoo on his tanned left forearm. One decorated word: MOTHER. Willi fought down a fresh wave of remorse. He had no time for that. Bauer had been all too right: it was hard enough to kill. Killing a frightened kid was intolerable.

He looked down at himself. The damage to his clothes was not great. He took off the jacket and dusted it down, walking back up the track to retrieve the knapsack. The tractor could stay where it was.

The sun suddenly seemed very hot. He looked up and judged he was still east of the White Horse itself and the road down to the floor of the Vale.

Wheeling the bicycle, he set off now, moving briskly. It was hard to do, but he pulled his expression into something that he hoped looked relaxed. As he stepped out he realised that though he couldn't recognise any feature in particular, he now remembered vividly the feel of the Ridgeway. Nothing seemed to have changed. Well why should it have? The old track had always been here, always looking very much like

105

this. And yet it was odd, somehow, to be back. He had the faintly spooked sensation of *déja-vu*. And then the even more odd thought . . . that he had been drawn here, that blissful summer before the war, as a kind of rehearsal—as a means of saving his own life.

The air was good, the scent of the fields and hedgerows intoxicating. Before he had gone far, his expression of relaxation or relief or euphoria was no longer a struggle.

19

Going back to Ronnie's flat after the Queen's Club Gardens bomb had been a funny way to start a holiday. But it had served at least one purpose. The experience had been so depressing that when Ronnie asked Harvey to go away with her for a few days, he didn't hesitate.

"Neither of us has had a holiday," she said. "We need one. Even if it's only for a few days. Will you try?"

"I'll do better," Harvey said. "I'll tell McNair."

McNair, when he was told, was relieved not to have been asked for more. He hid his relief. "If you must," he said, "do it now. There seems to be a full house this week. How long?"

"Four days," Harvey said, ready to accept three. McNair's grunt of assent was a genuine surprise.

He called Ronnie.

"Gwen is going to manage by herself here," she said. "I need not go in tonight. When could you be ready?"

"Where the hell are we going?"

"To Lammas, of course. Where else?"

Harvey had heard all about Lammas, the Croft estate near Newbury. He opened his mouth to object and realised he didn't really. Why not? A little luxury wouldn't hurt either of them.

A tremulous sound at the other end of the line nudged him. "How would three o'clock suit you?" Harvey said.

He began to look forward to it. The Queen's Club flat affair had shaken them both. They had to go back, and by daylight the damage was much worse than he'd thought. When they'd arrived by cab, a gang of workmen were working along the street, hammering white canvas across the tops of the gaping window frames and black canvas across the lower halves. Kids were playing again along the fronts and hedges, from which the railings and gates had long since been requisitioned for scrap.

Inside Ronnie's flat the mess was appalling. The porters had already opened the flat for the windows to have the black and white canvas treatment, but even in the gloom the white dust laying over everything made it look as if the room had been open to a major sandstorm. Glass still crunched thickly underfoot. It turned up in the bedclothes—it had seemed impossible they had made love there so comfortably only a short time earlier. It was in the cupboards, the rugs, even in the shelves of the cupboards which contained Ronnie's clothes.

They had worked steadily, Ronnie hampered by her arm, sweeping, vacuuming, setting each room to something like order. Workmen arrived to rehang the doors and removed the wicked-looking splinters hanging from the basic window frames.

Only when it was all done did Ronnie show signs of distress. It could be patched up, but it was still a mess. And Harvey understood; it was the only place she'd ever had which was entirely her own. She sank her head briefly on his chest. When she looked up her eyes were wet, though her voice was steady enough. "Your place for a while, I think," she said ruefully.

But the prospect of Lammas transformed her.

Harvey had been prepared to be faintly shocked by Lammas. By what he felt must be the waste of such a house, standing empty for most of the year. And by the servants, who had nothing to do except maintain an environment of luxury simply against the possibility that Croft or Ronnie might want to enjoy it at some moment.

Lammas changed his mind in less than forty-eight hours.

Such a house, he came to understand, needed no vindication. He was puzzled by this switch in his reactions, though willing to go along with it for the moment.

To begin with he was astonished by the wealth of produce which seemed to pour from the estate. It was a cornucopia that fed not just the estate workers, but supplied shops in all the surrounding villages and as far as Newbury itself.

The old walled kitchen garden was only a fraction of its wartime producing area. Former graceful lawns and arbours, the old grass tennis courts and the sweeping grasslands around the lake had all been patriotically ploughed up in the Dig for Victory fervour.

. As for the house itself, it seemed to deserve the labour of its upkeep. It had survived as a manor house since long before the Civil War and would be there for generations to come. Long after the Crofts were forgotten, Lammas would stand as the focal point of a community, giving life and purpose first to the estate itself, and then to those it employed and fed. It had dignity, whether or not its owners had. It had history, even if successive owners only marked time on it. The Crofts, like all its other owners, Harvey realised, were unimportant to Lammas. They held it just now. And that was all.

It was Harvey's first experience of a house of its kind. And it worked some kind of magic on him. He felt it at once and was amused. Ronnie watched him, also amused. She listened while Old Childs told his stories of former owners. One had been a judge under Cromwell. Another a notable eighteenth-century womaniser. Eccentrics had lived at Lammas. Straight-laced squires had bred there. A member of the Hellfire Club had died in the Judge's Suite. Two kings and one queen had enjoyed its hospitality. Harvey listened, got their names straight, laid them in order in his mind. In consequence, Childs told his wife over supper below stairs: "He won't do for Miss Ronnie, but he's a nice enough young chap." Mrs Childs was startled. The old man was not given to expressions of approval. A moment later, Childs added, thoughtfully: "For a Londoner."

Mrs Childs, younger by ten years, irretrievably motherly and looking like an advertising man's ideal grandmother, was grateful for the sudden appearance of Ronnie and Harvey. It had been months since Mr Croft had been to Lammas, though most of the huge house was kept in constant trim. Now that 'Mister David', as he was called by all the estate workers, was too busy to leave his war work, she felt the waste of their efforts keenly.

"Summer in the country needs to be shared," she told Ronnie obscurely. And again: "It seems terrible to us that flowers come and go and no-one sees them except us."

"Flowers?" Harvey was surprised.

"I'd sooner have dug the lawns for taters than touch the Lammas roses," Old Childs explained. "There ain't nothing worth shifting them for. Not even 'itler." In his round, Berkshire tones it came out as It-lerr.

"Flowers grows wild, too," Mrs Childs reproved him. She

shook her head. "You city people." And then: "Miss Ronnie knows."

Simple soul, Harvey thought. Or was she? When they retired to the cottage at the edge of the estate after dinner was cleared away, could they fail to know that he and their 'Miss Ronnie' made love in each other's bed, alternately, to average out the wrinkling. Did they care? Would they be shocked? He thought not.

He was entranced by them. And with the countryside. Like many Londoners he had previously fled to the sea whenever he'd had the free time and felt the need of change. His only experience of the country was of Sunday lunch in the not-too-well-hidden hotels and inns which Londoners are apt to 'discover' and then drop as soon as they're discovered by other Londoners. Living in the country, he saw now, was something entirely different.

In the old stable block Ronnie showed him a collection of old bicycles sufficient to set up as a minor museum and the first two days they rode through almost every village in the Vale of Kennett. On the third day Ronnie, saddle-sore and 'clean but not kempt' told him over breakfast that she was going to give herself assorted treatments.

"While I'm busy," she said, "you may have the so-called comfortable bicycle."

It was a ladies model, an old Rudge. But he took it, gratefully. "I'll be back about one," he told her.

Ronnie pouted. "So long?"

"We'll see. If I'm later, don't wait lunch." He was mildly pleased at the suggestion that she would miss him, but thankful once he got moving, that he was alone and relieved for the moment of the odd tensions of their relationship.

He headed north from Newbury towards the White Horse Hills. They had already made the trip, but there was enough of atmosphere to draw him back. He also knew the route and could ride without the need to think about it. As he rode, he puzzled over the change in Ronnie's manner. Perversely, he found himself piqued at the subtle withdrawal she had lately made.

Harvey recognised that women like Ronnie were often hard-headed about marriage. They chose carefully and then made it work. It wasn't always that way with the kind Harvey was used to. He doubted, though, that Ronnie's new reaction was anything to do with his background—however she saw that. If she loved him, that would be enough. She was proud of her father's achievement, while perfectly well aware of his very ordinary beginnings. It was at least possible though that the continuing defection of Justine Croft was making Ronnie doubtful about the desirability of marriage at all.

Ronnie was remarkable. He had never known anyone like her. Nor had many men. He tried not to think about where he and Ronnie stood now. He put his head down and pedalled fiercely. The old Rudge, which had been left behind by a house-parlourmaid who had long since left Lammas to join the ATS, was comfortable. He sped through Lambourn towards the higher ground. By eleven, the sun strong on his face, he was walking the Ridgeway, exulting in the warmth, the scents, the dramatic landscape spread out below. He saw no one. A lark sang incessantly, kiting in the unbroken breeze. The place had magic for him.

He had been walking for a long time, wheeling the old cycle, when he first heard gunfire.

"Christ, even here," he said bitterly, aloud.

Then he saw the aircraft.

When it came towards him, following the track, it was in the sun. It roared overhead and he saw no markings. He walked on, the mood disturbed, blinking into the bright sunshine. Harvey knew little or nothing about the Ridgeway, but in spite of that he sensed a great deal about its character, appeal and mystery.

When he heard the aircraft coming back he stopped dead in his tracks, watching. And this time as it came up over the spine of the hills he suddenly saw the black crosses on the undersides of the wings. He shoved the cycle into the hedgerow and tensed himself to follow it. He suddenly saw himself not so much an unlikely target as the only target on this high hunting ground. He'd seen enough newsreels of non-combatants being strafed.

The surprise of the encounter in this peaceful, lonely place slowed his thinking. Now he saw and evaluated the long plumes of smoke. The pilot seemingly had his hands full. He relaxed a little and watched. It was clearly a fighter. He couldn't tell what type.

Again the German approached, losing height rapidly. He flinched as it abruptly dropped to near tree-top height and howled past him on his left. It had to crash. He stood still, listening for it.

The explosion, when it came, took him by surprise. It

seemed oddly late. And yet very close. The wind of it whipped along the hedgerows. He was puzzled.

Harvey looked at his watch. It was still early. He had plenty of time. And what did it matter anyway? The crash was back the way he'd come. He hesitated only a second or two before recovering the Rudge and hurrying back.

Could the pilot have survived? It now occurred to Harvey that he might be the only person near. Would the man need help? And would he surrender peaceably? And if not, did he want to get involved? He began to trot anyway, crashing the old Rudge in and out of the deep, tramline ruts. Then he admitted to himself that he ought to have the answers to some of these questions before he rushed into anything.

It couldn't be far. And there ought to be smoke, whichever side of the track it was. The fool couldn't possibly have put his aircraft down on the track, could he? The sun was fierce on his back and he'd already slowed, feeling hot, when he finally saw someone coming towards him, wheeling a bicycle like himself.

Willi was determined to speak first. "Hullo . . ." he said when he was still at a distance.

Harvey stopped, waiting for him to come up. The man was about his own height, fair-haired, pale, well-built and swinging a knapsack. "Hi," he said, waiting for the other to come closer. "Did you see the German come down? Well of course you did. Is it far?"

"No, not far," Willi said carefully. "About two hundred—" he nearly said metres, checked and coughed elaborately "—about two hundred yards. It blew up. Frightened the life out of me."

Harvey took in the dusty sports coat. "You look a bit shook up," he said.

"So would you—that close," Willi grinned. "I dived into the hedge. And even so something clouted me. A piece of debris, I suppose." This was a lot of talk very soon. It was going nicely, but too far and too fast. Willi looked down at himself as if now realising that he might look ruffled. He began dusting himself down elaborately to give himself breathing space. He drew a few deep breaths and then looked up, grinning.

"It's on fire, is it?"

"Certainly is," Willi said. "Damn great blaze. I thought I ought to tell someone, and I had an idea the nearest road down was along this way. Not that they'll have missed it

111

down below." He saw that Harvey was framing questions. "Sorry . . . ?"

"What about the pilot?"

"Poor devil is presumably still inside. He's beyond help now anyway." Willi pushed the hair back out of his eyes and winced as his fingers caught the place where he'd hit the canopy. He looked earnestly at Harvey. "What's best do you think; wait up here, or go back down the road and give them an idea of where it is?"

Harvey considered. "Go back to the road, I suppose. You were walking away from it. There is one this way, but it's much, much further. Someone will be along, and they probably have an idea from the smoke which road up to take."

They turned together. The oil smoke flagged the site of the crash a long way before they got to it. As they walked, Harvey looked again at the other man. He now saw that he was an inch or two taller than himself. It was the face that drew his curiosity. It was unusual; boyish, freckled over an unnatural pallor and yet curiously mature and worn. It was the face of a 30-year-old who had given himself a hard time over something lately.

"Damn strange thing to happen," Harvey said. "I came down for a break from London and the V1's. But it's not so different here after all. You on leave or something?"

Willi was ready. "Holiday," he said. "Cycling about the countryside. I walked the Ridgeway years ago and I always said I'd do it again. I won't tackle the whole thing this time, but I couldn't resist a look." He smiled brilliantly.

Harvey beamed agreeably, too. Then he noticed that his companion was limping a little. "Hurt your leg?"

"Not today," Willi said. "Old surgery."

Harvey was pleased with the explanation. It accounted for the face, perhaps.

They stopped. The FW was burning steadily and burning fragments had ignited the stubble here and there. The aircraft was unrecognisable. The blast had turned it over. Part of the mottled tail section had buckled through 90 degrees and escaped the flames so far; the swastika was clearly visible.

Harvey moved a little closer, Willi following. They were standing by the gate. Harvey made to prop his cycle and move through into the field.

"I wouldn't do that," Willi said urgently. The body of the

boy lay unconcealed a few yards from their feet, screened only by the hedgerow.

Harvey, startled by the other's tone, drew back but doubtfully.

"Ammunition," Willi explained. "Bombs, fuel tanks, anything. Don't these things have cannon shells?"

Harvey nodded, acknowledging the sense of that. "You're right," he said. "In that case it's not safe to stand here, either. Let's get on."

Willi smiled. Nothing suited him better.

It took them some minutes to get to the junction with the narrow dirt road up from the valley floor. As they arrived a Standard 10 rattled into the tight passing place carved from the hedgerows for tractors and the occasional tourist car.

Two men bustled out in the cloud of dust. A uniformed police constable and a short, stocky, moustachioed man in a tweed jacket not unlike Willi's. They came towards them now briskly.

The short man, closing with them, offered no greeting. "You've just come off the track?" he said abruptly.

"That's right," Harvey said. "The plane came down in a field this side of the track." He gestured. "You can't very well miss it. No-one hurt, except the Jerry pilot. It seems he's still inside, poor sod."

The plain clothes man made no comment. He didn't smile. He produced his warrant card. "Inspector Bell," he said. "Can I see your identity cards, please, gentlemen."

Harvey turned his head a little and winked at Willi. He found his card in the back of his wallet and handed it to Bell. Out of the corner of his eye he saw Willi doing the same.

Willi was tensed. He was taking all his hurdles at once, it seemed. He watched Bell's face. He saw that his own card looked identical to the other, perhaps rather cleaner. Too clean? He'd attend to that. A pulse beat in his neck. He put his hand under his coat at the back and felt the reassuring bulk of the .22 in his belt. If he could survive the next hour he'd get rid of it. He couldn't think why he'd wanted it. He hadn't dared use it with the boy; a bullet was total negation of the story he wanted to build.

Beads of sweat had broken out again all over his face. The moment was unreal. He saw Bell pore over the cards, slow, stolid. Marsh was saying something about staying locally, but Bell was only half listening.

At last both cards were handed back to Harvey. Willi was

delighted with the assumption that they were together. Harvey held on to his own and held out the other to Willi.

"We'll have to get on up there," Bell said. "Do you know that the pilot is dead? Did you see the crash?"

"No," said Harvey promptly.

"Yes," said Willi simultaneously. Then, realising his mistake, added quickly: "There's no chance he got free."

Bell, who had begun to move off, turned back. "Well now," he said, "Which is it? Yes or No? You did see the crash or you didn't?"

Willi jumped in quickly, anxious to preserve the assumption that they were together. "I did see it," he said. "My friend here didn't. We were something like two or three hundred yards apart." He was pleased with the use of 'my friend'. Bell could take it to mean one thing and Harvey another. Before Bell could dissect the statement, Willi added: "We were both on the Ridgeway, but I was by the field, much further ahead. I thought it was going to come down on me. I even jumped into the hedge."

It worked. Bell nodded, impatiently. "I see. Well, we'd better not hang about anyway."

Harvey watched them go. He shook his head, amused. "I suppose he thought we were German spies." Willi laughed shortly.

"Christ," Harvey said, "at this stage of the war if you were a spy you'd sit tight, keep your head down and enjoy the war that someone else was fighting."

Willi grinned at him. "I must say you don't look much like a spy." He stopped short, changed the cycle to his left hand and held out his right. "Bill Ryder."

"Sorry," Harvey said. He pushed the Rudge ahead and walked round the back of it: "Harvey Marsh." And after a moment or two of the downhill trudge, too steep to attempt mounted, added: "Fancy a drink after all that?"

Willi was delighted. "Certainly. Where?"

Harvey nodded on. "There's a village about a mile off the main road. The signpost has gone, of course, and I can't remember the name of it, but I saw the roofs as I came up. Where there's a village there's a pub."

I ought to have been alert to that, Willi thought.

He made another mistake as they stood at the bar of a pub that looked like something gingerbread from Hansel & Gretel. The landlord, a heavily moustached man of about forty, who looked more like a veteran British flyer than a village publican, asked them what they'd have.

"Scotch and water," Willi said promptly. It was what he drank in England in the years before the war.

Tha landlord gave Harvey a wry smile and jerked his head at Willi. "Any particular brand he likes?"

"Two pints of bitter," Harvey said. "Not that we couldn't both use a Scotch if you had any. Some bloody Kraut has just banged his plane into a field up beside the Ridgeway. Damn near blew my friend apart. It's the sort of thing you can do without if you're out for a peaceful walk."

The landlord glanced round cautiously. A few old men were at a table in one corner. There was no one this side of the bar. He put two small glasses on the bar top, brought up a bottle of Johnny Walker from somewhere below, and measured two singles. He said loudly. "Two pints of bitter. Right, sir."

Willi smiled, but he was furious with himself. He told himself that for a while he had to couch everything in tentative terms. He could just as easily have said. "What we need is Scotch, but we'll have whatever's available." He put the Scotch down swiftly and watched the landlord draw the two bitters. He suddenly realised how badly he needed a drink of any kind. As soon as he decently could he sipped the beer. It was very good. He was mildly astonished that it was so readily available, even here in the smallest of villages.

"Londoner?" Harvey was asking.

"No!" Willi smiled, denying it fiercely; it was no part of his story. "No, I'm a mixture of Scots and Irish really. And born in Peterborough. I'm going to London in a day or two to stay."

"No wonder I couldn't place your accent," Harvey said.

"Accent?" Willi was instantly alarmed. "I didn't realise I had one."

Harvey considered it. "Well, not so much an accent. More a way of speaking."

Another hurdle. "You a Londoner?" Willi asked. He was pleased with his quick adoption of the clipped, telegrammatic way that Harvey spoke. It would serve well for a while.

"Right," Harvey smiled.

"And what do you do?" Willi could remember that sort of question, knew it to be acceptable. And he had a slight unease that this man might have some official function.

"News agency," Harvey said. "Night editor. And you?"

Willi breathed deeply. He should be ready for this. Better to get it over now. He produced his cover story, taking it

115

easily, breaking it up into parts so that it didn't sound rehearsed.

"Well," he said reflectively. "I'm unfit for service. Car accident a few years back." He tapped his left leg and then sipped his beer again. "There's a piece of plate in that which is all right most of the time. It's a bit limiting, though. So, for a few years I've been in the insurance business. But I'm tired of that." He affected to be choosing his words. "You could say that I'm between jobs. I quit and came down here for a holiday first. Then I thought perhaps I'd find something in London. What do you think?"

Harvey nodded reassuringly. "No question. Plenty of jobs in London. Lots of the firms who moved out during the bombing of '40 and '41 came back again when the raids dwindled to nothing. Now they wish they hadn't, of course. All the same, they won't move again. It isn't worth it. The V1's will stop just as soon as the launch sites are taken. So they're back, and they need lots of people."

"The V1's are bad?" Willi asked sympathetically.

"Right. Nasty things. Really frightening. One dropped about 50 yards from my girlfriend's flat earlier this week." He related the story of the V1 which had wrecked the Queen's Club flat. "It's why I'm here, really. We thought we could both do with a rest."

Willi was rediscovering an ear for colloquial English. He remembered the facility strongly now. He picked up the phrasing "We can do with" and fed it back almost immediately.

"And of course you can't do with things like that up on the Ridgeway." And then: "I hope you won't mind my asking— are you excused service, working as you do in a news agency?"

Harvey glanced at his companion with mild curiosity. He had an oddly formal way of speaking. "No. I'd have been willing, but I'm not acceptable. Rheumatic fever when I was a kid. I look healthy enough. I feel fine. But they won't have me even in the Catering Corps, stirring porridge. Pretty stupid, eh?"

Willi agreed. It did seem pretty stupid. He was mildly shocked at the contrast with Germany, where every adult who could walk was pressed into some kind of service. The Britain which he had begun to glimpse even in these last few minutes was not the one that had been pictured for the German people by Goebbels' propaganda machine. The thought occurred to him that if Hitler, Goering and Goebbels could see the peace and complacency of this village alone they'd surrender at once. In the effort to convince the Germans that the British were only a step from final defeat, they had almost convinced themselves. His eye fell on two posters pinned to the adzed beams at the side of the bar. One pictured a man in a telephone box excitedly telling his listener: "—But for Heaven's sake don't say I told you." A dozen cartoon Hitler faces peered from the top and sides of the box. CARELESS TALK COSTS LIVES, the poster warned in large letters. It took him a moment or two to assimilate. Then it struck him as enormously funny. He looked away, trying to control the laughter that bubbled inside him. Seeing Harvey's puzzlement, he said briskly: "When I get to London—" He stopped, unsure how to phrase it. And then finished it in a rush: "Is it easy to find somewhere to live?"

"Depends on what you want," Harvey told him. "A flat? Or just a room somewhere—lodging?"

Willi considered briefly: "A room, to begin with."

"You shouldn't have difficulty. Central London or outside a little?"

"Outside."

Harvey looked at him again. He seemed a decent sort. Carefully spoken. Well-educated probably. He was thinking about Frank's desire to let a room or two. The old devil couldn't be trusted with a woman. But a man . . . He hesitated only a moment longer. Then he took out his diary, wrote down Frank's Wembley telephone number and tore the page out for Willi. "Try this when you get to town," he said. "It's my father. He's alone now, living in a house with spare rooms. He was thinking of letting one or two." He grinned at Willi. "I can't be sure he hasn't done it already, of course. I don't think so. Anyway, give him a ring if you want."

"That's very nice of you," Willi said carefully. "If I stick to my plans, I'll do that. Thanks very much." He was anxious not to sound too eager. In fact he was stunned at this piece of luck.

Even so, he couldn't resist a look at his watch. He realised that he had to get moving. It was inconceivable that they wouldn't have found the body of the young boy by now. Once they found it they would have to consider seriously the possibility at least that the Focke-Wulf pilot hadn't died in the crash. That the escaping pilot had killed him wasn't the only possibility—the boy could have been struck by debris, or killed by the explosion and his body thrown some distance. And they wouldn't, yet, be able to get close enough to the FW to check whether or not it contained human remains. But they would, unless they were incredibly stupid, take the precaution of setting up road blocks for miles around and screening everyone passing through.

They would not, Willi thought, make any connection yet with the two men Bell had interviewed coming off the Ridgeway. For one thing the FW was a single-seater; which suggested one missing man, not two. Then, too, he had seen Bell's expression when Marsh said he was staying at a place locally—Lammas, was it? Bell had been impressed. Then again, it would be human nature for Bell to discount both himself and Marsh: he had checked them and let them go and he would uphold that judgement for a while yet.

He had learned a lot from this man Marsh in only a few minutes. And the offer of a room was tremendous luck. On the other hand, he had to go now. Once the road blocks were set up a different set of police and military would begin checking identities all over again—perhaps more carefully this time.

Will felt both exhilaration and panic. Less than 50 minutes ago he had been an enemy; a dangerous enemy and a legitimate target. In that short time he had landed, made an acquaintance, passed a police check, had a drink in an English pub and been offered a room in London. It was amazing luck. It was also too much, too soon. He had to get away and think. He was scarcely into his role. There was an acute danger of stage-fright unless he could absorb what had happened so far and practise a little at being Bill Ryder—alone. For the moment he would not think about the dead boy, but that, too, had to be absorbed.

On the other side of the room an elderly farm worker was having difficulty teaching two others the words of a song:

> Hitler has only got one ball
> Goering's, they say, are rather small
> Himmler's are very similar
> And poor old Goebbels has no balls at all . . .

Willi was only able to penetrate the thick Berkshire accents on the second time around. When he did he had a wild urge to shriek with laughter. He looked wildly round for something to distract him.

The smile died right there. The door opened. Two young men came in. Willi almost recoiled in shock. One of them looked almost identical with the boy he had left under the hedgerow up on the Ridgeway. Willi stared. They were of an age, they shared the same square and slightly concave look about the jawline. The hair was the same colour. They had to be related. If this was not a twin, then they were certainly brothers with only a year or so between them.

Even as he looked, both the newcomers stood for a moment apparently nonplussed not to find someone else here ahead of them. At the bar they asked something of the landlord that Willi didn't catch. "Not since I've been open," the landlord said cheerfully. "He's supposed to be, is he?" He turned away towards them with their full glasses and Willi lost the rest of the exchange.

"I must be off," Marsh said.

"See you again, perhaps," Willi managed. He was badly rattled by the boy on the other side of the bar. He drank up, shook hands with Marsh outside the pub, and watched him ride away smoothly. Willi thought he ought to head west and the sooner the better. He wasn't ready yet for London. He had a lot to learn and he must do it where the police and the military would be thinner on the ground.

20

Dieter Bauer drove back to Luftwaffe HQ thoughtfully, scarcely seeing the road. He had got Willi away! That was something to have done and he would not regret it, whatever happened now. But the exhilaration of the task was waning and anti-climax taking over. Now, he thought, I only have to pay the price. There was little chance that Willi's FW would not be logged all along its route across Germany and occupied Holland, or that its failure to blow itself out of the air, giving Willi a 'hero's death', would go unnoticed. And he had no illusions about the penalty he might have to pay.

There was just one chance. Goering, he thought, really had intended Willi to get away. The man might be gross, crude, cruel and a lot more besides, but he did respect real fliers— and he was a sentimental man. No matter what orders he, Bauer, had been given by his immediate superiors, Goering, he thought might well enjoy the joke: that Willi Reiter, hero and Luftwaffe bomber ace—the sort of man with whom Goering himself had once lived and fought—might by this time tomorrow be walking free among the British, his pockets full of counterfeit money and documents. He might even be amused that he, Bauer, had used influence, contacts and authorisations that had been given him over Goering's signature for earlier, quite different assignments, to produce all that Willi had needed. It was a chance, anyway.

He returned the ostentatious staff car to the motor pool and sat brooding in his own cell-like room. He re-read the latest letter from his sister, a naval cipher clerk stationed at Bremen, then he spread out his kit. He combed through it carefully, reducing his personal effects to the two good valises with which he had begun the war. Everything else he destroyed or gave to his orderly, Boll. Then he closed the door of his room and walked to the main building. Before Willi had appeared at Luftwaffe HQ, Bauer had been working, quite pointlessly, on the latest revision of some of the variable detail of the fighter-defence presentation which Goering had historically and unsuccessfully made to the Führer. It was a standing joke among HQ officers. Everyone knew that Hitler would never offer another chance to re-open the old offensive/defensive argument. So Goering now dreamed of a revitalised Luftwaffe fighter force sweeping British and American bombers from the sky and of saving the German people and industry from the fearful daily devastation; a sort of Battle of Britain in reverse.

He had been allotted Map Room G for the never-ending task of keeping the presentation in a state of permanent up-dating and he had been in residence so long that no-one ever came there hoping to use it for anything else. It had been his home for months, even when he was pulled out from time to time to tackle minor projects of a different order.

Bauer setted down in 'G' after dinner and remained there through the night. He still half hoped that the communications system was so battered and ragged that the FW's escape, even if logged, would somehow be lost in the minutiae of the seas of paperwork which befogged everyone. Communications were appalling. It was a chance, he told himself. And for a time would believe it and relieve the chill that had settled into the pit of his stomach.

Next morning after a shower and breakfast he made a few tentative enquiries to determine Goering's whereabouts. He didn't really think he could bluff himself into an interview with the Reich Marshal over some detail of his project. But he might be compelled to try. Goering, he was told, was aboard his armoured train HQ, and had been visiting devastated cities, spreading comradeship and cheer.

By mid-afternoon that day, though it was too early by far to start hoping, he had begun to wonder if he had done the right thing in disposing of so many things he had treasured for years.

At six he was disgusted with himself for cowering in 'G' for so long. He went back to his quarters, tidied himself up and walked unconcernedly into dinner. In the ante-room he was at once confronted by Prelle, a Colonel on Moller's staff.

"Bauer!" Prelle looked at him unbelievingly. "Where the hell have you been?"

"Here," Bauer shrugged. "Where else?"

"You were not in your quarters last night," Prelle said coldly.

"You could have found me in 'G'—working."

"If I were you I would report to Milch's aide as soon as possible," Prelle said with open satisfaction.

Bauer nodded. "I'll eat dinner first, I think."

He had little appetite. But it might be some time before he ate again. He sat on with his meal, swallowing with difficulty, his mouth dry with fear. His preoccupation was such that he neither saw nor heard anyone around him. The orderly serving his meal shook him by the elbow. "Herr Captain. Your orderly is in the ante-room with an urgent message."

So be it. Bauer drew a deep breath, composed himself and walked out to where Boll stood, stiffly at attention, effacing himself in a corner away from the ebb and flow of hungry officers.

"I'm sorry, Herr Captain, I had to call you out. You are ordered to report to Reich Marshal Goering as soon as you can. He is at Rominten Heath." He handed Bauer the signal.

It was a miracle. Bauer re-read the signal three times. He puffed like a winded runner. He beamed at Boll. "You did right, Boll. Thank you. Find me a car and a driver. I'll start at once. You will arrange a signal to the Reich Marshal's HQ train to that effect." Boll, a simple, fearful man, hustled away.

Boldly now, Bauer sped up two flights to Milch's suite. He walked into the outer office brusquely, startling a young duty officer who was eating a sandwich at his desk.

"Bauer. Dieter Bauer. I understand your chief is anxious to see me. Well, I'm afraid I can't stay. I am summoned to Rominten Heath by the Reich Marshal himself. You will see that your boss gets that message?"

The flustered duty officer, impressed, avowed that he would deliver the message, a small spray of crumbs falling on his spotless blotter.

Moving on air, yet warning himself he must be cautious, that it wasn't all over yet by a long way, Bauer sped down to the waiting car.

In under the hour he was being ushered into the coach Goering used as an office aboard the armoured train.

The great head lifted. The deep-set eyes looked him over. The huge bulk shifted on the swivel chair. Goering leaned to his left, lifting one vast buttock—and let wind loudly. He shook his head, a ghost of a smile hovering about the mouth. The smile jelled, grew into a grin. Goering threw back his head and roared with laughter. Bauer joined in, cautiously at first, then wholeheartedly, subsiding only by degrees.

"Marvellous," Goering said, wiping his eyes. "Bloody marvellous. You actually did it. You actually got our little hawk away." He wiped his forehead with the back of his hand, still rumbling with good humour.

"I'm glad you are pleased, Herr Reich Marshal," Dieter grinned.

Goering sniffed. "Pleased? I'm more than pleased, sonny. You did well. I wish—I only wish we could know what happens on the other side. But we never will know, I suppose."

"No sir," Bauer said. He hesitated. It was now or never. "But I have the impression that not everyone is pleased. You see, though I was given no direct order, nothing on paper, I was firmly given to understand that Reiter was not to reach England alive. A detonator, a charge—" he gestured vaguely. "I should not be wholly surprised to find myself under arrest shortly."

"Arrest!" Goering bellowed. "What prick would order a thing like that?"

Bauer feigned embarrassment. "General Moller?" he ventured. Prelle was Moller's man.

"No, hardly Moller," Goering mused. "In any case, forget it. I want you here. There is work here for any man who can deliver something well done once in a while." He heaved himself to his feet, stretching. "I'm off to Bremen. I want to see what new hell the Royal Air Force has caused there. I want to talk to the poor buggers who live there. They need me there. I'm a help to them in their agony. They crowd round me, you know, and I spend hours talking to them. They love it. I love it. It makes me feel I'm doing something useful." He let his arms fall, heavily. He frowned and cocked his head listening to the replay of his earlier words. "What was I saying? Oh, yes. Clear up in Berlin. Get your kit. Report to me here as soon as you can."

Bauer cracked to attention. "Yes sir," he said with enthusiasm. Goering waved him away.

An assortment of hovering aides stared at Bauer curiously as he left the Reich Marshal. He singled out one. "The Reich Marshal has indicated that I am to return to this HQ once I finish up a project," he said. "I am not sure when that will be, nor where you will be by then. How can I be sure to get through by telephone?" The aide, a friendly type who looked admiringly at Bauer's wound patch and collar facings, scribbled the details on a slip of paper for him. As he left the extraordinary train its staff hustled him aside, intent on their departure procedures.

Bauer laughed out loud as he drove back to HQ. He was under Goering's order's! He had got away with it after all. Ruefully he smiled over having cut his personal gear to the minimum like a condemned man. Never mind. He had taken a huge risk and got away with it. He felt the same kind of exhilaration as a parachutist does with his first jump—relief, elation, pride.

The sense of wellbeing lasted all the way back to the main gate.

He slowed for the barrier and plucked the HQ pass from his breast pocket. The sentry came quickly across. He took the pass, glanced at it nervously. "One moment, please, Herr Captain." He scuttled back into the guard-hut. Bauer saw him gesturing to a lean Feldwebel. The Feldwebel came out to look for himself, holding the pass.

"I am sorry for the delay, Herr Captain," he said. "We have certain orders."

Bauer felt a tremor of anxiety but pushed it away with the thought that Goering himself had commended him. The Feldwebel handed back the buff-coloured HQ pass and stood away from the car. But the barriers stayed down. "What's the problem?" Bauer demanded. The man only repeated:

"A moment, sir, please."

The original sentry reappeared in a moment and said

something in a low voice to the Feldwebel, who nodded and came forward again.

"Sir, you are requested to report to Colonel Prelle in Block 'B' of the New Building. The guard will go with you to direct you."

"I know where the New Building is," Bauer snapped. "I don't need an escort."

"Yes sir," the Feldwebel said. He came to attention respectfully. "However, sir, our orders are that you must be escorted directly to Block 'B'. Perhaps the Captain would help us in this respect. We cannot disobey the order."

"Very well," Bauer said.

The sentry opened the door and got in beside him. Bauer drove irritably, badly, round the main building to the so-called New Building, which had for some reason always been known as that. It contained, as far as he knew, only map supplies, photo-reconnaissance composites, personnel records, stationery and the like. Perhaps someone had at last decided to make some sensible use of it. He cut a wide arc round to the entrance to Block 'B'. The sentry got out. Bauer left the car and approached the entrance. As he did so, a large figure came towards him in the darkness. He recognised a man called Stiefel, a huge Gefreiter who was on someone-or-other's staff; Bauer was always seeing him about the headquarters.

"Herr Captain Bauer?" Stiefel came to attention. "Colonel Prelle asked me to look out for you. This way, sir." He turned and led the way into the building.

'Prelle!' Bauer thought. 'A typical bloody HQ loafer, puffed up with self-importance, a bloody parasite on the backside of the real Luftwaffe; the kind who spends most of the day either kissing the arses of generals or talking bravely in the bar. Well he'd got another think coming if he thought anyone was going to make something out of the Willi Reiter affair.' He grinned at Stiefel's back, imagining Prelle's—and anyone else's—discomfort when they heard he was under Goering's orders.

They came to the end of the corridor. Stiefel smiled and pressed the lift button. The cage sucked into position and the doors opened. Stiefel gave him a little bow and Bauer stepped forward into the lift, still smiling gently, maliciously.

He was conscious only of one stunning blow on the back of his neck. His eyes closed, and in closing saw only a line of

124

polished rivets set in the angle of the stainless steel lift-cage. They seemed to run upwards and away before darkness engulfed him.

Stiefel stepped into the lift behind him. It creaked under his weight. He lifted Bauer gently under the arms and held him propped against the wall while he pushed the button for the basement. He was respectful in handling this officer's body. He knew very little about him but had liked what he had seen. Pity the poor bugger had to come up against people with real power.

When the lift stopped he picked Bauer up like a child and carried him to the small room in which Eugen Reiter had died. He laid Bauer gently on the bed. Working quickly, he undid Bauer's tunic, felt for the ribs, and with the spread fingers of his left hand marking the spot, took the long pin from the back of his own left sleeve.

The pin pierced Bauer's ribs only once, leaving a tiny wound in the skin. But withdrawing all but the last inch of the weapon, Stiefel probed Bauer's heart again and again at different angles, raking the wall and the vagus nerve. Bauer died at the first penetration.

Satisfied, Stiefel checked the absence of pulse or breathing and buttoned Bauer's tunic. He put out the light, locked the door and retrieved Bauer's car from the front entrance to the building.

In the early hours of the following day, the body of a Luftwaffe captain was found at the back of a ruined office block on the edge of the Tiergarten district. The keys of the car were still in the ignition and the ignition switched on. The car was off the road, at an angle across the entrance to a car park. The battery was flat. The captain's head lolled back at an unnatural angle.

Police took charge of both the body and the car. They reported to Luftwaffe HQ later that an officer, one Captain Bauer, had apparently died in an air raid during the course of which he had unwisely failed to take shelter.

Bauer's body was claimed at once by a Luftwaffe detail and cremated with suitable honours. A signal recording the police opinion was sent at once to Goering's personal HQ with a supplementary note to the effect that the signal was being sent because Captain Bauer had recently come under the direct orders of the Reich Marshal.

Goering never read it. He had forgotten Dieter Bauer

already. The signal remained in his 'Important' tray for 48 hours. Then it was winnowed from the overflowing tray by an aide as being of much less importance than many others which also remained unread.

21

The failure of the Koch exercise was still rankling with Himmler. He was resigned, now, that the *Volkssturm* would be fully exploited by Party officials under the malign leadership of Bormann—and on a national scale—and that his own prestige and authority would suffer while his workload grew. That was inevitable. There were other troubling aspects.

Himmler was growing accustomed to losing to Bormann. He would find a way, one day, to settle that score. Sooner or later the man would put a foot wrong somewhere, and then . . .

But he could not sit still for losing to Goering. That was not to be borne. Koch, without ever knowing that his life had been in jeopardy, might be safe again now, but Himmler was not satisfied simply with the alleged disappearance of both Reiter brothers. He said nothing to Brandt, who was clearly relieved and anxious to forget his over-optimism. He summoned Gestapo Muller and gave him a carefully edited version of the story—one that could quite safely be repeated to Hitler himself.

"Understand," he told Muller, "I want an investigation so circumspect that even the men who undertake it are to know nothing. The Reiters are simply to be found, if they are still alive. Let me know when you get that far. If they're dead, then I'll want to know who killed them, when and why. If it takes more than one man, then each additional man must have only basic facts; one detail each, one aspect each to work on."

Muller nodded, intrigued. He was wondering if this was something of Himmler's that had come unstuck. And if so, whether it might some day be used to his own advantage. He was loyal, but not too loyal.

As he prepared to go, Himmler pointed a finger at him.

"And no comebacks, Heinrich. I don't want Goering on the phone. Easy does it."

Muller snapped his arm up into a salute and turned to leave. Himmler caught him at the door.

"And Muller . . ."

"Reichsführer?"

"Nothing on paper."

Muller smiled. "The Reichsfüfrer does me an injustice."

In forty-eight hours he was back. He was admitted to Himmler's room immediately, but Himmler's manner was distant. He was already having regrets about pursuing the thing this far. All he'd achieved was that now Muller, too, probably guessed that he had been outsmarted.

"Well?" Himmler demanded.

"Standartenführer Reiter left his uncle's home here in Berlin for a short walk on the evening after he was here," Muller said. "He had been at home all day, apparently fearful of leaving the telephone. He was never again seen alive. His uncle, his only living relative, is greatly disturbed. He is sure—"

Himmler held up his hand. "Never mind the details," he said. "Is it a reasonable assumption that he was killed—murdered?"

"It is."

Himmler pursed his lips. The brother, Willi? Or the Luftwaffe? Or Willi with the foreknowledge and connivance of the Luftwaffe?

"And the brother?"

"It is certain that Reiter spent several days at Wildpark-Werder, though not under arrest. He was given a room there, but not allowed to leave the building. He was treated the whole time as a respected officer. The only visitor he had was—" Muller consulted a note "—an officer called Bauer, a kind of specialist armourer."

Muller looked up to see if Himmler wanted to comment. He was motioned to continue. "We think it is not likely that he is dead. He was probably taken out, or sent out of the country. He could have flown out. There is no proof or direct connection, but on the other hand, one aircraft flew from Rangsdorf later last week and there is no record that it either returned or completed any logged flight. As far as the records go, the flight never took place. Though we know it did. And there are other unusual circumstances . . ."

"For instance?"

Muller shrugged. "Nothing concrete. This aircraft was an FW190. We are fairly sure it wasn't armed. It took off alone. So what do we have? A fighter mission without ammunition? A training flight from a field which does no training? A ferry mission performed by an officer on leave? And no record of any such flight anyway?" He raised his eyebrows at Himmler, who nodded, satisfied. It did, indeed, look as if the Luftwaffe had quietly put one over on him.

"One other thing," Muller said, "is very odd."

Himmler attempted an expression of indifference. None of this was palatable.

"The officer Bauer, was found by the *Ordnungspolizei* two days ago. He was sitting in a car, dead, apparently a blast victim of the last RAF raid. It took time for that to filter through to me. We weren't looking for Bauer, or even at him."

Himmler nodded repeatedly. It was an old favourite, much used of late by some of his own people. Muller looked as if he wanted to talk about it a little more, but Himmler cut him short. He wanted no questions. He patted Muller's shoulder, returned his 'Heil Hitler' and hustled him out. He wanted to think about it quietly for a moment. If Willi Reiter really was out of the country he was probably no longer a danger of any kind. The death of the brother, though, suggested aggressive Luftwaffe involvement, way beyond mere protection of their own. What was Goering up to? Was it all part of the silent skirmishing? And did it matter anyway?

He was inclined to forget the whole thing. But there was one more step he could take. And then he'd forget it.

22

Detective Inspector Andrew Musgrave Bell sat behind his desk hardly able to focus on the papers in front of him. He sweated, his mouth was dry and his hands clammy. Almost whimpering with fear, he brooded despondently on how differently he would have handled the last few hours if only he could begin them again, and how uncomplainingly he would handle a normal day of routine if only he could somehow survive the rest of this one.

He had made a hash of it. He knew that now. And he squirmed over the details.

His first mistake had been to react at once to the phone calls about the German aircraft. Many people had seen it crash up on the Ridgeway and dashed to the telephone. They were still calling in when he was out.

No planning. That was bad to begin with. He hadn't realised, either, just how long it would take to get up to the scene of the crash, or what limitations the ground itself would impose on him. He should have taken two men; he saw that now.

The problem of the aircraft alone would have been sufficient. German planes came down all over England, but he'd never had one on his patch before, and though the procedures were pretty much common sense, they needed to be taken in careful steps.

There had been no problem finding the crash. When he got there, the main fuselage still burned furiously and the column of black smoke could be seen intermittently between the trees as he and Dowson moved towards it along the track. They had stood just outside the field itself for a few moments. It did seem unlikely that the pilot had escaped from an upside-down burning machine. He looked at it carefully. It looked small enough to be a fighter. No danger, then, from a bomb-load. He was mildly surprised that cannon shells weren't exploding all over the place in that heat. Perhaps that had happened already, though the two 'eye-witnesses' hadn't mentioned it. A fighter without ammunition was somehow a contradiction. He was pleased with that much deduction and he would be sure to put it in the report.

It was only when he'd seen enough that he realised that he could not, with only one man, conduct a search for a possible escaped pilot, even if he believed in one. He was at once inclined not to believe in the possibility. But the comfort went out of that when he saw that he couldn't put the fire out, either. Or telephone from anywhere except back down on the road again. He ordered Dowson to stay on guard at the edge of the field and hurried off back to the car.

Before he had gone a hundred yards, he heard Dowson shouting his name. Irritably he stopped and waited for the young PC to catch up with him.

Dowson took his helmet off and wiped his forehead. He took a deep breath and announced: "We've got a body."

Bell brightened and walked back with him. Dowson, it seemed, had ventured into the field and at once seen the body of a youth. "What's more," he told Bell, holding down his excitement, "it isn't the pilot."

"How the hell do you know?" Bell snapped, his panic returning. A moment later, as they turned into the field, he wished he hadn't said that. The body was that of a boy of seventeen or eighteen at the most, and he was quite clearly a farm labourer. His clothes were as English as the hedgerow: muddy boots, torn flannel shirt and the trousers of what had once been a cheap blue suit.

Bell edged his way along, close to the hedgerow and knelt only where the ground might reasonably be thought untouched. Bending over the body, he tested for signs of life. There were none. The pockets contained a packet of ten Woodbines, a petrol lighter made from a spent .303 cartridge case and seven shillings and eightpence in small change. No keys no identity card, no handkerchief, nothing to identify the youth at all.

"Come back to the bar with me," Bell commanded. "I've got an old cape in the boot to cover him with." And, as they started back along the track: "Nothing changes. You stay put. I'll send somebody up to relieve you as soon as we can get things sorted out. And keep your big feet off the area."

Bell took the little car down the hill and pulled up at the first house he came to. He knocked imperiously and after a long wait a tiny woman came to the door. She wore the deceptive smile of someone who is still savouring the residual pleasure of a joke just heard. When Bell asked if she had a telephone she looked at him pityingly.

"Does it look like it?" she said. "Do you see the wires?" She smiled still more.

"Where's the nearest then?" Bell was annoyed with himself. He should have noticed.

"High Leas." She pointed east along the road. "The farm." Without waiting she turned and closed the door in his face, still smiling broadly.

He found the farm. An unshaven wisp of a man, shirt-sleeved, was cleaning out a cowshed behind the house. Impatient with rustics, Bell sought the front door of the farmhouse. Only after he had pulled an antique bell twice did he realise that he hadn't heard it ring.

The back door of the house was closed and locked. He called out several times. He was losing his temper. He turned to look for the man in the cowshed. In it, behind it, across the yard. No-one. He looked at his watch. He had already lost an hour and a quarter since leaving the station.

Hot and angry, Bell got in, turned the car around and headed for his own desk. He calmed himself. From there he could organise.

Immediately he arrived he checked the telephone number of the local Home Guard Commander from the list on his wall. There was no reply. He tried the area commander, got through and listened to a long explanation about patrol rotas. What it amounted to was that a full platoon, from which dusk to dawn patrols would be drawn, would normally stand-to early that evening after the day's work.

"I could come myself," the Home Guard CO offered. "And I can have someone here try to get in touch with men as they become available during the day."

Bell forgot himself. "Well that's a lot of help," he said caustically. "I've got a burning plane, a possible escape Nazi and a dead body. I'm sorry I can't offer anything really meaty, like an invasion. But perhaps that's just as well."

There was a long moment of silence at the other end of the line. In a less friendly, much more military tone, the Home Guard major said, gently: "Yes, well this is 1944, you know. We have rather tended to believe, of late, that Jerry has other things to worry about. I'm sorry if you're fussed. Call me if you need me." The disconnecting clicks as the major hung up sounded to Bell very much like a raspberry.

Frantic to do something right, Bell turned his attention to a bunch of folders in his bottom drawer. There were standing orders to cover crashed aircraft at least. If he could report something achieved, it would help. The Air Ministry, he knew, had to be informed as quickly as possible. RAF experts would want to examine the wreck, mount guard over it and, eventually, remove it or as much of it as they thought necessary. He made the call, which flowed perfectly, and relaxed slightly.

His next job was to get Dowson down again. He'd be wanted on the paperwork. He looked at his watch again and felt a fresh stab of anxiety. Two hours! He called his sergeant, arranged messages for two more PCs to report in urgently and then did what he should have done long since. He called his superintendent.

131

Superintendent Edwin Whisby listened to the essential facts. He asked no questions. "I'll be over directly," he said. "Don't do anything about the body, I'll bring the police surgeon and transport."

It wasn't until he relaxed a little and reviewed his actions that Inspector Bell had a new and terrible thought. He had, he now realised, got his priorities muddled. He had assumed that the crash and the death of the boy were both part of one event. That blast, or shock, or perhaps flying debris had been the cause of death.

What if none of these assumptions was true? Was if the pilot had not died in the crash? Had, in fact, killed in order to escape without an immediate alarm?

He'd been prepared to go through the routines of a search and had already tried to enlist the aid of the Home Guard, hadn't he? Now he began to wonder if that was enough. Perhaps the Army ought to have been called in. No, he couldn't do that. Whisby would make that decision.

He began his review again, this time assuming that the pilot had escaped. Because that was the greatest danger and therefore held the highest priority.

He had left Dowson up there alone. If there was a pilot he probably had a hand gun. He'd read they often had.

Bell shook his head. He was fussing unduly. It was regulations that something like the burning wreck had to be guarded. Dowson might be at risk, but so what?

Then the real blunder hit him. In the pressure of events he had forgotten the two men—what were their names? Marsh and—Ryder. Well they were in the clear. He'd seen their identity cards. Even as he reassured himself, Bell began to wilt. It wasn't all right. He had no addresses, and only the assurance that one of them was staying over at Lammas, near Newbury. He'd been a bit too impressed by that. Was either one or both totally excluded from suspicion of being the pilot? No. Or involvement in the death of the boy? No. What if the boy had been murdered—nothing to do with aircraft or Germans? What then would Whisby make of his letting them walk away, without statements or a deeper check on their bona fides? How could he have been so stupid?

For a moment or two he played with the idea of not mentioning Marsh or Ryder at all. He tried to justify such a course in his mind. He had cleared them, hadn't he? They were patently British anyway, for God's sake. That at least let them out of the aircraft thing. But in his heart he knew he was going to have to tell Whisby.

Then he had an idea. It was a measure of how the events of the day had rattled him that he hadn't thought of it before. Moving very quickly, he found the directory for the Newbury area. He knew, as all police in the county did, the names of every owner Lammas had had in the last thirty years. He dialled, praying that Whisby was still some minutes away.

At length the phone was answered by a woman. The housekeeper or the cook or someone. A local, anyway, judging by the Berkshire vowels.

Bell announced himself. There was a brief silence at the other end. The poor old sod probably associated police calls with bad news, he thought, just as they did with telegrams.

He wanted it right first time, so he spelled it out carefully. "A German aircraft crashed near here this morning, madam, and I believe that a gentleman I spoke to soon after the crash, and who may have seen exactly what happened, is presently staying at Lammas. A Mr Marsh?"

"Yes?"

"Good Christ!" Bell muttered. Before he could begin again, the woman said, uncertainly: "They're playing tennis. Did you want me to call them?"

"No!" Bell shouted. He was frantic she would put the phone down and be lost to him while she went waffling round to the tennis courts. Whisby would be arriving any moment. "No," he said in a gentler tone. "There is no need to bother them. All I need is confirmation that Mr Marsh is a guest at Lammas."

Again the pause, and then: "Miss Ronnie's guest."

"Very likely," Bell said. "This Mr Marsh—he's about six foot tall, light colouring, about 30 years old?" And to ram it home: "Is that your Mr Marsh? That's all I need to know."

This time the silence was even longer. "Yes. I can fetch him to the telephone if you want. They're playing tennis, you see."

"Don't bother," Bell said, and hung up.

It was his worst mistake of the day. In his anxiety to have his judgement confirmed, it had not occurred to him that 'they' who were playing tennis could be any other than Marsh and his friend Ryder. He sat back, more calmly now, and awaited Whisby.

The Superintendent was not a brilliant man. But his years of experience had taught him to manage men and events with a checklist mind. A tall, gaunt man, whose flowing moustache, pale looks and fidgety manner suggested only marginal vitality, he constantly surprised his subordinates.

Bell jumped up when he arrived and offered his desk. Instead Whisby folded himself in sections like a pocket-knife onto an old bentwood chair, seeming not to have noticed.

"Right," he said softly. "Let's check it out. Who's looking after the body?"

"PC Dowson, but I've got two more men should be in any time. Dowson hasn't eaten."

"Any idea of identity?"

"None as yet. There was nothing on him. He's obviously a labourer on that particular farm. That shouldn't be hard to establish. I'll send the first spare man up to the farm as soon as he gets in."

"Why not phone?"

"To see if anyone's missing, you mean?" Bell said. "Well I'd rather someone went to the door. The thing is, it could be a son, or a close relative. If I tell someone on the phone a boy's dead in a field, they'll be along there before we can take proper precautions. They almost certainly know exactly where he was working."

"Right. What killed him?"

"Nothing to show," Bell said. "I couldn't move the body around—just in case. I could have been trampling on evidence. The police surgeon will have to tell us."

"He's outside," Whisby nodded. "I'll get him started up there in a minute. He can go up in your car. Meanwhile, anyone else seen him? And any witnesses to the crash?"

"To the crash, yes—well, more or less. To the boy's death, I'd assume not. But I haven't had the men to check the other." Bell now related his check on Marsh and Ryder.

"How do you know they're OK?" Whisby looked at him sharply.

"I called Lammas at once," Bell lied. "Marsh is a guest there." He looked at Whisby straight in the eye. "And I checked his description with the housekeeper there to be sure we were talking about the same man."

Whisby nodded. "Air Ministry?"

"Done," Bell said, concealing his relief. "They're getting some people down here fast. Though how they'll get the thing down to the road is anyone's guess."

"Not our problem," Whisby waved it away. "We'll need the Army. I've got half an alert out now, as far as Reading and an

134

RAF fire team should be up there by now. They're used to this sort of thing. Once we know if there's a body in there we'll know if we need to start combing the countryside. We can't do that with the few men we've got. It will give the Home Guard something to do this evening, too." He pulled at his moustache. "Bloody nuisance it being on top of the Downs. No bloody phone, no nothing."

Bell nodded sagely. "It wasn't easy getting it started," he confessed. "Sodding about round the farms looking for a phone."

"Did you ask at any of the farms about the lad?"

Bell faltered for a moment. Then he decided to forget the cowman and the old woman. "No-one at home even," he lied. "It's market day. Everything stops on market day."

"What a game," Whisby sighed. "We don't know if we've got an escaped Jerry and a murder or just a crashed plane and an accident." He pulled his chair up to the corner of the desk and began mapping out the next steps.

"Here's what we do . . ."

23

Cycling furiously across the English countryside with only one good leg was something he hadn't thought out too well. Willi had wanted the bicycle primarily as camouflage. But because of the leg he was only just going to make it. The muscles ached badly, even though he'd put all the thrust into the right leg on the hilly stretches. When he at last free-wheeled into the grey suburbs of the old railway town of Swindon he was almost finished. He felt the streets close round him comfortably. Out on the open road he had dreaded interception every mile. Here, in an fairly busy town, it would be impossibly bad luck to be challenged.

Once in Swindon, too, he was back if not on familiar ground then at least in a place where he was not totally disoriented. He looked around keenly for buildings, streets—anything that might jog his memory, but he thought he knew where to find Swindon Junction. Then he would be back on the guidelines he had sketched out in Berlin. He knew that he wanted the GWR station, not the Town station. From the Junction he could get to Birmingham—with any luck by early evening. And be lost in the anonymity of a big city.

He turned a corner, breathing hard and within an ace of having to dismount to rest his leg—and there it was, the old dull, Bath-stone frontage with the long wall of the railway workshops streaming away down the road like the outer bastion of some grim fortress. He smiled grimly, sailed past the station itself and propped the bicycle against the high wall. Standing was a strain. The leg throbbed painfully. He gritted his teeth and limped into the station yard.

In the flagged booking hall he leaned against a wall gratefully, and took in the feel of the place. One fine evening in 1938, after just such a day as this, he'd arrived here on his way down from Birmingham. A bent and fragile old porter had taken his bags through to this hall and gone off to find him a cab. He'd set his watch by GWR time from the pendulum clock set on the wall by the ticket windows. And there it was still. He smiled at it as at an old friend.

There were plenty of travellers. Servicemen and women, civilians, uniforms he didn't recognise. He began to move about among them. He read the posters. This was the kind of stuff he must drink in, feed on, fattening the threadbare framework of his cover story. There were advertisements for real estate, farm sales, auctions. And for concerts, recitals, films, plays, lectures and evening classes. Most were simple enough and quickly absorbed. He couldn't make much of something called Pelmanism. But life in England seemed to have a great deal to offer, despite the war.

After a while he shifted ground to nearer the pokey ticket windows and without appearing to, watched several ticket transactions. Each person simply offered notes or notes and small change. The servicemen and women seemed to have travel vouchers, but none of the civilians offered anything at all that could have been either proof of identity or any kind of travel permit. It bore out what was implied by one poster that was much in evidence. IS YOUR JOURNEY REALLY NECESSARY? it demanded. So it was a matter of conscience whether or not you took up space on the trains, and not of showing need or gaining a permit.

He was hungry. He didn't believe that there were plain clothes police mingling with the travellers, but for the benefit of a possible watcher, he studied his watch, mimed surprise and moved off smartly down the tunnel to the buffet on the nearest platform. Again, that was territory he knew slightly. He had never used it, but remembered its existence. He found it crowded and the door blocked by a queue. Diffident still about servicemen, he waited until a woman harassed by four children joined the queue and then stepped in quickly behind her. The precautions were probably wasted. Unless it was their job, even German servicemen rarely took any kind of official interest in civilians; in England, Willi thought, it was even more unlikely.

The service was appallingly slow. In Germany the food always seemed to run out. He watched anxiously, keeping his eyes on each purchase. No coupons or tickets were handed over for the food. Another good break. Unless there was something special about this one, he would be able to eat in railway buffets if nowhere else.

When his turn came he simply repeated the last order he'd heard.

"Two cheese sandwiches and two teas, please."

"No more cheese, only brawn." A girl with strong cheekbones, pretty enough but with frizzy hair, her expression at once relaxing into a near-simper, waited on his decision. He nodded and she fluttered her eyelashes improbably. Turning with the food, he found there was no space anywhere to put it down. The girl immediately swept aside an empty glass display case and made room for him at the counter alongside her own station. Absurdly, Willi flushed. He could not refuse, though he'd bought the double order in the hope of suggesting that he was not alone. Now he had to eat the food almost in front of her. Each time she returned to her position her eyes flickered over him with incautious interest.

He wolfed the food. He had never eaten brawn, didn't quite know what it was. It seemed to be some sort of jellied meat. It tasted delicious. The tea, though was alien: weak, hot, sugarless. He drank that with the same relish. He felt better immediately. It was going to work. It was!

"You in the Forces?" The girl spoke almost in his ear. The queue had melted away. Willi smiled and nodded. "Raff?" she said. "My boyfriend's in the Raff." Her accent was West Country, the studied twitches of the mouth were pure Hollywood. She looked wholesome, Willi thought. He warmed to her. "Lucky man—on both counts," he said. "Yes, I'm on leave, that's all. Just passing through." She lowered her chin,

137

giving him a long stare. She put up both hands and teased the frizzed hair away from her face, at the same time thrusting her chest slightly forward. "It's always the bloody same here," she said. "Just passing through. Nobody ever comes here to stay here. Nobody interesting anyway . . ."

On impulse Willi put out a hand and touched her cheek gently with the back of his hand. "I'll look for you on my way back," he smiled. And turned away. He lifted a hand when he got as far as the door. The girl still stood there, stunned, her hand to her cheek and her dreams revitalised.

Willi returned to the booking hall. The queue at the tiny ticket window was shorter now. When his turn came he was tensed and ready for flight if he should make any mistake. He asked for a single to Birmingham and passed one of his five-pound notes through the tunnel-like aperture. The clerk took it and fed him back both ticket and change.

High on this success, Willi tackled a porter for the platform number and details of any change he would have to make. From the bookstall he bought a *Daily Express* and a *Picture Post* and was pleased to have added these to his camouflage. He toyed with going direct to his platform, but now that his hunger had been stilled the need for nicotine was resurgent. There was no sign of tobacco anywhere inside the station. He remembered passing a shop close by. He hurried across the road. The shop was roughly where he'd thought it to be. The interior was gloomy and smelled of tom-cat. A wizened woman, with eyes as bright as a girl's, perched on a stool behind the counter and a scrawled sign announcing: 'Sorry, No Virginia. Turkish Only.' The logistics of that baffled him.

He'd found he'd forgotten how to ask for cigarettes. By the pack? Quantity? He experimented. "Turkish?" he said doubtfully and wrinkled his nose.

"That's right," the woman told him. " 'Orrible, aren't they?" The button eyes looked warily past him at the door. "Here . . . you on leave?"

"Yes," Willi said. "Just checking the trains for tomorrow."

"Ah," she said softly. She slid her hand under the counter without taking her eyes off him. "Put them away quick," she said. She clapped something into his hand, leering at him. "I always keep a few for nice-looking boys."

Willi smiled his best smile; the one that produced rather odd-looking dimples. He covered the packet with one hand and held out a note with the other. "Thanks," he said, making it sound heartfelt. He was rewarded with a huge grin.

Back in the booking hall he looked at the packet. It was of pale blue paper, without foil or board. Players. He remembered.

He joined the rush to the Birmingham train. He had to change at Cheltenham. Smoking a Players, full of bread and brawn and tea, he felt better; confident enough to push in where he could. It was a short train and packed. He found himself jammed into a corridor between a neat young WAAF and a morose looking corporal wearing the red and white shoulder titles of the East Surrey regiment. The corporal sat on his kitbag. It had his name and service number stencilled baldly in white across the black canvas: Cpl. E. A. Carswell, 10548783. The WAAF looked tired and leaned against him companionably. It evidently meant nothing. She smiled at him wanly once or twice, but that was all.

The journey took twice as long as he had expected. He read the *Daily Express* and learned that the Russians had attacked Rumania with 900,000 men in an endeavour to encircle twenty-three German divisions, and that there were rumours that the Rumanians would seek a separate peace. He read it with little emotion. Or was he suppressing feeling? He supposed that his circumstances did it for him. He turned impatiently to the kind of information that could help him. Cricket seemed to be in full swing. There was racing at Newmarket and greyhound racing at White City, wherever that was, and at Wembley and Perry Barr, Birmingham. (He remembered that Marsh's father had a Wembley telephone number.) There were advertisements for cocoa, for fungicide with which to spray tomatoes, and for mushroom spore, tulip bulbs, roses, beer, shaving cream, hair tonic—and even second-hand cars. In the cinemas Ingrid Bergman and Gary Cooper were appearing in *For Whom the Bell Tolls,* Ginger Rogers in *Lady in the Dark,* and Rita Hayworth and Gene Kelly in *Cover Girl.*

The advertisements told him more about life in England now than he could take in immediately. The picture they drew was of a nation that was tired and stretched, certainly; but not to the limit. British servicemen were dying in theatres of war all over the world; on land, sea and in the air. At home, the V1's were causing thousands of casualties daily. And yet ... people were still going to the theatre, the cinema, still growing tomatoes, watching cricket matches, listening to music, and waiting, waiting. Waiting, no doubt, for the victory that they were quite sure they would soon embrace.

Willi was torn by the thought. He thought of the war that the German people had suffered; that his parents and friends had died in; of the pinched faces and empty bellies everywhere in Germany; above all, of that look of total war: deep and unremitting fatigue. He remembered and choked on the bitterness of it.

When he came out into the street from Birmingham Snow Hill station it was nearly seven. The evening was warm and airless. The first thing he noticed was a billboard alongside a man selling evening papers. It read: PARIS LIBERATED.

His eyes filled, but he wasn't sure why. Were they tears of despair, or relief?

24

Fleet Street usually gave Harvey a lift. He loved all newspapers indiscriminately, though he had no desire to work on any of them. Like many another agency man, he was even more in love with the sensation of being ahead even of them with the news. But he was part of them; they were his shop window and he felt affection for them impartially.

For once as he turned up Bouverie Street he got nothing out of the unique, bustling ethos. The roaring chutes of the two evening papers, the queues of vans waiting to be fed with lunch-time editions, the hum of giant machinery and the curiously paraffin smell of ink billowing from every doorway and vent were all familiar—but unlovable after the peace of Lammas.

He usually saw the area by night and it had been some time since he'd looked at it critically in the unkind brilliance of a day like this. The appearance of Fleet Street itself was mildly shocking. Between the bombed-out premises with their boarded fronts and eyeless upper storeys there were too many shops with To Let signs; their owners called up, called away, or perhaps killed in the raids on the suburbs they called home. The Black and White Milk Bar, which he usually found by torchlight and instinct at least once each night of shiftwork, by day looked seedy and depressed.

He was restless and dispirited. He'd called ABP as soon as he'd got to Temple Chambers, and learned McNair had written him into the schedule for four twelve-hour shifts from eight p.m. next day. It was what he preferred, yet illogically he was resentful. Now that he was back he would have preferred to go to work immediately. He had taken Ronnie home and left, her day fully planned. She was lunching with her father at Grosvenor House, had 'things to do' and would be back in the MOI canteen by seven. Having the day to brood in was something he didn't need. Lammas had made an impression. Without ever being awed by it, Croft's estate had put his own ambition uncomfortably into perspective. After wondering briefly if that had been at least some part of Ronnie's intention, he dismissed the idea as unworthy. Ronnie always said, straight on, what she thought. She never hinted or nudged. It was one of the things that made her so different—not only from other women, but from other people generally. It now struck him that Croft must be quite a man—not only to have got where he was, but at the same time to have won from Ronnie respect, affection and the unusual closeness they shared. He wondered about Justine Croft. He had once tended to think of Justine as one of those poor little rich girls trapped in luxurious boredom by the success and indifference of their husbands. Now he thought that was probably doing them both an injustice. And yet, though it didn't make a bit of difference to anyone, he was suddenly rather on Croft's side.

He walked aimlessly down the Strand. He hadn't done that for ages either. The Savoy still had Jack Buchanan and Coral Browne in *The Last of Mrs Cheyney* and across the road *Arsenic and Old Lace* was in its second year. He thought it was a minor miracle anyone could find the theatres; at night they allowed no lighted signs, no foyer lights, no glitter, no magnetism. Until you were past the heavily curtained entrances they were as dead as the ruined shops and offices that infected every block like some creeping disease. Yet the Strand was in slightly better shape than Fleet Street; there remained some tawdry appeal in the shops; the restaurants, the jewellers, the theatre-fronts with their stills and garish review boards. The smell of decay was fainter at this end of the long stretch.

He dodged a No 11 bus and took a turn round Trafalgar

Square. He couldn't waste the day. He thought briefly about seeing the matinee of Phyllis Dixey's *Peek—a—Boo*, smiled at the idea, changed course by Canadian Military Headquarters and found himself staring at the model P & O liners in Cockspur Street. That only brought back the world of Lammas and wealth. Three months on a P & O boat to the Far East and back was about as real, for him, as Fred Astaire's world of top hat, white tie and tails.

He halted abruptly. He'd go down to his father's office, pick him up after work and spend the evening out at Eastcote. The house he'd lived in as a child, as a teenager, still pulled at him occasionally. Was that a sign of immaturity? What if it was? He rather liked the idea of an evening out there. Without Ronnie they could talk, mooch about in the garden. Perhaps they could take home something to eat. After that, a pint or two at the local pub. The old man would enjoy that. Harvey felt better. And feeling it, acted out feeling better. He smiled, relaxed, slowed down, looked about him cheerfully. He told himself that if he had been born into money, came from some such home as Lammas, he would not have met Ronnie anyway, and even if he had, he would not have appealed to her. That in itself was compensation of a sort. Whatever happened between them, knowing Ronnie had been one of the best things that had ever happened to him. If he had wanted Ronnie, then his own fairly commonplace background was the right starting point; Ronnie admired men like her father who had begun with nothing and earned everything.

He waved a cab out of the slow-moving traffic emerging from the Mall under Admiralty Arch and on impulse decided to have lunch at the Press Club.

The place was full of familiar faces who wanted a word. A Reuter man, whose name he couldn't summon, obliquely offered him a job. Virgil Pinkley, of UPI, told him he was overdue for something better. Neither encounter seemed important. It was gone four by the time he'd walked down to the Underground at Blackfriars. On the Tube he read in the evening paper that the Germans were putting up a fight for the streets of Paris after all. A small item at the bottom of the paper caught his eye:

LONE RAIDER DOWNED

A lone German Frock-Wulf fighter crashed in a field yesterday beside the Ridgeway, the ancient trackway atop the White Horse Downs in Berkshire. An official Air Ministry and Ministry of Home Security communique today adds that no trace has been found of the pilot, who was earlier assumed to have died when the fighter exploded and caught fire on crashing. Police and Home Guard Units are searching the area.

He was mildly astonished. How on earth had the pilot got away without being seen? It was intriguing to think that while he and what's-his-name—Ryder—were walking along together the man might even then have been in hiding nearby. And what was the point of the man running anyway? They'd have him very quickly. They always did.

Frank Marsh was pleased, but looked faintly embarrassed to see him. There was something different, too, about his appearance, though Harvey couldn't pin it down. He disappeared, flustered, to wash his hands.

Harvey greeted Philomena Bedell and she smiled back at him brightly. They had met several times before. Now, as then, Harvey found himself wondering lewdly whether anyone at all had ever enjoyed those overflowing breasts, those majestic thighs. He realised he was staring. Miss Bedell was aware of it. She said, primly: "Still with the newspaper business, Harvey?"

"News agency," Harvey corrected, nodding.

"Ay'm afraid Ay don't really know the difference," she said. She looked at him nervously and then added: "Anyway, Ay'm sure it's very important work."

Harvey was irritated. "Yes, well, it's the best I can do. I know I look healthy enough. But they won't have me in the services at any price." He was at once aware that he had overreacted again and worried that he was letting the thing get out of hand. She was a simple woman and probably meant exactly what she'd said.

She pushed back her chair and stood, abruptly. Her face and neck were spreading crimson as far down at the tops of her breasts. She entangled herself in the telephone and pulled it to the floor.

Harvey was contrite. He rushed to help her. Then took her arm. "Take no notice of me. I get that way. After five years of explaining why you're not a Commando, a Marine or even an Army cook, you do get that way."

Philomena nodded and tried to pull away. But Harvey held on. "I'm sorry," he said softly.

Philomena peered myopically, intently at the front of her blouse. "You must think I'm very silly," she said. "After years of being an old maid, women get like that." She patted his hand. Harvey noticed for the first time that her hand was small, delicate, cool and beautifully shaped. She smelled delightful, too.

"I don't care how you got that way," he declared, moved, "but you ought to give lessons. There aren't enough like you."

Frank appeared, rubbing damp hands. "Get your hands off that woman," he demanded.

Philomena fled, the crimson returning.

Frank Marsh stared after her. "What was all that about?"

"A very brief misunderstanding," Harvey told him. "But quickly repaired."

When they emerged from the Tube at Eastcote the air had a cool and country smell. There was a blackboard in the booking hall that said: AIR RAID IN PROGRESS. It was a pleasant walk through the fresh little streets. The summer roses were hanging full-blown in the front gardens. Still newish, the houses had a rainwashed look. The All-Clear sounded as Frank put his key in the front door.

It was a perfect evening. His father changed into his old cardigan and flannels and took Harvey round the garden. Harvey inspected the onions and the runner beans hanging heavy on their bamboo frame.

Harvey rediscovered his mother's favourite bush, a beautiful Daphne that produced a summer evening scent always a delight to them both. Behind the Anderson shelter still lay the rusting remains of an old swing his father had bought him as a six-year-old; it had been removed to the new house by mistake, long after Harvey had outgrown it, and as long as Harvey could remember it had been kept because Frank thought it 'might come in useful for something'.

The sirens sounded again just after seven and then again as they set out for the pub, each alert lasting only a few minutes. The fourth warning of the evening came while they were still in the pub. They both found it amusing for some reason. Someone else was getting it, that was the only snag.

Harvey, in a relaxed mood, related something of the grandeur of Lammas. His father listened carefully.

"A bit out of your depth, isn't it?" he said at last.

Harvey scowled at him. "What is my depth? Croft never had reservations like that. He's a Central School boy, that's all."

144

His father had doubts. "Oh, it happens once in a while. Still, I thought your target was a big desk in New York. Even there you wouldn't make Croft's kind of money."

"That wouldn't bother Ronnie," Harvey said irritably. "For God's sake, Dad. You've met her."

"A beautiful girl," Frank Marsh agreed. "But money does change people."

"Balls."

A moment later, Frank frowned and, looking sideways at Harvey said: "I get lonely here at times. On my own an' all."

"Well, of course. And I'm not a lot of help. I ought to come out more often."

"You've got your own life," Frank muttered, embarrassed.

Harvey stood up and walked about. "Christ," he said. "This sounds like a fourpenny library dialogue." He looked at his father earnestly. "I should be here more often. Especially these days. You could be bombed out, dead and buried and I'd never know."

"Your name and address are on a piece of cardboard nailed to the back door," Frank reminded him.

"And if the bloody door is buried somewhere under the rest of the house? It isn't doors they collect up. It's bodies. You should have it in your wallet . . ."

There was silence for a few moments. Harvey fingered the old biscuit barrel and his mother's silver teapot standing on the sideboard. His father said suddenly:

"What if I were to get married?" He pulled out a handkerchief and blew his nose ferociously.

Harvey stared. "Married?"

Frank looked sheepish, but volunteered nothing further.

"Well," Harvey said at last. "I suppose I'd say it was a good idea." Then, with more conviction: "A damn good idea. You're not old, for God's sake." He suddenly looked at his father keenly: "That's what's different about you. You've had a different haircut and that was your best suit and you've got a new tie."

Frank Marsh grinned.

"A woman!" Harvey shouted. "You old bugger. You've found a woman." This time his pleasure was genuine. He was warming to the idea. "Who? Who is it? Anyone in the street?"

Frank Marsh shook his head. "It's just my fancy at the moment," he protested. "All in my head."

Harvey wouldn't be put off. He tried coaxing a little longer and then quite suddenly he knew. He sat down, struggling to find something to say. He was at a loss to understand his own reaction.

"It's Philomena Bedell, isn't it?" Harvey was aware that his grin was less than natural.

Frank Marsh looked suddenly old. His expression said he wasn't fooled by Harvey's limited signs of joy. "I'll make a cup of tea," he said to break the awkwardness.

Harvey watched him go: a rather pathetic figure in sad old carpet slippers and the lumpy bottle-green cardigan his mother had knitted years before the war. He was touched, yet vaguely resentful, anxious for his father's welfare but faintly scandalised that someone so ripe and improbable as Philomena Bedell might move in here. He almost heard this reaction from somewhere inside himself, and heard it with self-disgust. It wasn't as if it offended the memory of his mother, for she had been a cold and relentless woman. Even as a boy, Harvey had dimly recognised his father's plight. He could remember willing his father to hit back, to put his foot down, shoot her down, strike her, shake her, anything. Instead Frank had always acquiesced and done as he was told. For the sake of peace, perhaps, only to discover the old rule: that appeasement is no way to win a peace.

He went out into the kitchen. In a falsely hearty voice he couldn't do anything about, he said: "Look, Dad,"—he hadn't called his father 'Dad' for many years—"if I sounded less than thrilled, take no bloody notice. Don't let anyone put you off. If you think it's right, go ahead."

His father, hugging the kettle on the gas, looked at him wryly. For a moment Harvey didn't see his father in the tired, embattled man who stood there so downcast.

"Nice of you to say," Frank said. "But your first reaction was probably right."

"Oh, balls!" Harvey shouted. "Can't I have an infantile reaction without throwing out something as serious as this?" He thumped into a kitchen chair. "Christ knows what hangups I've got. I don't know why I reacted that way. But why should you care? Do it, please."

His father filled the old brown china teapot. The fragrance of hot water on tea curled up from it in the still air.

"Can you imagine," Frank said, his tone changing suddenly, "She's got to that age untouched by human hand. Well, almost. Preserved in gentility like some great mammoth locked up in a glacier. Warm her up, thaw her out and she'd have the passion of a young girl." He shook his head at the wonder of it.

"You're talking about my stepmother," Harvey said stiffly. "Besides, you'd probably kill yourself."

"Oh Christ," Frank said. "I'd forgotten the stepmother thing. Could you stand that? Would you do it for your old Dad?"

"It'll cost you," Harvey grinned.

Frank poured the tea, a little glazed. "She could make me young again. And without my looking silly."

Harvey smiled, but his father didn't notice.

"And don't think it's just the big tits, either," Frank said earnestly. "I'd be good to her. A warm, live woman like that about the place—just to look after me. Think of that."

"A novelty," Harvey agreed, beaming.

"I'd do anything for her," Frank ranted. He looked a little wild now, Harvey thought. "Go back to reading. Give up the beer. Do things around the place . . ."

"Mend the back door?" Harvey demanded.

Frank roared, clutching at his sides.

Harvey was relieved. The moment of awkwardness was gone. He was delighted his father could be this candid.

"Okay," he said briskly. "So you're convinced and I'm convinced." His approach sounded right, now. "It's a good idea. But is she keen?"

Frank snickered. "Probably not. I don't even know if she's ever had a man. Nobody knows. And I haven't dared to do anything about it."

"Well you should, and soon. She's—comfortable, obviously not stupid and she's alone and you're alone. She's got a lot to offer."

"Especially in front," Frank sniggered.

"And them, yes."

His father stared. "You mean it? You really do?"

"I do," Harvey said. "Get on with it."

The telephone rang. Frank went out to the hall stand where the phone stood. He came back after a rumbling exchange. "It's Ronnie," he said.

Ronnie's tone was brisk. "Darling, nothing to get excited about. I've had the police on to me. Apparently they tried to find you at Lammas."

"The police?" Harvey was still preoccupied with his father's pleasure.

147

"They're doing a routine check on you following up that crashed German plane. You spoke to an inspector there that day, remember?"

"Right. And not finding me at Lammas, they're following through, is that it?"

"Quite. And they also want to check on someone called Ryder—a man who was with you. They want to know if you can tell them how to get in touch with him. Who is Ryder? You didn't mention anyone . . ."

"I didn't know him," Harvey said. "He was just a chap who was walking the Ridgeway when the damn thing fell out of the sky and thumped down between where he was and where I was."

"Well, they'll have to find him some other way then if it's important." Ronnie was almost shouting against the background clatter of her canteen. "I gather they thought you were together. They expected to find him at Lammas, too. Anyway, darling, can I give you this number? They want you to call. I didn't want to spoil your evening so I said I'd give you a message when I located you. They're very nice, very humble, very apologetic."

"So they should be. They've checked us both already once. If they want to get me they can do it when I'm home—on their call." Harvey had other things on his mind.

"All right," Ronnie said. "I'll give them your flat number."

"You're an angel. I can't be bothered with police now. Big things are happening here. Frank has decided he wants to get married."

"I could have sworn you said Frank is getting married," Ronnie said, giggling. "There's a terrific din this end."

"Never mind," Harvey said. "Many in tonight?"

"Full," Ronnie shouted. "Someone must have leaked the news: we've got sausage and egg on the menu. That little Reuters man with the beard has been up twice in an hour and a half."

"Creep!" Harvey said. "Turn him in. Grass on him. It's probably a treasonable offense to get an extra egg by false pretences."

"I can't hear very well," Ronnie said. She blew him a kiss down the phone. "Ring me when you're home."

He told his father about the police as they sat on in the kitchen.

Frank Marsh only half listened, seemingly preoccupied

with the importance of what he had suddenly proposed. He wore a faintly distracted look.

"By the way, I told this man Ryder you might have a room for him. You said you'd thought about it."

"Thought about it, yes, but that's all." Frank Marsh looked dubious. "What's he like?"

"Seems a very nice sort. Well educated, I'd have thought. Unfit for service, like me. Wants to work in London for a while. If you're going to do anything at all about Philomena you could probably use the extra money from a letting—just while you're in the planning stages."

Frank thought about it and decided quickly, happily. "You're right, Harvey. Best thing I could do. A lodger will keep me up to the mark, too."

Harvey could hear his phone ringing as he climbed the stairs at Temple Chambers well after midnight.

Bell, the inspector he'd met on the Ridgeway, sounded testy and accusatory. "Miss Croft now tells us you didn't know this other man at all," he began. "Why did you say that you did?"

"I didn't, as I recall, say anything at all about him." Tired, Harvey was in no mood to be helpful.

"He distinctly said, referring to you, 'my friend here'," Bell fumed.

"An expression," Harvey said bleakly. "A figure of speech."

A long silence. Then: "Do you know where he can be found? Do you have any idea where he lives?"

Harvey considered. "No. He said he was on holiday. And later he said he might be moving to London—from the North or Midlands I think. As a matter of fact I gave him my father's address as a likely place if he wanted a room."

"You did?" Bell sounded delighted.

"Why not?"

"So you were totally satisfied that he was genuine and in no way connected with the crashed German aircraft?"

Harvey held the phone away from him, shaking his head. "I'm not sure I understand you," he said caustically. "Do you mean did I think that Ryder caused the crash—shot the thing down? Or did it strike me that he might be a German pilot in English tweeds who, having staggered from the blazing wreck of his aircraft, was now walking the Ridgeway in the company of an old bicycle? Either way, the answer is no."

He was astonished to hear Bell laugh heartily. Even on a poor line the relief of the man was painfully evident.

"Mr Marsh, you've been a great help. Of course the man was a genuine walker. We merely had to be sure. You've been very patient, sir. And we're most grateful. Goodnight to you."

25

Willi sat in his hotel room reviewing his position. He was tired yet cautiously pleased. Except for the boy he'd had to kill, everything had gone fairly well. His collection of newspapers told him little about the possibility of pursuit, but he thought it unlikely that he was sought very urgently in his role as Ryder. Despite the exhortation of posters everywhere, the British, at this stage of the war, seemed astonishingly unsuspicious. If they were looking at all, they were looking for an escaped pilot. Not for Bill Ryder.

The statement by the Berkshire County Constabulary on the discovery of the body of Perry Baynham, seventeen, a farm labourer of Shrivenham, was pushed out of most newspapers. The war news was too big, too much and too varied. Any remaining space was being filled with morale-building features on the shape and promise of post-war Britain.

The post-mortem on the boy had yet to take place, though the police surgeon had volunteered a possible cause of death: a clean break of the spinal column. But nothing was adduced about the manner of the blow, or fall, Baynham had sustained. It seemed unlikely to Willi that the Coroner's court verdict would ever be reported outside the local newspapers.

It was a comfort, too, that no-one called Ryder was named as someone the police wanted to see. Still, he would guard against complacency. It was possible the police would like to see him just the same, even if only as a possible witness to the crash and what might have happened immediately after it. Then, too, he wasn't going to ignore the possibility that some other agency, with wider powers, would start again with the identity and whereabouts of Ryder if they didn't quite soon find the missing German pilot.

For the moment, at least, he was reasonably safe. The hotel had been no trouble. Bauer had briefed him: "If you use a hotel, never stay more than two nights. That way you'll avoid having to surrender either your ration book or the supplementary coupons which are issued for travel. The ration book is genuine. Stolen, originally, but genuine. But there's no sense having it laying about on some hotel manager's desk."

He had picked a solid, Victorian-built hotel within a few yards of the station. He walked past it twice, working out a script for himself. Then he limped in with his haversack.

The foyer was quiet. The night porter was busy in his booth. Only two people were at the reception desk. One, a pale and sickly young man, looked up at him without interest.

Willi smiled and mimed extreme fatigue. "A room for tonight and tomorrow night?"

The young man, jaundiced about uniforms, haughty officers and the ill-assorted single-night 'married' couples who seemed to form a high percentage of current wartime trade, nodded agreeably.

"That's a relief," Willi murmured confidentially.

"A long journey?"

"Walking tour," Willi explained. "Well—I think I'll give it up now. It's doing me more harm than good."

"You do look a bit tired," the young man said. He bent over the register. "If you want dinner it's on for another hour." He offered a pen and Willi wrote in the address of the girl who had taught him English before the war, changing only the street number.

"Two-two-six." The clerk smiled wanly again and rapped his bell for a porter.

The room was large and comfortable. Willi shaved, washed and hung up his other clothes. Then he took his newspaper down to the dining room, ate a passable meal and went straight to bed. He was too tired to give any thought to his situation if he was caught now. He wouldn't be. He was beginning to be sure of that. If it was this easy, and provided he moved every two days, he could live quietly and very well in England with the money he had.

After the war—that was going to be the problem. There was no guessing what conditions and problems peace would bring. The only sure thing, perhaps, was that he ought now to be praying for Germany's early defeat. And he wouldn't be alone in that; many Germans already believed that the sooner their country's suffering and sacrifice were over the better. And he, in particular, needed to be sure that the whole National Socialist regime was going to be swept away. Only a new, democratic, constructive government would be likely to find excuses for his actions now.

He slept well enough and without fear. First thing after breakfast he began building a new background for himself. At one shop in the station precinct he bought a fibre suitcase. At another, a dozen or more secondhand books: Evelyn Waugh, Compton Mackenzie, Bertrand Russell, an Agatha Christie, a large volume on Indian history, a series of essay on cricket and a book of wartime poetry. He discovered that though coupons were required for new clothes, secondhand shops and market stalls could yield most things if you didn't quibble about price. He bought a fairly good raincoat which was just a little too small, a secondhand jacket and a pair of trousers that would need taking in a little at the waist. He also bought notepaper, envelopes, a Rexine identity-card holder, soap, toothbrushes, needles and thread, mending wool, aspirin, plasters, bandage, a gas mask case—which he considered superb camouflage, even if it was empty—and a small torch complete with a No. 7 battery. From a counter assistant in Woolworths he learned that No. 7's were hard to come by and he squirreled the information away. Tiny details like these were the sort of thing he could produce in conversation.

He packed all his purchases into the suitcase and checked it into Left Luggage at Snow Hill.

Now, well fed, rested, and only mildly anxious for his immediate future, Willi felt he was able to make rational decisions. He did not see how he could be traced here. If he had to move to a different hotel every two days anyway, it was unlikely that anyone could get nearer to him than one step behind.

The only area of worry was the £5 notes. Ultimately the Bank of England would recognise them as counterfeit. Even if they were near perfect, the serial numbers would at some moment be seen to be either unregistered or duplicated with real notes. How long? He had no idea, but he thought it would be hustling indeed if in less than two months they were first to find their way back via local banks to some inspectorate, be recognised and subsequently traced as passed in this hotel or that shop. In two months he ought to be able to change a very large number, building a reserve of 'good' one-pound notes from the change. Meanwhile, one job he had to do was to look at them all closely and see that he only used notes from the same serials. That way any counterfeit warnings circulated, and any investigation launched as to their source, would have to be limited to serials that had shown up so far, and he would be free to pass quite different serials for an equal period before they too were returned, discovered, and added to the list.

The other minor worry was that he must reckon that the forces of pursuit might not be limited wholly to police looking for a William Ryder, an innocent Englishman who might have seen something significant in Berkshire, or even quite different police looking for the source of counterfeit money. There was also just a faint possibility that the long arm of the Gestapo could reach him, even here. It didn't seem likely, and it didn't seem worth their while. What harm could be done to the omnipotent SS by a man alone and irretrievably out of the game?

The second night he lay awake, listening to the night sounds from the street. He felt rested, refreshed, alert. For the moment at least he could stop running. His need now was to soak up the mannerisms, the slang, the colloquial speech, the threads and details of English life. He must learn to act and think as William Ryder might. Because once he was seriously challenged he would never get away with it. It followed that he must not be challenged. He must blend with the crowd, thinking as they thought, sounding as they did. His performance must be perfect, even where it hurt. The only good German is a dead German. Bloody Luftwaffe. Poor old Hermann. Don't You Know There's a War On? Business as Usual. Hitler has only got one ball. Under the counter. Is Your Journey Really Necessary? Put That Light Out! Open The Second Front Now!

The newspapers were his tutor. And to begin with he would read the *Express*, not the *Daily Express*. Its leader would be his Thought for the Day. He memorised and rehearsed tones of voice for lines he might use or hear as opening conversation in pubs, trains, anywhere: 'What's Jane doing today?'; 'Any idea of the lunchtime score?'; 'I see South London got it again last night.' He must remember always to employ the disdainful British habit of referring to public figures by nicknames or surnames only: Winnie, Roosevelt, Woolton, Beaverbrook. Only Germans, he recognised, accorded such people their formal titles. It was always 'Monty' or Mountbatten. Only entertainers and the well-loved were given

153

their full names: Bruce Belfrag, Vic Oliver, Alvar Lidell, Ben Lyon, Tommy Handley . . .

On the morning of the third day he went down to settle his bill. The middle-aged woman acting as cashier already had two people at her counter. Willie smiled absently, watching carefully. Again his luck held. He had a five-pound note ready in his hand. So had the man in front of him. The woman totalled the account and, to Willi's astonishment, took the note and wrote a number and the date on the back. The room number? It looked like it. Only then did she count out the change and receipt the bill. Willi quickly put his own note away and took out several one pound notes instead.

His transaction went smoothly. He had learned something. The woman had barely glanced at the note itself, so there was evidently no check on serial numbers. He couldn't remember having seen this done in England before the war. He thought about it. The five-pound note was neither very rare nor very common. Just unusual enough, perhaps, that in hotels and restaurants, where there was a routine for everything and the staff with time enough to take the trouble, they took this minor precaution against counterfeit. He would watch that, paying hotels and the like in one pound or ten shilling notes.

He walked confidently to the station, retrieved his suitcase and, emerging as a newly-arrived traveller, took a cab to another large and impersonal hotel which he had already scouted. He was still less than half a mile from the station.

This time the doorman took his bag and carried it to Reception for him. This time Willi stood at the desk freshly shaven with the *Express* in his hand and a raincoat on his arm. His suitcase was imposing luggage. This time, in the retrievable impressions of the receptionist there was nothing whatever that could be gleaned by subsequent police enquiry for a man without luggage, a man perhaps not quite English . . .

"I'll look forward to getting some sleep tonight," he told the receptionist cheerfully. "London got a pasting again last night. No sleep for anyone. Not even in the shelters."

"You'll be all right here," the under-manager said, coming forward. "They're bringing expectant mothers and young children back to the Midlands again now." He looked at Willy sympathetically. "Bad, was it?"

"Frightful," Willi said. He was pleased with that word.

He had begun to enjoy himself. It seemed all too easy.

It was while he was at a third hotel, four days later, that he narrowly avoided a street identity check. It was a grey day. He was drifting through the lunchtime crowds with his head down against a breeze that carried the threat of rain. When he looked up he was at first confused. The street was suddenly congested. The crowd ahead had slowed to a shuffle. At first he thought there had been a street accident. Then he saw the police and army uniforms and knots of people passing through a pavement cordon. Three or four police were strung out in a line, watching the oncoming crowd and funnelling them to bottleneck on the inside of the pavement.

He moved quickly. As the policeman nearest him looked away for a second, Willi made an abrupt left turn into a shop.

It took him a moment or two to focus. He was in a large electrical store. In the corner on the nearest counter was a sign: *Number 7's: One Only Per Customer*. It seemed a good omen. He bought one and left, turning smartly away from danger this time. He imagined eyes on his back but he got round the next corner and away from the locality without problems.

The incident had unnerved him a little. He told himself repeatedly that he could have passed the check without trouble. Yet the thought persisted that the check might have been specifically for him.

He sought quiet in the reading room of the public library. And in the cinemas. He saw *This Happy Breed* and wanted to see *The Way Ahead* next. He walked a great deal, ate well and was developing a real liking for public houses. Already he knew the names of the beers, local and otherwise. He liked pubs so much he had to ration himself.

It wasn't the daytime that presented the problems. Out on the streets he felt safe so long as he remained alert. But in the evenings, after he had eaten his final meal, he was becoming restless and anxious when he should have been relaxed. The face of the dead boy returned disturbingly again and again. He had seen plenty of death. He had brought dead crew home from bombing missions many times—some of them close friends. He was proof against hideous wounds, too. But that was war and the enemy's victims had at least been remote. Killing the boy, though, was something he had done coldbloodedly. As an act of survival, true—but against all his instincts. He tensed suddenly when he heard footsteps outside his room. When it was too quiet he had moments of irrational panic, sometimes finding himself listening at the door. He tried reading, but the silence was too threatening.

He took to going out again after dinner, mostly to reassure himself that the world outside the room was not waiting to burst in on him. After one particular restless night with little sleep he found himself jumpy, even on the street, imagining that people were looking at him strangely. That was absurd, he knew. If he was suspected at all he would be arrested at once. His rationalisations worked for only a few minutes at a time. On the evening of the sixth day, with his unease at a peak, he rang the London number Harvey Marsh had given him.

"Oh yes, I remember," Frank Marsh said. "Harvey spoke to me about you. Still looking for a room, are you?"

"Well, I'm in Bristol," Willi lied. "But I do want to come down to London and find something to do. I've had enough of a holiday."

"Right, well come along and let's talk about it. It's not much, but perhaps we can fix it up to your liking. Come straight here, if you like. Even if you don't want to stay I can put you up for the night." Frank Marsh read him the address.

"You're very kind," Willi said. He hung up, enormously relieved. Birmingham had begun to close in on him. He was unable to shake off the notion that pursuit was only one step behind him. He resolved to clear out by an early train.

26

Above his shop, just off High Street Kensington, Jerome Judson Fairbrother's sign read, simply, *Jerome*. In the back of the dusty window, a card described 'Jerome' as an antiquarian jeweller.

It was a useful nominal trade. In wartime London it explained the lack of callers and customers and it provided him with a small workshop and an address away from home. More by chance than design, he still did occasionally buy and sell the odd piece.

The shop was really half a shop, split by a desperate estate agent. There were two shop doors together at an angle, each letting onto a narrow shell. There were two shop windows facing each other across a narrow tiled entry.

Fairbrother came to it more or less by accident. In 1940 he had taken a one-room bachelor flat in the small, discreet block above the rest of the parade of shops. At that time he'd had a dark and high-ceilinged shop in West Brompton, an area languishing badly even then. Kensington had more class, but property prices had slumped so badly that he got the new place on terms he couldn't ignore. He reasoned that after the war, prices would rocket up again, especially if the Germans knocked down much more of London, so if he took a 30-year lease he could hardly lose. And anyway it was much more convenient in the blackout. He had only to lock up, take a turn round the block out of pure caution, and he was home.

In the last year or two the shop had begun to look seedy. The only window display was a rather good jade Buddha, arranged on a length of ruched, old gold velvet. Once it had looked fairly opulent. The effect was spoiled now by time and the criss-crossing tension wires holding an anti-blast pad in position in the centre of the plate glass.

Fairbrother himself was a neat and pleasant-looking man. He was rather small, with startling white hair and looked in his early sixties. For some months it had been unusual for him to be in the shop at all, far less early in the day. But a telephone call from Dublin to the number of his widowed sister in Herne Hill had led to an early appointment. He had promised Thelma that he would spend the day with her and he never disappointed her if it was humanly possible. He had offered 8.30 a.m., had it accepted, and now awaited his caller with pleasure.

Dublin had been a good source of income for some time now. The war news, of course was such that he must reckon this might be his very last commission. So be it. His new profession would, in all probability, be just as valuable in the post-war world. If not, there was always antique jewellery.

He read *The Times* complacently until, exactly at eight-thirty, the doorbell rang. Fairbrother walked through from behind his curtained alcove, raised the shop blind and studied his visitor. This was not a man he knew. Neatly dressed. About fifty, well-fed looking. And without the tired, strained look so common among Londoners nowadays. He hesitated only briefly before unlocking the door.

"Good morning, good morning," Fairbrother said heartily. And after a pause: "A good crossing?"

"A necessary one," his visitor said. He waited, unsmiling.

"Capital. But we haven't met before, I think?" He stood aside, now, and latched the door behind him.

"No," the other admitted. "We have not. But our friends in Dublin—"

"Ah!" Fairbrother held up a warning finger. "Excuse me. Your friends in Dublin. Not mine. Customers, perhaps. Clients, if you will. Hardly friends."

The visitor smiled thinly. He had been told all about Fairbrother. Picking his words more carefully, he said: "Dublin ... have a commission they feel you may wish to undertake."

"Splendid, splendid," Fairbrother said affably. "Come through." He led the way back to the alcove and sat down behind the neat little walnut reproduction kneehole desk he'd bought at Harrods because it looked like the sort of piece that might be found in an antique jeweller's.

For a moment the two men sat in silence. The man from Dublin seemed to be waiting for Fairbrother to speak.

"I'm Fairbrother, of course. You're satisfied about that?" The other nodded. "And you are?"

The visitor shrugged. "Malone?" he offered.

"Why not?" Fairbrother said. The idea seemed to please him. "Well now, Mr Malone, anything I can do, I will. Before you tell me the details, may I make a little speech?"

"Do," Malone said.

"Your friends—your Dublin friends, will lose the war. Of course I was always sure of that. All of us in Britain always were. Now even they must know it, too. They already have lost it. Nothing they can do will change that." Fairbrother spoke jovially, his face alive with goodwill. His pink skin and remarkable hair gave him a rather jolly and antiseptic appearance which he knew and constantly exploited. Together with the smile—a smile so clearly without reservation or guile—it made him a hard man to resist. He sat back, smiling even more joyously. "That is why I don't mind helping. I can't do any harm. Mind—" he lifted a warning finger "—I'll do nothing really unpatriotic. You must understand that. On that basis, sir—" He encouraged Malone with an open, uplifted palm.

Malone looked at him coldly. "It's nothing to me. I'd heard about your—conscience."

"Excellent, excellent. Now then?"

Malone hesitated. "Perhaps I should explain something, too," he said. "The principals in this matter ... are, of course, at some distance from our present client. Their belief is however, that if the matter can be resolved quickly and without fuss, then it is worth the undertaking. On the other hand, they do not want the matter to become protracted, or to attract any attention of any kind at all. They do not, it seems, believe that the principals will care much either way in a couple of months from now." He frowned. "I wonder if I'm making myself clear?"

"Perfectly," Fairbrother assured him blandly. "The German Embassy in Dublin is stuck with a request from Berlin. In two months' time who can tell what may be the situation in Berlin. On the other hand so long as Berlin is giving the orders, and for only that length of time, they have to be seen to be taking them. Is that a fair analysis?"

Malone sat up straight. He no longer looked calm and confident. "For God's sake . . ."

"Oh, my dear chap," Fairbrother said quickly. "I've shocked you. I am sorry. But you know you may have been a bit infected with their attitudes. I mean, you surely didn't want to exchange passwords and secret handshakes or anything like that, did you?"

Malone sighed and relaxed by degrees. It was clear that everything they'd told him about Fairbrother was true then. "All right," he said at last. "Shall we get on with the details?"

"Capital, capital," Fairbrother beamed. "And the nature of the enquiry?"

"Shall we say—a missing person?"

"Yes, by all means let's say that," Fairbrother agreed impishly. "He needs tracing, of course."

"Yes."

"And once traced?"

"Killing," Malone said pleasantly.

Fairbrother's smile broadened still further. "It sounds very straightforward," he said. "Is it?"

"No."

Fairbrother laughed delightedly. "Oh, Mr. Malone, you have a sense of humour after all. I was beginning to think you'd lost it by constant association with the German mind."

At last Malone smiled. He relaxed further. He had had very little briefing. He was reassured by the way this foxy little man worked and by the way he accepted everything so easily. With luck, he thought, he could be back in Dublin in no time at all. "There are a few problems," he warned.

Fairbrother nodded vigorously. "There always are. First I have to know the nationality of the, ah, missing person."

"German," Malone said promptly. "A young man. A Luftwaffe pilot." He waited.

"Well that's all right then," Fairbrother said. "And the difficulties?"

"It is believed that he crash-landed his aircraft on the top of a hill in Berkshire earlier in the month. Other than that we can't give you much at all to go on."

Fairbrother looked thoughtful. He stroked his immaculate white hair. "A difficulty indeed," he admitted. "But not insuperable."

Malone was clearly surprised. "I'm impressed," he said. "You must have a fine—technique."

"It's my training, you see. I did work of this kind for many years before I—retired. This young man. He has a description, distinguishing marks, a photograph, a name, a history?"

Malone opened his wallet and handed Fairbrother a post-card-sized photograph. The reverse was filled with tiny handwriting. "Everything relevant is on here."

Fairbrother transferred the picture to his own wallet.

Malone now unbuttoned his raincoat and withdrew four bulky envelopes from the pockets of his grey tweed suit. He laid them on Fairbrother's blotter.

"I'll hear from you?" he said.

"You will," Fairbrother told him, rising. "But only when I have the news which your client requires. Then," he patted his visitor's back encouragingly, "you may bring me the rest of the money."

"The price?"

"Open," Fairbrother said firmly. "A great deal depends on the difficulties of the search. I'll find a way to let you know," he said cheerfully. He held out his hand.

"A pleasure to do business with you," Malone said.

"How nice of you to say that. Goodbye now."

27

There was one moment in every day on the coal wharf when a lull fell on the whole place. The trolleys and wagons had rumbled out across the weighbridge, the big shires between the shafts, to deliver their loads of kitchen nuts to properly registered customers. The big trucks had gone to load large coke at Wandsworth gasworks. And inside the little row of offices, the next loads were already docketed and allocated. If tea was available, this was tea time.

Wearing his best suit, Frank wrote up a couple of orders in his regular copperplate, but his mind wasn't on it. Was this the right day, he wondered, to propose to Phil? With Harvey's approval comfortingly in hand he had no doubt that he should do it. But today? Well that's what he was wearing the suit for, wasn't it? If not now, then when? But today? One half of him quaked at the thought of it. It had to be here, too, that was the trouble. It was the only world they shared. His new lease of life, his new spirit of adventure pushed him on. What about now. In the Lull?

It was certainly quiet outside. A bright, glaring day, more like spring than late summer, the sun bouncing off the coal hills with dazzling brilliance. What about inside? He looked about him. On the wharf side all the doors seemed to be wide open. Townsend was out there somewhere, searching for a rogue wagon, notified but seemingly never shunted onto their dock. He'd been looking for it for days, roaming the coal hills in search of his stray—like some bloody blue-serge cowboy.

Redheaded Arthur's stool was empty. God knew where he'd gone. And the damn kid had disappeared, too. The little sod was always missing. Probably sitting in the shunters' hut again, drinking tea and looking at their obscene graffiti that covered every blackened wall.

Now? he thought. Seize the moment? He looked round again. Still quiet. Even if the kid came back suddenly he could always be sent out to look for cigarettes; it would take him an hour to find Turkish even. That only left Old Mr Spencer and he was as deaf as a coot, poor old lad.

Now? Sweat broke out on his hands. He wiped them on his handkerchief, squinted down at his appearance, dropped ash over himself and bent to brush it off. The smoke from his cigarette went into his eyes and up his nose. He broke out into a fit of coughing and wheezing. Christ! he thought. Some catch! He put the cigarette out.

Phil was quiet, checking over a letter in her machine. He wished, suddenly, she wouldn't plait her hair that way. The coiled up plaits over the ears, with the earphone effect, were bad enough. But to do it she had to sweep her hair savagely away on both sides of her head at the back, leaving a huge parting. He looked at her again and melted. She looked pretty good though. Another cream-coloured dress, all lace down the front. The light from her window gave her profile an oddly ethereal look.

He took a step towards her. Or, as it might be, into the next room if his courage failed him. His heart banged. Now! This time!

Watson came in, banging the street door and hullooing. At the same moment Townsend stepped in at the back. Frank rubbed his forehead as if he'd forgotten something on his desk and turned back to the safety of his corner.

It became clear that Watson had something. He carried it, hefted it. Bigger than a cricket ball and black and heavy.

"Here you are . . ." On a note of triumph he tossed it to Townsend. "What do you make of that?" At once everyone crowded into the same room. Except Old Mr Spencer.

"Bit of a German plane," Arthur suggested over Townsend's shoulder.

"Right my lad!" Watson bellowed. "Not just any plane, either. This is a bit of the one that came down through the roof of Victoria station. Bloody Dornier." His triumph was complete. He held it up for all to see. "A long-range bomber, the Dornier."

"I thought it was a Heinkel that came down at Victoria," Arthur said. "Shot down in a dogfight." There ensued a brief skirmish between Arthur and the older man until Watson swung on him angrily. "Back to your stool, sonny. If I tell you it's a bit of a Dornier then that's what it is, all right?"

The incident was closed and the morning resumed its natural pattern. Townsend nervously added up the contents of his cash drawer again. Watson waited, lolling in a corner.

No-one put the kettle on for tea because there wasn't any. At last it was twelve-thirty and Townsend, Watson, Arthur and the boy had all gone about their lunchtime business.

Frank lingered still, watching Phil out of the corner of his eye. She paused in her typing briefly and produced her sandwiches. She nibbled delicately at them, working through.

"What's in yours?" Frank asked in the painful silence. His courage had fled and he was beginning to think that Watson and his bloody Dornier had ruined his chance for the day.

"Ham paste," she said.

"Try one of mine—Marmite," Frank offered. She smiled, took one, tried it.

"All right?" Frank asked.

"A bit strong for me."

"Good for you," he said. "Yeast, you know. I probably shouldn't eat the stuff. It stirs up the old blood. Just when I'm alone with you." No trouble there. It was easy to say things like that. He always had.

Philomena dimpled at him.

"Sorry," Frank said, suddenly inspired. "Ridiculous, really, all us old chaps making jokes all the time. It's all talk you know."

"I know," she said. She pushed her typewriter back and sat at rest. That was a good sign, Frank thought. Cosier. But she didn't look at him directly.

"You must get bored with us all lusting after you in this ridiculous way," Frank tried again.

She stopped eating, laid down a minute piece of sandwich and flushed. "I don't believe," she said evenly, "that people lust as you say—not after an old spinster."

And there it was! The right opening. But he funked it. "Why didn't you ever marry?" he said tensely instead.

"Oho," she smiled a little fixedly. "No-one ever asked me." He was about to rush in then, only she spoiled it by adding: "Proof, I should think, that no-one thinks of me that way."

"I do," Frank said quickly. The sweat broke out on his hands again. Oh, God! he thought. Come on! It's now or never! You won't get another chance like this one, old son. There was a roaring in his ears. They'll be back from the pub soon.

"What if I asked you?" he croaked. Thank Christ! It was out!

"Asked me?" She looked baffled for a moment. He groaned inside and managed: "To marry me . . ."

163

Her face flooded with colour at once and she laughed nervously. Her fingers twittered round her sandwich tin, closing it with a snap, opening it . . . "Mr. Marsh!" she giggled.

Somehow, now that the words were out, he was more in command. "Well?" he demanded.

"You don't expect me to take you seriously?" She looked at the floor, at her shoes, the ceiling, the front of her dress.

"Of course I do."

Philomena stood up, gathered her towel from her bottom drawer and made ready to escape. At once Frank bounded to the doorway, barring her way. He seized her hands, her forearms, pulled her closer. Where was he getting all this dash? He felt masterful. She had to put her hands on his chest to hold him gently off.

"Of course I expect to be taken seriously," he repeated. "I'm not young, not handsome. But I have got a sense of humour and a nice little house. I'll look after you. You need looking after. A great big meringue of a woman like you—someone is going to take a great big bite out of you someday."

She looked as if she was going to cry.

"None of that," Frank said firmly. "Just Yes or No. Crying doesn't come into it." He was into his stride now. They could all come back if they wanted to. He wasn't going to stop now.

She looked at him doubtfully.

Frank remembered something he'd heard. Or read. In a story or a poem? "I need you," he said very distinctly.

She looked up at once, astonished. "You do?" she said.

Great God, it worked! "Yes, I do."

"And it isn't a joke?"

"No. Not a joke."

"Yes or No?"

"That's right."

"Now?"

"Before they come back," he said, his courage waning already.

She dabbed at her nose with a tiny lace handkerchief. He had to let her loose. She at once picked up her towel again, but as she turned she said. "Well then, Yes. Now I must go and wash."

"You're not going anywhere," Frank said gleefully. "Not until I've had a great big kiss."

Ten minutes later work resumed. Phil was typing. Frank was back in his corner, hardly able to believe he had done it.

Why hadn't he done it long ago? His eyes watered a little and his blood sang.

At three he passed through into the next room, carrying a batch of orders for Arthur. Watson dozed in a corner. Frank prodded him awake.

"Whaa?" Watson blinked. "What's up?"

"It was a Heinkel that came down at Victoria," Frank said. He was using a voice he had never before managed with Watson. "You've got it all wrong."

Watson gaped.

On his way back he did something else he'd never done before. He closed the door between the two rooms. As he sat down he winked at Phil.

On the other side of the door he heard Watson grumbling: "What in the name of God has got into the old fool?"

28

Harvey woke from his deep, after-shift sleep to find Ronnie, petal-fresh and gorgeous slipping out of her street clothes by the side of his bed. His clock had stopped. His watch was in a pocket somewhere. To judge by the thin slant of the strips of dust-laden sunlight through the closed curtains, it was about four in the afternoon.

Ronnie, straight-faced, threw her clothes at the old basket chair and bounced onto the bed beside him.

"No decent girl does this sort of thing," Harvey complained. "I haven't shaved and I have a mohair tongue." But he was silenced by the perfection of her. He reached out and pulled her close. Without thought or warning, he heard himself say: "Why don't you marry me? Then you can be legally indecent."

Ronnie's close-up gaze was dark and enigmatic, but her tone was light enough. "And we'll be happy forever—or, say, until Thursday week when you're called to the War Office."

That part of his mind which always looked after his ego and his image of himself prompted him to say: "Oh, well, if you're going to quibble about details, let's stick to the script we've got." He fastened his mouth on hers and lifted her bodily to lie on top of him. Elsewhere in his mind, he noted that it was true after all: Ronnie had changed. And perversely, his ego was bruised even though he had told himself a score of times that marriage was out.

He held her still, restricting her for a time. Her breathing became more and more ragged and she struggled. He let her lie on her back while he kissed her mouth and breasts, but when he tried to reach down to her she brought up her knees at once and pulled at him determinedly. She would not wait. For a time the noise of the street, the sound of distant explosions and the whole world at war fell away. Their own sensations and the roar of their breathing enclosed them totally.

"Marry me, for God's sake," Harvey almost shouted towards the end. He was dazzled and gratified by the frenzy of her need.

Ronnie only thrashed her head from side to side, her mouth frozen in anticipation of the final ecstasy, her body and hands urging him on.

Then they lay still for nearly an hour, Ronnie watching him from heavy-lidded eyes. Harvey sat, cross-legged, admiring the curves and hollows of her body, touching here and there as if to confirm their visual perfection by a more reliable faculty. There was no repeat performance.

When he judged she was calm and quiet, Harvey got up and looked in his jacket for the note from McNair he'd found pinned to his corner of the ABP board.

"I wouldn't have nagged about marriage," he said, "but for this, from McNair."

Ronnie appeared to stop breathing for a moment. She lay perfectly still on her side, her eyes followed him. "Read it to me," she said finally.

Harvey found a cigarette. He sat on the edge of the bed and tried to make McNair's memo sound both unimportant and inconclusive. "We have War Office approval in principle," he skimmed. "Accreditation will follow almost immediately. You will need to report to Public Relations at the War Office for briefing, documentation and identity papers." He skipped the bit about the booklet on Do's and Don'ts and proper behaviour for war correspondents, and read on: "Suggest you use this as letter of authorisation to get yourself fitted for both service and battledress, field kit, etc etc, a list of which is attached for your guidance."

For a moment he feared an outburst. When she reacted differently though perfectly in character, he was again perversely hurt. She sat up, suddenly, her face aglow. "You did it," she whooped. "You did it." She looked at him eagerly. "Are you happy?"

Harvey hesitated. He realised her pleasure was genuine and though he was, now, bound to leave here, he found it unbearable that she should be so detached. "Yes," he said, soberly. "I'm happy." But he couldn't quite manage to look it.

"Oh, come on!" Ronnie urged. "It's what you wanted. What you planned. And you kept on wanting it, long after we met. This is the first big step."

"And you won't marry me?"

Ronnie looked puzzled. "Is that what you thought? That when the papers came I'd melt at the last minute and say yes, yes, on any terms?" She shook her head sadly. "Oh, Harvey don't say you believed that. We've been through all this. It can't be. It's not what I want, and not what I mean to have. I'm not the kind to be moved into something as serious as marriage by bugles and a sad, station goodbye. I want life and love. Not a film script to live by."

Harvey was seared by this and not a little bitter. Though not with Ronnie. He had badly misjudged her, even though he had known she was quite, quite different. Somewhere at the back of his mind he had believed that when it came to the pinch, to the putting on of the uniform and of his going off to what was left of the war, Ronnie would be affected, weakened, pliable. To be wholly fair, he'd imagined he would be able to play that scene any way he felt at the last: yes or no. His own script had been No, no, no, all the way through; but he'd held open the idea that, consonant with all the sentimental words of all the sentimental love songs, he'd always have a choice of ending.

He got up and began picking up her clothes. When he thought about it a little longer he realised that Ronnie, at least, was blameless. She had given generously, asking nothing. She had said from the start that she wouldn't wait at home. He managed a grin. "Right," he said. "But you can't blame me for trying." He assumed an artless affability he didn't altogether feel—yet. "Come on, I said I'd go down and see Dad. I want to find out how he's managing with his new lodger. And I want to see what he's done about securing Philomena. You work on him, too, will you?" He marched about, purposefully. Ronnie stalked about naked while running their bath.

Harvey's bathroom was Victorian with Edwardian additions. It had no shower and the gas geyser projected threateningly a good foot over the end of the huge tub. They soaped each other furiously. Harvey's erection almost diverted them back to bed, but Ronnie's mind was already on Frank's problems. By six they were on their way.

A station man was folding away the air raid boards when they emerged at Eastcote and the All Clear howled triumphantly from too close at hand.

At Lindsey Gardens, an altogether brighter, smarter and younger-looking Frank opened the door. He seized Ronnie and began nuzzling her neck.

"God's sake," Harvey said. "Find your own women." He was cheered by his father's unaccustomed bounce. "Have you asked her yet?"

"Ah, well," Frank said mysteriously. "It isn't wholly finalised." He pulled them into the kitchen, holding tightly to an arm of each. "But the answer's yes. What woman of her age could resist? Christ! Sound in wind and limb. Educated byond natural need. Randy as a snake. What a package! What a prize!"

"That's who, you or Philomena?" Ronnie demanded.

"Have you asked her yet?" Harvey persisted.

"Asked her? Asked her?" Frank affected bewilderment. "There was no asking. I told her."

"Great. When?"

"A detail," Frank said briskly. "Come and meet my lodger."

Willi was in the garden, sleeves rolled up, marching up and down the tiny lawn with an antique mower. He looked bronzed and fit.

"Look at him," Frank shouted. "He's already picked the beans and tied up the tomatoes. He's a bloody treasure. Why didn't you send him to me sooner?"

Willi came forward, grinning. He shook hands with Harvey and turned to Ronnie. At once he made a small blunder. Automatically he gave her a little formal bow and only then extended his hand. He was momentarily confused.

"Good God, the man's shy," Frank beamed.

"Overheated, more likely," Ronnie said. "Someone get him a drink." Frank hurried away, exclaiming to himself.

"I want to thank you for suggesting this," Willi said, gesturing at the house. "It's very nice here. I'm happy. Your father and I get along very well." Harvey said something about being glad it was working out, then remembered the police call. He explained the problem. "They really only

168

wanted to be sure that we were who we said we were." He saw Willi's expression, interpreted it correctly as concern and added: "But you can forget about ringing them. I told them you might even come to stay here. They didn't seem very interested after all. Once, this is, I'd told them we saw no sign of any German pilot. That's right, isn't it?"

"Right," Willi said. He could have embraced Harvey.

Harvey turned to Ronnie, opened his mouth to say something and never formulated it. It was a moment he remembered for many years, always with wistful anguish, always with bewilderment. She was looking at Willi, saying something unimportant. But about her stance, her expression, her tone, there was something startlingly different. That same evening and many times afterwards, Harvey replayed that moment in his mind, hoping to pin down the exact nature of the change he saw in Ronnie then. He was always unsuccessful. There were no words spoken that meant anything, no new attitude struck. And yet the difference was there. No-one who had ever been close to Ronnie could have missed it, no-one who hadn't would have seen it. It was as subtle as a shift in the permutations of the thousands of face muscles that make up expression, elusive as the difference between a face with a smile and a smiling face, indeterminate as well-feigned passion. But Harvey saw it and for the third time that day was unaccountably and quite unreasonably hurt by it.

It was another perfect evening. The sun, a giant orange ball, slid imperceptibly down a promising mackerel sky. It flared across the tops of trees and garden fences with an agreeable warmth. For a while they were all taken with it, looking about and sniffing the still air like connoisseurs with a rare vintage.

Harvey found himself helping Ryder empty grass cuttings onto the compost heap. "So you came after all," he said. He was aware of testing out his own reactions to the man, on the watch for childish chagrin in himself. "I'm glad. The old man looks and sounds years younger."

"I think that is the lady—Philomena?"

"Not altogether, I think," Harvey said generously. He was aware of being careful to give credit—and on the instant impatient with himself.

Frank brought out water and a bottle of Scotch, shrugging off astonishment and applause. He poured liberal measures and went to sit on the crumbling garden seat with his arm around Ronnie's waist. "I've got to practise this sort of thing," he told her seriously.

"I have an announcement," Ronnie said. It was clear that she had been waiting for the moment. She caught permission from Harvey's expression and related the contents of McNair's note. Harvey tried to look modest. Frank was delighted. Even Willi found himself clapping Harvey on the back.

Willi was beginning to find his situation bizarre. He was developing a second personality the way a secondary circulation develops around some constriction or obstruction in the system. His old entity as a loyal German and as a Luftwaffe pilot had been pinched out and was beginning to fall back and grow faint under the impact of another but no less real world that made quite different demands upon his feelings. It was impossible to dislike these people. The Marshes, father and son, were likeable people not very different from others he had known. He could not feel antagonism towards them simply because they were British; they were too close. And towards Ronnie his feelings were developing in an alarming way. He was conscious of her every moment. It would have been unthinkable to conduct himself in any special artificial way in order to gain her good opinion, but he became self-conscious whenever she turned towards him and then curious about what she saw. He found her incomparably attractive and puzzlingly so. When he was quite sure that she would not notice, he stared. He found the poise of her head, the soft feathered curl of her hair, the movements of her body and her hands all quite superb without ever being able to pin down exactly how they were so special. He told himself sternly that his almost immediate attraction must remain a curiosity, that anything else was dangerous and futile. The next moment he found himself watching her again.

The evening became still more bizarre when, in the middle of a buzz of talk, the Warning sounded for the sixth raid of the day. Willi had forgotten his earlier *faux pas* and much else. He was relaxed, for the moment, as with real friends. And was only mildly astonished when he heard himself groan, along with the rest: "Oh no!"

Within seconds the chilling roar of a V1 grew on the unnatural hush. There was no gunfire.

"There," Harvey pointed, unmoved.

Clear and low and level the V1 came on, the flaming tail no less eerie for being a familiar sight. It flew past, diminishing with astonishing speed, before the jet motor cut. Willi, along with the rest, held his breath for the distant crump of the explosion. A tall column of smoke climbed rapidly on the skyline and hung seemingly motionless in the still evening air.

"Harlesden," Frank announced. Willi had noticed that someone always did immediately ascribe a location for each tragedy. Without thinking, he added the customary epitaph: "Poor devils." It wasn't his first V1. As soon as he had moved into the broad sweep of V1 flight-paths he had noticed this facile acceptance of death and destruction. He had been compelled, not wanting to seem different, to use street shelters with all types of people and been astonished by the British attitude to the attacks. He had long since realised, too, that it was not possible to crush people in this way. At least, not these people. They simply did not see the possibility of defeat or subjection, possibly never had.

The V1 and the failing light, though, did drive them indoors. There were other explosions, some nearer. The house shook and the windows rattled. But inside, behind the blackout, the evening was a success. Ronnie made toast. Frank produced a piece of cheese. "It's his back rations," he explained, pointing at Willi. "The bugger is a goldmine of unused rations."

They stared at Willi. Unused rations set a man apart. "Hotels, you see . . ." he shrugged off their surprise easily, not in the least worried.

Ronnie quizzed him a few minutes later. "You're from the North?" she said.

"How can you tell?" He was relaxed but careful despite his third large Scotch.

"It's the way you sound your a's," she told him. "Long, as here in the South, but not as though you'd done it for a lifetime."

Willi gestured disappointment. "And I thought I spoke BBC English."

Ronnie smiled politely and then for some reason seemed embarrassed. She dropped her gaze and without moving away from him, turned to hear what Harvey was saying.

"While I'm away in France—or Germany, I suppose by the time the War Office gets round to the paperwork—I'd like to think you were tucked up safely here with the luckless Philomena," he said.

"Right!" Ronnie said cheerfully. "What about that?"

"What's the hurry?" Frank grumbled. "Everyone is pushing me into the arms of this woman. Prurient buggers. Just because you two can't think of anything else."

It seemed an innocent remark, under the circumstances. It produced an effect that was disturbing for Willi. Harvey grinned, amiably enough, until he noticed that Ronnie was patently embarrassed. She turned, imperceptibly, and looked directly for Willi's reaction. Willi saw both results and was stunned by them. It was at once clear that Ronnie was both ruffled by the easy reference to her relationship with Harvey and concerned with the effect it had on himself.

"No, seriously," Harvey persisted. "If you want my new uniform and officer-like status to lend tone to the wedding photographs, you'll have to be quick. Why not next week by special licence?"

The moment of awkwardness was over. But Willi was preoccupied with the meaning of that instant reaction from Ronnie. His mind buzzed with it.

"Christ's sake," Frank grumbled. "I'm only just learning to like widowerhood. And what about my new pal here?"

Willi was startled. He hadn't thought about his own position in relation to Frank and marriage. Once a week or so ago it had seemed something well in the future.

"I shall go, of course," he said immediately. "I can easily find somewhere else."

Frank shouted him down. "This place is more like a home than it has been for years," he protested. "I won't let you go."

Willi noticed that Ronnie said nothing more. She had enthusiastically endorsed Harvey's first statement, but had fallen silent now. More than once Willi either found her watching him or had the feeling that she had looked away only a split second before.

He was grateful when Harvey announced that he and Ronnie would have to go. He needed time to think about what he had seen and sensed.

When they were alone again, he again raised with Frank his anxiety to be out of the way.

"Balls," Frank said. "Why shouldn't you stay? Even if I do get married—I rather like the idea of a pal to fall back on if I don't like it. We'd outnumber her."

"It doesn't sound very practical," Willi smiled. He began putting plates and glasses into the kitchen sink. "Let's see what happens. Who knows—perhaps the lady will change her mind."

Frank considered that seriously. "Women are odd," he

agreed. And when Willi laughed out loud, he became first indignant, then puzzled and, finally, helpless with laughter.

Harvey, too, had reservations. On the long walk and tube ride back, he talked about Frank a great deal. Something of the atmosphere of the house prompted him to talk about his parents' marriage and their life together before the war. Ronnie listened, fitting some of the pieces into her understanding of both Frank and Harvey, but she said very little.

"What do you think of Bill Ryder, then?" Harvey asked suddenly. He was sitting on the edge of the bed at Temple Chambers, watching the breathtaking business of Ronnie preparing for bed.

Ronnie thought a while. "What does he do?" she asked eventually.

"No idea," Harvey said. And after a moment: "Why?"

"He's very—agreeable," Ronnie said evasively.

"You have reservations?"

"No," Ronnie frowned. "It's just that he's hard to label."

Harvey, alert to something in her voice that was as close to irritation as he'd ever heard from her, considered it for a moment or two and then said quietly: "Oh?"

"You don't feel it?" She looked at him with impatience. Harvey had the sensation of having been moved, at one stroke, outside her confidence.

For the moment he had no answers. He sat down on the bed, aware of a net discontent with a day that had seemed to go so well. He wanted no more talk about anyone else. He held out a hand, and in a moment or two Ronnie slipped into his arms. Did he imagine the hesitation?

It was not until very much later, as he lay, wakeful, listening to Ronnie's soft breathing, that he recognised that she had changed in some other ways, too. Their love-making had been warm, fond, selfless on both sides, but oddly separate from the patterns he had come to expect; different, even, to the state and nature of it only a few hours earlier.

He at once remembered Ronnie's apparent reaction to Ryder and though he couldn't characterise that either, was instinctively aware of a link and instinctively again disconcerted by it.

29

Until Fairbrother studied the Ordnance Survey map of the Berkshire countryside he had no idea of the size and complexity of his assignment.

Newspaper reports of the crash which had almost certainly been Reiter's had variously given the site as 'on White Horse Hill', 'near the White Horse', 'on the Ridgeway by the White Horse' and 'in the White Horse Hills'. Experience had taught him that you took nothing for granted. It could be anywhere within a twenty-mile radius and still, roughly, conform to those locations.

There were other, more serious problems. Moving about the countryside without a car was one. He had never been able to show a pre-war need entitling him to wartime Pool petrol coupons. He would also have to add the hazards of deceptive distances, unsignposted roads, irregular and much-curtailed bus services and restricted areas now used as army and air force camps, high-security hostels and the like.

It wasn't easy even choosing a starting point. The nearest town of size, and then move outward; that seemed the most sensible way. But which was the nearest town? There was a wide choice.

In the end he chose Newbury. He rang the RAC hotel there and booked a room for one night only. His train left late, delayed by repairs to the Great Western tracks which had been badly hit in the western suburbs of London. He didn't mind too much. All these assignments were an adventure. He made the best of them, whatever the problems. Each one was a sort of holiday. There was a special pleasure for him, always, in the opening stages. The unknown, unknowable, delighted him every time.

That night he sat down to a good, if plain, meal in the hotel's fine old dining room and followed it with a brandy and coffee in the lounge. The manager, harassed by the shortage of staff, was looking after the lounge bar himself. He accepted Fairbrother's offer of a brandy, but reacted only vaguely when his guest referred chattily to the 'bit of local excitement on the Downs'. Fairbrother wasn't disappointed. Hotel people, he knew, led an enclosed life full of their own crises and had little knowledge of the world's problems.

After half an hour, Fairbrother excused himself, said he had to have his constitutional, turned left outside the hotel and walked directly into the nearest pub. It was a busy night. A darts match was in progress at one end of the saloon bar; an excitable affair involving half a dozen elderly Home Guard, an assortment of men who might have been farm workers, and up to twenty committed supporters. Fairbrother was lucky to find another brandy and took it to a table at the far end of the room. He sat quietly, projecting amiability. It hardly ever failed. In a few moments a spruce little man, with the blotched hands and slow eye movements of the elderly, nodded at him and sat down at the far corner of Fairbrother's table.

"They seem to be enjoying themselves," Fairbrother said.

"It's a regular battle," the little man explained. "Home Guard versus the pub team. It's a big draw, too. Been going on two, three year now."

Fairbrother smiled very amiably. "They do a great job, the Home Guard," he said reflectively. "It's not easy, turning out three nights a week." He let it lay for a moment, seemingly following the match with interest. Then, without taking his eye off the game, said: "Is this the bunch that had the excitement over the German plane?"

The old man's lips muttered soundlessly. He looked as if he was spelling the question out again. Finally he managed: "The German plane?"

"Up on the Downs?" Fairbrother prompted.

The old man nodded comprehension vigorously. "No, no! That was the other side."

"The other side?"

"Not the Newbury side. No, not this side. No, it was up on the White Horse. By the side of the Ridgeway."

Fairbrother thought it over. He feigned interest in the game for a moment or two and then affected to remember his brandy. As he turned back to it, he asked carelessly: "Did they catch him?"

"Catch him? Catch who?"

"The pilot."

"Who?"

"The pilot," Fairbrother said patiently. "Of the German plane."

The tortoise stare blinked heavily at him. "Course they didn't catch him," the old man said testily. "Burnt to death, that's why."

"Really?"

"Oh yes. All alone, you see. Never stood a chance poor devil. Burnt to a crisp. Never stood a chance—a single plane like that."

Fairbrother was puzzled by the logic, but at least he had something else to think about. Back in the hotel he studied his map again. He saw now what the old man meant about 'the other side'. He had not appreciated, for all the thought that he'd put into it, that if an event takes place on a high plateau, the ripples—whether administrative or simple in terms of local gossip—will inevitably be felt more on one side than the other.

It was, no doubt, a matter of from which side the police took charge and, in consequence, which side claimed the affair as a local event. It was, in any case, something you couldn't see from a map, read from a report or appreciate in any way at all until it was made clear on the ground itself. He did not grudge the time lost. But it was clear that he must move. Sitting up in bed, he gave half an hour to the maps again before picking up his novel. This time he pinpointed the village of Uffington as his next base.

After an early breakfast he turned his back on Newbury. With some difficulty, he established that there was a bus running to Shrivenham across the Wiltshire border. He waited more than an hour for it and by the time that he got down at his mid-route stop, Ashbury, it was already well into the morning.

He considered walking east to Uffington at once, but a comfortable looking pub was opening, offering a chance of an early lunch and an opportunity to cross-check his thinking. He was in no great hurry. The weather held fine. He took his newspaper to a bench outside and, over a truly delightful piece of pie which would have been a credit to Fortnum's, read that the British 12th Corps were across the Somme and the Americans into Verdun. Again the thought occurred to him that this might be the last time that Malone or anyone else would bring him a commission from the German Embassy in Dublin. Not that it mattered very much. There would be others needing his kind of service. But it was important to bear in mind that he would have to deliver Willi Reiter soon if he wanted to be paid before the whole Third

Reich crumbled and began to suffer a fine loss of concentration about anything except self-preservation.

He was genuinely, patriotically pleased with the war news. It bore out what he'd said to Malone.

A Land Army girl, in grass-green sweater and tight breeches, smiled at him, carrying a covered basket round to the back door of the pub. He suspected illicit eggs and felt a rush of righteous indignation. On the way back, she gave him almost a map reference for the site of the crash. "Straight up White Horse Hill and out left onto the Ridgeway," she told him. "Put roses in your cheeks, that climb, Dad."

Fairbrother beamed at her, not minding the 'dad' at all. He wondered what she got in return for the eggs. The landlord, a ruddy, cheerful-looking man with a dramatic limp, was whispering to her across the bar, his head almost touching hers as Fairbrother, before he left, interrupted to try him for a room for the night.

"Can't do it," the man told him without much regret. "Haven't really got the room. If you want to stay in the area for a day or so, try Uffington. You should be all right there."

Fairbrother smiled, wondering how much the refusal had to do with the Land Girl's after-hours activity.

It would have been a long walk if a truck, loaded top-heavy with baled hay, hadn't overtaken him after the first half-mile, and by tea-time he was unpacking in a cool green-washed room with dormer windows looking out into a meadow. It was an inn so snug that he almost hoped he would not be through too quickly. On his bedside table he laid out two H.E. Bates, a C.S. Forester and the new Evelyn Waugh. Even the thought of the long climb next morning could not diminish his sense of wellbeing, progress and anticipation.

In the event, getting up the hill was easier than he'd expected. He took it slowly, resting his legs and letting his breathing settle every few minutes.

Once up, finding the site was easy enough, too. There were not too many places for either a controlled or a crash landing. He walked east and found it almost at once. An RAF Regiment guard watched over the wreckage; a single blue figure, unarmed as far as he could see, only the web-equipment marking his attendance as in any way official. The man took no notice of him. Fairbrother stood looking over a closed gate across the high plateau of the field, taking in the detail. He could tell nothing much from the terrain. It was open; no broken-off branches, nothing to indicate the angle of the

FW's final run. If there had been a long skid, the marks were obscured now. The wheat stubble had been burned off and the whole area was uniformly scorched. The aircraft itself was barely recognisable as such. The charred, twisted metal looked as if it had been broken down further by RAF experts looking for explanations of the crash; or perhaps just for souvenirs. They would have left nothing of value and the remains would stay here until they were ready to haul it away.

One thing he saw clearly now was why nothing much of the affair was known in Newbury. Screened from the South by the line of the Downs, it was plainly an affair of the area from which he had just climbed; and that was a whole small world of its own.

Heartened by this piece of orientation, he thought he would give up for the day and spend the evening pleasantly with his books.

Next day he began his slow investigation in the villages. He took care to project the same image everywhere: a quiet, casual and perhaps even lonely man looking for a little peace and quiet and some exercise. A senior civil servant, possibly. It was a pose he'd often found useful and it fitted his appearance and manner. Better still, it explained him. In these country areas, he knew, a label was a useful device. The country people had been invaded by servicemen of all nations, they had suffered the same privation and tragedies as the city dwellers, and yet London was still remote and a Londoner was still as much a foreigner as a Pole, an American or even a German; they were all simply people who had an alien way of life. So it was important here to become almost a caricature. Fairbrother, with his neat, dark suit, bowler hat and immaculately furled umbrella, was the more immediately acceptable for being readily identifiable.

As he moved through the villages, acting his role of a tired man looking for a breath of a country air, he was everywhere treated with amiable respect—tinged, perhaps, with tolerant amusement at his clothes. But he learned nothing.

Or almost nothing.

In one pub he learned which police station had been involved. In another, almost without asking a question, he was told the name of the police inspector who had been first on the scene and that of the superintendent who had later assumed responsibility.

There was some indignation that a coroner's court still had

not produced a verdict that would somehow apportion cause and blame for the death, however obvious, so that the parents of the youth could digest his death and begin to feel that the matter was, at least in official terms, closed. Fairbrother expressed sympathy.

In his room after supper that evening, he turned once more to the map. There were a great many villages. Most had a pub. Since they were the only natural setting for conversations of the kind he needed, he would have to tackle them all until he got some kind of lead. He could manage two, perhaps three, at lunchtimes, and another one or two more in the evenings. So be it.

He had brought comfortable walking shoes, but his calf and thigh muscles soon stiffened. Yet he had to look casual and with time to spare; even if he had a car at his disposal it would not have been right to use it. To be unremarkable, unmemorable, it must appear that he walked chiefly for the exercise and that the places he visited were wholly and simply an opportunity to rest. He was grateful that Double British Summer Time gave him light enough until nearly ten to make this look natural.

After two days, Fairbrother had a good colour, but his legs were giving out. He felt fit, though, and promised himself that if this worked out well he might return and take it easy, watching the onset of autumn. He admired the Berkshire skies, a dome of such spectacular evening drama that he sometimes lost precious time watching the changing patterns and colours. He put this down as a plus; a soothing benefit to offset the growing disappointment of his search.

He was not yet willing to concede defeat, though he had begun to think about returning to London to rest and think the problem out differently. He toyed with the idea of going to the police with some such excuse as a lost pocket watch, in the hope that while he was there he could engage someone in a gossip about the German aircraft. It was thin. Still if he didn't get a break soon he might have to fall back on something like that. There was, after all, nothing suspicious about his interest. What had happened was public knowledge. He began to practise the necessary conversational gambits, right down to the facial expressions.

That evening he had a stroke of luck.

The landlord of his own inn was on duty with the Home Guard. In his place a big man, in his early forties and with a substantial beer belly, had taken over behind the bar. The atmosphere was a good deal more relaxed than usual. The customers, Fairbrother noticed, were more at ease with the relief man than they were with the licensee.

On the spur of the moment, while he was waiting for his drink, Fairbrother aired his story of a lost pocket watch. He had first to reassure the man that it wasn't worth turning the pub over to look for it; that he was almost sure he'd lost it on his travels.

"Never you mind about that," the barman told him. "Ken? Got a minute?" He beckoned to a burly man with an Errol Flynn moustache leaning on the other side of the bar.

"Ken's in the pleece," the barman said. "PC Bicknell. He can save you the walk to the police station."

"Gentlemen?" The big policeman slid into a comfortable slouch beside them at the bar. The barman outlined the problem.

The policeman looked at Fairbrother with insolent care. "Visitor, are you sir?"

Fairbrother said he was. "I thought you could report it for him," the barman suggested. "Save him coming in."

"Better if he does, I think."

Fairbrother preferred it, too. For one thing he could change his mind and forget the whole thing; otherwise his name and address would be recorded here and now.

"I'll come in tomorrow," Fairbrother said. "It's lovely here, isn't it? Always been a favourite of mine, this part of the country."

His scrutiny over, and his routine suspicion allayed by Fairbrother's manner and voice, Bicknell relaxed and became more friendly.

"You're local are you?" Fairbrother asked after a while.

"That's right."

"I had a walk today up on the Ridgeway," Fairbrother said. "I wouldn't envy you that climb."

"I don't climb it," Bicknell said. "Not unless there's a very good reason."

"You don't patrol the Downs?" Even as he asked it, Fairbrother realised it sounded pretty silly. He also knew that people love to point out silliness.

"The Home Guard does enough up there," Bicknell said.

Fairbrother bought a pint of ale for both men. As he put away his change he said: "The Home Guard, eh? Still, I suppose the German that crashed up there gave you plenty of trouble."

"Not me," Bicknell said at once. He had the awkward manner of instant contradiction that many policemen exhibit. He gave a thoughtful sideways smile as if to revive an old joke. "My inspector, though, he gave himself a mess of trouble over it."

It was clear that Bicknell and his inspector were not close. Fairbrother smiled polite encouragement, though the story was going to be told anyway.

"Two chaps come down off the Ridgeway that very day," Bicknell said in a low confidential tone. He clearly relished the tale, had told it a few times already. "He stops them, has a look at their identity cards and then lets them by with a thank you and have-a-nice-day." He shook his head at the folly of it, but said nothing more.

After a moment or two, Fairbrother said, as he was required to: "I'm mystified, constable. What should he have done?"

Bicknell looked at him as if he were witless. "No address taken, nothing down on paper, you see. Nothing to check on."

"But they did have identity cards?" Fairbrother contrived to look only mildly interested, sensing at once that there was something in this for him.

Bicknell shook his head again as if his story wasn't being appreciated. "Identity cards are nothing," he said heavily. "Suppose one of the men was the pilot from the crash?"

"I'm sorry," Fairbrother said. "Silly of me. I imagined when you said there were two men that they came down together."

Bicknell now shot a look at the barman as if blaming him for getting him into conversation of such absurdity. He sighed, took a pull from his pint, looked round the bar and finally brought his gaze back to Fairbrother as if for one last try. "One of them might have been the pilot. The other might have been his contact. It all sounds a bit like the pictures, of course. But in police work you don't take chances. You work by the book. And the book says you assume nothing. You check, check, check." Bicknell assumed the look of a man unlikely to make such a mistake.

"Yes, I see," Fairbrother said, disappointed. "Very careless."

Bicknell snorted, satisfied.

"So two perfect strangers were seen coming away from the crash?"

Bicknell smiled in a superior manner. "Not quite, sir. One of them happened to be staying over at Lammas—that's a big estate outside of Newbury."

"And the other?"

"That's it!" Bicknell came alive. He took another long pull at his beer. His timing was quite nicely judged, Fairbrother thought. "You've hit it exactly. They did come down together. But one of them was a stranger. That's why old Ding Dong got his balls chewed off by the super. We'd still like to talk to the other one. Not for anything, mind. Just to eliminate."

Fairbrother's pulse moved up a notch or two. He had the sensation, as so often before, that he was on the point of a breakthrough. In the end someone, somewhere, always knew what you wanted to know. Sometimes they didn't realise they knew. You had to go on probing, peeling away the layers, uncovering scraps about time, or place, or event which—unmemorable to them—were the pieces you needed to make sense of the whole.

"But why," he said slowly, as if trying to piece it together to please Bicknell, "why couldn't the man from Lammas give your inspector the details he needed?" He thought he knew the answer. Nonetheless he wanted to hear it spoken.

Bicknell now clearly warmed to Fairbrother. It was clear that his tale of police intricacies didn't always engage an audience in this way. "Why?" he said. "Because he didn't know him. The other man was just a passing cyclist. They'd only met a minute or two before." He leaned back to see what Fairbrother made of this, smiling hugely. When Fairbrother had nodded his appreciation of the joke sufficiently, he added: "Make no assumptions. Always check, check, check."

As if conscious that he had said too much, or that anyone might think that he had, Bicknell drew himself up and breathed deeply and looked around vaguely. His posture suggested that he was ready to leave. Unless there were any questions.

There were. Fairbrother needed one more piece and he thought Bicknell was just enough of an idiot to give it if he had it. "As it happens," he lied. "I have a friend who sometimes stays at Lammas—or says he does. It wasn't a man called Marriott by any chance, was it?" He wondered briefly where he'd got that name from.

"No," said Bicknell promptly. "Marsh. Harvey Marsh. A London man."

"Ah," Fairbrother said. "Just a thought. Another drink anyone?"

Fairbrother stayed one more night. He slept late, spent most of the day in a deckchair in the garden beside the inn, and got an early night. His legs were less stiff, but he felt he'd deserved the rest.

When he bought newspapers to read in the train back to London he was suddenly back in the war. Capture of the main V1 bases in northern France and Belgium, it seemed, meant that London and the South had seen the last of the German flying bombs. Evacuees, though, were warned not to return to the capital . . . yet. There was an end-of-the-war flavour about the leaders in *The Times*, which, though he was warmed by it in one way, reminded him sharply that he couldn't really spare this resting time.

London looked dreadful to him. Shabby, dirty and not in the least defiant. On a bus from Paddington he looked down into endless bomb-sites now converted to hold emergency water tanks. Like most Londoners, he had been used to the optimist's view of the bombing: it was so comforting to see how much of the city was still standing that one tended to underrate how much had been flattened.

By five he was busy with the telephone. There were a good many entries in the book for Marsh, H. He ruled through all those who were Marsh, Henry, or Marsh, Harry. And for the moment ignored those, too, with more than one initial.

It took time. Some subscribers were plainly out all day. Others away from home. There was no guarantee that he could even do it this way. If he could it was quicker.

Late on Saturday morning he had whittled the list down to five. He went down to the shop to see that all was well there. A few circulars lay in his mail box. The place was dusty, but the windows were intact and the phone was working. On impulse he took out his list of remaining possibles and dialled the first. It was a Central number.

On the fourth ring a man answered.

"Harvey?" Fairbrother began genially. "Harvey Marsh?"

"Right," a man's voice said. "Who is this?"

"Harvey," Fairbrother began, "I'm glad to have caught you. I've been trying to—" He cut himself off abruptly, as if the link had broken accidentally. It sounded less suspicious than a caller who backed off once he had identification.

So that was that. He'd found Harvey Marsh.

Where did that take him? Fairbrother considered. He now knew where to find a man who had been at the scene of the crash at the very moment it took place, or at least almost immediately afterwards. A man, moreover, who had come down from the crash site with another, as yet not satisfactorily identified or eliminated by the police.

He was pleased with his investigation, but it had taken time and he wasn't sure that he was any closer to Willi Reiter. Had the man with Marsh been Reiter? It seemed more than possible. And if he was Reiter, did Marsh know it? PC Bicknell would not, of course, be privy to the results of further police investigation. But it was sure that they had looked into Marsh, both at the Lammas end and at his home. If they were satisfied with his bona fides they wouldn't be likely to bother Marsh further, beyond taking an expanded statement from him.

Fairbrother would have liked to believe that if the police were satisfied with Marsh then he would be saving himself trouble if he, too, now proceeded to the assumption that either the stranger with Marsh was a chance cyclist, or that he was Reiter and Marsh had no knowledge of it. But he couldn't. The police handling of the incident so far had been appalling. By now, perhaps, Special Branch were looking into it. But if so, Reiter—if Reiter it was—was already through their net and away.

It was clear that he needed to know a lot more about Harvey Marsh and enough to be able to establish for himself the nature of the relationship between the two men. The police were overworked and undermanned. At this stage of the war, he wondered whether even Special Branch would take a very serious view of a lone pilot, saboteur or spy who chose such a risky and dramatic method of infiltration as crashing a plane in broad daylight on top of the Berkshire Downs. As to the various branches of military intelligence who might also have the affair in hand, Fairbrother smiled; he had no great opinion of them, either.

He would check Marsh himself. What was the connection with Lammas? The proximity of the crash to the Croft estate could be pure coincidence. Reiter might have put his plane down anywhere in England and still been within a mile or two of such a property. And anyone from it might well find themselves the only immediate eye-witness to the crash. But it needed checking. And quickly.

And indeed, if he was going to persevere with this line of enquiry it was his only possible lead.

30

At the junction of Bouverie Street with Tudor Street, Fairbrother paid off his cab and walked slowly down towards the Embankment. It was still a little too light for detective work, but this was one locality in which his appearance helped tremendously; a small, mild, dapper man in city clothes was so much at home in these wig-and-pen streets that Chesterton's invisible man principle had some validity. And Marsh himself was safely on duty at ABP; a quick phone call there had established that his shift started at eight p.m.

He walked first past Temple Chambers on the other side of the street. In red brick, with Victorian embellishments in stone, it looked as if it might have been built as chambers to accommodate an overspill from The Temple, a little to the west. The block told him nothing about Marsh. At first glance it was a more likely address for an office than a home.

The river looked three parts red-gold, one part lead-grey. A tram rumbled by on the Embankment, eastbound. When it was gone the silence was somehow deeper. The life had ebbed out of the city. It breathed shallowly, its only pulses faint and remote in the first stirrings of the newspaper nightworld. The streets were empty; lonely almost. Fairbrother crossed swiftly to Temple Chambers, studied the bells, mastered the complicated numbering and identified Marsh's staircase. It was stone, gloomy, badly lit. Fairbrother was relieved.

Yellow expressionless eyes watched him approach with interest. A large tabby cat sat patiently at Marsh's door, perhaps in a nightly vigil. Fairbrother stroked it, picked it up, tucked it under his arm and studied the door. He was delighted to see it had only a simple Yale lock. He was not a skilled housebreaker, but it presented no problems at all. The cat clung, purring, to the collar of his coat while he manipulated a simple tongue of stainless steel. The door pushed open easily.

He had no fears. He had many times talked himself out of situations as difficult as this with a 'God-bless-my-soul' or a

'Good-heavens-what-will-you-think-of-me'. Open and artless, that was the thing. He waited a moment before stepping inside. He stood quite still, listening. The whole building was quiet. The bell-plates in the hallway suggested only a few of the units were being used as flats; most were offices for one-man-stamp-dealing firms, an accountant or two and unidentifiable businesses with a need for a city address.

In the hallway the darkness was intense. He used a small torch to get his bearings, then switched on the hall light. It was clear that Marsh had completed his blackout before he left. Though it was cool enough in the street, it was hot and airless in the flat. He pulled up the inner doormat so that it would cover the crack of light under the door. The cat jumped from his arms and ran straight ahead. Three doors before that one: kitchen, bathroom and lavatory to the right. The end one was evidently a bed-sitting-room—unless there was another room leading off that one.

He switched on the overhead light. There were no other doors. This was the whole of the flat. He took in the big room carefully. A large bed in an alcove; a gateleg table with two almost-matching chairs on the left-hand wall; a bureau, open and spilling papers, under the window, with heavy curtains drawn behind it; two armchairs facing a gas fire on the righthand wall.

Fairbrother sat down at the bureau. The cat nuzzled his ankle. Underneath the top layer of letters, notes and bills, Marsh's address book—the most promising target. He took out a notebook and began. Family first. Under 'M' for Marsh he found only Dad/Wembley 0048. He was lucky there. A son doesn't normally need to write down the address or telephone number of a parent. Marsh had, perhaps, done it in a rush of efficiency when he first acquired the book. There were no other Marshes. And the rest of the book was disappointing. There were almost no addresses, just telephone numbers. The only full entries were for a solicitor, a bookshop, a jeweller, the Press Club, Harrods, Fortnum's, and two or three restaurants. All of these were written in the same bright blue ink as the entry for Marsh's father. Fairbrother smiled. He was right. Marsh had begun his book diligently and carefully, as most did, and thereafter skimped and scribbled. More than half the entries were for men, from whom there was both Christian name and surname, but there was no indication of their relationship to Marsh. One entry did look important. It was printed in capitals:

MCNAIR AT HOME—Prospect 6263

There were numbers alongside several girls' names: Sally, Diane, Janet, Susan, Clair and Joan S. He wrote them all down hopefully. In all probability they were useless, but you never knew.

"Disappointing, pussy," he said aloud. The cat rubbed its head in a melancholy fashion against the leg of his chair, purring sycophantically. Fairbrother sat back and looked around.

Now he saw the picture. How could he have missed that? It was a framed photograph of a beautiful girl with a stunning mouth and perfect teeth. Her hair was carefully groomed and held. She was clearly important. No man keeps a picture of a beautiful girl in a prominent place unless she is, for the moment, the girl. And this was no ordinary girl. The style and pose looked like the work of a society photographer. The shot might have been taken for the portrait page of *The Tatler*.

There was one oddity about the picture. It was signed, simply: Love, Ronnie. Fairbrother mused over that. 'Love, Ronnie' did not promise love enduring, love exclusive or love exceptional. It was such a careful statement.

And Ronnie? An odd name for a girl. Veronica?

He tried the book again. There was no Ronnie or Veronica. He worked quickly through the papers in the bureau: bills, an empty diary, a bus map, an unused cashbook, an envelope full of bus tickets, one of each colour, and an envelope containing two photographs. That was better. He studied them carefully. In the first, a tall young man with rather solid good looks stood between a small, dumpy, frowning woman in her early fifties and a rather handsome, leonine, but seedily dressed man of about the same age. The clothes suggested the early thirties, but it was hard to be sure. In the second, which suggested a few years later, the young man was pictured only with the older man. There was a real difference between the two groups. In the group of three, all stood stiffly and unhappily in self-conscious pose in what looked like a small back garden. Alone, the two men were relaxed and each had an arm round the shoulders of the other. Their faces showed genuine pleasure and spontaneity.

"Is this Harvey Marsh, puss?" Fairbrother mused. He memorised both faces. He got up, found a saucer in the kitchen and a bottle of milk standing in a bowl of water in the sink. He poured the cat a drink, added water, and took it into the other room. The cat vocalised its gratitude and slurped undaintily.

He returned to the search. In the drawer under the open flap of the bureau he found what he wanted. The birth certificate of Harvey Marsh. He read that Marsh was the son of Francis Harper Marsh, at that time a teacher, and Edith Eithne Holt, a nurse, then both living at Humboldt Gardens, Pinner, Middlesex. He knew now that Marsh was 28 years old. He looked again at the photographs. It was facile, of course, to suggest that the elder man in the picture looked like a schoolteacher and the woman like a nurse, or former nurse. But time was running short. In the absence of many photographs it was reasonable to assume that the only two kept by a young man might be of his parents. He thought he'd gamble that much.

There was another envelope in the drawer. It contained a letter on the heading of Associated British Press. It was from McNair, the Managing Editor, advising Marsh that the War Office would shortly document his accreditation as a War Correspondent for ABP with the Allied Expeditionary Forces. An enclosure suggested a list of field kit and uniform items that Marsh should buy at ABP's expense. Across the outside of the envelope was scrawled, probably in Marsh's writing:

> Public Relations Department
> War Office
> Brigadier Vine

As he replaced the papers, Fairbrother saw a small strip of four passport size photographs caught in the bottom of the big envelope. His luck was holding. There was no need to compare these pictures with the snapshots. They were of the same man. So this was Harvey Marsh. He studied the face again. Regular features, squarish, the mouth a little hard, a flat and rather arrogant stare—offset, to some extent, by the smallest hint of a self-mocking smile.

Some things now made sense. McNair at Home now dropped into place—as distinct from an ABP, obviously. Then, too, though he would be very lucky to find the elder Marsh still at Humboldt Gardens, Pinner, he did have both the initials and phone number of Marsh's father.

The rest of the flat revealed nothing. Fairbrother was mildly surprised. His experience of examining people's private things had almost always revealed one or two giveaways: items so private, so embarrassing that their owners would have given anything for them to have remained hidden.

He prepared to leave. "Out you go, pussy. It wouldn't do for you to be found on the inside." He went to the door with the cat and then came back to the bureau. On impulse he picked up the address book again.

Marsh was a tidy man. The little flat was sparsely furnished, clean and ordered—monkish, almost. It bothered him that 'Ronnie' was not on record somewhere. Marsh might have no need of such a note now. But what of when he had first met her? Sometimes . . . He flipped open the address book just inside the front cover. Nothing. Inside the back cover? There is was!

> RONNIE Flat Fulham 2266
> Lammas, Newbury, Berks 288980
> MOI Canteen MUS 7296

Fairbrother was quite inordinately pleased with himself. At least Marsh had conformed to one of his rules. It was common enough. If the contact was special enough, people wrote the details in a special place.

Some more questions were answered. Ronnie was a Croft— the daughter, presumably, of David Croft, the film distributor and the owner of Lammas. This Ronnie had a flat somewhere in the West Ken section of Fulham. And she could also, at times, be found at the MOI canteen. This last sounded like war work of some kind. Marsh's appearance in the countryside at all, and at Lammas in particular, had been puzzling him. A relationship with Ronnie Croft made it all clear. And Marsh's appointment as a War Correspondent explained, didn't it, why a youngish man should have the leisure, in wartime, to be there at all, instead of away in one of the services?

Armed with this much, he peeled back the bedspread and sniffed the pillows. Unless Marsh wore perfume, a woman had slept on the right side of the bed lately. No hairpins, that he could see, but Ronnie Croft didn't look the type anyway. In the cupboards and bathroom he found no signs of occupation other than Marsh's. Without checking more closely he couldn't be sure, but at least he had established it was improbable that anyone other than Marsh and a girl used the place.

Fairbrother let himself out, slipping the mat back into position. Before he had turned the stair, the cat had taken up its station on the doormat to the left side of the door.

31

Harvey put the phone down unhappily. He had agreed to lunching with David Croft and at once regretted it. There could be only one subject Croft might want to talk to him about alone, and over lunch.

He had only been up for half an hour, moving leisurely towards his bath by way of the coffee pot and several cigarettes. The informed, considerate timing of the call irritated him; it was so efficient. And he'd been intimidated, thrown off his guard by his own unshaven, sleep-smelling scruffiness as if the crisp, barbered Croft on the other end of the line could somehow see him.

He hurried through the shower and dressing and set out an hour in advance to regain the initiative. From St James's tube station he walked up through Green Park, kicking at the first fallen leaves. He tried out crushing responses to anything Croft might say. He liked the man, admired him even, but what happened between Ronnie and himself was none of his business. She was not only of age, but demonstrably well able to take care of herself.

The park calmed his spirit. The indignation died away and his mood softened. The far-off rumble of the Piccadilly traffic sounded like the boom of surf. The park was like a calm, island oasis. It was hard to believe, here at the heart of it all, that the war wasn't just a bad dream. If you didn't look around. American servicemen, looking more at home than the British, hunted unattached girls in small packs. Nannies in grey uniforms and white collars pushed prams along under the trees; though they were all grey-haired now, the pretty

190

ones were in factories, hospitals, on farms. He mourned again the loss of the grand old railings, sacrificed to the war scrap drive. But the dapple and dazzle of the sun through the trees was the same as ever. By the time he turned right to the grey colonnade of the sandbagged Ritz he was calmer. He told himself he would give Croft a polite and understanding hearing.

He sat up on a stool in the downstairs American Bar and tried to recall any one of the little speeches he had rehearsed. Instead of found himself nervous and defensive. His timing had been poor. There was still ten minutes to go before Croft appeared.

He was on a second drink when he sensed Croft's arrival in the way the barman's glance slid past his right ear, breaking off their desultory exchange. Harvey doggedly refused to turn on his stool, but the barman was already reaching for the makings of Croft's Gibson.

Croft touched him on the shoulder: They shook hands, smiling. Harvey could not resist looking at his watch. The man was dead on time; he might have been waiting for the very moment of the hour.

"I hope I haven't kept you," Croft said. Harvey felt ungracious when he didn't comment. They sat down at a table in a corner of the room.

"I have to tell you that I was in two minds about this lunch," Croft said. "I thought you might resent it. It was a struggle of conscience." He smiled at Harvey encouragingly over the rim of his glass. "Cheers."

"But you won?" Harvey couldn't resist it.

Croft's smile acknowledged the shaft, then relaxed to a lesser brilliance. "That's right. I did. I always do when it's a choice between delicacy and peace of mind."

He gave Harvey no chance to develop a counterattack. Instead he asked a string of concerned questions about the timing of the ABP accreditation, Harvey's kit, likely date of departure and the number and disposition of ABP correspondents already in the field. Harvey was surprised by Croft's grasp of the procedures and knowledge of his likely role. There were, he realised, some aspects he hadn't fully explored himself.

"An exciting life," Croft said thoughtfully. "Anything at all I can do to smooth the way?"

At one time Harvey would have been grateful for the suggestion. Now his irritation returned. It was on the tip of his tongue to urge Croft to the point of this meeting when Croft said abruptly: "Shall we go up, then? We can talk comfortably over lunch."

They both ordered asparagus and lemon sole with salad. Harvey didn't hear the white wine order, couldn't see the label in the bucket and didn't want to ask. It was good. He thought how odd it was to be here at all while most men of his age were trying to stay alive on battlefields all over the world. He ate sole and drank white wine. They ate K-ration and drank water if they were lucky. For all that the Park wall of the Ritz grillroom wore sand-bags, it was still the incomparable Ritz, and a long way from real war.

"Would you like to say your opening piece?" he said when Croft began to dissect his fish. He looked at his watch again.

"Of course," Croft said. "Where to begin . . . ?"

Harvey put down his knife. He looked at Croft impatiently. "Would it help if I suggested it had to do with my giving up the ABP job and not rocking the boat for Ronnie?"

Croft looked up mildly. "Why? Did you want to change your mind and do that?"

Harvey snorted. "Stay behind, take the ready-made job, marry the boss's daughter and live happily ever after?"

Croft thought a moment, his fork halfway to his mouth. "That's not possible?" It was a question couched as a statement.

Harvey stopped eating and regarded him steadily for some moments. "I suppose you get the chance to play God fairly often," he said sourly. "What's it like?"

When Croft said nothing, he added, by way of justification: "It isn't even as if Ronnie is so sure of her feelings."

"I've heard Ronnie on the subject of Harvey Marsh," Croft said patiently, "and it's perhaps true that at times what she has said tended to be too much about the prospects and too little about the man." He munched a little salad. "That's her mistake, perhaps. Obsession even." He paused and stared at Harvey intently: "But you're not suggesting that you have at any time believed that that's all she feels about you? I mean, you're not suggesting that she's been sleeping with you all these months as a means of securing you as a piece of husbandly clay to be moulded to her own design?"

Harvey reddened, more out of embarrassment than anger. He did not trust himself to answer for the moment. And because the question was startling, he found himself considering whether that wasn't at least possible. He had always found Ronnie to be disarmingly honest, disturbingly direct.

But was it possible? No. He dismissed the idea first, then grew still more angry that he should have been asked it.

"What the hell does all that mean?" he said at last.

"Mean?" Croft leaned toward him earnestly. "I simply wanted to know if you had begun to think that Ronnie doesn't so much love—as rationalise."

"No, what you mean is, do I think she will ever actually love anyone at all? Except her father, that is?"

Croft thought about it. "If you like." He resumed eating, taking the tension out of the exchange.

"I hadn't thought about it deeply," Harvey said. "Don't get me wrong. I have nothing to complain about. Ronnie has always told me where I stood. Meeting her—" he reached for a better word "—knowing her has been the best thing that ever happened to me. Good God, that sounds like the worst of Hollywood. But Ronnie is like that. Whoever she ends up with, she'll eclipse anyone that man has ever known. She's wonderful." He ended it on an up note, and Croft waited for the rest.

Harvey was silent for a long time. At last he said: "But love . . . ?" He shrugged.

Croft's cool, anticipatory smile flagged at last. "That's your reaction," he said coldly. "You're only one man. How Ronnie might react to someone else entirely remains to be seen." He smiled thinly. "Not that I'm a great believer in love. It's good for business, but—" he shrugged in turn. "A lot of guff is talked about love. If it's around it must be a nice thing to have. It's a fairweather factor in marriage, though. It remains regrettably true that love doesn't last too well when life gets sordid. It flourishes well enough in some fine, dramatic circumstances—wartime separations for instance. But it wears badly under monotony, drab life-style, deprivation." He looked at Harvey for comment, and when he got nothing, went on: "On the other hand, it's quite wonderful how love stays fresh if you have the money to look and dress like a million dollars. Love, or something that looks and sounds and feels very like it, is a commodity quite easy to manufacture with the right surroundings—with mood, atmosphere, fine clothes and all the time in the world." He grinned at Harvey; "I could make you into a screen idol to break any heart. Or turn a shop girl into a love goddess adored by millions."

Harvey looked at him impassively. "Fascinating," he said flatly. "Except the formula doesn't seem to have worked for you."

He regretted it as soon as he'd said it. Croft simply ducked his head, acknowledging the point.

"I'm sorry," Harvey said. "I was getting fed up with grow-up-Harvey time. Which is it that you're trying to convince me of? That Ronnie can give love, or that if she can't it isn't as good as having money?"

Croft nodded. He signalled the waiter and ordered coffee, then went straight on: "It's a pity about you, you know. I don't know what Ronnie wants, but I'd have liked to have you with me. You have a nice edge. And edge is almost everything—in business, anyway."

"Fine," Harvey said. "I appreciate the compliment. I really do. But what did you call me here for?"

Croft looked down at his manicured hands. For the moment he looked vulnerable and Harvey warmed to him. He was, after all, a Dad. A rich one, perhaps. But just an anxious Dad.

"I was simply curious to know whether you have really touched Ronnie, or simply been an excitement for her."

"Is it any of your business?" Harvey said sharply.

"You say yourself that Ronnie isn't like anyone else you've ever known," Croft said gently. "I would very much like to know if you are going to wear off quite quickly, once you're gone, or whether she'll be hurt." He put out a restraining hand and added, urgently: "Neither way is it your fault. You've stuck to your terms. And by anyone else's standards they're perfectly reasonable." He looked at Harvey appealingly: "Will she survive?"

At last Harvey understood. He felt sorry for Croft and reflective about the possible need for the man's concern. He couldn't really answer the question. Ronnie, at least in that way, had been a steel-plated enigma.

"I don't know," he said at last.

"All right," Croft said. "I accept that. My problem then, not yours." He sat back. "A brandy?"

Harvey shook his head.

They came out into the sunlight. There was a breath of autumn in the air. They shook hands, awkwardly, like strangers. Croft turned a little as if to bid him goodbye and then seemed to remember something.

"One thing," he said.

"Yes?"

"Our secret, this lunch?"

"Why should you care?" Harvey was genuinely surprised.

Croft shrugged. "I'm not keen on Ronnie thinking I interfere."

"I'm not keen on her thinking I've turned you down flat at this late stage. You did make the offer again, didn't you? Anyway, if I keep my mouth shut can I rely on you to let her make up her own mind—right up to the last minute?" He grinned. "I could always get an eleventh-hour stay of execution from ABP for something as serious as marriage."

"Agreed!" Croft squeezed his arm, pleased. "But why? Do you still think you may get her on your terms?"

Harvey shook his head. "No," he said. "It's just that I don't want her hurt, either. Or if she has to hurt, I don't want it on my conscience. If she makes the decision it may hurt less. That's all."

Croft nodded happily. "You do care. It's a deal."

Harvey watched him cross to the Berkeley Street corner, whisking through the swirling afternoon traffic. He liked Croft better now than ever before.

A mood of nostalgia descended on him. A couple of weeks more and he might not see all this for some months. For a few moments longer he watched Croft out of sight. The Ritz, the nightingale and Berkeley Square. He grinned sentimentally and turned back to the park.

32

When Fairbrother went down to the shop on Friday morning to clean up a little, there was a picture postcard in the letterbox behind the front door. He knew at once it would have a Belfast postmark. Little enough mail ever reached Jerome at all, and none of it these days had anything at all to do with antique jewellery.

Scrawled in the message section, he read:

> *Will you be able to make it?*
> *MY friends are anxious to accommodate*
> *you, but quickly, before their house*
> *comes down.*
>
> *Malone*

Fairbrother was neither surprised nor troubled by the message. Malone exaggerated a little, he thought. The people Reiter had offended looked still to be firmly in the saddle. And their malice was more likely to grow, rather than diminish, with their own growing insecurity. He tore the card carefully and put the pieces in his pocket. For safety's sake they would go into a street litterbin.

He was philosophical. Unless the Marshes, father and son, led him to Reiter—and there was only a hope that they might—he would, in any case, have to start again from scratch with a different angle.

Meanwhile, he thought the chances were that Reiter was in London. That at least made sense. London was at once the most obvious and yet the most secure hiding place of all; it was already succouring a whole underworld of deserters, black market operators and racketeers. With his command of English and his pre-war experience, Reiter could probably pass as British. If he couldn't, then London, with its bloated population of refugees, Free-French, Dutch, Belgians, Poles, Czechs and oddly-spoken Commonwealth nationals, was the only place a foreigner should hide. In any city less cosmopolitan a foreigner with doubtful English would attract immediate attention.

The problem with Reiter being in London was one of time. It would take time, perhaps too much. In which case he would lose the commission.

Fairbrother was not too concerned. Not since 1936 had his income been dependent on any kind of steady profit from dealing in jewellery. And while there weren't, perhaps, too many clients for his other services, he didn't need more than one or two. Who could tell?—perhaps even the new Germany, when it came, would have need of him. There would be many old scores to settle, not all of them democratically.

Meanwhile, it would be as well if he lost no time. With the names and telephone numbers, the addresses for Frank Marsh and Ronnie Croft had been readily forthcoming from Directory Enquiry. He would tackle those today—in his own special way.

He adjusted the CLOSED sign on the shop door and hurried upstairs to his flat.

It would not do to look too prosperous. The clothes he chose were the same kind he always wore—black jacket, striped trousers, silver grey tie, white shirt and bowler hat. These were all well worn. In the suburbs he ought to be wholly indistinguishable from the buttonholed hordes who went up to London every day on the lines to Victoria, Waterloo, Charing Cross and London Bridge from the green dormitories of the south and west.

In the tiny hall he hesitated over taking Stella. Stella had her own special place on the hallstand. It was unlikely, but he might just need her today. If he did, then she was always ready. He took up the silver-capped ebony stick lovingly. She was a comfort: a weapon totally disarming and innocent in appearance, yet more fearsome than any firearm. She was silent, swift, sure and very final. She was more than a tool of his trade; she *was* his trade. Without Stella he could never have succeeded. She had been his friend since 1933 when he had found her in Venice and bought her from a curio dealer who insisted she was unique, almost certainly a century old—a very special weapon specially commissioned and specially crafted. Fairbrother had carried her for years before he found her name quite by chance. It was chased minutely between details of the fine silver-leaf pattern which climbed the four inches immediately below the knob. Since then he had always thought of her as Stella, delighted by the mystery of the name's origin.

The elder Marsh, he saw from a street atlas, was on the very edge of Metroland. It was a chore and might yield nothing. But he could not sensibly contemplate combing London until he had at least disposed of the possibility that either one or both of the Marshes had some kind of direct connection with Reiter. He set out to complete the exercise with an open mind.

Eastcote was a dead suburb during the day, deserted by much more than half of its population. He saw only a half-dozen men on the long walk from the tube station.

The whole area seemed to have been developed by a single builder just before the war. Every street and house looked alike. He knew everything about them at one glance. They had sold then for £5 down and £450 over twenty years. Each had a garden of about sixty feet, three rooms upstairs, two down, and a little donkey boiler in the kitchen. Lindsey Gardens was like every other street, with its grass verge, alternate pink and white pavement slabs and ornamental trees; but it was locked into an open fan of similar streets on the far edge of the development.

As he turned into the street he could see that there could be no breaking into a house here, under the inquisition of the close-packed porches and windows of neighbours. But there was another way to find what he wanted, and Fairbrother was prepared for it.

He stopped short of 29 on the other side of the road and after a moment of hesitation rang the bell at No. 24.

It was opened by a motherly sort of woman in her fifties. She looked surprised by Fairbrother and stood with the door only half open, shielding her body.

Fairbrother lifted his hat and beamed cordially.

"Mrs Warren?" he said confidently.

The woman blinked and then shook her head. "Warren? No, Flax is our name. You've got the wrong address." She looked enormously relieved. Then, as Fairbrother knew it would, curiosity brought her out from behind the door. She looked at the paper in Fairbrother's hand. "What number did you want?"

"Ah, let's see. Number twenty-four. Mrs. Warren. Elizabeth Nola Warren." Fairbrother had another glance at the sheet himself, seemingly perplexed.

"No," Mrs Flax said less timidly. "Wrong number entirely. I don't even know a Mrs Warren—not in this street. But then I don't know them all." She now came out onto the step and looked up and down the street companionably, as if a fresh look might give her inspiration.

"Um," said Fairbrother. "Bless my soul, how careless of them. Well, I'm awfully sorry to have bothered you." He gave the woman a beautiful smile, tipped his hat again and made to turn back down the path, again studying the paper in his hand.

It was an old routine, but it worked nine times out of ten. Mrs Flax watched him go rather regretfully. Such a courtly little man. Smiling, she watched him unlatch the gate, and then hesitate. She smiled more brightly still, folded her arms across her bosom and inclined her head helpfully.

Fairbrother laughed. It was a short, gentle, self-derisive sound. "I think I've got the answer," he said, waving the form. "It's badly written, you see. That's all. It could equally well be a badly written seven. So it's number twenty-seven I want." Again he tapped his hat. He was through the gate before Mrs Flax reacted.

"I don't think it's twenty-seven you want, either," she

called. She found she was enjoying this little encounter. It was a nice little moment of human contact which cut across the boredom of her day. She added, almost with pleasure and warming to the mystery: "Twenty-seven is a Mr and Mrs Firth."

"Oh dear," Fairbrother said. He adopted a look of total desolation, to which Mrs Flax warmed instantly. "Firth you say? I wonder—did they have a married daughter living with them at some time, perhaps—or another relative?" He had not so much asked Mrs Flax for the information as mused aloud on the possibility.

The woman shook her head at once, her lips pursed very positively. "No, there's just the two of them. Always has been. He's retired and they don't have any children at all." She felt rather sorry for Fairbrother. She wondered if he had come far on his fruitless errand.

While she spoke, Fairbrother looked down at his paper once more. He looked up cheerfully. "I've got it," he announced. "It could just as easily be a nine, too, d'you see?" He folded the paper discreetly, offering only the fraudulent memo heading of a solicitor with a Chancery Lane address. To one side, at the top, was an address panel in which there was, indeed, a scribbled address for an Elizabeth Nola Warren of 24 Lindsey Gardens. Now totally involved, Mrs Flax peered at the form herself. The second digit did indeed look like a four, or a slovenly seven, or just possibly a very open nine. She giggled nervously, then decided to commit her local knowledge. "No," she said eagerly. "That won't do either. I'm afraid it isn't your lucky day. Twenty-nine can't be right, either."

Fairbrother looked so crestfallen that she was tempted to indulge her curiosity further. "It's a Mr Marsh at 29," she said. And then: "It's not bad news, is it? I couldn't help seeing the solicitor's name."

Fairbrother looked surprised. He hesitated for just the right count. "Bad news? Oh, I see. Oh, no. Very definitely not. That's why we're so anxious to contact Mrs Warren. But this is the only address we have apparently."

Mrs Flax was sympathetic, pleased to be taken thus much into Fairbrother's confidence, sharing his dilemma. She made no move to return inside. She was wondering if she could offer him a cup of tea, after coming all this way. Would it be permissible? Would he accept? If he did, would she hear more, perhaps, about the legacy? It was all rather exciting. She would not have admitted it even to herself, but she also found Fairbrother rather attractive. He was so clean, so . . . gentlemanly.

After a moment, Fairbrother said, in the lowered tones of a friendly conspirator: "Marsh is the name at twenty-nine, you say?"

"That's right."

"No Mrs Marsh? Who might at one time have been a Mrs Warren? You see our information is out of date. That's clear. And we do know that Mr Warren is dead. So it's entirely possible that she has a new name now."

Mrs Flax was amused at the idea. She was enjoying herself hugely. "No," she said. "Mrs Marsh died—oh, before the war. Long before."

Fairbrother nodded unhappily. Then rather roguishly he said: "A married daughter, perhaps living there?"

Mrs Flax laughed, delighted with him. "No daughter at all, I'm afraid. Only a son, and he doesn't live here now."

Fairbrother turned on her his most charming smile. It begged her indulgence. It invited her help while acknowledging that she had already done enough.

"A lodger?" he said whimsically. "A lady lodger?"

"Well, yes, he does have a lodger, just lately. But that's a young man."

Fairbrother shook his head to show that he was beaten, ready to abandon the enquiry. To prove it he folded the paper in his breast pocket. Once more he smiled beautifully and turned to go—and turned partly back, rather comically, frozen in a pose of arrested departure.

"I suppose—" he laughed at himself for asking it "—the young man's name isn't Warren? He could have a wife. There could be some mix-up. No?" He grasped the tip of his bowler apologetically ready to raise it the moment she dismissed him with her answer.

Mrs Flax laughed aloud. She was really quite taken with Fairbrother. She had enjoyed his call and she was sorry to see him go. She had half a mind to invite him in to rest.

"No, I'm afraid not," she said between gusts of laughter. "I think I've heard at the shops that his name is Ryder."

Fairbrother mimed defeat and began to move away. Rather regretfully Mrs Flax closed the door on his beautiful smile and beautiful manners. She had no sense of having given any information at all about her neighbours.

Ryder? Reiter?

It had to be. Fairbrother had no doubts.

He began the long walk back to the station. It seemed a very short step. He was delighted with himself. The old methods were best. A simple job, well done.

It wasn't easy to see how the Marshes were linked to Reiter. Had he known them, perhaps, before the war? If so, how had they dared to harbour him now? Was his being here now simply a long-odds result of that meeting on the Berkshire Downs? If so, it was long-odds indeed.But then life was entirely made up from long-odds meetings with even longer-odds results. A man went out to a party when he'd almost made up his mind to stay at home—and met his future wife, who should have been, perhaps, on a train to Carlisle or somewhere else altogether. Another met a man in a train, struck up a friendship, ended up in partnership years later, and finally, perhaps, was driven to suicide or murder by the other's folly or deceit. Life was like that. In wartime, even more so.

The relationship angle was something he could satisfy himself about in due time. First there was the final check. He knew what Reiter should look like. He knew his height, weight, age, scars, colouring, limp, and much more besides. He would know the man on sight.

This was a piece of superb luck. Fairbrother glowed. His beatific smile so unnerved a woman sitting opposite him in the Piccadilly Line train back to Earl's Court that she moved to a seat further down the train, sure that he must be 'mental or something'.

33

Willi's cover at Lindsey Gardens seemed to grow daily more comfortable and secure. They had quickly developed morning and evening domestic routines. Frank would prepare breakfast while Willi was in the bathroom. After breakfast Willi would do the dishes while Frank got himself ready for work. Then they started out to the station together, caught the same train.

Having Frank with him enhanced Willi's feeling of safety, bolstered his confidence to face the day. When Frank got out at his stop, Willi went on into the West End. He had quickly learned to leave the Underground at Green Park. Piccadilly Circus was too much a magnet for deserters, the booking-hall in particular too much a hunting ground for military police. He was growing in confidence and his identity card had been checked more than once, but he still avoided the redcaps' favourite hunting grounds. At the same time, he was learning that he was reasonably safe. No deserter or serving soldier out of uniform had an identity card at all. Once one was produced, neither police or redcaps were really interested.

On his arrival at Frank's he had let it be known that he had been able to find work readily, and had then crushed any further curiosity by suggesting, rather than saying, that he was not at liberty to discuss the job. "A sort of clerk's job, really," Willi said, thereby hinting that it was nothing of the kind. Frank was immediately apologetic. So many people did have jobs of that kind; even if the work itself was unimportant, the subject matter might be top secret. Nobody pried.

So they both ostensibly 'went to work'. Willi usually spent his day in what had quickly become a routine. In the mornings he walked the streets, or read newspapers in parks or churchyards. If it rained he read them travelling round and round on the Circle Line. It was dry down there and comfortable, though some of the trains took on the sickly smell which billowed in at the stations used as shelters. Thousands still spent their nights below ground from long-standing habit, drowsing, talking, smoking, sleeping, even singing. Bed spaces were stencilled on the platforms to within a yard of the platform edge. Late night travellers had to pick their way among the sprawled bodies and their portable treasures: bags containing photographs, letters, jewellery, marriage lines, identity cards—even the family silver.

Towards the lunch hour, Willi liked to be near Fleet Street. Unable to stomach English cigarettes, he had turned first to the *Turkish Only* signs at every tobacconist. Then he found Weingotts at the Strand end of Fleet Street. They kept Menzalas Brazilian cigarettes—and had begun saving him a pack a day. The black tobacco was much closer to his native smoke.

Afternoons Willi spent mostly in the safety of the dark. He had become a cinema buff. He had seen Gary Cooper in *The Story of Dr Wassell*, had been moved by Deanna Durbin's

Christmas Holiday and entranced by *Fantasia*. News theatres he had given up. They were too painful. The weekly Gaumont-British footage of British troops advancing relentlessly into Germany in overwhelming strength set up emotions which disturbed his efforts to look, act, sound like an Englishman. Every newsreel now contained its shots of the *Feldgrau* marching into captivity, their hands on their heads and their faces stunned, exhausted, despairing. Their eyes, looking straight into the camera, accused him. One such newsreel left him so shaken he was sure as he left that the cause of his distress must somehow be obvious to the casual passer-by. He couldn't afford the luxury of patriotism, even in the dark. He learned, in scores of ways, all day and every day. It wasn't living and it wasn't liberty, though he had hopes of both. Meanwhile, the fantasy world he inhabited was comfortable enough. To the British, to Frank, perhaps, it was total war, but if the newsreels were true, his own people alone knew the meaning of that phrase. The paralysing day and night raids on German cities surpassed anything he'd heard of happening in Britain. They were a final agony that his own people were still enduring and the thought often left him drained by both compassion and guilt.

On the whole he liked the English. What suffering they had experienced, they had accepted bravely and with calm. Perversely, he sometimes caught himself longing for one last stinging defeat to jolt them out of their unquestioning certainty of victory. The rest of the time he couldn't wait for that victory—not so much for himself, but to end the suffering of Germany.

On Saturday morning, he sat with Frank longer than usual over breakfast. It was at moments like this that he found his situation unbelievable. He was safe—in a suburb of London, breakfast and the morning paper discarded between them. Dempsey's 2nd Army, according to Berlin Radio, had linked up with the British paratroops at Nijmegen. The Arnhem misadventure was over. Still Willi was unable to react. He wanted the war over. He needed that like any other prisoner. Yet each fresh German defeat brought him fresh agony of spirit. He liked Frank. He liked Harvey—and he dared not think about his feelings for Ronnie. Their suffering, though, like that of most non-combatants, was minimal. It was different for servicemen; they had to take it as it came—rough, or, as the British called it, 'cushy'. But he raged, silently, at the complacency of the Home Front. After five bitter years of war, the newspaper in front of him still advertised chocolate, biscuits, soap, toothpaste, patent medicines for minor ailments, dog powders, new clothes and scores of things which no German family had seen for years. Already here in Britain, debate had begun on the master plan for demobilisation, announced earlier in the month. The British were already arguing about the problems of peace. It irritated him deeply.

"You ready for tonight?" Frank asked him.

"Yes, I have the new suit. Thanks for sorting out the clothes coupons thing for me. Never did understand it."

"I haven't had a night Up West for—oh, I don't know how long," Frank mused. "I'll probably get pissed."

"Phil coming?"

"Course she is."

"And you're sure Ronnie knows I'm coming?"

Frank stared. "Of course. Six of us: you, me, Harvey, Ronnie, Phil and David Croft." He looked sideways at Willi, gathering the plates. "Do you know, you've asked me that three times already?"

A few minutes later he wandered into Willi's room, knotting his Saturday cravat into an open shirt. "I've got to be off now," he said. "I'll pick you up here at about six. All right? That'll be in plenty of time for 7:30 at the Savoy." He caught sight of the new, dark blue suit hanging on the outside of the wardrobe. "Hullo, is that it? Very nice. Where did you get that?" He unbuttoned the jacket and looked at the label. "Good God, Harrods! You really do chuck your money about don't you. I thought all suits were supposed to be utility; I suppose they don't know the meaning of the word at Harrods."

"You like it?" Willi was mildly embarrassed.

"Like it? It's beautiful. You must earn big money old son." He grinned. "What exactly do you do for a living?"

Willi smiled mysteriously. That was his regular routine. "Well," he said slyly: "You know you shouldn't ask." He tapped the side of his nose.

"Secretive bugger. It's probably not secret at all. If you made the bloody tea at the War Office you couldn't say so; it would still come under the Official Secrets Act."

"That's right," Willi grinned. "More than my job's worth."

Frank made a noise of disgust. "See you at six."

Willi was glad to be alone. On weekdays he was exposed. At weekends he could relax in this, his hiding place. He was content to sit. He walked miles most days; his shoes already needed a repair. He could sit quietly and think and read. His glance went to the framed picture on the scarred dressing table under the window. He picked it up and looked at it a long time.

He unzipped his briefcase and checked through the contents carefully. The case went with him everywhere. It contained one or two letters he had written to himself at Lindsey Gardens in carefully disguised hands. One purported to be from a colleague in an office he'd worked in, another from a girl who wrote that she might be in London in October briefly and would like to see him. He'd spent a lot of fantasy time composing both letters, enjoying creating characters for both people, embroidering their styles with idiosyncratic bits of language and a whole history for each, which was only minimally hinted at on the letters themselves. He had become attached to them both and regularly put them into fresh envelopes and mailed them to himself again. Frank had commented on the frequency with which the girl 'Connie'— Willi had revealed her existence with suitable modesty— wrote.

He kept his cheque book in the briefcase, too. He had opened an account at the local branch of Lloyds and was feeding it with 'clean' money he took in during the week. He changed his five-pound notes all over the West End, though never at the same place twice. For the moment he was working south from the Goodge Street area of Tottenham Court Road down to Charing Cross; he was only halfway, at Cambridge Circus.

The original wads of £5 notes were a great deal thinner. He had paid for the suit by cheque. None of the counterfeit money had ever paid for anything that could be traced to him. He also kept in the briefcase an envelope full of National Savings Certificates. Not that they could be useful to him; if he ever had to move from Frank's place in a hurry they would be lost to him. But they were nice 'colour'. Somehow they added to his own picture of himself as an innocent British citizen, though he knew perfectly well that his identity wouldn't withstand much investigation: he had no job, for instance, and no insurance cards.

He zipped the case, locked it and put it away on top of the wardrobe, out of sight behind the moulding.

Towards noon, having read a little and shaved and bathed slowly, listening to *Worker's Playtime* and Reginald Foort at the organ, he went out for a walk. He thought he might fetch some fish and chips for his lunch from the shop near the station. It was a long walk, different, somehow, from his fretful, weekday wanderings. He felt hidden, safely, in this quiet suburb.

It had rained in the night, heavily. Mushy leaves were beginning to plaster the pavement. Out here, where the bomb damage was far less, it was peaceful. There was a suburb of Berlin very much like this. He wondered how it looked now. Or if it even still existed at all. The air was clean and had an early autumnal sparkle. There was no bomb-site smell here. Probably wouldn't be now; there had been only one 20-minute alert yesterday. The V1 bases were now in British hands and the launchings had come to an abrupt end. The war was moving to an end after all. He felt alive and well.

And he was going to see Ronnie.

He had covered something like half the distance to the station, absorbed in his thoughts, when he had a moment of panic. For a few minutes he had forgotten completely the habit of stealth, had actually believed in his security within his new life, and was in consequence suddenly naked, like an animal forced to break cover.

He faltered in his stride. The street seemed deserted. Then he became aware that his own footsteps were being echoed, pace for pace. He looked back over his shoulder, nervously.

A small, neat man, dressed in city clothes, with a bowler hat and carrying an impeccably furled umbrella, came on behind him, perhaps ten yards away.

The man smiled cheerfully and nodded. Instinctively Willi half-raised a hand in greeting. He walked on.

Willi's mood had been so light he almost dismissed it. Instead, he found himself wondering. He turned the corner, past the deserted children's playground. Someone from the pub? He couldn't remember. From the street? He couldn't place the face.

Stealth returned. He slowed his pace fractionally, hoping to be overtaken. By half way down the long street the little man remained obstinately behind. Willi speeded up slightly.

Abruptly the footsteps behind stopped dead. The street was still empty. There was a pause of a second or two more. Then the man called out:

"Reiter?"

Willi's world shook and began to crumble. He took a few more steps, unable to believe what he'd heard. Then he

206

faltered and stopped. Turning was somehow incredibly difficult. He had no proper command of his limbs. He stayed that way; half-turned.

Fairbrother drew abreast of his quarry, smiling affably. "It is Willi Reiter, isn't it?" Fairbrother made it a statement, but there was as much of sympathy as of challenge in it. He lifted his bowler briefly, politely. "Yes, I thought so."

With an enormous effort, Willi focussed on him at last. The germ of some action began to move in the back of his mind. He looked up and down the street. Still empty.

"I wouldn't bother, dear boy," Fairbrother said gently. He seemed to sense in Willi the need to react strongly. He took Willi's elbow and urged him forward. "Let's go and talk about it somewhere."

Willi shook the hand off. He forced a nervous smile. "My name's Ryder," he said heavily. "Bill Ryder. Have we met somewhere?"

Fairbrother chuckled appreciatively. "Yes, yes, of course. Bill Ryder. Just as you say." He cocked his head to one side. "But a very short time ago you were Willi Reiter, too. Major Willi Reiter, Knight's Cross and all that. Can we talk about it somewhere? We must find a place to talk."

Willi stared at him. He couldn't believe it. He was out in the open, after all. His run was over. Or was it? He looked wildly about him. This little man couldn't stop him if he ran. But perhaps he wasn't alone. It seemed unlikely that he would be. Willi's pulses hammered in his ears and a hard knot in the pit of his gut began to weigh like a stone. He thought about smashing the pink, smiling, neatly barbered face that seemed so intolerably close.

And remembered the boy on the Ridgeway. He sighed and turned to walk on. Fairbrother, content that he wasn't going to run, quick-stepped along beside him. For perhaps a hundred yards neither spoke.

"How did you find me?" Willi said at last. He was astonished by the sound of his own voice.

"It wasn't difficult," Fairbrother said quietly. "Well, not very difficult." He chuckled. "Although the police didn't manage it." He looked Willi steadily in the eye. "Your English is very good, isn't it? Of course your mother was English, wasn't she?"

They walked on in an almost companionable silence. Willi had not noticed that they were walking now in a circle, round

207

the block. It took some moments for Fairbrother's comment to penetrate. When it did, Willi stopped dead.

"You're not the police?"

"My dear chap!" Fairbrother smiled reproachfully. "Do I look like the police?"

"M15?" Willi hazarded. "Or six, or whatever?"

"None of those," Fairbrother protested. "No," he gestured that they should walk on, "—a friend, almost."

Willi heard it, but could not take it in. He was grappling with the implications of his discovery. Somehow, though he had accepted the dangers, he had begun, in his solitary, fantasy days, to lose his grip on the reality of capture. Capture? By this pink and white little man? Why not? There had to be others. He just hadn't expected this. What now? Out of uniform, one part of his mind insisted, he would be shot for sure. The thought occurred to him, quite absurdly: in the Tower?

"A friend?" Willi said heavily.

"Perhaps I should explain," Fairbrother said softly.

"Why not?" Willi said.

They walked on, turning the corner and approaching Lindsey Gardens again. "A man came to see me," Fairbrother began cheerfully. "From Dublin. Not one of yours—simply a minion. But acting for your former friends. Am I making myself clear?"

· Willi heard him but could make nothing of it. "Not really," he said.

"Their idea *was*," Fairbrother stressed the word heavily, "that they would rather not have the embarrassment of you." He chuckled again. "Tidy minds, d'you see?"

He looked sideways at Willi, very keenly, and Willi nodded, dully.

"I am,—" Fairbrother reached for the right word—"a freelance. A rank amateur, of course," he added modestly. He paused again.

Willi breathed a little more easily. There was room to manoeuvre here. He thought he saw a ray of hope. "And you are to do the tidying up?" His voice was still a croak and he heard, too, that something of his careful accent was slipping. Bill Ryder was crumbling, like a heap of clothes and a last hope that he was.

Fairbrother seemed delighted. "That's right!" he exclaimed. "Absolutely right. You're with me every step of the way. Capital, capital." He grasped the stick he was holding close to the middle and hammered the air enthusiastically with it to underline his pleasure.

Wili thought about it. There was hope. His pulse was slowing and he felt a lot better. He said, drily: "Ambitious, wouldn't you say?" He was absurdly pleased that it came out like Ryder again.

For a moment Fairbrother looked puzzled. He stopped suddenly and Willi turned to look at him. "You surely don't mean—because I'm such a little chap?"

Willi said nothing.

Fairbrother shook his head. He resumed walking. "Not a lot of comfort for you in that, I wouldn't think. But I agree it's a risk you might feel you want to take."

"What's the alternative?" Willi said quickly. He sensed, now, that there was one.

Fairbrother nodded, vigorously, evidently pleased to be on more friendly ground. "Much better, my dear chap. Much better. We'll come to that."

34

It seemed to Ronnie that everything was going wrong with Harvey's party. They had been an hour in the Savoy's restaurant foyer bar before finally being called to their table and it had taken another fifteen minutes to order. The others seemed happy enough, but the noise and the formality of sitting down purposefully together heightened the sense Ronnie had of being two separate entities: one, the old Ronnie, and another a spectator, looking out from behind her own eyes. She smiled, she laughed, she chatted, but she had been hit by a wholly new and unexpected emotion which appeared to have stunned her normal personality, leaving only a caretaker to make the expected responses.

And the cause was Ryder.

She had been prepared for this second meeting and for any effect on her at all. She had thought about him only marginally since the evening at Eastcote. Once or twice she had speculated about him and his history. But she had thought herself no more than mildly attracted. This evening when she had arrived at the Savoy with her father and found them all waiting there, Ryder included, she had been badly jolted. For one thing he looked so different. At Eastcote, in his casual tweed jacket, he had appeared younger, more relaxed, just another agreeable young man. Tonight, in a dark suit and white shirt, he looked elegant. And more than that: mature, serious, tense. And she saw at once that when he looked at her at all, he looked at her quite differently.

She saw her father's lips move and leaned to hear what he was saying, but made nothing of it. The Carroll Gibbons orchestra, making an effort to be heard above the hum of the Savoy's peak hour for dinner, began a strident version of "It Could Happen To You".

Philomena Bedell, on her right, turned to her. "This is nice. All of us celebrating something." She blinked, nervously, as if uncertain that she'd said something suitable. And then: "What a beautiful dress . . ."

Ronnie thought the dress was a mistake. Halter-necked, bare-backed, in startling emerald satin, she'd had to go to Mount Street to look for it among her other 'rarely worn' clothes. It was out of place in a sea of khaki battledress and carefully preserved pre-war civilian suits. So was her father's dinner jacket: perfect, bought in Saks Fifth Avenue before the war as one of three, and looking now like a peacock among pigeons.

She heard herself say: "I can't even take credit for it." She turned a smile of sun-like warmth on Philomena. "It was made for Gloria Grahame in *Save Tomorrow*. A perk of the trade . . ."

She ought to have returned the compliment. Philomena wore a dress of brown silk which clung to every rounded inch of her and her remarkable hair was tonight piled high and folded into a long French pleat. Even with her astonishing proportions she managed to project a good deal of style. Too late, Ronnie heard her father supply the right words. Philomena blushed furiously, the stain blotching her neck down to the breastbone.

"I know I'm invited," her father was saying now, "but when is the wedding?" He was almost shouting above the clatter.

Ronnie looked up. Ryder was watching her. She looked away at once and was angry with herself. She looked past him instead. A youthful looking major-general at a table for two, only partly screened by a pillar, was massaging the

210

upper thigh of a very young girl with a cap of shining, short blonde hair.

"You've got a choice of Thursday or Friday," Harvey said. "After that, Dad, the photography will be short on class."

Harvey was wearing his new uniform for the first time, revelling in his officer status and the shoulder patches announcing him as a War Correspondent, which drew many second glances. He half turned to Ronnie and dropped his hand over hers. Ronnie's confusion grew. Her instinct was to pull away. All that was over! Harvey had chosen. She steeled herself to leave her hand where it was, anxious to know if Ryder had noticed. He had. She felt flushed. This was ridiculous, she thought. She was behaving like a schoolgirl.

Ryder asked if she would like to dance. She nodded and stood up. At once he was at the back of her chair.

"Your consommé will get cold," Harvey said cheerfully.

"My consommé is cold consommé," Ronnie said bleakly. That was the wrong tone, too. She didn't seem to be able to adjust.

At the edge of the floor she hesitated. There were no other dancers. Ryder was insistent. The orchestra began on "Rum and Coca-Cola". There was a muted cheer from a group of American fliers at dinner with a girl in the stunning blue uniform of the American Red Cross, who looked astonishingly like Betty Grable.

After a few steps Ronnie relaxed a little. "At least there's one thing I know about you," she said.

Ryder inclined his head.

"You're a superb dancer. Where did you learn the rhumba?"

"I travel a lot."

"You're a traveller?"

"More of a fugitive," Willi said recklessly. His mind was grappling with the problem of Ronnie. Now that he had been 'found' he did not dare stay at Eastcote after tonight. How then would he ever see Ronnie again? And what the hell did it matter if he didn't? As against staying alive, that is? He would have to tell Frank tonight that he was moving on. He thought Frank would be upset. He would be upset himself. He liked Frank. In a very short time, the randy old devil had become a sort of surrogate father to him. He like Harvey, too . . . It was all a mess. He reminded himself again to be careful with what he drank. He was becoming maudlin.

"Who are you?" Ronnie repeated.

Willi lost the beat and made a little performance of hesitating before picking it up again.

"Who?" Ronnie persisted.

What on earth could he answer to that? "It matters?" he said finally.

"Yes."

"Harvey hasn't even left yet," Willi reproached her.

"Hasn't he?" She regretted that. It gave all the wrong impression. But she couldn't bring herself to explain.

"The wedding is Thursday next," Harvey announced as they came back. "Special licence."

"Special woman!" Frank said. "Wait until all those old goats in the office hear about this," he crowed. "Sorry about this, old chap, but I won't be in on Thursday. Neither will Phil. We're getting married." He banged the table, making the cutlery jump. "Christ! I can't wait to get in there on Monday."

Philomena sparkled, Croft offered a toast, Harvey was beginning to sound thick of speech. Ronnie smiled brightly and watched it all. She was back in control. Something had happened out there on the dance floor. She saw them all clearly now. She saw everything clearly. She was suddenly deliriously happy that Harvey had not wanted her enough. It had been fun. It had been more than that, perhaps. But it had never been something to re-shape her life, splinter her secret self, vanquish her dreams.

Now she saw everything. Eyes, lips, hands, movements. She saw Harvey spill some wine, saw the major-general's hand move under the girl's skirt, saw Philomena dabbing her lips daintily. She returned her father's wink, decided that it *was* Betty Grable with the fliers and, at the same time noticed, fascinated, that Ryder moved his hands with a deft economy that was almost like precision machinery. Through the meal she watched him covertly.

Her father was explaining to Frank that there was room in the Civil Service for both himself and Phil, that they ought to move.

"It's the wrong time, surely?" Frank said. "At the end of the war?"

Croft laughed. "It's exactly the right time. The civil service has had a taste of expansion and loves it. Once it's over there'll be no stopping them. They'll have ministries for things you haven't dreamed of."

Ronnie yawned nervously. Harvey had his arm along the back of her chair. He had lit a cigar. She thought there was nothing left to recognise of the man she had made love with all summer. "Next week," she told him, "You'll be glad of a Woodbine, a cheese sandwich and a cup of Army tea. How will you like them apples?" Harvey gestured happily, blowing out a cloud of smoke. "If the second edition of the brave new world is anything like the first, I'll still be better off," he said cheerfully. "At least I'll be sure of my creature comforts. Who knows, it may be the best of both worlds. Neither threadbare civilian nor risk-taking serviceman." He stood up, asked Croft to order the coffee and transfer to the lounge and excused himself.

"I'll come with you," Willi stood up. "Me, too," Frank said.

Harvey led the way. He looked back at Willi once and Willi had the impression he was on the point of saying something. Instead a small silence grew between them. Willi's conscience was clear. So far, nothing had happened with Ronnie with which Harvey could reproach him.

Two lines of mirrored basins were almost all free. They washed briefly. Willi was preoccupied. He saw no-one else until it was too late.

"Ryder! My dear chap, there you are again. How extraordinary to see you again so soon."

Fairbrother. Nodding and smiling benignly, turning from the opposite side of the room, hands held up like a surgeon scrubbing up.

Willi, taken completely by surprise, could not disguise his shock. At once he was aware of Harvey's interest, somewhere just behind him. He murmured something suitable.

"What a surprise," Fairbrother repeated. "Still, see you shortly, eh? We'll have that meeting." He gave a series of short laughs, shot his cuffs, adjusted his tie in a mirror and was gone.

"Friend of yours?" Harvey murmured.

"Works—in my department," Willi said briefly. He was shaken and wanted to get away. It was clear that Fairbrother had arranged the incident simply to demonstrate his ability to put his finger on Willi at any moment, anywhere. It was effective as far as it went. A second-rate private detective could do as much. Fairbrother no doubt had superior talents, but he wasn't omnipotent. It ought not to be difficult to lose him tomorrow sometime.

Ronnie was waiting for him outside, looking about anxiously. She pulled him round a corner of the corridor. Out of sight she suddenly took both his hands.

"Next week . . ." she said.

"Yes?"

"You'll call me?"

Willi shook his head, dazzled and distracted.

Ronnie was puzzled. "You're married?"

"No."

"In love?"

"Hardly."

She pressed his hands between her own. "We have only a few moments," she said flatly. "Tell me you like me."

"I like you."

"And so?"

Willi shifted uncomfortably. Seconds yawned between them. "I'm . . . bad news." He realised he'd heard that line in a film.

Ronnie hesitated. "You're in trouble?" It was as if she told herself: 'I knew it.'

"Yes."

"What kind?"

"The worst kind."

"I'll help."

"Impossible."

She looked at him helplessly. "Who are you?"

"Bill Ryder."

She shook her head impatiently. "You know what I mean. There's something . . . I don't know, something about you that's different—very different. Why do I know that, and not the others?"

Willi said, troubled. "If you want to help, please don't say that to anyone else. Especially to someone like your father."

"He would help."

"Believe me, no-one can." Willi was growing restive. If anyone came to look for them how would this corridor tête-à-tête be explained?

Ronnie touched his arm. A man with the engorged face of the hard drinker and a woman, bony and submissive, rustled by in evening clothes, glancing at them curiously.

Ronnie watched them out of sight. "If it's that bad," she urged, "you need a friend. Will you call me?"

Willi considered quickly. He didn't want to think about next week. Tonight, tomorrow, Fairbrother. Those were his

214

immediate problems. Yet there was a tiny note of good sense in what Ronnie was saying. He *did* need a friend. But how could he see her again and not involve her? Impossible. And there was risk enough in that, even with Ronnie Croft. The only good German is a dead German. It wasn't only the working class who believed that.

"Yes," he said finally.

She appeared satisfied. She pressed his arm. "Go on back," she said softly.

As she spoke, Fairbrother reappeared, as if from nowhere, moving fast. He nodded at Willi, smiled politely at Ronnie as he passed. A new anxiety stabbed at Willi. Had Fairbrother heard anything?

Go on back? His instinct was to run. Now, tonight. From Fairbrother. From Ronnie, even.

His legs took him back to the glass doors to the bar. He smiled as he pushed through. There was no sense running blind. Fairbrother might find him anyway, but if he was to stand a chance he would need every asset he'd been able to assemble. And everything he had in the world was at Frank's place.

35

Sunday morning. Bill Ryder had been gone an hour already, refusing even help as far as the station with his bags. Once the front door had closed behind him the Eastcote house had resumed its oppressive loneliness. Frank couldn't get used to the idea that he was on his own again, even if it was only for a short time. He gloomed about the house, twice checking that his lodger had left nothing behind in his room. The silence was so irritating he switched on the radio for the Forces programme to cheer himself up, then switched it off again because he couldn't hear himself think.

About eleven the phone rang. Frank brightened, hoping it was Phil; he'd be able to tell her what had happened and perhaps even get her to come over.

"Good morning." It wasn't Phil. Instead it was a cheerful,

cultured, male voice. "I wonder if I might have a word with Mr Ryder."

"I'm sorry. He's not here," Frank said.

"Ah. I thought perhaps Sunday morning might be a good time to catch him."

"It would be normally. But he's left I'm afraid." There was a long silence at the other end of the line. Less cheerfully, the voice said: "I would very much have liked to talk to him today. Did he perhaps say where he was going?"

"Sorry, no. No forwarding address. He did say he'd ring or write when he was settled. Anything I can do? A message, if he should ring? Are you a colleague of his?"

"Thank you, no." The caller hung up.

Frank decided to ring Phil anyway once he'd tidied the house. He needed to talk to her about their appearance in the office tomorrow for one thing, and for another he wanted to tell her about Bill Ryder. One less at the wedding.

The speed of it all still bothered him. Bill had said nothing until they got in from the Savoy. They had been fairly high and pretty well numb with all that drink. And then the evening had to end like that.

"Frank, I know this is short notice, but I have to leave tomorrow. Early."

Frank was hanging onto the kettle, coaxing it to boil for a last cup of tea. He looked up, astonished. "Leave? Move on, you mean."

"Exactly that. Move on. It's a change of jobs. Or rather something I have to do out of town."

"Tomorrow!"

"Yes. I'm sorry. It'll throw you out, I know."

"You'll be able to make Thursday, surely?"

"No. I'm sorry. There it is."

"Orders?" Frank nodded.

"Orders."

He'd taken a big breath as the disappointment finally hit him. "Oh Jesus!" Then it had occurred to him that Bill might not be exactly delighted either. "Well never mind about us. We'll get along. What will *you* do for a pillow?"

"I expect they'll find something for me."

"Good job you weren't my best man," Frank said. "Here, have this tea. Your gut will be delighted after all that hard stuff. What sort of time do you want to be off?"

"Let's say right after breakfast."

Frank had meant to ask if he knew where he was being sent. Probably he wouldn't have been able to say, in any case. Everything was secret these days.

There was some comfort now in going from room to room tidying in case Phil agreed to come over. He considered. She'd have made plans for her own lunch, so he'd better have something himself. He passed the vacuum cleaner lightly over the hall and living room, then took it up to Bill's room. Pulling out the dressing table to clean behind it he found Bill's family photograph in its unsteady metal frame. He didn't look at it. Bill had always kept it there. It had probably skittered off the back of the dressing table when Bill opened a drawer. He'd be upset not to have it. When he went downstairs he put the picture in an envelope and scribbled Bill's name on the front. Right, then! Lunch. He put the cleaner away and looked in the meat safe. Meat safe! That was a joke these days. There were some pieces of stewing lamb, part of which was Bill's by rights because it was their joint ration for the week. He put the radio back on again while he fudged together some sort of casserole and put it into the oven. His mind kept going back to Bill's bombshell announcement. At one point he'd said, accusingly: "You might have said something earlier . . ."

"Before we went out? And spoil the night of nights?"

And later: "Any chance of coming back?" He thought Bill had looked sceptical at first, then suddenly optimistic. "It's possible. But you'll have Phil here then. Who needs a third party around the place when they're newly married?"

"Oh balls!" Frank said. "You know we'd love to have you. There's three bedrooms, for God's sake. One for you, one for us and one for sound insulation." He grinned lewdly. "Anyway, come back if you can. Do us a favour."

So that was it. Breakfast. A handshake and he was away. Funny how he missed Bill about the place. Two men living together could work sometimes. About now, he thought, they would be going down to the pub together. He thought about going anyway. Best not. His stomach had had enough.

The radio was making such a noise he almost missed the doorbell.

Frank recognised the man on the doorstep at once. It was the one Bill had spoken to in the washroom at the Savoy last night. Neat little chap. Bowler hat, city clothes, the sort of man you half expected to be wearing spats.

"Mr Marsh?" It was not quite a question.

"Yes?"

"My name is Jerome. I wonder if I might have a word with you?"

"Certainly." Frank made no move to open the door. "Are you the one that rang a while back?"

"Yes I am. I'm most awfully sorry to have to disturb you twice on a Sunday morning like this. The matter is urgent."

"Well, as I've already said," Frank shrugged. "I have no idea where you'll find Ryder now. There's no way I can help."

Fairbrother nodded gently, good humour crinkling the corners of his honest grey eyes. "Well," he said, "I think you'll find you can, actually." He made a move forwards so that Frank backed off, opening the door for him.

Fairbrother needed information badly. He accepted that Willi had left without a forwarding address. It was bitter gall, but he accepted it. He could not accept, though, that there were no leads of any kind. It had been a mistake to let Reiter run with the hook already in him. He might now shake it off altogether and then he'd be back where he started. The intention had simply been to show Reiter that his situation was desperate and that it was futile to run. The Savoy incident had shown, or should have shown, that he, Fairbrother, had put his finger on him all the way.

But he had mishandled the thing. He had been overconfident. It was not, simply, that his demonstration of omnipotence in turning up at the Savoy like that had not worked. He had also reasoned that Reiter, given time to consider his position, would decide that even if he paid over the money Fairbrother had asked for, there would be no guarantee that he would be free from there on—that his pursuer might easily take the money from him and still collect his pay as an assassin. No, letting Reiter run free to think it over had been, as much as anything, a gesture of good faith. It was the con man's basic device to instil confidence. Why, Reiter *should* have reasoned, was he given a chance to run at all if the offer were not genuine? Why not just insist on the money at once and double-cross him afterwards?

But Reiter had not thought that way. He had looked, and sounded, as if he had given in. He had sounded defeated, resigned and willing to pay when Fairbrother left him to continue his walk. Either he had got his nerve back rather quickly, or he hadn't meant to pay anyway. Fairbrother had learned a lesson he would never forget. Never again. He'd had Reiter in his hands and let him slip. Even now the postcard could be on its way to Dublin . . .

"Come in here," Frank said. He led the way through to the kitchen. The warm, encouraging smell of the casserole was heavy in the air. "Hang on a tick, I forgot to salt my casserole. Have a seat, Mr—"

"Jerome," Fairbrother supplied. He sat down at the small kitchen table, laid his bowler hat down on the cloth and Stella by the side of it.

Frank retrieved his casserole, salted it and put it back. He adjusted the thermostat on the oven and turned to look at his visitor. The glossy little man made the kitchen look drab, he thought. That ebony stick, with the silver leaves at the top. A nice thing. It looked very fine lying there on the old red chenille table cover. He was conscious, suddenly, of the hideous whale-shaped inkstain right in the centre. It had been there, oh, fifteen years it must be, since Harvey sat there as a lad, night after night, wrestling with his homework.

"Now, then . . ."

"I'm afraid," Fairbrother said gently, "that I must ask you some questions." He smiled apologetically.

Frank was startled. "Police?"

"Not . . . quite," Fairbrother said judiciously.

"Security!" Frank guessed.

"Something of the sort."

Frank nodded. "May I see your credentials?"

"No," Fairbrother said firmly. He decided to bluff it through. "You may not. I'm very much afraid that you'll have to take me on trust. In my line of—ah—business, we are scarcely likely to carry warrant cards and the like."

Frank thought about it. There was a brief silence. "Well," he said at last, "it depends on the questions. If they're about Bill Ryder I may have to disappoint you. I like Bill—a lot."

"Possibly," Fairbrother said. "I wonder, though, if you would have liked him if you had known who he is."

"Who he is?" Frank laughed. "He's Bill Ryder. Some sort of civil servant. Though he'd never quite say what sort. I rather thought you and he were colleagues."

Fairbrother shook his head slowly. His smile was sad.

"Not a colleague? Not a civil servant?"

"Not even Bill Ryder."

Frank was too surprised to respond immediately. The

219

statement was not just astonishing. If it was true, he thought, then Bill lied to all of us. How did he feel about that? He didn't know, yet. Was it true? And if it was, could Bill have had his reasons?

"So you see," Fairbrother was saying, "I'm afraid I'll have to insist on your answering some questions."

"Insist?" Frank bristled. He got up and turning his back on Fairbrother stood for a moment looking out of the window into the back yard. Marie Gilchrist was at the end of her garden, hanging a blanket on the line to dry. Her breasts strained interestingly upward and outward as she pegged at the thing, and he liked the way her short sweater rode up, exposing several inches of creamy midriff. He smiled at his own randiness and turned back to his visitor. He didn't know what to say. So he said: "Insist all you like."

Fairbrother shook his head sadly. "Now, now, Mr Marsh, you're being foolish. If you won't answer me, you'll answer in custody. And in time of war, who knows how many kinds of charge might be brought against you under the Defence of the Realm regulations." Marsh, he thought, didn't look the kind who would take much intimidating. He was mildly surprised at the spirited reaction so far. So if he was going to bluff he had to do it fairly strongly.

Frank, however, was unmoved. "Balls!" he said. "The war is nearly over. What are you threatening me with? The Tower? What I'm asking is reasonable. How do I know you have the right to ask anyone anything? Show me, even, that you have some identity card from some Ministry and I'll concede your right to come in here chucking your weight about. If you can't, no-one is going to charge me with anything for simply being careful. It's my duty to be careful. For all I know, it's you who are suspect. I do know that Bill Ryder worked on something fairly secret."

Frank decided he didn't like Jerome, or whatever his name was. Smooth little bugger. Too smooth.

Fairbrother said equably. "I understand your reactions," he said. "You're right to be suspicious, as you say. I can see that I will have to take you into my confidence a little . . ." He rubbed his chin thoughtfully. It was too bad about Marsh. It was tiresome, it was messy, unnecessary and exasperating— but Marsh would have to die.

He was into the algebra of it again. There were two possibilities still. One was that Marsh knew perfectly well

220

who Ryder was. In which case Marsh would perhaps reveal that somehow, if he could be kept talking. If, on the other hand, he did not know, then it was inconceivable that Reiter had lived here closely with Marsh without making some small, revealing slips which, though insignificant while his role as Ryder went unchallenged, would raise immediate doubts in Marsh's mind once he was told the truth about the man.

"Bill Ryder," Fairbrother said slowly, "doesn't exist, Mr Marsh. Your lodger's name was Willi Reiter. That's spelt R-e-i-t-e-r." He watched closely and was at once rewarded by Marsh's expression of total shock and bewilderment.

"Bill?" was all Frank could manage. And then: "A German? Is that what you're saying? Good God! A spy?"

"No. Not a spy. If I tell you a little more, will you agree to answer one simple question for me? I don't have a lot of time to go through the procedures for forcing you to answer. One department to another—that alone could cost as much as twenty-four hours' delay. I don't have that kind of time to spare." His tone was reasonable, but guarded. "You agree?"

Frank nodded, dumbly.

"Very well. Reiter is a Luftwaffe officer. Quite simply he is the pilot of a Focke-Wulf fighter aircraft which crash-landed on the Berkshire Downs some weeks back. He was a bomber pilot. If it makes any difference he took part in some of the first heavy night bombing of London and other cities. He was decorated for it. He also knows England, and lived here before the war. Indeed, his mother was English." He could see that he was getting through to Marsh now. It was almost possible to watch Marsh's mind reviewing what little he knew of 'Bill Ryder'. "Now," he went on, "doesn't something of this sit with what you know of the man? Were there not some . . . differences between 'Bill Ryder' and most other people, now that you come to think of it?"

"What's he doing here?" Frank ignored that.

"Will you answer one question first?"

"Go ahead."

"When, how and where did you meet him?"

"My son, Harvey, met him—in Berkshire, as it happens. Come to think of it, they both—" Frank stopped and chewed his lip "—saw that plane come down," he finished lamely.

Fairbrother uttered a short laugh, a bark almost, of triumph.

"It was a chance meeting? Neither of you knew him before this event?"

"No. He happened to mention to Harvey that he was looking for a room. Harvey knew I wanted to let one, so he gave him my number." Frank was feeling dazed. He couldn't quite believe that this was all happening.

"What's he doing here?" Frank repeated.

Fairbrother said nothing until he thought Marsh had recovered and was paying full attention. "We believe he's harmless," he said. And then: "One theory is that he is escaping his own people."

They sat on in silence. Marsh appeared to be preoccupied. He was looking out of the window again. Fairbrother was grateful. Before he made any other move he wanted to check his algebra once more quickly. First, Marsh must die. Was that inevitable? Yes. Because Reiter's identity was a commodity in which he, Fairbrother, could not deal. He couldn't share the revelation with Marsh, who might, if left alive, at any moment decide to tell the police about both Reiter and what he'd been told—and about himself. The latter wouldn't be too dangerous. He hadn't used his own name. But it was surprising, sometimes, what the police could do with an intelligent description and an alias. He didn't want that risk. More importantly, his deal with Reiter would be threatened, perhaps even pre-empted. Then there was Reiter himself. Fairbrother was satisfied now that there was only an accidental connection between Reiter and the Marshes, so he was unlikely to return here. However, if for any reason Reiter was caught by the police or security men as a result of information laid by the elder Marsh, it was fairly certain that Reiter would assume he had been double-crossed by Fairbrother and in his turn reveal Fairbrother's trade. Even if he did not, and even if he simply ended up, perhaps with some relief, in a German POW camp somewhere in the country, Reiter would immediately come within reach of whoever he had offended in Berlin. That was an old story. Once more, at the very least, he, Fairbrother, would lose his deal.

Finally, if he concentrated now on finding Reiter and actually succeeded quickly, there was always the chance—if he left Marsh alive—that the death would be reported, that Marsh would remember it and decide to tell the story of his Sunday-morning with a 'security' man.

Fairbrother was upset. He did not like killing. It caused him no great pang of conscience. But each time was a danger. He stood up, lifting the stick from the table. He settled it in his hand, the silver knob in his palm, the first and second fingers braced under the silver ferns, like a giant syringe.

"You have been very foolish, Mr Marsh," he said. "Even now I am not sure that there will not be some charge preferred against you, though naturally I shall be able to say that you collaborated with me satisfactorily." He picked up his bowler with his left hand. The stick swung in his right.

Frank turned, frowning. He said indignantly: "But he had an identity card and ration book! How was I to know?"

Fairbrother froze. Ration book. Of course. He shivered a little at the thought that he might have made a serious blunder. "You have the ration book?"

Frank shook his head. "Of course not! He took it with him."

Fairbrother was satisfied. He took one, two steps towards the door as if to leave, then turned sharply back. Frank had made to follow him out.

"Don't bother to see me out," he said blandly. He raised the stick, found the right spot on Marsh's chest and gave him a little push with it.

Frank Marsh had time to look down in astonishment at the stick. He had a moment in which to be surprised and indignant at the arrogance of the gesture. His hand even began to travel upward.

At that moment, Fairbrother clenched his right hand. There was a heavy metallic thump.

Frank heard it. It was the last thing he heard. His eyes glazed and closed in a moment of agony. Eight inches of fine steel, burying itself in his chest with stunning force, penetrated the costal cartilage and sliced into the muscle and tissue of the left ventricle of his heart. He made no sound. His legs buckled and he was dead when he hit the floor. His weight, pulling on the blade, jerked Fairbrother forward, causing him to stumble. But the blade was free when he regained his balance.

Fairbrother straightened up, his breathing only slightly affected. The blade looked clean enough, but he wiped it carefully on a corner of the chenille table cloth.

He picked a spot on the floor, pointed Stella's tip at it, and leaning with both hands on the knob, pressed heavily down against the ferocious spring. The blade clicked back into place. From his pocket he took a tough rubber ferrule and covered the end.

223

Fairbrother picked up his hat. He looked round, reminding himself not to hurry. From the front room window he looked out at the street cautiously. A group of young people, the girls wearing Sunday coats with the hideously square shoulders of the current fashion, were ambling down the street one way. An elderly man, with a senile bull terrier panting two paces behind him, took some minutes to pass out of sight in the other direction. Fairbrother watched until the street was quite clear. Then he stepped smartly out onto the doorstep, pulling the door closed behind him.

At the gate he checked again. A woman opposite had opened her door and was coming out. Or was she?

Too late, Fairbrother recognised the lone and vulnerable Mrs Flax. He could not turn back. He hesitated only briefly. He tipped his hat in recognition and crossed the street to her slantwise.

"Hullo," she called when he was still some yards from her gate.

Fairbrother smiled pleasantly. He opened the gate.

"You didn't find her then?" she said.

"Mrs Flax, isn't it?" Fairbrother purred. "No. I'm still on the trail though, I'm afraid."

Mrs Flax looked at him oddly. "I didn't think Mr Marsh could help you. I told you that."

"I had to be sure," Fairbrother said apologetically. He looked up and down the street. It was still clear.

"They do keep you working, don't they?" she said. "Even on a Sunday!"

"Well, of course, that's the time when most people are at home," Fairbrother muttered. He had to get inside somehow. He was frantically framing something when the woman added:

"You wouldn't like a cup of tea, would you?" She said it too quickly, meaning to be casual but somehow not managing it. "Only I've just made myself one."

"I couldn't think of intruding on you and your family like this—on a Sunday, too," Fairbrother said. But he was already moving up the path.

"Haw!" Mrs Flax made a yelping sound of derision. "I'm on my own. Mr Flax died, oh," she said airily, "years and years ago."

Fairbrother hadn't time to pretend indecision. "Thanks—that's awfully kind," he said. "You lead the way."

224

Mrs Flax let him in, closed the door and moved on down the hall past him. "This way," she said.

She took only a few steps. Fairbrother removed the ferrule, aimed the stick a little to the right of the curve of her left shoulderblade. There was no time for finesse, but he was lucky. He squeezed. The spring blade impaled Mrs Flax in mid-stride. She fell forward. She had a moment in which to say "Oh" in a soft tone such as she might have used in surprise to find herself wearing the wrong spectacles.

This time Fairbrother was rattled. Damn silly woman! If she had stayed inside, if she had not seen him leave the Marsh house, she would be alive now enjoying her tea.

Stepping over her body, he moved cautiously toward the kitchen. Keeping well away from the window, he angled himself to look out on the gardens at either side. Both were empty and quiet. On the table, just as Mrs Flax had said, a brown teapot with a knitted cover fitting it like a dog's jacket, sat next to two cups and a jug of milk.

He poured himself half a cup, added milk and drank it down. He was annoyed with himself when he recognised that he had a dry mouth. Perhaps he was getting too old for this sort of thing after all.

He stepped over Mrs Flax again on the way out. She looked very peaceful, her head resting on her sprawled right arm.

The street was still empty. He walked rapidly towards Eastcote station. It was impossible for him not to feel that he had made more problems than he had solved.

36

When his phone rang on Sunday night, Ted Gilchrist was standing in his garden; just standing there in the dark, delighted with being able to see lights in the windows of most of his neighbours. Except when the sirens sounded, the blackout was over. It was a real milestone. The beginning of the end, and more heartening than all the grandiose words being pumped out now by the propaganda machine about the new Britain they were all going to enjoy and all the marvellous privileges this man Beveridge had dreamed up for them.

Marie came to the French window. "For you, Ted. It's Harvey."

Gilchrist was surprised. He'd known Harvey since he was a lad, but never once had he called him on the phone.

"I'm sorry to bother you Mr Gilchrist," Harvey said. "I'm worried about Dad. I've been calling him all day, but he doesn't answer the phone. For a start—you haven't had any bombs out there, have you?"

"Nothing old son. Not a thing. Couldn't be that. What you've probably done is missed him this morning while he was at the pub and again this evening."

"No," Harvey said. "I called several times this afternoon, too. The thing is that I thought he might be with his fiancée, but when I rang she was worried, too, that she couldn't get through."

"His what!" Gilchrist howled.

"His fiancée! He hadn't told you? Oh, Dad's getting married on Thursday. In fact we had a sort of party last night to celebrate. But look, the oddest thing is—if everything's all right, why doesn't his lodger, Bill Ryder, answer?"

"Well they could be out together, of course," Gilchrist said reasonably. "That's good news about your Dad getting married. I was only saying to Marie a couple of weeks back that he'd been on his own far too long. Marie will be pleased."

"Great, yes." Harvey said. No bombs. He was tempted to let it go. Though he had promised Phil he'd ring with some news or reassurance. "Still, it is odd, Dad not answering. I wonder—just to ease both our minds—if you'd mind taking a look?"

"Might as well be on the safe side," Gilchrist agreed. "Give me the number you're at, and I'll call you back in a bit—save you hanging on."

Gilchrist took the number and hung up, shaking his head. He looked into the kitchen where Marie was pickling onions. "Here listen, Frank's getting married again. On Thursday, would you believe? That'll suit you. A new neighbour to fuss over." He took his old torch down from the hook above the boiler. "Harvey can't get him on the phone and he's worried about him." He grinned. "I suppose he thinks the excitement may have seen the randy old bugger off. Won't be a minute."

Frank had never been known to lock his back door. Gilchrist walked the length of his own garden. In the early days of the war, he and Frank had dug the pits for both Anderson shelters as one, back to back, taking away a section of the fence. It had been a useful idea to join forces with the labour and at the same time provide an alternative way out if either of the houses sustained a direct hit. Now Gilchrist simply walked up the slope of his own shelter, across the top of Frank's and down the other side. The smell of Frank's honeysuckle was strong in the cool night air.

There were no lights showing in the house. So both of them were probably out, he reasoned.

The back door was unlocked. Gilchrist opened it and stepped into the dark kitchen. "Frank!" he called out. He listened but there was no sound except the ticking of the kitchen clock.

The light switch for the kitchen was in the same spot as his own—across the room, by the hall door. He pinpointed it with the narrow beam of his torch and moved towards it. At once he tripped and fell headlong, catching his forehead on one corner of the kitchen table and knowing, with instant crawling fear, that he had tripped on a body. He let out a small, stifled scream and scrambled up, scrabbling at the wall for the door and switch. He put the light on.

Frank Marsh lay on his back, eyes wide, mouth slightly open baring tobacco-stained teeth, quite unmistakably dead. The face didn't altogether look like Frank at all. The lips, drawn back, gave the mouth a snarling, almost fierce appearance.

Gilchrist stood quite still, staring, and adjusting to his old friend's death. He had been in the BEF in France during the First World War and was used to death. Even so it took him a moment or two to recover his composure. Frank's skin was yellow-white. He had been dead for some time. No sense calling an ambulance. The police . . .

He looked closer. Frank's cardigan, unbuttoned, had ridden up over a considerable red stain on his white shirt. Gilchrist thought it looked like a knife wound rather than gunshot. He bent to touch the cheek. Ice-cold. He drew his fingers over the eyes, but they remained stubbornly half open.

Gilchrist went through to the hall, put on a light there, checked the other rooms. It was odd, but the spare room, Bill Ryder's, was as bare as if he had gone. There were no clothes, no personal effects, nothing.

Gilchrist returned to his own house the way he'd come. His own kitchen, bright and cheerful, was filled with the acrid fumes of spices and hot pickling vinegar.

"Put that down, Marie," he said. "And ring the police for

me. Frank is dead." He saw her eyes glaze and her mouth open wide with shock. He patted her on the back, sensing that if he said anything at all kindly she would let go. "Come on, girl. Get on to it. I'm going back to stay with him and I'll ring Harvey from there. All right?" The details would wait, he thought. He turned back through the door quickly so that she would have to cope.

37

His mind still cringing, Harvey went into that curious behavioural overdrive which, even in the shock of a confrontation with death, allows rational thinking and planning. His first action was to call Ronnie at the MOI.

For a moment after he had delivered the scant information he had, Harvey heard only the rattle of canteen plates and cutlery echoing down a suddenly cavernous-sounding line. Then for Ronnie too, the levers dropped and the emergency-only wheels began to turn. She asked no questions, but at once in a low voice said she would start out for Eastcote station within fifteen minutes—by car if she could find someone to break the law for her. With muzzy astonishment at himself, Harvey found himself able to think wryly that with Ronnie's looks half the men in the canteen would almost certainly forsake conscience and duty for her. He made no protest. It was one of those rare times when you need give no thought to selfishness. It would be good to have her there. He was reassured.

What next? He put his head in his hands and tried to cover his ears against the roar of the ABP newsroom. Ring McNair. One of the kids would have to take over. Grow-up time for someone. How would he get out to the house? Worry about that later. Which kid? He beckoned Dixon, the smoothie, and motioned for him to listen. He rang McNair. His wife, Dorothy, answered. McNair was playing bridge. She would fetch him, she said. She sounded more resigned, defeated than annoyed. That, of course, was what Ronnie had wanted to avoid: the long arm of the job.

"Mac?" he said shakily. "I don't know if I can say any of this twice. My father has been found dead at home." He hesitated only marginally before stepping round the word 'murdered'. "It is possible he was killed. A neighbour has called the police, but I have to go there and go now. I'm leaving Dixon on the Desk. Can you come, or cope or something?"

McNair was superb. "Sod the Desk," he said. This is dreadful, laddie. Right! Now tell Dixon to take over at once. Tell him it's now-or-never time for him. That's all there is to that problem. Next—how are you going to get to Eastcote? I'll tell you! You'll go out and get a cab to Earl's Court station. I'll start out now and meet you there and lift you on. Right, now get you gone." He hung up.

Impatiently, Harvey gave Dixon some instructions and set out to find a cab, grateful to McNair. He was in uniform. He'd worn it out of sheer vanity to impress his shift. They were impressed. He had the vague thought, as he hurried out into Fleet Street, that the uniform might be of some use now . . . With the police at the house? Or in simply staving off any question of using Pool petrol for a non-official journey?

McNair, coming from Richmond, arrived only a few moments behind Harvey's cab in his sleek blue and black Wolseley. They drove at reckless speed through Ealing and Harrow, saying nothing. Again Harvey was grateful. It gave him a chance to think. Where, then, was Ryder—that Frank should have lain dead for so long? He realised he knew very little about Ryder or his habits. Perhaps he always came home in the small hours. Come to think of it, he didn't even know if Ryder worked office hours or shifts. But he still felt an unreasonable irritation that Ryder should be out of the house on this particular day; if he'd been there perhaps whatever had happened might not have. He shook his head, dazedly. There were too many questions, too little information. Ryder might have arrived by now.

"Direct me from the station," McNair said quietly. He peered ahead into the dark of the deserted, Sunday-night, empty, lonely-looking, sodium-lit suburban streets, his bony cheeks and jutting forehead grimly intent.

Turning into Lindsey Gardens, McNair drew up outside the wrong house—attracted by a knot of police and a patrol car in a tableau of activity under the blazing lights of No. 24, across the street. What were they doing there? Bewildered, Harvey indicated his own old home and began his thanks.

229

"I'll wait here," McNair told him. "You can't dismiss me. And anyway, you don't know yet what I might be able to help with." Harvey nodded "Here . . ." McNair held something out to him. He took it. It was a hip flask.

Ronnie was there. She had heard the car and come out onto the step, her arms out to him. He embraced her briefly. Over her shoulder he saw Ted Gilchrist hovering.

"Better come into the front room," Gilchrist said. "The police are all over the kitchen. They don't want anyone in there for a bit. But I'll tell the man in charge that you're here."

38

The kitchen was full of police and police specialists. Harvey had tried to get round the door but it was standing-room only. Now he was sitting at the big table in the dining room with a Detective Chief Inspector opposite him and a shorthand writer over in one corner. Harvey was having difficulty holding to the essentials. The gross bulk of the man fascinated him. When he sat down, Edith's solid mahogany Victorian dining chair had groaned and he kept wanting to warn the man that if he leaned his weight against the curved back it would snap off because it was only dowelled in; that all the chairs had been mended a dozen times. The man's name was Ainslie, he remembered. He tried to get his mind off the chair back and on to something else. He fixed on Edith's cracked peach-coloured Venetian glass fruit bowl, which, ever since Harvey could remember, had stood in the exact centre of a gold runner which was exactly the width of the table's centre-panel when the gate-leg sides were let down. The bowl had left a faded circle where it sat on the runner. Why faded, he wondered. Why not darker?

It was late. It had been a long wait. Ted Gilchrist had gone next door and brought back Marie. Marie had made tea first for them and then for the police. Ronnie was outside in the car with McNair. That much Harvey knew. The rest was a blur. He wanted to get up and turn off the overhead light and turn on the side lamps but was afraid that it would seem frivolous to Ainslie and his shorthand man. His head ached and he could not believe, at all, that Frank was dead. He had tried McNair's flask, but it was full of brandy, which always gave him heartburn. Or perhaps it was the cigarettes. He had been smoking incessantly and they were awful. He'd sent a copy boy out earlier in the evening—this evening?—yes, only this evening—and he'd come back with Sunripe, the one brand he disliked even more than Frank's old Goldflake. He smiled a little, thinking of his father's obsession with Goldflake. At one time he had been livid when he'd been unable to get them. "The war only became real for you the first time you had to smoke something else," he'd once told his father.

Harvey realised that Ainslie was looking at him, waiting patiently. For so big a man—but why should only small and medium-sized men have a monopoly?—Ainslie, was, he realised, an unusually sensitive one. He seemed to know exactly the pace at which they ought to go.

They had been through Harvey's movements carefully but apologetically. And what Harvey knew of the domestic arrangements at Lindsey Gardens during the time Ryder had been there. Together they had looked at Bill's room. There was no doubt. All his things had gone. Ryder had gone.

Ainslie said now: "So you were with Ryder last night? At the Savoy?" He said it in the recording, non-committal tones of a doctor entering facts about his patient's bowel movements.

"We all were. We had this party, as I said."

"And then Mr Marsh came home with Ryder?"

"I assume so," Harvey said. He wondered why it was Mister Marsh but plain Ryder. What did Ainslie know?

"And up to that point, neither Ryder nor your father had said anything about Ryder leaving?"

"No. I expected him to be here tonight. I even expected him to have turned up—" Harvey shrugged "—half an hour ago. He could still come in, any minute. Or perhaps he's away for a day or two."

"Taking all his things? Everything?"

Harvey conceded the point. "That is odd."

There was a pause. Ainslie said: "Of course we can assume nothing. But one thing is clear. We do need to talk to Ryder as soon as possible, if only to establish when and why he left and that he had nothing to do with—" he gestured, "all this." And then: "And so suddenly, it would seem, if nothing was said to you."

"Yes." It was the only comment Harvey could muster.

"And you can't suggest where we might begin looking for him?"

"No. I only met him by chance, you know. In the country. In Berkshire, specifically. During a short holiday with Miss Croft. You've met her? We got to talking. He told me he was thinking of coming to London for a while. When he asked if I had any suggestions about accommodation in London, or just outside, I gave him my father's number here."

Ainslie nodded. "You don't know where he works?"

"I don't. My father told me once or twice he thought Bill was a civil servant of some sort. He used to joke about Bill being very secretive about exactly what he did."

Ainslie asked for a description and set himself to note it down very carefully. Harvey thought about it, making an effort, and came up with: age about 28 or 30, 150 pounds, height about six feet, fairish colouring and hair, squarish cleanshaven features and a limp.

"A limp?" Ainslie looked astonished.

Harvey couldn't help smiling. "Yes. He limped."

"Why do I keep saying 'was' and 'did'? He's not dead." He forgot for a moment what he was saying. "Bill Ryder limps with his left leg. He has a piece of tinplate in it, I think. A car accident before the war, he told me. It made him unfit for war service." He watched Ainslie enter it in his tiny notebook with a gold pen squeezed tightly in his huge fist. Harvey fought down a sickly grin. "Bit of a policeman's dream that, isn't it? A limp. The limping man and all that." He frowned suddenly. "Or would be, in a suspect. But he isn't is he?" He hoped not.

"I don't know," Ainslie said. "It's early days." He looked up mildly. "Do you think he is?"

"No!" Harvey said emphatically.

"Why?" Ainslie looked up at once.

Harvey thought about it. "I suppose I said that because I like him." It sounded feeble, so he added: "Another thing is they got on so well together, he and Frank. I gathered from Dad he was an ideal lodger. He fell in with anything Dad proposed. They would go down to the pub together in the evenings—and on Sunday mornings . . ."

Ainslie murmured, encouragingly.

"Then again, you know how it is, it's hard to say quite why people get on. I certainly saw that Bill—Ryder—liked Dad." He saw Ainslie's eyebrows shoot up. "I know it's only a short time. But you can tell things like that. One person likes another and they watch that person when they speak, smile while they're speaking, seem to enjoy what's said. If there's either antipathy or nothing that doesn't happen."

"Fine," Ainslie said. "We'll assume a good relationship." He made another note. Then looked up as if to open a fresh chapter. "Did Ryder know Mrs Flax?"

Harvey frowned. "What is this about Mrs Flax? You said you'd tell me later. It is later."

Ainslie rubbed his forehead, leaving red marks. "There isn't a lot to tell. An inquest will reveal more. But . . . Mrs Flax is dead. She was killed about the same time as your father. That's an estimate, of course." He breathed heavily down his nose. "What more? Well, the wound she died from— or the only suggested cause of death at the moment at any rate—is similar to your father's." He looked as if he would have liked to leave it there, and then added shortly. "A long knife, perhaps."

The thought set Harvey back considerably. "It's unbelievable," he said jaggedly. He shook his head helplessly. "Just so—fucking unbelievable."

"*Did* Ryder know her?"

"I wouldn't have thought so."

"Was she ever a visitor to this house?"

"Not that I know of. Frank wouldn't have liked that much."

Ainslie inclined his head.

"Well, Dad sometimes—" he choked momentarily on the thought of Frank's obscene comments on Mrs Flax, poor old sod "—he would often say that she fancied moving in here— being a widow . . ." He bit his lip, unable to go on.

Ainslie got up. Was he being diplomatic? "Hang on a moment, will you, Mr Marsh." Harvey heard him open the front door and trudge across the street. Why? What had he said? Did he imagine that Frank and Mrs Flax had somehow stabbed each other and then staggered back to their respective houses to lie down and die? The edge of hysteria flicked at him.

It was all fantastic. And yet—Frank was dead. And Mrs Flax. And Ryder was gone. Bill Ryder? Harvey summoned the image of the smiling man he knew very little about. He was having difficulty in hanging on to the impressions he'd sustained to date. One minute a quiet, amiable, unassuming man lodged happily with his father—and the next a bloody maniac? How could that be true? On the other hand, where the hell was he? And why? When?

The shorthand writer was looking at him compassionately. "Won't be long now, I shouldn't think."

Harvey got up and walked through to the kitchen. The police seemed to have finished in there. Ronnie was sitting with Marie and Noah, close up to the little broiler. It was chilly out and they'd got it alight. They looked up at him anxiously, waiting for him to speak first. Harvey said nothing. He carefully avoided looking at the floor. He didn't know if there had been blood, but he didn't want to look in case. The red table cover was gone, for some reason. He went to stand outside the back door for a few moments, breathing deeply. There were signs of grey light on the horizon. He looked at his watch. It was four, or near enough.

"I must go and see McNair," Harvey said on his way through again. "There's nothing he can do." Ronnie touched his hand softly as he passed and gravely watched him go.

He gave McNair back his flask. "Good stuff that, thanks. I'll be staying here, I think, but you go, will you, Mac? There's nothing you can do." McNair didn't argue. Simply sat up straighter and waited.

"I'm grateful," Harvey insisted. "If you bugger off it will be one less thing for me to worry about. I wish you could take Ronnie, too, but I know if I try to send her I'll have a fight on my hands."

"Very wise," McNair said. He paused a moment and then added: "Look, you probably hadn't even thought about it. But when you get round to worrying about next Saturday—don't. We'll get you a new movement order from the War Office. All right?"

"Fine. And thanks again."

"You'd still want to go?"

Harvey gestured, suddenly too full to speak. After a pause he managed: "Of course. Even more so, perhaps."

McNair agreed: "It's best, I think, whatever the police find out. If there is anything you have to come back for, well, you can just come. I'll keep you in touch with every step, too. But what am I blathering about. All that can wait."

Satisfied, McNair looked to his front and the Wolseley moved away quietly. Harvey watched the tail light out of sight. Ainslie emerged from No. 24 and started back across the road.

Harvey didn't feel like beginning again at once, even if it was going to be short. He went down to the kitchen. He

234

wanted to say something to Ronnie, though he hadn't analysed why he wanted to say it.

He waited until he had her whole attention and then told her: "They want to find Bill Ryder. I think he's their prime suspect." He watched her face closely.

It was as if he had slapped her. She opened her mouth to say something and it closed again as if on a weak, slow spring. Even in his fuddled state, Harvey could see that the idea offended her deeply. And seeing it was himself silenced by the revelation of feelings that took him totally by surprise.

Ronnie flushed. "Absurd," she said tightly. She looked down at her spread hands, at the Croft-crested signet ring she always wore.

Harvey wanted to agree, but Ainslie's worm of doubt was already eating away inside him.

"I think that's a bit far-fetched," Ronnie said shakily. "Bill isn't here, where he's expected, that's all. There's probably a reason for that." She ventured a tight smile. "You can see that, can't you?"

For a slow count of five Harvey said nothing. Then, with a ragged edge of malice that surprised him even as he spoke, he said: "Yes, I do. I see that. If he shows up within 24 hours that is. Otherwise—" He cut off Bill Ryder's credibility with a curt, flat-handed gesture.

"You're tired," Ronnie said softly.

"Tired?" Harvey cackled querulously. "Yes, I'm tired." He nodded ponderously. "And so bloody sad and bitter and angry and vengeful I couldn't begin to tell you."

He turned about and stamped back into the dining room.

Ainslie was waiting. He looked up sympathetically. Harvey thought if anyone else looked at him with sympathy in the next half-hour he'd smash their bloody face in.

Ainslie let him settle, fidgeting with his little notebook and his pen, like a giant playing with the fiddly artifacts of a vanished race of midgets. He looked apologetic.

"I think I can skip some questions now," he said. "But there is one thing I'd like you to tell me . . ."

Harvey nodded dully.

"And if you wouldn't mind, Mr Marsh, I'd be grateful if you wouldn't repeat the question to anyone else outside this room."

"Right."

"And I don't want to elaborate in any way on the reason for

the question. I just want you to consider what I've asked and then give me a straight answer. Okay?"

Harvey gave him what he thought was the last gleam of his intelligence before fatigue and shock took over and drowned him, nodding to ram it home.

"Fine." Ainslie said. "The question is this . . ." He looked up into the air, as if to conceal anything on his jowly face that might offer a clue to Harvey. "Have you at any time . . . noticed anything at all about Mr Ryder . . . which either then or now . . . might have caused you to suppose that he might be not William Ryder at all, but perhaps someone else—someone not even British?"

39

After leaving Eastcote, Willi checked his bags into Left Luggage at Charing Cross, ate in a snack bar, rode the trains for a while trying to decide what to do next, and finally left a Circle train too late to claim a comfortable shelter space for the night.

Thousands were again packing into the Underground system for shelter. At their peak, flying bombs had fallen on London and the south-east at a rate of 100 to 150 a day. As their launch sites were overrun and the flying bombs dwindled away, evacuees had swarmed back into London. The blackout became a dim-out. But now a new menace had shattered the brief euphoria. Official statements spoke only of 'exploding gas mains'. Londoners enjoyed the flying gas main joke only for a day or two. Now they knew better. Giant rockets, moving faster than sound, seemed to be the new terror weapon. They arrived without warning. There was no looking up to watch and to decide if you were going to live. One minute you were there, and the next you and the whole street had vanished. There were fewer of the V-2's, as they were already being called, but quite enough to ensure that all the shelters were full from 7 p.m. to 7 a.m.

Willi was now tired, stale and demoralised after Sunday night spent dozing fitfully on the immobilised Down escalator at Earl's Court tube station. He was also torn between getting out of the city fast, in the hope of shaking off his pursuer and staying behind in the hope of somehow seeing Ronnie again. Good sense told him to run. And there were a dozen reasons why he shouldn't attempt to see her. But what he wanted to do was stay.

He told himself he would clean up, find a phone and ring her as he'd promised. What did he hope for? Love? Sex? Shelter? All of those were a pretty poor second to staying alive. And yet . . .

He sat in a snack bar in Charing Cross Road with a 'meat' pie and a cup of coffee, trying to reach a decision. He would have liked to hold out a few days before he did anything at all about Ronnie. By Saturday, Harvey would have left. It wasn't a matter of delicacy; simply that with Harvey gone there would be no further distraction, no pressure on Ronnie, no more chance of last-minute reconciliation between them. Any move she made then would be unhampered by the final hurdle of their traumatic goodbyes. But could he wait until Saturday?

Living with Frank he'd grown timid, instead of confident. He now distrusted hotels, large or small. He vividly remembered the trapped feeling he'd had in Birmingham of being in a hotel room alone and isolated—and the sense, each time he went in or out, of walking into a trap; of waiting predators.

He had sat long enough. He was drawing stares from the elderly counterman. He walked slowly down to the Strand, and then, remembering that he needed cigarettes, on to Weingotts. When he arrived back at Charing Cross on foot he washed and shaved in the Men's toilet, picked up his bags and took a cab to the Wilberforce Hotel in South Kensington. He'd let the cabbie suggest it—as being close enough to central London without being too far 'in'. In no way suburban, it was nonetheless far enough from police or redcaps.

It was a quiet hotel. Too quiet, he quickly discovered. Again he found himself listening for creaking boards in the corridor. He spent one sleepless night quite certain, in the haunted early hours that he had somehow given himself away. On Tuesday night, exhausted, he slept a little better. About 10.30, after breakfast, he walked out with his bags again, found a passing cab, and put the bags back into Charing Cross Left Luggage.

In a quiet moment of Wednesday afternoon, the receptionist at the Wilberforce borrowed the early edition of the *Evening News* from the table in the foyer. The first four pages were dominated by the war news. On the fifth was a report of the adjourned inquest on a man and a woman who had been murdered in separate houses in the same street in Eastcote, Middlesex. Police were 'anxious to interview' a man calling himself William Ryder. Bubbling with excitement, the receptionist showed the newspaper to the manager, who telephoned the police. Within the hour they were rewarded by a visit from a Detective Chief Inspector. They were only slightly disappointed that he was not from Scotland Yard.

By that time, Willi was sitting in the dark safety of a cinema, watching Fred MacMurray, Barbara Stanwyck and Edward G. Robinson in *Double Indemnity*. He saw the programme once to take his mind off his troubles and then sat on a second time to doze. He still could not bring himself to a decision on ringing Ronnie. It was a terrible gamble at best, he argued. Away from the fevered atmosphere of Harvey's party, and on the run like this, he found it difficult to credit that his conversation with Ronnie had been as intense and meaningful as he had at first believed. He put the decision off. He was wearing his oldest clothes and his old raincoat. He would sleep tonight on the tube, even if he had to explore the whole system, station by station to find an empty bunk or a free bedspace on the platform. The nights were beginning to be colder. He would be warm there at least.

When he roused himself, the cinema's pink-glowing clock said six-thirty. That still left an hour. Shelterers were allowed onto the platforms of the tube after four-thirty, but until seven-thirty they were confined to spaces that were eight feet from the platform edge. After that, they would take up any space up to four feet from the line. Willi thought he had time to get something to eat. He wasn't really hungry, but in a Leicester Square snack bar he ate a cheese roll and washed it down with some thin coffee. He bought a tube ticket to Earl's Court. That gave him a good piece of the Northern and Piccadilly lines to explore.

He was moderately lucky at once. On the northbound platform of the Northern Line he found a small space at the end of a row of bunks. It was far enough from the entrances that he couldn't be surprised by a sudden visitation from the police. The tunnel mouth gaped only a few yards away. It was the quiet end of the available area. He nodded to an old man who was sitting on the bottom bunk of the first pair to his left. He spread out his *Express* and *The Times*, bundled his raincoat into a pillow, and sat down gratefully. Perhaps later he would be able to sleep.

Though the rush hour was over, there were plenty of people still boarding and leaving the trains. One or two glanced his way curiously. He felt slightly conspicuous; most of the early shelterers were elderly people, the younger ones would only drift in later. He pretended interest in the current *Picture Post* and told himself that for all they knew he was only holding the place for a relative; he could be killing time between trains—a serviceman, even, displaced from a proper bed by bombing, anything.

About nine he woke from a doze, wincing, the end of his spine numbed and painful. The old man on his left was saying something.

"I wake you up? Sorry, son." He was about 70, warmly dressed despite the stuffiness, in a flat cap and ruined gabardine raincoat. He wore old-fashioned boots, the laces crisscrossed, then tied twice round the ankles.

Willi smiled encouragingly. It was good cover to be 'with' someone.

"I was saying," the old man wheezed, "if you want this top bunk for the night you can have it." He nodded several times reassuringly.

The bunk had a bedding bundle and an old coat on it. "I don't think it's free," Willi said.

"Course it's free. I put that stuff there. That's the old woman's. But it's gone nine, now, innit? So she won't be coming. Said she wouldn't if she didn't feel like it. Reckons she has to have one good night's sleep a week, like, and that's enough to see her through. So she's stopping in bed at home tonight, rockets or buzz-bombs or whatever she gets."

"Well, if you really don't mind," Willi said. "Most grateful." He stood up painfully.

"Course I don't mind. I'd keep the old woman company, like, except we'd lose the place then, you see. This is our bunk most nights. Only you have to be down here like a bloody rabbit sharp at half-four if you want to keep it. So you'll be doing me a favour if you like to think of it that way." He stood up and reached for the bundle. "All this stuff can go down here at the end."

"Great!" Willi said. He transferred his coat and papers to the top bunk and hoisted himself up.

The old man rubbed his chin, yawned, stretched and looked at Willi closely. "What—you on leave then?"

"Yes," Willi said without hesitation.

"Army?"

"Air Force."

"Don't seem a sensible place to spend a leave. On your own down a shelter. If I was young, like you, I'd be up top, mate. Have a bloody good time. Never mind about shelters." He leered at Willi with watery eyes. "Best time of their lives, some of 'em, you know. Specially some of the women. Plenty of them, too, upstairs."

Willi drew his feet up and looked down at the old man seriously. "I know," he said. And then: "But there are reasons."

"Had a row with the wife? That's the usual. See a lot of that, down here. Hear some stories, too."

"How did you know?" Willi was grateful for the idea. He might use it elsewhere.

The old man snorted. "That's the usual reason. See a lot of that down here. Hear some funny stories, too." He wrapped his coat tightly round himself, eased himself into the bottom bunk and lay back. His watery eyes looked up at Willi through the bare wire springs of the top bunk. "Get some kip while you can. My advice. They'll be on with the bloody singsong later."

Willi nodded. He lay back in what seemed like luxury after the hardness of the platform. He dozed immediately.

Trains rumbled and hissed through the platform regularly. He was only marginally aware of them. He woke once and looked down the platform wearily. The whole of the space up to the 4-foot mark was taken, and passengers waiting for, and getting off, trains were having to pick their way gingerly through arms, legs, rumps, sleeping bags and hold-alls that strayed outside the demarcation lines. The sleepless sat up, staring resentfully. At the far end of the platform the predicted singsong was in progress. The air had become thick and sickening. But in the sprawling tangle of bodies, bedding and belongings Willi found comfort in anonymity. He surrendered himself to sleep again.

When he opened his eyes again the old man was shaking him gently. He looked down. "Cup of tea here, if you want it." Willi did. His head ached, his neck ached and the diamond pattern of the bunk springs had imprinted itself deeply on his clothes. He reached down gratefully and the old man poured brown liquid from an old blue enamelled pot with a wire handle. "My old brewing up can, this is," he said.

"Where did you brew it?"

"No, lad, I didn't brew it." He saw Willi's puzzlement.

"There's a canteen up at the far end by the Way Out." He grinned. "You can fetch it next time, all right?"

"Right." Willi sipped greedily. The tea was strong and sweet. He wondered why he had ever thought he hadn't liked tea. "When do you want it brought?"

"I'll tell you when. Tom's my name, by the way."

"Bill," Willi acknowledged. He drained the mug and settled himself again.

Much later, Willi woke with the same sensation of anxiety that he'd had in hotels. He sat up cautiously. It was quiet at this end of the platform.

Two policemen and two military police were at the far end of the platform. As he watched, one redcap bent to a half-recumbent figure, laughed and straightened. The four moved on a yard or two closer, studying the sleeping figures. It was clear that they were going to make a sweep of the platform.

He moved warily. They were still a long way off. He didn't want to attract attention by sudden movement. He put his legs over the side and dropped down softly.

"If you're looking for the toilets you can find 'em by the smell; just follow your nose down that end," the old man said quietly from the bottom bunk. He opened one eye.

Willi was startled. He rubbed his legs. "I might stretch my legs a bit, too," he said. "Want anything? What about tea? Anything to eat?"

"Just the tea. Take the old pot." Tom, still wearing his cap, nodded at the end of the bed. The pot hung like a lantern from a bent loop of Willi's bunk springs.

"Right," he said. The police and redcaps were now about halfway along the sprawl. To avoid them he would have to walk half the distance between them and then cut through the passage between the north and southbound platforms. What if they shouted at him to stop? He took a deep breath and set out along the four-foot gap between the sleepers and the platform's edge.

He reached the passageway without attracting attention. But as he turned sharp left to it his foot struck a leather Gladstone bag by a sleeper's head. Jolted by the bag, the sleeper sat up. It was a woman, fortyish, in curlers and headscarf, wrapped in a plaid blanket. "Christ!" she said loudly. She watched him tread cautiously towards the passageway. "You'll never get through there," she said. Her normal speaking voice sounded very loud.

It was true. The passageway, in theory not a part of the

shelterer's domain, was evidently a favoured spot, out of the tunnel winds from the trains and secluded from the general mass of bodies. Sleepers were packed closely, their heads against the curvature of the walls, their feet jumbled together. There was no way he could move through them.

He thought about running quickly through them anyway, even if it meant treading on every one of them. But that would cause uproar.

He fought down panic, turned, shrugged at the woman and retraced his steps. He had time to notice that the police were only a few yards away.

"That was quick," old Tom rumbled.

"I forgot some money in my raincoat," Willi said quickly. He cut a look left. He was going to be caught. There was no doubt of it. The only escape was on the line itself. Into the tunnel. There might be room in there, somewhere among the cables and tunnel supports. But he would be seen just the same, the alarm raised.

This is the worst, he told himself. Worse than anything so far. If I get out of this, even hotels would be better and safer. Never again!

He fumbled with his raincoat. He found some change in his trouser pocket and tried to give the appearance of combining the resources of both pockets.

The tunnel draught grew, suddenly. There was a far-off rumble. At this time of night the trains were few. There hadn't been one for half an hour or more. He folded the raincoat again, elaborately, one eye on the tunnel.

Gradually, the deep murk at the end of it took on a faint glow. The rumble increased in volume. In seconds more, headlights swung into the approach slope. It was a train. Perhaps the last. If he could get on it he might be safe.

"You're sure you don't want anything else?" He bent to the bottom bunk.

"Just the tea." The old man wheezed and then broke into a fit of coughing.

The train roared up the slope and into the station level, drowning all other sound. It was almost entirely empty. The doors hissed open. There were no passengers on or off, but it stood there.

If he moved too soon it would alert the police, who were now only a dozen yards away. If he moved too late he would have to undergo a check on his identity for which he wasn't psychologically ready. He had his identity card, but here and in these circumstances they might very well want more. The military police particularly would be suspicious. There was the danger, too, of being overheard telling a different story than the one he'd already told Tom.

Willi gritted his teeth. The old man was looking up at him with bleary curiosity. And still the train doors stood open. The police moved three or four yards nearer. One of them looked up and ahead at him with interest.

"Right, I'll be off then," Willi said. He looked complacently toward the police and moved forward, swinging the blue can with what he hoped was nonchalance.

At last the hiss of the pneumatic doors. They began to rumble shut. Willi jumped sideways. They closed him off from the platform. The train trembled, jerked, began to move and then to gather speed.

He peered through the close, green anti-blast netting on the door. The police had crowded to the edge of the platform, alerted at last. Old Tom, his mouth wide with astonishment, had scrambled up and stood frozen in an attitude of disbelief.

Breathing hard, Willi watched the platform whirr by like a too-fast camera pan. The safety of the tunnel engulfed him. He put the can down on an empty seat, put on the raincoat and poised himself in the doorway for a quick exit at the next stop. Not that there was much chance of anyone phoning ahead to intercept him; in the few seconds between stations they would be lucky to get anyone to answer the telephone . . . And anyway, no-one had been able to have a good look at him. He was safe. He was just another late-night traveller.

He walked out into the night at Tottenham Court Road and turned south in the direction of the river. He thought he would walk over one of the bridges, keep on the move until the first trains were running, then get some sleep on the Circle Line again. Later he would shave in the washroom somewhere—say, Victoria. After that, breakfast and a stroll round some of the department stores. If he felt settled again he would go and see someone called Esther Williams in a new film called *Bathing Beauty*. Though it was on in the relatively risky area of Leicester Square, there were also plenty of eating places there.

He had survived another day, perhaps. Nonetheless he would ring Ronnie. He didn't know if he could hold out until the weekend. Next time he might not be so lucky.

40

Phil's flat in Gunnersbury Park seemed to be in the basement of a solid Victorian house hidden behind a ring of gloomy laurels. The whole area was one which Harvey didn't know and immediately found alien. He could not imagine what sort of people lived in—had ever lived in—a district of such heavy and isolated respectability. Maiden ladies, perhaps, preoccupied with the piano, lavender polish and embittered pedigree cats.

Both the road and the house were oppressively quiet. There were four doorbells: the Misses E. A. and A. E. Bucknell; Donald Prince, piano tuner; R.J. Whitaker; Miss P. Bedell. Harvey grimaced in a melancholy fashion.

When he pressed the bell, the curtains of the basement window whisked aside and Phil smiled up at him.

Thunder rattled overhead. The air had stopped moving and the stillness was threatening. He thought Phil looked terrible, though it may have been the light. She backed away to let him in and he was mildly surprised to see that she was not wearing black, not even a touch.

The stairs down to her flat cracked loudly despite heavy carpeting. The room that she let him into seemed to be a combined living room and dining room. It gleamed with loving attention.

Harvey kissed her cheek. She seemed very calm. "Harvey," she said. "I am sorry."

Harvey managed a smile. "I should be saying that to you."

She sat down on one side of the dead fireplace. It was cold in the room. Harvey sat in the other huge armchair. There was a moment of awkwardness.

"I'll get you some tea in a minute," Phil said. Her hand flew to her mouth. "Oh dear, perhaps I should have got something stronger." She looked mildly distrait.

"Tea will do fine," Harvey said. "I came to see you."

She faltered, looking down at her lap. "I—I didn't really know Frank well at all, really." She twisted a small handker-

244

chief round and round her forefinger. "He seemed like a very nice man."

"He was," Harvey nodded. "But somehow not a lucky one. He was nearly lucky with you."

She gave him a grateful smile. Harvey asked: "What are you going to do now?"

"I don't know," she said. She smiled rigidly, nervously. "Work is good for grief, isn't it?"

"Phil," Harvey began. "There is one thing I'd like you to do for me." He had meant to save it, but was suddenly anxious to get it over.

"Anything," she said warmly.

"I'd like you to have the house."

She was astonished. She looked away, down at her hands, at the fireplace, anywhere. "I couldn't," she said at last.

"You could," Harvey insisted. "In a day or two it would have been legally yours anyway if what Frank planned had happened."

She didn't understand.

"Frank planned to have the house transferred to your name anyway as soon as you were married," he explained. "I happen to know that." It was a lie, but a good one. "He would want this now."

Phil continued shaking her head.

"For one thing," Harvey went on, "I don't want it. If my plans go right, the last thing I'll want is a suburban house."

"You could sell it," she said quickly.

"For another," Harvey persisted, "I know that Frank would like to think that you were not entirely dependent upon your job and the people in your office." He grinned, hoping to bury the proposition in something else. "He didn't like them very much, you know."

"Not difficult to imagine," she smiled. Harvey thought she looked nicer every time he saw her. Her small smile was especially attractive.

"Anyway," he said, "his idea was that if anything happened to him you could either live in it and take a lodger, or you could sell it. One way or the other it would be something."

She had been listening, watching with huge brown eyes moist. "I can't take it," she blurted. "It's too—" She broke off and dabbed at her eyes. A sniff seemed to fortify her. "You know, I don't think I was meant to marry after all."

"Balls!" Harvey said. "If I believed that, I'd have to believe that Frank was meant to be murdered. Because that's the only thing that stopped you being his wife. And there's not a lot of sense in that."

"No, I see that," she whispered.

"Then you'll accept the house?"

"May I think about it?"

"Of course. And then accept it. Meanwhile, I'll have Frank's solicitor note that when probate is through, that's what he must attend to next. It may be a little time." Harvey scratched his head. "I know this sounds strange, but in the interim, I wonder if you could go and live there? Somehow, I have the feeling that you and I—and Frank—will all feel better if you do that. No matter that it happened there. I don't think you'll find it bothering you. It will be a house that loves you." Harvey heard himself say it with genuine surprise.

She looked surprised too. She sat on for a moment and then got up and came over to him. "You are the most surprising person, Harvey." She combined a shaky laugh with a liquid snuffle. "But I know what you mean. Yes, I would like to live there. Now how could you know that?" She bent and kissed him on the forehead. Harvey put an arm round him and patted her on the back. That was too much. She muttered something in which he caught the word 'tea' as she fled.

She was back with tea and scones before he had taken in the room properly. He guessed the furniture had been her parents'. There was a red-plush chaise longue in the window. The dining-table, ornate, claw-footed, was glowing yew. There were miniatures of placid, gentle-looking people grouped on two of the walls. It was a room salvaged from another, better time.

"Harvey," she said, pouring the tea, "did you really want him to marry?"

"You? Or at all?"

"Either."

"Both," he said. Their smiles collided again.

"If you hadn't killed him off yourself," Harvey said gruffly, "you'd have been good for him."

Her eyes opened wide in shock.

"What do you mean?"

"Oh come on, Phil. Frank was close to his sixties. He was randy beyond his means. I can say that, knowing he'd only have laughed."

She laughed and coloured at the same time.

"Mind," Harvey added. "He'd have died happy."

246

She looked at him reflectively. "You're a lot like him. Kindly, stubborn, and a bit too—"

"Frank?"

Harvey was fascinated by the way she covered her mouth when she laughed inordinately. It was a touch of innocence quite captivating in its effect on the observer.

"Let's keep in touch, Phil," he said warmly. "I don't want anything much from you. But we're both alone, and we both loved him in our ways." He hooted with laughter suddenly. "And you'd have been my stepmother on Friday."

It was the wrong thing to have said. Harvey couldn't tell whether it was their sudden closeness or what he'd said about Friday, but she broke down at once, sobbing bitterly. He made no attempt to comfort her.

"Good," he said. "Great! Get it out of your system." It sounded like a Godawful cliché and yet it had some validity.

"Why?" she sobbed. "Why?"

It was a moment or two before he realised what she meant. "I don't know."

By degrees she got it under control. She blew her nose and took a few deep breaths. "It couldn't have been Bill Ryder, could it?" she asked more steadily.

Harvey shrugged. "It's hard to believe. The police were hinting at all sorts of odd things about him." He was thoughtful for a moment. "Listen, did Frank ever say anything much to you about Bill?"

"What sort of thing?"

"I don't know. The police asked me if I had at any time thought of him as being anything other than Bill Ryder. Had I noticed anything about him."

"No," Phil said. And then shook him by adding: "But I know what they mean."

"You do?"

"In a way." She screwed her face up. "There was just something about him. I can't find the right word. Mysterious is the best I can do."

"Mysterious? For God's sake, Phil!"

"I know," she admitted. "Even I don't know what I mean by that. Nothing bad, certainly. Nothing against him." She was quiet for a moment. "Frank liked him very much, you know."

Harvey nodded. "I did, too. Why not? There was nothing to dislike. And yet—"

"Yes?"

"Someone killed Frank."

"Not Bill," she said firmly.

Harvey was irritated. That was Ronnie's stance. He could not accept it just like that. He dismissed Ronnie's view now more vigorously for hearing it echoed by Phil. Two women had come out strongly against the evidence. Women's intuition or something. You couldn't accept it and you couldn't argue against it.

He hoped they would find Ryder soon. He was quite suddenly filled with an anguished sense of futility and waste. Poor old Frank. He never did get his hands on the lush body he had so coveted. Poor old Phil, too, who would be lucky to get another chance. In an odd way he wished she were younger. Phil was the kind of woman, plain though she might be, who could hold a man: artless, loyal, innocent, able to wait while he got on with life on both their accounts. Poor sods. A bubble of grief rose in him. The urge to tears was suddenly much too close. He stood up abruptly. "I have to go," he said, looking away. He touched his lips to her hair. "I'll ring later and make an arrangement to take you to the inquest. You'll want to go?"

"No," she said. "Unless you want it."

"Of course not." He got to the foot of the steps to the upper hall. "I won't be leaving now until it's all over. So I'll see you again."

She took his hand in the hall and held it until they were out on the steps. He was surprised to find the street wet. He hadn't heard the rain. The air was fresh and moving again sweetly.

He hurried away without looking back. Only now, for some reason, was anger beginning to build in him. It wasn't just that he had lost a father and a dear friend. Frank, poor old Frank, had lost what might have been his best and happiest years. Some bastard had robbed him of that. Robbed Phil, too, as life had robbed her before.

Someone was to blame. It had to be Ryder. Why did both women insist that it wasn't? The police weren't so bloody sure! Women were so easy for a bastard to conquer. They could be won with a smile, imprisoned with a kind word, deceived any old time by a bit of devious insincerity.

He raged on. Again and again it came back to Ryder . . .

41

By Wednesday, emerging from the initial shock state, Harvey was beginning to feel both Frank's death and the mounting pressures. There was the house at Eastcote to close up until Phil could get there. The inquest and then the funeral on Friday if everyone was satisfied. Meanwhile, Frank's body was still in the coroner's mortuary.

Ronnie was being wonderful. She had insisted on making the first trip to Eastcote with him and he didn't protest too much. "It isn't something you want to tackle alone," she told him. Could he pick her up on the way, about lunchtime? Harvey wanted to give her lunch but she was on regular nightshift and pleaded that she needed to sleep as long as she could. Perhaps she did, Harvey thought. And yet . . . she never, now, shared time with him, even innocently. He had the impression she would do anything for him: pack his cases, carry them to the station, wave him goodbye—just as long as she didn't have to be with him in the relaxed sense. "And who can blame her?" he asked himself reasonably, aware that a flicker of resentment burned in him just the same.

McNair lent him the Wolseley to get out there. That was a help; there would be stuff to carry away. This time though McNair had a price. Would he sit in once with Dixon on his first official nightshift alone on the Desk? Harvey agreed with a show of appreciation, yet was immediately oppressed by the thought of it.

On the way to Mount Street he gloomed about the remaining hurdles. Once today was over . . . The thought of having Ronnie there warmed him a little. He wasn't sure how he might react to the house on his own. There was, he knew, a broad vein of treacherous sentiment just below the surface of his self-assurance; one that he was careful never to tap. With Ronnie along he would have to be practical, efficient and cool.

Ronnie left him no time to brood. She kept him talking about the war and his immediate problems of getting into it. When he finally arrived at the house he found he was totally unprepared for it and panic rose swiftly. She sensed that, too.

"Frank did a great job with the roses this year," she said, defusing the moment. She walked all round the little front garden, postponing the moment, giving him time to bite on it. "Look at these, they're beautiful." Harvey loved her deeply at that moment. That mouth, those legs, that body and so much more perception than any other woman he'd ever met. Was he making a terrible mistake? Could he still grab her and go to work on Monday morning, bright and early, for Croft? Would she, even now, melt as she did once—provided he said the right words of capitulation? He stood on the doorstep, momentarily ravished by the appeal of it all. He watched her bend to the roses, cupping and inhaling their sweetness. His lips practised the words silently.

Instead he took a deep breath and unlocked the door. On the instant Ronnie was at his elbow.

"After the war," he said, hanging his raincoat on the newel post, "when weather forecasts come back, it will be nice to be allowed to know if you're going to get soaked or not."

"Who says it will rain after the war?" Ronnie said. "Only bluebirds, surely. Sun and laughter and joy ever after . . ."

"There's nothing in the song about Eastcote," Harvey said drily. "Only the White Cliffs. And wherever *you* stand, I hope." He smiled. "Shall we start at the top?"

He followed her up, again wanting to grab her. Good old unfailing lust, he thought. Perhaps the only thing in the world with the power to dispel, at least for a space, his sense of loss and defeat. "If you take the two small bedrooms," he said, "I'll do Frank's room. Shout if you're doubtful."

There was a bit of sun coming through the clouds now. Dust swam in the bright beams that poured in round Edith's battered old dressing table backed up to the window. He could remember her sitting there once, reproachful back and set mouth, scolding him with silence over something that he'd done or hadn't done.

He looked round helplessly. None of the furniture would be wanted by Phil, who had her own portable memory material—it was too heavy for such a small house, but she would bring it anyway, moving all this stuff out. It didn't matter. It had once meant something to Frank and Edith. It had always been cheap; now it was just junk. He started folding sheets and blankets in use and piling them on the bare mattress. Frank's suit, his overcoat, raincoat, shoes, galoshes, summer blazer, old pairs of slacks . . . where were his slippers? He found them under the bed along with a well-thumbed copy of

250

Lilliput. It was a nasty moment. Aware that he shouldn't, he flicked through to the page with the tasteful light-and-shade nude and ended up smiling. She was too skinny, too bee-sting breasted to have given Frank much edge. He carried the first pile of clothes down to the boot of the Wolseley. The dressing table was empty. Frank had evidently never used it. That just left the difficult stuff in the chest of drawers and tallboy. Shirts, separate collars, a couple of old stiff collars in a round, padded, laundry collar-box. Winter underpants—the kind with loops that you hung over your braces. Vests, socks, pullovers, the intensely personal things Frank was probably using only a few days ago. More than once Harvey felt a rising bubble of grief threaten to choke him. It was such a bloody waste. Christ! He found an ashtray, lit a cigarette and pulled hard on it. Handkerchiefs, ties, two old wallets . . . A small drawer full of rubbish: foreign coins, a letter from Phil, safety pins, spare buttons, cufflinks, armbands, spare black and brown shoelaces, razor blades, a propelling pencil with a broken clip, two mildewed fountain pens. He took it all down to the rubbish bin.

In the bureau he found Frank's Will. He was startled that Frank had even thought of making one. Miserably he read that the house, the contents of his bank account 'and all my assets' had been left to 'my dear son'. Again the bubble. He pressed on. There were other letters and papers that looked important and he set them to one side. He could hear Ronnie moving briskly in the room Ryder used.

Ryder. Where was that bastard now? How could he be innocent of this?

Finished with the room at last he stood for a moment by the window. Lindsey Gardens steamed in the unexpected sun. Some ten-year-olds jostled by, yelping, scuffling, their world almost secure now as the war receded. He envied them. "Here I am, sweeping up the bric-à-brac of my father's life," he told himself. "In the next room the woman who has meant most to me in all my adult life is doing the same before I leave her behind. In a few days, two weeks at most, I'll have turned my back on the whole thing at once. How can that be happening?"

Ryder! That's how!

"I'm glad that's over," he told Ronnie quietly. "War can only be easier." And he was astonished when she took his face in both her hands and kissed him hard on the mouth.

251

"What did I say?" he laughed shakily. "I want to repeat myself."

Ronnie smiled. "It's called overlaying one sensation with another. Are you finished in Frank's room?"

"When I've put this stuff into the boot there will be nothing left to give Phil a bad time. What was in the other rooms?"

"Spare linens, covers, curtains, that sort of thing. Nothing to upset anyone. Nothing she won't be glad of. That just leaves downstairs and we can have a cup of coffee. There may be more down there that you would want to take, don't you think?"

"Not really. Books and things like that I took away long since. But if you see the family album, grab it for me. And anything that looks like a bill unpaid, or whatever."

They spent five minutes in the garden and waved to Marie. She was holding Noah, who had found a soft berth without even changing his dominion. "I must send her flowers," Harvey said. "And make an arrangement for her to keep an eye on the place, forward the mail and such."

Ronnie took the kitchen and left him alone in the dining room, assaulted by half-formed thoughts and images he didn't permit himself to explore. He found the album and avoided opening it. He put it out on the hall chair with other things to go. In half-an-hour he was done. Ronnie had tidied the kitchen, checked the cupboards, disposed of perishable food, emptied the ice-box and washed up everything including the vases. As a final act they stood the houseplants outside to give them a chance of survival.

"That's all that's left." Ronnie indicated a small pile on the kitchen table. She produced the coffee.

Harvey sat down with no intention of looking at anything at all. There was a small pile looking like bills, receipts, postcards from other people's holidays—and a thick buff envelope. He riffled idly.

"Christ! What's this?" He was jolted when he saw that the envelope was addressed to *Mr W. Ryder*—in Frank's handwriting.

Ronnie studied it, unmoved. "An envelope addressed to Bill." Her tone was warily non-committal.

"In Frank's handwriting?"

Ronnie lit a cigarette suddenly clumsy. "He forgot something," she suggested flatly. "He would have sent it on when he'd heard from Bill."

It was a moment or two before the significance of that hit

her. She grabbed his hand. "Why would Frank address a letter to Bill if Bill hadn't already left—quietly?"

Harvey glared at her. At once the issue between them was not what the envelope contained, or at what point Bill Ryder had left, but the triumphant note of defence in Ronnie's voice.

"Fine," he said grimly. "I'll send it on to him—when I get his address. Meanwhile—" He ripped the packet open, shook out a postcard-sized photograph in a Woolworth frame.

The photograph was in sepia. Four people in a family group. A grey-haired man, the gaze and set of the features unsmiling and faintly disapproving, sat with a handsome woman perhaps as tall as himself. Her serene smile softened a strong jawline and cool, level gaze. Behind them, two young men stood. One aloof, his hands behind his back, the face self-assured, disdainful, almost girlishly good-looking. The other was clearly Bill Ryder, barely into his twenties; the hair fairer, longer and with something of a wave in it—the square, boyish face was relaxed in a wry grin and his hands rested on his mother's shoulders.

Harvey stared at it closely for a long time, Ronnie looking over his shoulder. There was something about the picture . . . Something about the clothes. Ainslie's last question—about Ryder—at once dropped into his mind. He turned the frame over, thumbed the tin latches on the backing, and took the photograph out. On the back the photographer's name was printed in two lines along the bottom:

Studio Wasserman, Berlin

The significance of the three words hit him. He stood up abruptly. "Ainslie has to see this." He moved about, breathlessly agitated. "Christ! Now I see what he meant about Ryder. And the bugger was right."

Ronnie picked up the photograph and looked at both sides for a long time. She said nothing.

"Don't tell me you don't find it significant," Harvey said aggressively. "Just as poor old Frank did." He kneaded his fists fiercely. "Christ, was I slow! Think about it, Ronnie. Think about the way I met him. Up there on the Ridgeway, with that fucking plane still burning. And I only see it now. Only now!" He gritted his teeth in a frenzy of self-reproach.

Ronnie bit her lip. "I think," she said dully, "that he was the pilot."

"Or was there to meet the plane." Harvey could not control

the shaking in his voice. "Either way he's a Kraut. A bloody Kraut! And I sent him here." His breathing became ragged. Ronnie watched his distress anxiously.

"You don't know that any harm came to Frank by that," she said. It was half reassurance, half challenge.

"Oh, come on!" Harvey turned on her. "You can't believe that. What is it with you and Ryder, anyway?" He was half aware that he was going too far, but his rage and indignation carried him on. "I mean why all this effort on your part to keep his nose clean?" He stopped pacing about, arrested by a further thought. He looked at her wildly. "You don't know where he is, do you?"

"No." Ronnie looked at him squarely. "I don't. But just because we were wrong about who he is, Harvey, it doesn't mean that we were wrong about the man himself."

"Crap!" Harvey was shouting now. "Ainslie needs this anyway. I'll apologise to Mister Bloody Kraut Ryder if and when they find him dead somewhere, too."

Ronnie looked at him with something close to contempt. "The only good German is a dead German, right?" she said coldly.

Harvey was shaken. He drew a deep breath and dropped his hands. "I don't know," he said more calmly. He put the photograph away in his wallet. "I have to get to Ainslie with this."

"Whatever you say," Ronnie said evenly. "But we might as well finish what we came to do. Let's do that first."

Harvey wrestled with his feelings, setting everything good that he knew about Ronnie against her odd attitude about Ryder. She still came out well in credit. He touched her hand and went up to fetch the bundles on the bed.

On the way back, Ronnie sat with her head back, eyes closed, all the way. Harvey was grateful. He had no idea what to say to her next.

She kissed him on the cheek for goodbye until Friday.

"Thanks," Harvey said. It was sincere.

At Hammersmith he stopped outside Nazareth House and handed in the things from the boot to the nuns there.

Hurrying back to Temple Chambers he could think of nothing but Ryder. He had the photograph on the seat beside him and looked at it repeatedly. It was unbelievable. And yet it was nothing of the sort. If Ryder was unbelievable, then so was the uniform that he, Harvey Marsh, was wearing, and so were Himmler and Hitler, thousand-bomber raids, Dunkirk,

D-Day, Lord Haw-Haw, pilotless jet aircraft falling on London by the score every day of the week, and all the rest of it. It was a mad world. His father was dead. Killed by a German who had dropped from the sky onto the Berkshire Downs. Was that any more mad than people dying every day of the week over breakfast in Fulham or Stanmore, or at Ludgate Circus in their lunch hour from their City offices, or on the way home in the 5.15 to Brighton? He braked sharply to avoid a bus inching round Hyde Park Corner. That was bloody mad, too. A London bloody bus—pulling a coal-burning gas producer. The whole damn world was mad, mad, mad!

He shook his head, aware that tears of rage and frustration were rolling down his face.

42

Willi walked into a phone box by the gardens at the Embankment end of Villiers Street. At once his mouth went dry and his palms sweated. He had tried to ring Ronnie before. A bunch of soldiers had immediately surrounded the box and begun a mild harassment, peering in and puckering their lips at him. He had surrendered the box to them at once and almost walked away. But two Land Girls emerged giggling from the next box. There was no reason to put it off.

He had been less nervous flying five thousand feet over London with a full bomb-load and the searchlights groping the night sky for him. He put his two pennies in the box and dialled the MOI's Museum number. When the switchboard answered he asked for the·canteen. The operator left him hanging on a dead line. On the instant he was all impatience. He had got this far . . . The line opened again with a ping, and a cheerful voice announced the canteen. He asked for Miss Croft and had to repeat it, louder, to be heard. There was a wait. He heard the first voice call out: "Ronnie—for you."

There was no mistaking her voice.

"It's Bill," he said flatly. He thought he heard a muffled sound. Astonishment? "You asked me to call," he reminded her. Again the canteen noises filled the line. "Ronnie?"

"That was before . . ." she said mysteriously.

Willi was mystified. "Before what?" he asked.

There was a short silence. Then: "Nothing. Where are you?"

"Charing Cross."

"The hotel?"

"The station."

She seemed to be thinking. Willi grew anxious. A WAAF came to stand outside the door of the phone box, ostentatiously establishing her right to the box next. She smiled at him faintly, perhaps content that she had only the one call to wait through. Willi turned his back.

"Can you come to me?" Ronnie said. Her voice was barely audible.

"At the canteen?" he said anxiously.

"No. At home. I have a flat in West Ken. I haven't been there much lately, but it would be a suitable place to meet." Willi was desolate that her tone was chilly, remote.

"Surely. When?"

This time the hesitation was only marginal. "Tonight at seven?"

"Fine," he said. His breathing seemed to ease. He stood a little straighter.

"I'll see you then," Ronnie said. "I have to go now. We're very busy."

Panic hit him. "Wait!" he shouted. "You haven't told me where." She gave him the address and he repeated it back to her.

"Are you all right?" he persisted. "You don't mind my calling you? If you've changed your mind . . ."

"Tonight at seven," Ronnie repeated. She hung up.

Willi surrendered the box to the WAAF and stood irresolutely on the kerb. The narrow street swarmed with servicemen and women carrying kitbags and valises. Two military police were descending the steps from the Villiers Street entrance to the station. Willi hurried by on the other side of the street, then cut through the front of the station. In the courtyard tired-looking RAF men were bundling out of Dodge 3-tonners and clustering round the boarded and sandbagged Cross built by Edward I. They wore the dull, resigned look of all troops in transit.

Willi walked north. His stomach griped with hunger. He had slept at Balham, on the other side of the river where neither police nor the military were much of a problem. He had at last discovered that all bunks in the tube shelters were held by season-ticket, though south of the river they were often not taken up. He'd crawled into one after waiting until past midnight for the owner to appear. No-one had disturbed him, and he'd slept a little. Even so, his head throbbed painfully from long hours in the foetid air and the small of his back ached. A hotel would solve most of his immediate problems, but he had lost his nerve. He couldn't now imagine how he had walked into a hotel in Birmingham only hours after landing in England. Perhaps his morale had been higher. Getting away at all and then getting down alive had seemed like a miracle—an omen that he must succeed. His confidence had fled since Jerome had been able to find him so easily. Twice.

Should he eat now or wait? It was eight-thirty. He had more than ten hours to fill. He decided to eat at once and then again in the afternoon. Leicester Square and the police patrols were ahead, but it was a good spot for food. And it had a public lavatory.

At the Moo Cow in the Square he ordered a Vienna steak and chips, without knowing what it was. It was a long time coming, but when he got it he thought he hadn't eaten anything so good for years.

He spent the afternoon in Green Park, huddling in a damp deckchair against a chill East wind. He dozed and grew stiff, moved the chair to the shelter of a huge plane tree, and watched the afternoon dwindle down. At four, again ravenous, he returned to the Square and ate the same meal, washing it down with three cups of weak unsweetened tea.

In the rush hour he stood for a while at the Embankment, near Temple Steps. The river was high, but the now familiar smell of its mud was heavy on the air. There were a few first lights on the South Bank. A collier, moving upstream to a power station or gas works, thrummed briskly by, low in the water, navigation lights on. On its lower deck a cook in whites stood at the rail, smoking, a warm gleam of light from the galley behind him. Willi envied him deeply. Envied him the warmth, the food, a place to sleep. The collier's wash slapped up on the granite walls below him. Willi shivered.

Perhaps tomorrow would be different. He decided at that moment that he would risk Ronnie with the truth. If she screamed, took fright, was outraged, he would still have time to run. He was already running. There was nothing to lose. He might as well try Ronnie. He was sure that if she once said she would help he could trust her. He reassured himself of that endlessly.

Ronnie left the MOI soon after Willi's call. She had already phoned Mount Street to say that she would be going down to Queen's Club Gardens and staying the night.

She unlocked the white door of her flat just before ten. The chill of the place struck through her at once. The windows had been replaced and the rooms were tidy enough, but dust was thick everywhere. Ministry circulars littered the hall floor; a 'Doctor Carrot' leaflet, advising her to eat National Wholemeal Bread, had kited through into the living room. The kitchen floor sounded as if she were walking a gravel path. Her house plants were dead.

Refusing to think, she set about cleaning up, her tiny Ekco radio grinding out *Music While You Work*. At twelve, lightheaded from lack of sleep, she went out to the shops for milk, margarine, bread, coffee, saccharin and whatever else she could get. Then she heated some tinned soup, ate it with a slice of toast, made some coffee, changed the bed linen and climbed in, exhausted. She set the alarm clock for five. Only then did she allow herself to think about 'Bill Ryder'.

She did not believe, could not believe, that he had anything to do with Frank's death. That was impossible. Nor had Bill sounded like a man who feared to ring, or feared what she might do or say in the hours between his call and his coming here. That was the acid test. If he came, knowing that he might walk into the police, he *must* be innocent.

It did not occur to her to be afraid. She tried to imagine that she was wrong, badly wrong. And that this was a man wanted by the police in connection with a brutal killing.

She fell asleep, smiling at the absurdity of it.

43

Tea time in Herne Hill. Thelma Franks, well-trained widow of a dull, conventional, insurance broker, was right on time with the tray. Everything just so. Strong tea, white-metal pot (never china, which didn't draw as well she thought), wafer-thin brown bread and butter. Milk in the cups first, sugar last. That was the drill.

She knew exactly where to find her brother Jerome; in the conservatory, pretending to read and more likely enjoying forty winks. She would be delighted if he had slept a little. The dear man did work so hard, just like Poor Norman. Business had not left him entirely alone, even on this short stay with her. There had been the phone calls. And the worried frown afterwards. It was all so draining for him, she thought. Not many men had been able to sustain a one-man business right through the war. But Jerome had kept going; even seemed to be doing well. She was proud of him and if there was any little thing she could do for him, well then she would ferret it out of him and go right ahead and do it.

She carried the tray through, thinking how nice it would be if he could only see her point of view about giving up that poky little flat in Kensington and moving out here with her, where the air was better and he'd have the garden all the time. He'd be so happy here. She was sure he didn't look after himself properly in Kensington. She sighed. It was a lost cause. They had been over this ground many times. Once Jerome had almost—not quite, but almost—shown a flash of temper when she had, perhaps, gone on a little too long about it. That was most unusual for him.

"Here you are, my dear," she said. "Right on time." She set the tray down on a whicker table beside him and took the basket chair opposite him.

Jerome Judson Fairbrother looked up from his book appreciatively. He did enjoy Thelma's teas. Very civilised, they were. He was sure that she deprived herself of her minimal butter and tea rations so that she could provide them freely when he was at Herne Hill, but it was so obviously something

e enjoyed doing that he wasn't going to interfere. He
. Ayn Rand's *The Fountainhead* cheerfully. It was a
.rmed Forces edition, printed two columns to the page
.nd the pages bound broad rather than long. He'd picked it
up secondhand in Charing Cross Road. The type was rather
small, but it was an amusing novelty.

He treated his sister to a special smile. He felt mellow
towards her. It had been a pleasant few days. Warm enough,
except for today, under the protective glass, and for the most
part bright and peaceful. There was still a lot of colour in
Thelma's garden; unpatriotically she had kept her flowers,
claiming that the Dig for Victory heavy work demanded by
growing one's own vegetables was beyond her. It was nonsense of course. Thelma was as strong as a carthorse, for all
her greying, wispy daintiness.

The week had done him good. Arriving in time for Sunday tea,
he'd allowed Thelma to press him to stay. This was Thursday.
He sighed and stretched. A pity the weather was breaking
up. He squinted at the heavy cloud bunched in the south-
west, just above Thelma's plank-built gazebo. He wouldn't
get another good day in. But that was just as well, perhaps.
Something had to be done about Reiter. Oh, there was no
question of his starting all over again, this time to comb the
streets of London. Reiter might not even be in London.
Likely, perhaps, but by no means certain; and even if he had
a dozen men working on it they might still come up with
nothing at all. Either way he wasn't willing to risk personal
involvement again, even if Reiter could be found. He already
regretted the affair of Marsh and Mrs Flax. Not their deaths
so much as the risks he had been forced to take to make quite
sure that he was totally clear of involvement. No, if Reiter
could be found—it must be done at one careful remove from
himself. Only when Reiter had settled, as a sitting duck,
could he, Fairbrother, risk another dangerous step.

Meanwhile, there was always hope that Hands would have
something to report.

"Marvellous," he said aloud, setting down his cup. "You
know, you do everything quite beautifully, my dear."

Thelma glowed. Jerome always appreciated what she did
for him. It was one of his nicest qualities. She was glad, as
she had been a thousand times before, that Jerome had never
married. It probably wouldn't have worked, of course. For one
thing, Jerome was far too fastidious for any woman to bear.

And for her part she couldn't have borne to see him looked after sloppily. "Another cup?" she said, already pouring.

Fairbrother didn't like using Hands, or any other help. It was always a risk. And usually limited. And he felt that his contact with the kind of people he was forced to use in some way brought him down to their level: that of the common criminal—because, of course, that was the only kind of help he could use reliably and the only kind that was of use. Billy Hands, for example.

Billy Hands was very much a creature of the shadows. A deserter since 1941 from the Pioneer Corps, he made a good living in the black market, on various racecourses and, once in a while, from violence to order. His real name was Meakin, but Hands was the name on the identity card he had stolen, along with much else, from a man he had found dying in the mean streets of Earlsfield, moments after a parachute landmine had drifted down one night to blast a huge crater in the road only fifty yards away. Incredibly, Meakin had been thrown bodily onto the flat roofs of a line of lock-up garages nearby. Shaken and scarcely able to believe his luck, he had crawled down with only a few bruises—and almost at once found his passport to respectability. His victim had a broken back and multiple head injuries. By some freak he was still alive; just. It was possible that he died at the moment Meakin rolled him over. Clearly, Hands had no use for an identity card any longer and Meakin, taking the man's wallet with the card in it, had limped away into the chaotic fiery gloom even as the fire and ambulance bells sounded close by.

Before employing him for the first time, Fairbrother had taken the precaution of exploring the personal history of Victor William Hands. When he was quite sure that his Billy Hands could not possibly be the original, he had let Hands know that—quietly and without threat. He also hinted at more knowledge than he actually had. From there on they enjoyed a trouble-free relationship. Fairbrother posed as a respectable solicitor with clients who were, perhaps, less than respectable. It afforded him a credible reason for demanding unusual services from Hands, without ever jeopardising his own safety from counter-action. At least it satisfied Hands. So much so that he even found acceptable Fairbrother's use of an unorthodox base from which to conduct the kind of affairs that might otherwise have soiled the dignity of the Lincoln's Inn practice at which Fairbrother sometimes hinted. He called Fairbrother 'Mr Jerome' with the accent on the first syllable.

He had the phone number of the shop and of Thelma Franks, whose relationship to Fairbrother also went unexplained. Hands was too scared to probe it.

"I think," Fairbrother said now, "that I really ought to be getting back to work tomorrow, you know. I've been very neglectful." He mimed regret very winsomely and made up for it a little by accepting another piece of Thelma's brown bread and butter.

Thelma shrugged, smiling, remembering what she had been feeling herself about not badgering him. "I know. But it did you good, dear." She felt disappointed, but at the same time lucky to have had him for so long this time.

"By the way," Fairbrother said. "I wonder if you have a postcard?"

"A postcard?" Thelma was surprised. "Plain or picture? I think I have one or two picture postcards somewhere. But doesn't it matter of what?" Fairbrother assured her it did not. She bustled away and came back with a nice card with a pre-war view of Beach Head. "Will this do?"

"Very nicely."

"But you haven't been to Beach Head." It was illogical in Thelma's mind to send anyone a card from anywhere unless you were actually there or had, at a pinch, just come back.

The telephone rang. Out on the hallstand, through two rooms, it was barely audible. They both listened to be sure it was Thelma's and not the Donnellys' next door; from the conservatory it was often difficult to be sure.

"It'll be business for you, dear," Thelma said. "No-one ever rings me. Especially not at tea time."

Fairbrother smiled at the idea that all England was either at business or at tea. Perhaps she was right. He hurried through.

It was Hands. "This is a waste of time, Mr Jer-ome," he began cheerlessly. "Like looking for a flea in a feather bed."

"You are being paid," Fairbrother said stiffly.

Hands snorted. "I don't like to take the money," he said. "If all three of us stood on Rainbow Corner and just waited for him to come by we'd stand just as good a chance of finding him."

"Then do that," Fairbrother snapped. He almost hung up. "What about Mount Street?" He had no great expectation from that, either.

Hands' sharp exhalation was derisive. "She goes to work, she comes home." He was careful not to add that they had actually lost Ronnie Croft for the whole of the previous afternoon; that she had been called for by the man Marsh, driving a Wolseley '38 saloon and catching Hands' man off guard.

"And she's still at Mount Street as far as you can tell?"

An apologetic note in the voice: "Well no. This morning she went directly from Russell Square to the Queen's Club Gardens place. She's there now."

"She didn't go out all day?"

"Only to the shops."

"And that's all?" Fairbrother was puzzled. He had rather expected her to attend the inquest with Marsh. She had to sleep, of course. Or Marsh might not have wanted her there. Too upsetting. It was plausible.

He stood for a moment undecided. Hands made a small, tentative sound. "Wait, I'm thinking," Fairbrother said coldly. It was entirely understandable that during her association with Marsh she might use the Queen's Club address rather than her father's home in Mount Street. But her association with Marsh was minimal now. That was clear from Hands' reports, and it made some kind of sense of his deductions. He had sensed, the first time he had seen her signed photograph in Marsh's flat that the relationship was not a lasting one. It was clearly winding down now. If Marsh's father were not presently laying in the coroner's mortuary he would probably be overseas already. Suddenly the Croft girl had elected to return to her own flat. Why? It was interesting.

On the instant the scene in the corridor at the Savoy returned vividly. Ronnie Croft and Willi Reiter. Standing close. Out of sight, round a corner and away from the restaurant. He felt a stir of intuitive certainty. And distrusting it, decided to check.

"All right," he told Hands. "Forget the West End. It is, as you say, a waste of time . . ."

"I always thought so," Hands growled insubordinately.

"Be quiet!" Fairbrother snapped. "This is important. Put your best people on Queen's Club, instead. Have them relieved frequently. I want to know everything that happens there: who goes in, who comes out, how long they stay. Round the clock."

He hung up, hopeful. The more he thought about it the more he liked it. That had been an odd little cameo at the Savoy. He couldn't begin to understand what it meant. Nor where, despite what he had seen for himself and what Frank Marsh had protested, the Marshes and the Crofts fitted into the Willi Reiter story. But he was hopeful.

He looked down at the postcard in his hand. He smiled. He'd send it to Malone. With just one more bluff.

He took out his fountain pen and wrote, in a small, beautiful hand:

> Am hopeful I shall not
> disappoint you friends.
> Go ahead and prepare for a
> happy result.
>
> Jerome.

44

Ainslie was waiting for Harvey as he emerged from the gloom of the coroner's court. The big man looked at his watch. "They're open. Would you like a quick drink? You look as if you could use one."

Harvey nodded and stepped out smartly, so that Ainslie had to exert himself to keep up. The short and scruffy private road to the court looked more like the entrance to a builder's yard and the court itself had the neglected, Victorian seediness of a workhouse chapel. Harvey was anxious to be away from both. It was over at last. The verdict was the only one possible under the circumstances, but it had been painful. The quiet misery of the medical detail had further eroded his balance. He had not expected to feel more, but he did—with every horrific technicality of the length and width of the stab wound. A short sword or a long dagger . . . a bayonet? It was preposterous, unimaginable.

Ainslie shouldered him to the right. He didn't know where they were going. They turned into the lounge of a newish pub with a large forecourt. It was empty, though there was clearly life in the public bar. "Scotch and water," Harvey said hopefully. Ainslie again nudged him with his bulk to sit down. He approached the bar and spoke briefly to a girl with feather-cut hair and chalk-white breasts billowing from a flower-print summer dress.

Miraculously, Ainslie returned with the Scotch. "Somehow they always have it for me," Ainslie told him. The girl remained at the bar, smiling encouragingly across at them. She wore a gold brooch of miniature RAF wings across the bottom of her cleavage. The smile died after a few moments and she withdrew, defeated, to the promise of the Public.

"This Ryder," Ainslie began. "He's important to us now. I appreciate you're numb just now. But if you think of anything—anything at all . . ."

"Of course."

"We will be doing everything we can. But meanwhile, I'd be obliged if you would tell me what your own thinking is now. Are you any nearer to believing that Ryder might, just might, have killed your father?"

Harvey tried to look as if he was thinking about it objectively. Then he gave up. He said bitterly: "First catch the bastard. Then give him to me for half an hour. Then I'll tell you whether or not the bastard did it."

"Very natural feelings," Ainslie said. "And it answers my question." He looked at Harvey's glass. "Another?"

"No thanks. You?"

Ainslie shook his head. "I must get along. Something tells me that 'catching the bastard' isn't going to be easy, though the photograph will help. That was a break. Meanwhile, the man seems to have vanished. We've got checks out everywhere, of course. We're doing everything, trying everything. I want you to be sure of that. And we've had to let the Ministry of Defense people have prints of the photograph, too. It's a reasonable assumption that Ryder is the pilot of the aircraft you saw, is an enemy alien at the very least, and possibly much more. They, of course, have their own methods. I can't tell you much about that. They're a close-mouthed lot."

Harvey shrugged. His thoughts had switched to Phil. Poor old Phil! He was glad she had not been there. Likewise Ronnie. "Why no funeral until Monday?" he said suddenly.

"Pretty much as we said in court. We'd like one or two more opinions on the—wound. I'd like to give you the green light for tomorrow but the Home Office man can't cope until tomorrow. Monday's the earliest then, you see? Your man will have his green slip by tomorrow evening, so it's best you keep in touch with him and arrange Monday for sure. Okay?"

"Sure." He remembered Mrs Flax. "Is she the same?" Ainslie said she was. He began buttoning his raincoat.

Harvey found the tube station after walking past it. He booked to Temple, sat brooding and sightless, missed the stop and decided to walk back from Blackfriars along the Embankment.

The flat was a haven. He need not talk to anyone here. He lay down on the bed without taking his coat off. He felt tired though his eyes remained stubbornly open. After a while he got up, put a Harry Parry record on the turntable and found, pacing the floor, that the moody repetitions of *Thrust and Parry* helped in some way. He listened intently, found some Glen Miller and without even realising it began to get a scratch meal together while he listened. He turned on the radio, ready for the 6 p.m. news, but kept it low. Halfway through *In the Mood* he realised Ronnie had to know about Monday.

She sounded distant and nervous. He told her about the verdict and the further postponement of the funeral.

"Monday?"

He explained. There was a silence. He puzzled over that; there wasn't a lot to be said, but it was odd just the same.

"You're getting ready to go, of course," he said.

"I'm in a bit of a rush," she said tightly. "But listen, about Monday—shall I come to you?"

"No, that's the wrong way round. It's nearer you than I am. We'll pick you up on the way. I'll give you the time as soon as I know it. And—thanks."

"Don't be silly . . ." she laughed harshly, in a splintered sort of way.

"You're all right?" he persisted.

"Of course."

He hung up, reluctantly. Time was . . .

45

He was late getting to Ronnie's. It had taken him longer than he calculated to retrieve his suitcase, change into clean clothes in the Victoria Station washroom, and return the repacked case to Left Luggage. The station swarmed with troops. A long queue of army ambulances stood waiting on the inner road and curling out into the bus area. The tube was choked with the last of the rush hour and the first of the shelterers. His train, battered veteran coaches which would have been retired but for the war, went out of service before Barons Court and he had to wait for the next. By the time he stood outside Ronnie's he was tacky with running and harassed by the thought that she might have given him up and left the flat for the night.

She came to the door, but her tight expression at once only multiplied his fears. She was wearing a skirt of heather-coloured tweed and a carefully matched sweater. Her hair fell in soft, dark waves around her shoulders. Against such grooming he felt grubby and suppliant. For a brief moment, pride alone almost drove him back to the shelters.

"Perhaps this is a mistake," he muttered.

"Come in," Ronnie said stiffly. "I want you to come in. I have to know."

He followed her into the comfortable living room. An electric log-fire glowed in the fireplace. The room was warm. He shivered gratefully.

"Know?" He stood in the middle of the room, looking round and seeing nothing. A tall, slightly hunched figure, stiff and suddenly awkward.

"A great deal," Ronnie said. She looked equally nervous, backing away from him towards the fire. She held her hands out to it. "About Frank first. And then about you." Her voice was a flat, even monotone without clues to her mood.

Willi was puzzled. "About Frank?"

"Harvey's father," Ronnie said irritably.

Willi shrugged, glad enough of another topic to open with. He smiled a little. "Frank's a good sort. He's been very kind to

267

me. I wish I could have stayed there. I'll have to explain why . . ."

"Yes, why didn't you?" Willi heard the hard edge of panic in her tone and was baffled by it. He had told her nothing yet. The truth was too improbable for her to guess at. So . . . ? He stared at her, trying to read her mood. "Well, that's the rest of the story," he said lamely. Here it came. The impossible moment.

"So tell me!"

Willi stood straighter, took a deep breath. In his unease he patrolled one end of the room slowly, touching the furniture, not knowing how or where to begin. Forget it? Run? Risk her? He'd been all through that. He could risk her and then run if it didn't turn out well. "It's not easy," he managed. Ronnie watched him, tensely, still as if any movement might kill a beginning.

"My name is not Ryder." Willi turned and looked at her over his shoulder from halfway across the room.

"No?"

"It is Reiter. R-e-i-t-e-r. Willi Reiter."

Ronnie's expression didn't change, but she seemed to gulp air and hold her breath. She looked pale.

"Yes," Willi managed a small, grim smile. "I'm German. I'm a Luftwaffe officer. If I'm caught I'll be shot as a spy." He laughed; a short, barking sound. "You can't get more trouble than that."

Ronnie's face told him nothing. She stood to the side of the fire, holding tightly to the mantel, unmoved. Willi didn't understand. He had expected hysteria, tears, fear, loathing, something. But she seemed to take that much in her stride and to be waiting for something else.

"Go on," she said.

He told her. About his mother, the war, the raids, the death of his parents. He walked about, picking up things, putting them down. But he kept his distance from her, wanting her to hear everything before she made her judgement and her decision. He told her about Eugen, Goering, Bauer and the escape. About the landing on the Ridgeway, meeting Harvey and feeling himself able to stay, secure at last until the end of the war. At some point she found cigarettes and lit them in a steady stream. She sat down on the floor by the fire, supporting herself with one arm.

He talked for nearly an hour. There was a table lamp in

one corner and the red glow from the fire, staining her cheek. The room was full of shadows. Willi stopped, abruptly, hoarse and jumpy, his head aching painfully. He felt utterly spent.

She said, staring at her hand on the rug: "You killed the boy." It was a flat statement, without emotion. It sounded as if she were drawing up a balance sheet.

But in a moment she seemed to crumple. She brought both hands up to her face and sobbed briefly. It was a small, quiet sound—so quiet he wasn't at first even sure of it. He watched and waited, keeping his distance.

"I had no choice," he said finally. "He would have gone straight to the police or the military. I had to decide in a matter of seconds."

Ronnie produced a handkerchief and blew into it. She looked up. "So you're a Nazi and a killer."

Willi stiffened. "I'm a German," he corrected. "A German escaping from all the killing. I had no option with the boy. Any more than if I had been British and on the run in Germany. What would I do then, under those circumstances? Let the first German I meet run me in? Or silence him if I could?"

"This was a boy," Ronnie protested. "A young boy!"

Willi uttered a short, angry sound. "What is a boy? Boys are shot down every day of the week. Boys die on the Russian front by the thousand every week. Boys of the same age, near enough, are dropping bombs on Berlin every night of the week."

Ronnie shook her head, pushing the idea away. Tears on her cheek glistened in the fire-glow.

For a while Willi watched her. When there seemed to be no end to whatever struggle she was having with herself, he said quietly: "I'll go."

"No," she said sharply. Her head came up and she stared at him angrily.

Willi said: "I've lived here now. People have been kind to me. Now, perhaps, I would do something else. Run and risk it. But then, at the moment, I was still at war. I have been at war for four years with your farm boy and his brother and his father and all his relatives. Perhaps his father is away now, killing Germans in Italy or even in Germany."

"You had a choice," Ronnie said bitterly. "You could have given yourself up."

Willi shrugged. "A choice of deaths. Even in the POW

269

camps here I wouldn't have been safe. The Gestapo has a long arm. It's happened before. In a week or so I'd have been found hanging in the showers and marked down as a melancholic suicide."

Ronnie got up slowly and switched on another lamp. When she returned to the fire her back was turned to him.

"I'm not ashamed of what I did," Willi said. "But involving you. Yes, that was a mistake. I'm sorry."

"And Frank?"

"Maybe he would be alive now." Ronnie had turned to watch his face, recording the movement of every muscle.

"Frank?" he said again dully.

"Yes, Frank. He is dead."

"But how? When?" Willi moved towards her. His shock and anxiety clear and simple.

"Sunday night," Ronnie said. She sidestepped the hand he reached out to her.

Willi digested that. "How?" It was a long, anguished sound.

"He was stabbed," Ronnie said, her voice disintegrating. "Stabbed in his own kitchen. He was found by a neighbour on Sunday night after Harvey had been unable to get him on the phone." She covered her mouth with both hands briefly. "He had already been dead some hours."

"But I only left him on Sunday morning . . ." Willi's mind reeled. It was bad enough to hear Frank was dead. But Sunday night! The implications were staggering.

"What do the police think?" he asked, already knowing the answer.

"That you killed him," Ronnie said. Her voice was steely.

Willi stared. So they were looking, now, for Bill Ryder. God! He'd been lucky to get away the other night. They had been looking for him.

For perhaps a minute nothing was said. Ronnie stood straight and still, her eyes avoiding him. Willi couldn't go into all the implications. There was a thread here he had to follow. "And still you asked me to come here?" he said. "Why?"

"To see if you killed Frank," Ronnie said calmly.

"And you've seen?"

Her lips parted to say something and she moved fractionally towards him. Then she drew back. "Tell me," she whispered.

"I did not kill Frank," Willi said calmly. "I had no need. I liked Frank. He was kind to me. We liked each other. The thought of his being dead . . ." He broke off, speechless. And then: "You know, once or twice I had the idea that if he had known about me, if I had told him, he would have kept quiet just the same. Sometimes I wanted to tell him, wanted to put it to the test. Telling someone would have been—a weight off me."

"But he is dead," Ronnie persisted.

Willi thought about it. At last he whispered: "Jerome!"

Ronnie looked at him, baffled. He explained.

"But why?" She seemed to accept the possibility at once and to be troubled only by a lack of motive.

"I don't know. Perhaps he went there looking for me. Perhaps Frank grew suspicious. You're right in one way. It was me Jerome was looking for. And he found only Frank. In one way, I did kill Frank; I'm the cause."

Again the silence grew. Willi sat down, preoccupied. Ronnie watched him, her face less stony. At last Willi looked up: "Perhaps you had better fetch the police," he said. "I have to tell them about Jerome. He must pay. He can't be allowed to get away with it."

"No!" Ronnie said fiercely.

"I'll see them," Willi said urgently.

"It doesn't help."

Again the silence. A new horror struck Willi. "What about Harvey? Does he think I killed Frank?"

She nodded miserably.

He sat stunned. It had all come down to this, then, after all. This was the end of his run.

"I'll go," he said in a moment.

"No," Ronnie said decisively. "I'll help you."

"Why? Why would you do that?"

The answer was a long time coming. Willi had almost decided there wasn't going to be one. Nothing could, in any case, be based on such an impulse on her part. He got up and moved to the door. Ronnie got there first and blocked the door. Her right hand found his left and rested there.

Willi began to lose his grip on reality. It was a small movement, but it at once ranged Ronnie alongside him. It gave him a friend. Her acceptance of him in that one small and unspectacular gesture was cathartic. It lifted some of the burden of guilt over the boy he'd killed. He hadn't realised how heavy it had weighed on him until now. It was the same with the identity of Bill Ryder. At last there was someone with whom he could step out of that. It was like taking off layers of heavy clothing, a sensation almost exalting. He didn't dare think further than that. The idea of Ronnie had invaded him when they first met and a hunger for her had been building in him ever since. Now, unbelievably, she had stepped towards him more than a little. It was enough, and it was also too much. He struggled with his feelings of release, gratitude, protectiveness all at once. He was too astonished to be anything but cautious. He patted her shoulder gently, and when she stepped closer still, kissed her forehead lightly.

"I'm still running," he said. "It will take time to stop and find out where I am."

Ronnie was at once solicitous. She demanded to know what he needed first.

He was sure of that, at least. "A bath," he said. "Is that possible?"

"And food?"

"That too," Willi said apologetically. "But a bath is more important."

Ronnie was glad to have something to do. She ran the bath, pushed him into the bathroom and shut herself in the kitchen.

She stood stock still in the middle of the kitchen, willing herself to stop thinking. She could never justify what she was doing, what she was about to do, to anyone else. Harvey would be shocked and outraged, perhaps rightly. Her father would be horrified. The police . . . she didn't dare think of the penalties. She must not think! This was what she wanted to do, so it was better to do it blindly. She rummaged in her cupboard and found a tin of Spam she had saved. She sliced it and began to fry it while mixing dried egg for a large omelette. She cut bread, set coffee to heat. For a while she was able to ignore the turmoil that suddenly raged in her mind.

When Willi emerged from the bathroom, very tentatively, the fragrance of the cooking hit him like a physical pain. His stomach growled noisily. He watched her move about, wondering. Like Ronnie he didn't want to think too much about next steps.

They ate together at the kitchen table, saying little. At one point she put out a hand and touched his. "Just before you arrived," she said, "Harvey rang. He was at the inquest." She poured coffee, her hand trembling a little.

"Yes?"

"Murder by persons unknown. I'm afraid you are the principal police suspect. They were looking for you anyway. After today they'll be really trying."

"I was about to give up sleeping in shelters," Willi said. He related his near capture in the Underground. "I was going to try a hotel again."

"You have to have an identity card," Ronnie objected.

"I have one. It's forged, but it's got me by in the past. That's no use now. A different name is no good without a matching card to back it up." The news filled him with gloom.

"Then hotels are out," Ronnie smiled. "You're stuck with me."

"You?"

"You can stay here," Ronnie said. She lifted her eyebrows at him. "Unless you'll feel . . . menaced?"

Willi opened his mouth to say something but found no suitable words. His pulse stepped up appreciably. The hunger for Ronnie returned at once, rekindled and blotting out everything else. A touch of hysteria gripped him. He assumed a dramatic expression. "I can never repay you," he said. It was another line from a film he'd seen.

Ronnie giggled and found it difficult to stop. The hysteria had touched her, too. "Don't be so sure," she said, between fits of laughter. "You don't know what you're capable of until you're rested."

Willi grinned, embarrassed. He hoped the stomp of his heartbeat wasn't audible.

They washed the dishes. Ronnie sat him in the largest armchair. She sat on the floor at his feet, her arm hooked over his knees. After a minute or two he stroked her hair. It was very quiet for a time. Someone in a flat on the floor below began to play Chopin on an untuned piano, a melancholy sound. She looked up and Willi grinned down, unbelieving.

Outside the sky went dramatic. Huge clouds, which had darkened the day down to winter grey, rolled aside and revealed a crimson and gold dying of the sun of a day in Double British Summer Time. Neither spoke. They watched the colours move and change. She rested her head on his knee. Sometimes, despite everything, his eyelids drooped. At last she stood up and drew the curtains. Willi stirred and stretched, his legs cramped and lifeless.

Somehow they stood, uncertain, facing each other. Willi had no idea how the next step was to be managed either.

After a moment of hesitation he simply scooped her up and carried her into the bedroom. He stood her on her feet and sat on the bed to watch. Ronnie shed her skirt and sweater.

"And?"

"The rest," Willi said.

Ronnie considered. "Can I clean my teeth?"

Willi shook his head. He hoped he looked impassive and controlled. Breathless, he watched her strip and stand submissive as a child. He forgot he was tired and hunted, trapped and helpless. He found he could think of nothing but her body. He gloated over the full breasts, flat stomach and long legs. The thought flitted unwelcome through his mind that Harvey was mad to lose her. And, sadly, that Frank, at the same age, would not have. He winced over the thought of Frank. Poor old Frank. His vision clouded for a moment. Then Ronnie bent to him, unwilling that he should hesitate. And he surrendered to pure pleasure in a way that he was sure he never had before.

Much later, as they lay, coupled still, exquisitely postponing the final act, Ronnie murmured close to his ear: "I lied to you."

"Yes?"

"At the Savoy. I said I wanted to help you—as a friend."

"And?"

"Lies, all lies. I just want you."

"There will be a penalty," Willi said, one part of him marvelling at his ability—after months of deprivation—to keep still.

"I'll pay," Ronnie said. "I'll pay."

46

Willi woke, suddenly apprehensive in the alien darkness. He lay still for a long moment of terror, unable to account for the bed, the time or the place. Gradually he pieced it together. Ronnie's flat. Ronnie. He found her on his left, lifted himself on one elbow and looked down at her. She lay still as death, her lips parted, seeming not to breathe.

He came wide awake and trod softly to the window. All

seemed well, but he had to be sure. He looked out over the wet rooftops and chimneys, the railed gardens, torn and squalid with the rusting corrugated fronts of shelters and the debris of too-close bombings. There were no lights and nothing moved in the blue-grey pre-dawn. It had been another quiet night. He couldn't see the front of the flats, but the back looked peaceful enough.

He was reassured. His spirits lifted suddenly. Were things so bad after all? It could easily have gone very much worse—right from the start. There was Frank Marsh, of course, and that was bad enough. And the farm kid. But he had got away with it so far. And would he have minded so much, even back at the starting point at Rangsdorf, if he could have known then that this was the worst he would suffer—hiding in the flat of a beautiful girl? What would Bauer have thought? He grinned in the dark. "Palmy bastard" probably. He could imagine Dieter's expression of joyful incredulity.

And now? He must try to be content with the fact that Ronnie seemed to want to befriend him, indeed—to want him; and against all her judgement and training was willing to protect him. He pushed away the word 'love'—with some regret. This was time out of war, when all normal emotions and motives were suspended, magnified or distorted. It was a wild dream being here at all.

He looked across at the bed. What could he give her in return? Comfort? Passion? The hope of something better at some time in the hazy future? Perhaps more; he didn't understand much about her. He had heard of other alliances between Italian and German prisoners-of-war and English girls. That was in the rural areas, surely? This was no inexperienced farm girl; no ordinary woman at all ... and there was no accounting for her. But, by Christ, he admired her! If he could stay alive, if he could get through the next few weeks, he would try to claim her, keep her and so arrange his life that she came first.

He padded to the bathroom and rinsed his mouth. Ronnie had scarcely moved. One white arm had escaped from the covers. She had beautiful shoulders, he thought. He eased himself back into the bed and lay studying her face in the gloom.

When he woke again, Ronnie was already moving about in the kitchen. Frank Phillips was reading the eight o'clock news of the night's chaos somewhere else. She came in, breathtakingly fresh and natural, her hair coiled, her eyes

275

bright. She dropped a lush towel on his head. "Five inches of bath water, no more," she said. "Coffee and toast when you're ready."

Willi was hungry again. They ate, beaming at each other. They smoked several cigarettes. What now?

"Well you can't go out during the day," Ronnie said. "But after dark we could walk somewhere. Two of us will look better."

"What about the Ministry?"

Ronnie thought about it. "I'll ring Gwen. I have some unused holiday. She won't mind."

Willi thought it would look strange—suddenly to claim a holiday right after pleading that she hadn't been well.

Ronnie didn't think so. "What more natural? I'm tired, run down, need a break. Leave it to me. Gwen's not the nosey kind. Do you know your voice has changed?"

"My voice?"

"Your accent. I can hear the German now." She was delighted with his instant alarm. "It isn't much, but it's there. I'm glad. You don't have to be someone else any more."

"Outside I do," Willi said grimly. He heard it himself then; a crisp division of the word 'outside' into two separate syllables each with a hard terminal consonant. He said it again, this time hearing the word in English in his head. "Outside I do," he drawled.

"Very good." She patted his hand. She saw that he had begun to worry about it. "Oh, come on," she said. "How long is it, after all? Weeks?"

Willi scowled. "I can't stay here until the war ends. You couldn't keep a secret like this for that long. Other people will come here . . ."

"No-one comes here," Ronnie insisted. "That was the whole idea. Well, Harvey did. But not any longer."

"What about food?" Willi objected. "If the police are looking for Bill Ryder then I have no ration book, nothing."

"Oh, food!" Ronnie dismissed it. "If you have money enough you can always buy something to eat. We'll manage."

"Money!" Willi jumped up. His briefcase was in the hall with his coat. He brought it in triumphantly and emptied it onto the carpet. "What about this lot?" Much of the money, he realised with sick anxiety, was in the bank account of William Ryder. That, too, was now closed to him. His enthusiasm died completely when he saw he had forgotten the gun. It lay amid the piles of used notes as evil and incongruous in that room as a cudgel in a nursery.

"I'm sorry about that," Willy said dully. "It was Dieter's idea. I'll get rid of it. Perhaps tonight when we're out . . ."

She couldn't believe the money was real. "Oh, it's real enough," he told her. "I didn't rob a bank. Well, perhaps I did in a way. It started off as counterfeit fivers. I've been changing it gradually . . ." He didn't understand her expression. She was fighting down a giggle.

"Say fivers," she demanded.

"Fivers . . ."

"No five-ers—with a vee."

"Fivers," he corrected. "God, I will have to watch it."

"Ja," Ronnie said. "You vill."

He caught her wrist. She struggled, giggling, then melted suddenly, her mouth insistent on his.

They needed more food. At his insistence Ronnie went out armed with money from one of Willi's bundles of £100. As soon as the door closed behind her he began to worry—he couldn't have said about what. To pass the time he tried visualising her trip: downstairs, along the length of the street, perhaps as far as that again to the shops, picking up purchases, filling her basket, paying, and then the journey back. When she'd been gone twice the time it had taken in his mind he began to pace, watching her modern electric clock inch round. When she let herself in, loaded, he felt foolish and said nothing.

She rang Gwen and arranged her absence. Somehow, during the making of a salad, they switched from Gwen's life and hard times to Willi's. He talked about his mother, about his pre-war holiday in England, even about the girl from Dollis Hill. Ronnie smiled at that. "Some teacher," she said, rolling her eyes. "Some pupil." The one thing he couldn't bring himself to talk about was Eugen. He was outside her experience. Oh, she could learn to shudder at the implications of the SS, but she couldn't be expected to understand how that kind of thing had split father and son, mother and daughter, brother and brother. He found that the recitation had brought on memories he had no use for now. It was difficult shaking them off. He sat over the litter of their lunch, staring moodily at his plate.

Ronnie watched him for a while, then took him by the hand and led him into the bedroom. The sun shone brilliantly on this side of the flat, flooding the ivory walls with light. She undressed and lay down on the bed, her body seeming to blend with the rich oyster brocade of the spread in a sunlit mother-of-pearl.

"Okay, Doctor," Willi said. "This is what you prescribe?"

"Three times a day after meals," Ronnie assured him.

He grinned and threw off his clothes. He forgot about Eugen. He forgot his fears. The frustrations of being confined in the flat vanished. His last thought, as he put his arms round her, was that the real danger lay in coming to enjoy his prison. The quarry had to remain always cautious and vigilant, however deep the cover.

47

At this stage of the war not too many young men walked the streets of London in civilian clothes. Fewer still were tall, dark and rugged. It made the job of logging Willi's arrival at Queen's Club Gardens fairly simple for the man called Darby.

He did it neatly, quickly and professionally in the first hour of his shift. He had spent some time in a doorway of the flats one block along to the right, chain-smoking and building a litter of cigarette ends at his feet. One or two residents on their way in or out had looked at him curiously, but no porter had disturbed him. His procedure was simple. The moment a 'possible' entered the square from the main road he stepped out smartly and walked fast to the doorway of the Croft girl's block, reaching it seconds before the other man. That gave him a moment or two in which they directly walked towards each other. If the description didn't match he walked on past. If it did he would make a sharp turn into the doorway of the Croft block and bound up to the floor above. It was a distance nicely judged. It worked just as well for an arrival by cab. If the fare looked right, all he had to do was to use the seconds while the cab was being paid off to climb to his observation point.

The light was going. He had only one false alarm. The bearing, height and weight were about right, but as he drew close Darby saw that his first try was a man nearer sixty than thirty. He circled the square and came to rest again in his hallway.

He had only ten minutes more to wait. A woman walked her dog, calling to it in Polish. A teenage girl came from the Queen's Club direction, carrying a tennis racket. And then, almost immediately, another 'possible'. As they drew close, Darby made the snap decision. This was the one. He turned abruptly into the block, leaving the door swinging as the other man reached it, pounded up the stairs and dropped into a crouch on the landing above. The other man came up the stairs fast, hesitated and then came to rest outside the Croft girl's door. Darby was delighted. With any luck he would be free for the rest of the evening. His listened carefully, watching the legs of his man.

"Perhaps this is a mistake?" he heard the man mutter. He didn't hear the woman's reply. The door closed on them both. He waited only a second or two longer and then headed briskly for the phone box on the far corner.

Fifteen minutes later, Thelma Franks was ringing Fairbrother. "That Mr Hands wants you to ring," she said. "Though I must say it seems awfully late for any kind of business. Can't you at least arrange to have your evenings free, dear?"

Fairbrother digested the report from Hands. He remained baffled. It was a piece of good luck, but he still knew nothing about the motives of the people in the affair. And he was reluctant to move while that was so. He had ordered the observation continued, of course. That might yield something more. Ryder was to be followed wherever he went and however far afield that might lead. He could not risk losing him again. He would have liked to know a great deal more. He could not believe that the Savoy corridor thing explained anything very much. There was the connection with the Marshes still slightly in doubt, for example. And now? He sensed that even Harvey Marsh would be surprised by this development.

He had been preparing for bed. Now he dressed again and paced a little. At least he knew where Reiter was. Should he seize this opportunity? He did not relish tackling Reiter inside the Croft flat . . . unless, of course, the girl was first safely out of it.

He had other worries. Reiter on his own had simply been a rogue who could be plucked down at any time. But what if he were now to confide in the girl? It was true that the name

'Jerome' was the only one that Reiter could link him with. Still, even that might bring a really clever policeman uncomfortably close.

He made up his mind. He could not afford to wait any longer. He must try to resolve the problem of Reiter at once. After that . . . he must fudge his own trail. Close the shop. He would see the agent, pay what was necessary to end the lease and then remove all traces of himself. He knew of no slip he had made so far, and he would tread very carefully from now on. When Reiter was found dead the police would have to look for someone else to blame for the death of Frank Marsh and Mrs Flax. He had, perhaps, had the shop too long anyway. He looked briefly round his comfortable little flat. This too, he thought. But his sense of caution was growing. He would start again somewhere else. And in between times he would go to Thelma.

As he let himself out he had no clear idea of his next move. Reiter was at the girl's flat. If he wanted Reiter quickly, that's where he had to be.

48

McNair had suggested a drink at the Press Club and a talk about his role in the field. Suspended between the postmortem and the funeral, Harvey was less than enthusiastic. Yet McNair had been good to him and perhaps it was sensible to get his mind on to something else. He was on his way downstairs when he remembered he hadn't told Ronnie the time of the funeral. How odd she didn't ask, either. He walked back up and dialled the MOI. But when he got through to the canteen it was Gwen who answered.

"She was off sick last night and she has these days in hand, so I'm hoping she'll use them sensibly," Gwen said. "She said she might even go down to Lammas."

Harvey couldn't miss a slightly mocking note in Gwen's tone. He was surprised at Gwen. She was evidently one of those women who, when they scented a change of course by a friend, were ever anxious to be there first. He wanted to ask her what Ronnie had been sick with, but he hung up instead.

He got as far as the door, turned back and rang Lammas. She couldn't be there, surely? Mrs Childs confirmed it. "Miss Ronnie isn't here, sir, and isn't expected." Frustrated, he rang Mount Street, which is what he ought to have done first. She wasn't there either.

So where was she? At Queen's Club? On her own? He was then unsettled by the thought of Ronnie sick and alone there. He pictured it as being the way he'd last seen it: glass in the bed, plaster dust everywhere. It was no place to be. And what was wrong with her anyway? She had seemed all right when he'd seen her last. He picked up the phone again, got McNair, explained hurriedly and almost ran up to Fleet Street in the hope of a cab.

He had a feeling of being in limbo. He had made arrangements to cover his mail, the rent of the flat, someone to look in now and then in case the block was bombed. He'd notified the police he'd be away within a week. Now there was nothing left to do. There were no more shifts at ABP. A few goodbyes were all that remained. On the way out to West Kensington he told himself he wouldn't have time to feel anything at all once he reported to 12th Army Group HQ. It did nothing to lessen his heavy depression.

Passing the old Kinema, now derelict, he stopped the cab, feeling the need to walk the last half-mile. It now occurred to him that Ronnie might have had a purpose in going back to Queen's Club; indeed for reporting sick. Someone else? Someone new? He didn't seriously believe it, but it slowed him up and on the instant he was just a little embarrassed at the idea of turning up on her doorstep. He needed a moment to think.

The night was cool and clear. Brilliant moonlight lit up the devastation caused by the flying-bomb which had wrecked Ronnie's flat. On the corner where he'd found the dead couple that night he paused and peered morbidly into the shop doorway. On the next corner a night-school class was emerging. An unseasonable baked-potato man, his brazier a bright and savoury oasis in a desert of shabby brick and soiled concrete, had already claimed a dozen or more noisy teenage students.

By the time he'd rung Ronnie's bell he'd dispelled his doubts. This was Ronnie, for God's sake, not some stranger. He had a right to be concerned about her, if nothing else.

She took a long time answering. When she did her eyes widened with shock. She said nothing. Just stared.

Disconcerted, he said: "Are you all right? I heard you weren't well."

Ronnie stood holding the door. She made no move to let him in. Her expression didn't help. She looked—frightened. "I'm fine," she said at last. It hadn't sounded too convincing, so she cleared her throat and said it again.

Her behaviour made him still more anxious. He couldn't, after coming all this way, simply go back without finding out what it was all about. "I'm not allowed in?" he said reproachfully.

Ronnie hesitated. "Can we keep it brief, Harvey? I have a lot to do." She stood aside reluctantly.

"Are you going to Lammas?" he asked. But she didn't reply. She looked round the room wildly as if she had lost something. Not finding it, she offered him a drink. "I only have beer, I'm afraid." Beer? He'd never known Ronnie to have any in the house.

"What's all this about you not being well?"

"What?" Furrows of irritability appeared between her eyebrows. It struck him at once as wholly uncharacteristic.

"I thought you'd be at the MOI, so I rang to tell you the time of the funeral."

She shrugged. "And they said I was having a few days off. What's wrong with that?"

"Nothing, except Gwen said you'd been off last night, feeling low. She sounded concerned." It wasn't quite true, but it would do. "She also said you might be at Lammas."

"I thought of it," Ronnie said. She circled the room, restlessly.

"So I rang you there . . ."

She stared at him angrily. "Why are you chasing me like this?"

He was astounded. And then angry in turn. "I'm concerned," he said heavily. "For heaven's sake . . . a month or so ago we were lovers. Aren't we even caring friends now?"

"Of course," her tone relented a little.

"So I decided you were at Mount Street."

"And rang me there, too?" Her irritation was barely under control.

"Yes."

"And now you've found me."

"And you're all right?"

"I said so." She had relented, made an effort to smile. "Yes, I'm all right. I just haven't had too much holiday. Once in a while—well you know what night work does to you."

282

"Sure."

There was an awkward silence.

"When *is* the funeral?" she asked.

"Ten. So if you like I'll pick you up on the way."

"Fine. I'll see about flowers and so on first thing tomorrow." Another silence.

Harvey was now determined to sit out her temper. He sipped at his beer, saying nothing. At last she perched on the arm of a chair and said: "When will you be off?"

"Hard to say. Next week, perhaps. The War Office is going slow. I think it's a reprisal for letting a death in the family interfere with their original timing."

"Is there anything else to keep you?"

"No. I can't do any good here. Mac will let me know if anything comes up with the police. Or they grab Ryder, or whatever his name is. Aren't you having anything?"

"No—I might have some coffee later." The suggestion of when I've got rid of you' was painfully clear. Doggedly, he offered her a cigarette.

She reached for it and then looked apathetically at the brand. She smiled faintly. "Best you could get? I think I've done better." She looked around vaguely.

Harvey also looked about him helpfully, saw cigarettes on a drum table. Churchmans No. I. "They're here . . ." He got up, helped himself, passed her the packet. There was a lighter on the table, too. He lit his cigarette, lit hers and wondered why her hand shook.

He clicked the lighter closed, looked at it and set it down on the arm of the chair. He stared at it, picked it up again. A leather-covered Thorens.

Dumbly he held it out to her on the palm of his hand. She stood up and walked away. "Harvey," she said tremulously. "I'm very tired. Would you mind going now? I'll see you on Monday." She stood with her back to him, looking down at the electric fire.

Harvey looked at the lighter again. "It *is* Ryder's. I've seen him use it dozens of times."

"Harvey . . . please . . ." She sounded close to tears.

Incredulity engulfed him for a moment or two. But her back told him he wasn't wrong. He felt outrage and fury kindle and catch fire. Shock drove the blood from his face; he actually felt it drain. He also had the eerie sensation of watching himself from somewhere above and to the right. From that position he saw his own choler rising.

"He's here!" he whispered. "Isn't he? Here, by God!" He stepped about agitatedly, hardly knowing what he was doing. "What the hell are you doing, Ronnie! Christ!"

She turned then and reached for him, her expression one of anguish.

For a moment or two longer he was immobilised by his own indignation and astonishment. He looked round, wildly. It occurred to him only vaguely that he had no right to search the rooms. "Have I not, by God!" He was conscious of striding into the kitchen and throwing open the door. Then the bathroom. He came back into the living room, breathing hard. There was only one other place. He bore down on the bedroom door, moved by his rage and with no clear idea of what he intended. Ronnie got there first and set her back to the door. Her face was crumpled and silent tears poured down her cheeks.

"Get away from it," he said harshly.

"Go away, Harvey. Just go away."

"Do you know what you're doing?" He still hesitated to handle her roughly.

Behind her the door opened. Ryder sood there.

Ronnie let her arms fall. "Now you know," she said.

Willi said calmly: "I understand your anger. But it is misplaced. I was not responsible for your father's death. You must listen. I can satisfy you . . ."

For a moment or two Harvey had been immobilised by the shock of Willi's sudden appearance. It took him seconds more to do what his brain commanded. He leapt at Ryder, bearing him backwards through the door, and struggled to get a grip on his throat. Willi was taken by surprise. Off-balance he was up against the side of the bed before he could recover. He struggled to speak, but Harvey's hands were locked tight on his throat.

Harvey held on a moment longer. Then his arms were knocked away and he felt a fierce stabbing pain under the ribs. He slid down to the floor beside the bed, winded and unable to speak or even move. His rasping breath sounded oddly amplified inside his head in some way. It was a full minute before he sat up, painfully. Then stood up. He attempted to straighten himself, focused on Willi, standing close, and aimed a furious blow at his head. It missed wildly, and Willi appeared on his left.

"Listen Harvey, I can satisfy you about—" Harvey shambled forwards and brought his head up brutally against

284

Willi's chin. He heard the grunt of pain and wondered whether it was Ryder's or his own; the top if his head felt as if it had been slammed by a bar of steel. At once he was hurled to the floor.

He looked up, fuming. Ronnie stood in the background, her mouth clamped over her knuckles. Willi stood over him. Harvey came off the floor, roaring with pain and anger, but Willi simply stepped back neatly and hit him hard on the side of the head.

Panting, Harvey lay on the floor, his teeth, his mind, his body clenched against the pain of the blow.

"Willi," he heard Ronnie say, fearfully: "No more, please . . ."

"Willi! For Christ's sake! He came up again, murderously. He actually wanted to kill now. He felt the drive of it, lifting him, soaking up his pain. But before he could focus, a thunderclap clouted him over the right ear and he fell, consciousness draining away. He heard his own last, dry rattle before he passed out completely.

Seconds or minutes later, feeling returned with a wash of pain. He was lying on the bed. Ryder stood at the foot. In his hand was a gun, a small, lethal-looking thing. Ronnie . . . his eyes hurt as they moved to find her, watched, distressed, her back to the window.

"Now will you listen?" Willi said.

Harvey glared at him, hatred and outrage supercharged by his pain and the humiliation of being so demonstrably unable to hold his own with the man. "I'll kill you," he said grimly. But he watched the gun with fear. He wondered, feverishly, if these were going to be his last few minutes.

"Listen," Willi said. "Quite correctly, you have reasoned it all out. That I am a German. The German, in fact, from the aircraft that crashed that day. And so? Have you always wanted to kill all Germans yourself, barehanded?" He drew a long breath and comforted his jaw with his left hand. The barrel of the gun came up and pointed at Harvey's head. "I could very easily kill you right now and then run," Willi said.

Even Ronnie believed it for a second. "Willi!" she half-screamed. "Put it down, now!"

"I will," Willi told her. "In a moment. First he must listen." He looked at Harvey again.

"I did not kill your father. One of your own countrymen did that. A man called Jerome. You can have the whole story if you will be sensible and sit still. Just listen, that's all I ask of you."

So he was not to die provided he was a good boy. Harvey breathed a little more freely. He avoided looking at the man Ryder. He focused on Ronnie instead, his expression one of loathing and contempt. She saw it and her eyes slid away from his. She moved out of his range of vision.

"I mean you no harm," Willi told him. "I ask only that you listen to the truth. Will you do that?"

"Put the gun away," Harvey said weakly.

Willi looked down at it, almost surprised to find himself holding it. After a moment he said: "All right . . ." He dropped his arm to his side.

"Better still," Harvey said, "give it to me." He was astonished to hear that he sounded exactly as he had intended: resigned, calm, no longer intent on violence. What had happened, his tone suggested, was only what anyone could expect as a first reaction.

"You'll listen?" Willi demanded.

"I'll listen," Harvey said dully. He sat up slowly, wincing, hoping to look and sound so preoccupied with his own condition as to forestall any reaction. After a moment he swung his legs over the side of the bed and held his head in his hands for a moment. Then, carefully, he stood and straightened, once or twice sucking in his breath sharply as his brain located new areas of pain. "Give me the gun," he repeated wearily.

For a moment only, Willi hesitated. Harvey seemed more rational. He had not ever intended to use the gun, only to demand a breathing space, talking space with it. Handing it over might be one way of convincing Harvey of that. He reversed it in his hand and held it out.

Harvey took it with his left hand, transferred it to his right, fitted the butt neatly in his palm, felt for the trigger and brought the gun up in a low, arching movement. He saw, with triumph, Ryder's immediate knowledge of his mistake.

"Harvey, no!" Ronnie screamed.

Harvey pointed the gun and squeezed the trigger.

Nothing happened.

Harvey couldn't believe it.

Willi exploded sideways through the door and vanished.

Harvey withdrew the gun and looked at it stupidly for a moment before he realised that the safety catch was on. By the time he'd located it and thumbed it down, the front door had slammed.

Ronnie flung herself at him. "Harvey! For God's sake, stop

and think!" She hung on his right arm. In an effort to free himself he brought up the arm so that at one moment he had the gun pointing directly at her face.

He used the same ploy he'd used a moment or two ago. He lowered his arms, slowly. She relaxed her grip and stood back. On the instant he had thrust her aside and was moving in pursuit. He tore the front door open, burst out onto the landing and stopped short to listen. Below, he heard the swing doors to the street flap wildly—and the receding sound of Ryder's running feet. He launched himself down the stairs. Ryder was not going to get away again.

He was totally unaware of Ronnie, close behind them both. Unaware, too, of Fairbrother who, watching from the telephone box that Hand's man, Darby, had used earlier, was suddenly alert and smiling exultantly.

Fairbrother left the box and moved quickly along the opposite side of the square. He had been right to come. Again he had trusted his instinct and triumphed. The moonlight troubled him not at all. It was clear that all three protagonists were much too preoccupied with their own drama to notice a lone walker.

It was beginning to make sense. Reiter was in full flight, Marsh in pursuit. And from their order of arrival at the flat it was at last clear that Reiter's being there had been a shock and an affront to Marsh. Now he would have to follow, of course, as best he could. If Marsh did his work for him, all to the good. It would provide the police with a neat case, with no need to look further. Reiter would seem to have killed the elder Marsh and Mrs Flax and to have been killed, in his turn, by the younger Marsh. Neat. Very neat. How to bring it about?

He must keep close to them. But he must watch the girl. She wouldn't be able to keep up and it would be awkward if she turned back suddenly, between himself and the two men.

He reasoned that the chase could not go far beyond this huddle of streets. Once out on a main road it would be inhibited by traffic, passers-by, police even. If it went on long, it was more likely to turn back this way. If he wanted to stay alive, Reiter had to shake off Marsh before others joined in.

Fairbrother broke into a gentle trot, emerging warily from the square just as the Croft girl faltered, as expected, and stood helplessly uncertain of what to do next. He thought quickly. There was one other exit from the square—a narrow footpath leading from the inside end of the garden strip at the back of the block of flats behind him to the right. Provided for the tenants of the flats, it had three concrete posts across its mouth to hinder bicycle-riding, the intrusion of trademen's carts and other ungenteel nuisances. But for the tenants it cut through to the road beyond the square.

Fairbrother about-turned smartly. When he again emerged into the road, the girl had gone. Presumably back towards her flat. He was delighted. He'd cut the corner, avoided the girl and saved time.

He heard a shot and hurried on.

49

Running hard, Willi turned sharp left away from the main road area. Any fuss, pursuit or shouting out there and he'd be surrounded in a few moments; wartime London at night crawled with wardens, rescue teams, AFS, fire-watchers—the city was never totally asleep. He was out of the area of the flats and into a minor road before he heard the runner behind him. It had to be Harvey. He didn't like it. What the hell was he to do next? Get clear, get clear! Out of the district. Once he lost Harvey he would be free to go wherever he wanted. But it was clear that Harvey was going to use the gun if he caught up. He had to go on.

The moon didn't help. It was riding in a cloudless sky. The open spaces were bathed in the milk-white glare of it, the shadows deep and sharp-edged as under a cold sun.

An additional problem was that he didn't know the area. Or anywhere round here, except the main road. He would have to try to work round to that in a wide curve, once he'd outrun Harvey.

There was no traffic this late. The road ran straight for perhaps two hundred yards and then curved to the left out of sight. He'd have to take it on trust. He made for the bend, legs pumping, the old wound not hindering too much at this stage. On the corner he slowed and looked back. He saw Harvey emerge from Queen's Club. Worse, Harvey saw him. And came on fast. He thought he heard Ronnie, but didn't see her. He swore as he saw that Harvey had already cut a big piece off his lead.

He was running beside a high brick wall. A sign. An elementary school, whatever that was. He swept past a gate. And another. And stopped and came back to it. The road ahead was too straight and long. The gate was tall, iron and closed. He tried the huge iron knob. It turned, the gate swung open with an appalling noise. On the other side of the wall the shadows were black. He passed the inside of another gate, and came to rest in a dark angle at the end of the wall. He squatted gratefully, feeling the relief in his thigh and calf muscles. The only trouble was that his lower left leg throbbed painfully, as though the metal plate had been torn forcibly away from its moorings in the flesh below the calf. He controlled his breathing, slowing it, using each mouthful before exhaling. Little by little he ironed out the raggedness and the knot of pain in his chest melted.

He heard Harvey come on, fast. He could almost see him scan the road ahead, check at once, and look around. His ears strained for the sound of movement.

Almost at once he heard a gate yawn. In full moonlight Harvey shouldered his way into the hard-surfaced school yard, stood for a moment, looking around, and then came on again. Willi could see why. The largest expanse of the school yard was ahead of Harvey and in full moonlight—and empty. He ought to have moved into the narrower passage between the bulk of the school building and the high wall running away from him now at right angles. That was the only area of concealment. Harvey was only a few yards away. Any nearer and he couldn't fail to be seen in the shadows.

No sense waiting. Willi launched himself out of the shadows, going like a hundred-yards sprinter. Once across the patch of moonlight he'd be swallowed up in real darkness. He heard Harvey exclaim and spring into action. For a few seconds his back was a perfect target, but no shot came. He'd taken Harvey by surprise.

Willi sped down the alleyway to the back of the school, praying that there was an opening at the other end. The darkness was impenetrable. He stared frantically into the gloom, slowing inevitably. It felt like running off the edge of the earth.

The shot, when it came, unnerved him. It resounded deafeningly in the narrow area, seeming to go on for seconds. His skin crawled. The next one might find him easily.

A wall loomed ahead. He fought down panic. On his right was what looked like a bicycle shelter with a corrugated iron roof, the high perimeter wall serving as back and end. He ran at it, dug his heels into the support timbers, and was up on the roof. But the noise advertised every step he took.

At the end of the roof the outer wall rose only three feet higher. But the top was surmounted by wire netting adding another four feet. He booted the netting at the bottom edge to get a foothold on the top of the wall and then folded his weight over the top edge. The stuff crumpled and gave. He worked it down, swung a leg over and transferred his footing to the other side of the netting.

A second shot slammed into the darkness, the sound uncomfortably near and rattling off the walls below. Willi looked down, anxiously.

Out of the shadow of the school, what looked like a short private road gleamed a blotchy, concrete-white below him. On the right, some distance away, rose the back of a four-storey factory or warehouse with another low building running at right angles from it towards him. To his left a pole barrier and weighbridge hut sat astride the road. By the side of the hut was a railed slope down into the ground. The word SHELTER gleamed white on black above it. As he looked, four or five men came up the slope at a run. They wore steel helmets, overalls and rubber boots, the standard uniform of the volunteer fire-watcher. At the top of the slope they milled about. One man spotted him and pointed up.

Willi couldn't go back. He could already hear Harvey scrabbling at the corrugated iron roof. The only way to go was down.

There was a chance further along. The netting provided something to steady him on the top of the wall. Halfway between himself and far end of the yard below him was a pile of wooden crates. It looked unstable, but better than the 12-foot drop with his leg in this shape. Clinging to the netting, he worked his way along briskly, speeding up as he heard Harvey make it to the roof and begin pounding along. The men in the yard below him watched his progress, following him along, shouting and gesticulating.

He reached the crates, dropped onto them at the highest level. They crumpled. His left leg drove straight through one, imprisoning his foot, the fractured wood gouging deep into the skin of his shin and calf. The pile teetered. He leapt down one stage, clumsily bringing with him the box still clamped round his foot. He lost his balance, clutched at the swaying mass and shredded his hands on a mess of nails and ribboned-metal strapping. He bent, rolled and ended up on the ground.

The men moved in around him. Willi bent and stove the sides of the crate in, freeing his foot. One of the men, bolder than the rest, grasped him by the shoulder. "Just what d'you think you're playing at?" He hardly had the words out when Willi hit him in the throat. The man collapsed, his strangled scream momentarily freezing the valour of the others. But more men were piling out of the shelter now. Willi charged through the four who still barred his way. A boy's face loomed at him, all eyes and teeth under his too-big steel helmet. Willi smashed his fist into the face and the boy fell, instantly, silently. A fat man grappled with him. Willi drove his fist deep into the man's gut. The hands dropped away and the fat man shrank down into a kneeling position like a punctured rabbit.

He was clear and running to the low building now. Looking back over his shoulder he thought he saw Harvey rolling down the pile of crates.

The nearest door to the building was unlocked. Inside there was one long brick corridor painted in institutional green. Four rooms, all open, led off on the right, like a rail car. The whole place smelled of food. He saw why. The first room was all sinks and racks. The next was fitted with ovens, giant boilers and utensils. In the next, huge trays of vegetables and some sort of baked fish dish lay cold on wooden tables. None of these rooms, he saw at once, had any other door. Nor did the last, which seemed to be a glass and crockery store.

That left only one door, straight ahead, at right angles to all the rest. If there was a way out—and there must be—it was somewhere through there.

The door was closed. He grasped the handle and paused to listen. Voices, laughter, the rattle of plates. No-one had yet appeared behind him. There had to be more than one way out. Still he hesitated. The door behind him burst open. He didn't wait to look.

The room was brilliantly lit, softly carpeted. He blinked. There was the way out, surely—the door opposite. He had the impression of six or eight men in overalls round a table, eating a meal. Conversation stopped. They stared at him. A chair or two scraped back. He heard one of them begin: "Just a minute. Do you mind telling me who you are and—"

But Willi had jumped at the far door. It opened inwards. He

dived through it—and walked straight into a tall, majestic figure coming in: a man of more than 200 pounds and at least a head taller than six feet. His weight and size bore Willi back into the room. He held Willi by the upper arms, more in surprise than outrage. "You are in a hurry!" he said.

Someone who had got up from the table was behind him now, a hand on his shoulder. "Just a minute, just a minute," he repeated angrily.

The door from the corridor slammed open and Harvey stood there, the gun in his hand. More men milled into the room behind him, shouting. One struck at Harvey's arm daringly, taking the gun and the stance as evidence of some form of unlawful aggression.

Willi moved. He slammed the edge of his hand against the big man's throat and, whipping round behind him, pushed him staggering, choking towards Harvey. He was through the door and out into the night immediately.

The door had opened under a flimsy canopy. He was now at the front of the factory, which bulked sombrely on his left. He turned right this time, back the way he'd come. He ought to have stayed within the complex of back streets in the first place. He raced diagonally across the road, lengthening his stride with a loping hop which helped the leg.

Chest heaving, muttering to himself, Willi put everything he had into this last attempt. He couldn't keep this up. Yet far from getting clear, he'd twice come within inches of being shot—with his own gun. As if to remind him of his folly, a third shot battered the night behind him. Not too dangerous, with Harvey still perhaps two hundred yards behind. He couldn't break his stride to look back to check that. He kept his eye on the turning which led back to the flats and the safety of the maze of small streets. Harvey evidently knew very little about guns or how unlikely it was he'd hit anything with a .22 automatic at that distance, but Willi fervently hoped he'd keep trying. He had a limited number of shots and each time he steadied to aim the damn thing he was probably giving away fifty yards.

As he swept into the 'square' a searing pain shot the whole length of his leg, from the plate up to the knee and above. He almost stumbled and fell. He didn't know what had gone wrong, but the excruciating pain and the numbness which was closing on the muscles of the leg slowed him at once. Panic returned. It might be possible to lose Harvey now in these streets, but the pain itself raised a new problem. What

292

if he now needed a doctor? Before this, Ronnie might have been able to help. Now she would be watched continuously; Harvey would see to that. It occurred to Willi now for the first time that she might face charges.

He limped across the open ground between the flats, every step an agony. The leg began to feel heavy. He forced himself another fifty yards, dragging the leg. That was all he could manage. Harvey was seconds behind him. And he wouldn't now make it to the main road. He looked around, distractedly.

A narrow strip of garden ran along the backs of the blocks of flats here. There were no railings, only a sparse hedge. He crashed through and moved deep into shadows. And even as he did so, Harvey's running footsteps came in from the road. Nonsensically, the urgent ring of a police-car bell thrummed by away to his left. Towards the factory, perhaps. He heard other men running into the square.

Moving stealthily, feeling his way round obstacles, he worked along the strip until he was halfway in and invisible from the corner. The ground underfoot was broken, uneven. He could make out some sort of vegetable crop. His one hope now was that Harvey and anyone else who had joined the chase would assume that he had made it to the main road after all. It was certainly possible and they didn't know he was hampered by the leg.

In front of him now loomed some sort of iron rig, as tall as the block itself almost. At first he took it to be a fire escape. He had navigated round two such structures in his anxiety to get deep into the strip. He strained to see in the gloom. Then he realised what it was. The thing was a kind of external dumb-waiter, presumably serving kitchen hatches at each level. He almost moved on. But if he went any further now he'd be past the middle of the strip and moving out towards the other end. He examined the lift again. The goods platform seemed to be an open-sided box, running in a skeleton shaft. It looked big enough to squeeze into. The base felt solid enough. He turned his back to it, planted his feet firmly on the rusting iron supports and backed into it, folding up into a squatting position as he went.

The wooden platform had been up an inch or two from the base level and his weight dropped it noisily down into the stop position. The sound set adrenalin pumping anew round his system.

With his head bent sufficiently he could fit inside comfortably enough, though his legs still dangled. He shifted

293

further back to make room for them. Again the platform jolted noisily on its runners. He froze, one leg in and one out. When he was sure that nothing moved near him he reached forward and grabbed his left leg to wedge it up into the box. The noise from the square was louder now. It sounded as if dozens of people had gathered there.

The left leg bent easily enough at the knee, but when he caught it lower down he was shocked by the size of the swelling. He still couldn't see, but the flesh was tender and puffed to perhaps twice the normal size. When he got the leg in, too, the strain on the calf made him sweat with pain.

A torch probed from the road end of the garden strip and finding nothing swept on. For three of four minutes there was silence. Then footsteps returned. The torch beam swept the strip again and blinked off. He sensed that whoever it was had turned away.

In some ways he was well concealed inside the hoist. Yet anyone taking a close look would find him quickly enough. Now he reached out for one of the cables and exerted a steady downward pressure. Nothing happened. It was the wrong one. He eased his position, throwing his left shoulder against the side of the box both to relieve the pressure on the foot and to tilt himself a little. He tried the other cable. This time he felt the hoist move upward—steadily, easily and with only a minimum of well-oiled rumble. He heaved again and glided up three feet. He repeated the process until he was about twelve feet off the ground.

He hung there motionless, cramped but relieved.

There was a new sound from the road end of the garden. He strained to intercept it. Someone was searching—steadily, carefully, making no attempt at stealth. He turned his head, but his vision from the box was limited to a narrow area behind his right shoulder. With his shoulders wedged it was impossible to screw his neck far enough around.

It had to be Harvey.

He froze again and began breathing through his open mouth, though Harvey was making enough covering noises.

Either the hoist or Harvey's efforts had attracted the attention of a tenant. Above him a window sash rattled up and he heard curtains swish aside. He could see nothing, but a man's voice grumbling to someone else inside the room, sounded suddenly very close at hand. As close as the first floor. He glanced down and was appalled to see that a long

294

yellow rectangle of light from the open window now lay over the garden directly below him.

Willi sweated anew. He couldn't be seen by the man above, but if Harvey got to this point before the man turned off the light he would almost certainly be seen clearly and at once from the ground. He ducked his head between his knees, offering the least white area to any upward glance. Why hadn't he gone up further? It was too late now. He heard Harvey thrashing through some taller crop than he had encountered. It sounded only yards away.

The light remained stubbornly on. He could even see the glimmer of it on the lower lip of his box.

He knew the moment Harvey stepped into the pool of light. The man above leaned out further and called down: "What the hell is going on down there? Do you know that's a private garden?" And when there was no answer: "What the hell are you doing?"

He heard Harvey mutter something and turn away. The man above him, apparently satisfied he had been effective, slammed down his window. A moment later the light was switched off. A police car swept by at the top of the strip, its bell ringing frantically. Then there was silence.

The pain in Willi's leg was now aggravated by his cramped position. He heard himself breathing noisily again and at once opened his mouth to control and soften the sound. With his arms wedged in tightly he was unable to check his watch; he began counting off sixty-second intervals. After three such he risked inching forward to look down. Nothing. And no sound. It seemed Harvey was satisfied that he had checked the garden. Willi began to feel that he was a little safer. But if he were Harvey, and given the rage which Harvey felt, he wouldn't give up too easily. The apparent arrival of the police in the area might impede his actions, but he would remain at hand, hoping to get one clear shot at his quarry.

Gingerly, Willi edged his way to the front of the box and eased his left leg over the edge. Hanging it that way made no appreciable difference to the level of the pain, but it might, perhaps, prevent worse pain or disabling cramp. And with one leg out there was more room for the other. He sat like that for a time. It was an odd sensation, dangling there above the sooty crops of this unlikely vegetable garden. But he began to feel strangely at peace. It was still possible, perhaps, to get free and clear. He began to toy with the idea that if he did get clear it might be possible, in another town, to

295

stage an innocent accident which would enable him to get treatment for his leg. Or would a surgeon recognise un-British surgery? He shook his head, impatiently.

He grasped the cables of the hoist and pulled steadily, imperceptibly. No sound. An inch or two at a time, it seemed, could be managed noiselessly. He set himself to manage the whole descent that way. He stopped, suddenly, struck by a new thought. Harvey had seemed to move deeper into the garden, rather than turning back below him. What remained of the garden he had certainly checked by now. So that unless he was waiting in the shadows ahead he had found an alternative way out. Was that useful? It might be.

There were voices again from the road end. What if Harvey was already under police restraint? If he was he was also explaining his motives and the whole area would soon be swarming with police. Willi gritted his teeth. He would have to move soon. He resumed his gentle pulling on the cables. The wheels rumbled once, but softly. He waited, then began again.

When he finally touched bottom his hands were dark with old grease. He stepped out and stretched his aching body. He felt much better. The pain had diminished a little. His spirits soared and he moved down the garden carefully, like a man balancing on shaky stepping-stones. He saw the three posts in the moonlight ahead.

He was halfway between the hoist and the end of the garden when he sensed a movement in the deep shadows on his left. He froze.

The man Jerome stepped from behind the last of the iron hoists and stood squarely on to him, his feet on a narrow path through some root crop.

Willi was stunned but not unduly apprehensive. He stood his ground, trying to read Jerome's intention from his stance, from what he could see of his face. Nothing had been said. Willi mimed a kind of defeat. "All right," he whispered. "You shall have the money." He moved a step nearer.

At once the little man raised his stick, holding Willi off with it.

Like Frank Marsh, Willi glanced down at the tip of the stick, thrust against his chest. "Not here," he said softly. "There's no time to—"

He heard an odd metallic sound. He began the thought that Jerome must have punched at him hard with the stick. But he never completed it. His weight had been on his good right leg. And it was that way that he fell, soundlessly, into the neat rows of swedes.

Fairbrother moved swiftly. He winced at the idea of depressing Stella's spring here on the concrete path. But it was a matter of urgency. He replaced the ferrule.

As he had hoped, the chase had come full circle. He had entered the garden behind Harvey, confident that he, too, anxious to avoid the mounting activity in the square, would leave by the narrow inner path.

Only by chance had he discovered Willi. While he waited for Harvey to check the last third of the garden strip he had heard the gentle rumble of the hoist.

Not really luck, he told himself. Painstaking attention to detail. Following the thing through. Taking one's time. That is what paid off and always had.

He pulled the brim of his bowler a little lower over his eyes and stepped smartly out onto the footpath. He crossed the road and walked steadily out of the area and towards West Ken underground station.

50

A cordon of blue-painted police steel-helmets began to blossom across the mouth of the garden strip behind the blocks of flats opposite Ronnie's and on the far right end. Despite the efforts of the police, a small crowd was forming, being dispersed and reforming again in shifting patterns like leaves in an erratic wind. Unanswered questions hung excitedly in the moonlit confusion.

Frustrated and fearful, but still in control, Ronnie watched from the hallway of her own block. She had been standing there when the first police car swept by. She gave no thought to the flat. No news would reach her there, and Willi would never, now, risk returning. She had waited, hoping that he would somehow double back, eluding Harvey. He had left things in the flat he would need. She had them ready.

Still she hesitated. It was just possible that he had got away. He might, she thought, be anywhere in the shadows, even now, waiting a chance to get clear. A few seconds with

297

her, a few whispered words, would be enough to set up a rendezvous. He would need her for every kind of help now.

Five minutes passed. It began to look as if the police activity on her right was not just incidental, but was focused there. She began to walk that way, peering into the shadows for Willi as she went.

Two more police cars had arrived there by the time she got to the corner. Frightened, she pushed through the crowd and came up against a wall of uniformed police.

A hand gripped her shoulder. "Come on now, Miss, it's nothing you want to see."

"I have to get through," she muttered. She pushed hard and the man looked down at her. Taken aback perhaps by her looks and her obvious distress, he yielded fractionally for a moment. It was enough. Ronnie broke free and ran past him into the garden.

Lights from half a dozen flats had banished most of the shadows. More uniformed police and two or three men in plain clothes were clustered round a service hatch. She saw Harvey, flanked by police. She ran forward, tripped, fell headlong. A hand reached for her and grasped her arm. She shook it off, bursting through the knot of men, using her arms like a swimmer. Another constable caught her round the waist as she plunged forward, but he was off-balance and again she broke free.

She looked where everyone else looked.

It was Willi. As she had known it would be. His face was bloodless, eerie in the searching moonlight. No-one bothered her now. She stared distractedly as two men lifted him on a street-shelter stretcher. A police cape was handed through and his head was covered with it.

Harvey, moving between two policemen, struggled forward. "For God's sake!" he said. The words meant nothing to her. She turned to look at him. He shook his head sadly at her. And again his meaning was lost on her.

She stepped back half a pace, steadied herself and at once crashed her fist into his face, using every ounce of her strength. Harvey staggered back and would have fallen, but for the men flanking him, who caught at his jacket and pulled him upright. Police closed round them both.

Willi is dead. Ronnie allowed herself, as if in a dream, to be marched out of the gardens to one of the police cars. Two ambulance men with a stretcher passed her on the way in. By the car there was a wait. A burly man with apopleptic cheeks was striding about, demanding to know from subordinates: "Where's the gun? Who's looking after that?" Another produced it, wrapped carefully in a handerchief. "Right," the other said. "I'll take the girl with me. You fetch the man."

In the car behind, Harvey sat between two uniformed constables. People peered in at him. Nothing was said as the car nosed out into the main road and turned away.

At last Harvey said: "I want to talk to a Chief Inspector Ainslie." And then: "The man in charge of the Eastcote murders."

"Christ!" the driver exclaimed. "What have we got? A mass murderer?"

One of the uniformed men now reached over and took Harvey's wallet and identity card from his inside breast pocket. Harvey suffered the indignity without comment. Ryder was dead. He had failed to kill him. All right, Frank? No, not all right. But at least I tried. He knew he should feel exultant anyway because someone had killed Ryder, but his mind treacherously gave priority to an endless play of Ronnie's expression of loathing. His nose still ran blood. His face was bruised and aching. What the hell would McNair make of all this?

"Jesus!" the constable said, reading from Harvey's wallet. "You aren't going to believe this. He's a war correspondent."

"A bit off his course," the driver said drily. "The war's in Germany, not West Ken."

Trying hard to keep touch with reality, Harvey stared at the fat neck of the driver. A police car, he told himself. Arrested. I just tried to kill a German and failed. But someone else had the same idea. Something clicked in his mind. What was it Ryder had said? One of your own countrymen. A man called . . . Jerome?

He felt hysteria rise. Had he nearly killed the wrong man? Had he wanted to believe that Ryder killed Frank? Because of Ronnie?

There was no way to put that right. If Ronnie's face had not been enough, then he was guilty anyway because he'd tried, by God, he tried! If not for his intrusion, Ryder might be alive and in Ronnie's flat now. At worst, sometime, a POW. He choked back what might have been a sob of anguish, confusion, despair. Not knowing which he felt most, it turned into a choking laugh. Perhaps not liking the sound of that they put him in an interview room to cool off.

51

Time, as it does under the impress of shock, had collapsed for Ronnie. Released almost immediately by the police and driven home, she had almost no memory of what had been said to her. Only two circumstances penetrated the fog of her isolation and fatigue: it was almost daylight when she returned to the flat, and her door still stood wide open.

Moving with what seemed rational intent, she bathed, put on a long woollen robe, lay down on her bed and fell asleep at once.

Either in minutes or hours, she surfaced wretchedly and with difficulty. The doorbell was ringing insistently.

Ainslie stood in the hallway, unashamedly watched by little Miss Fletcher across the landing, who could not, apparently, find her key. Ronnie let him in and followed him into the living room.

She looked at him dully, frowning. She was horrified that she had slept at all; she should have been awake. "He was only killed a few hours ago," she said, puzzled. For the first time she noticed Willi's old Thorens and his cigarettes on the seat of a chair, where Harvey had dropped them. She picked up the lighter and held it as if she might warm it into life. She began to cry and Ainslie sat for a time watching her.

At last Ainslie said, gently: "Mr Marsh says he is a German. Was German. You knew that?"

Ronnie nodded, more composed.

"His name?"

"Willi Reiter. R-e-i-t-e-r. Major, Luftwaffe."

Ainslie wrote it down as if it were the most normal thing in the world. "Why was he here?" he said, still writing.

Ronnie looked at him, but over and over her eyes cut out while she saw Willi's pale face in her mind's eye. She put up her hand slowly, to cover her face and it was some time before Ainslie realised that she was crying again.

"I mean, it isn't as if killing old people in Eastcote was much of a contribution to the German war effort," Ainslie said.

"No!" Ronnie shouted. She shook her head furiously, unable to speak.

"No?"

"That—was Jerome," Ronnie sobbed.

"Are you saying Jerome?"

"Yes."

Ainslie waited a minute or two. "Suppose you tell me," he said kindly.

"I'll make some coffee," Ronnie said in a shaky but near-normal voice. "It's a long story."

Ainslie was a good listener. He made notes, never once interrupting her flow. Once, when the coffee cups were empty, he got up, took them to the kitchen and returned with refills. He set his own down by the bureau, alongside his notes, and took Ronnie's across to a low table. He bent then and did up half a dozen of the tiny buttons of her robe, closing it across her thighs. Startled, Ronnie buttoned some at the top. She had been sprawled, half-kneeling in the chair, naked under the robe and with only one or two buttons closed. She blushed. "I'm sorry," she said.

"Don't apologise," Ainslie said without rancour. "Fat men, of course, don't have normal instincts. It's a widespread belief."

"What do you know about Jerome?" He picked up his gold pencil again.

"I saw him once."

"You did?" He looked up sharply.

"So did Harvey—Marsh. At the Savoy on the night of Harvey's party. You know about the party?"

"Yes."

"Jerome passed us—Willi—" she choked on his name and had to begin again "—Willi and I. In a corridor. Harvey would have seen him for longer in the washroom. Willi told me that."

"But of course Marsh didn't know that the man he saw was the man Jerome?"

"I suppose not."

"How would you describe Jerome?" Ainslie poised his pencil.

Encouraged, Ronnie became animated, urgent. "He was short, a little man in every way. Perhaps five feet four inches. White hair, about sixty. Dapper. Dressed as if for the City. Public school manner. Genial. Polished." She looked at Ainslie, petitioning his belief. "He killed Frank and the woman across the street. Not Willi."

"You told me."

"He wanted money to stay away from Willi," she persisted.

"Perhaps."

"He did! He had been paid to kill Willi. I told you all that. He called them 'your friends'. 'Your friends want you dead', he told Willi. He meant that—"

"Yes," Ainslie interrupted. "You said so." He hurried on: "You may have to tell this all over again to Special Branch."

"Gladly," Ronnie said with warmth. She went out to the kitchen and returned eating a biscuit. "And Harvey?"

"What about him?"

"What will happen?"

Ainslie considered. "The police—the Army, too, for that matter—are not terribly keen on people who take it on themselves to attempt the work of the armed forces. Killing Germans is Army work. He should have handed Reiter over to the police."

"And then?"

"Reiter would have been tried."

"But he hadn't done anything . . ."

Ainslie simply looked at her. Ronnie saw he could not be moved, that he was a fair man, that he was treating her with some kindness. She let it go. "And Harvey?" she repeated.

"I doubt if there will be any charge—under the circumstances. But I wouldn't be surprised if he has an uncomfortable few days while he waits to find that out."

Ronnie thrust Harvey out of her mind. That was over. She hoped not to see him again. If she did, she would at once attack him again. She shivered and seemed to gather herself together. "Can I ask you something?"

Ainslie looked away. "What would that be?"

"Major Reiter . . . Where will he be buried?"

Ainslie inclined his head, but he took a long time to answer. "I'm one of the few people who can answer that authoritatively," he said. "As it happens. And I only know by accident." He put away his notebook. "Always assuming his identity can be checked, there are three places a German serviceman killed in this country might be buried. It happens from time to time of course. They get shot down, pulled out of wreckage . . ."

"Where?"

"Well, Greenwich is one place. Woolwich is another. And Fulham."

"That's right. Fulham Old Cemetery," Ainslie nodded. "It's no more than half a mile or so from here. In which case I'd say

that was the most likely bet. There are others there already."
He said it gently, meaning it to be of some comfort to her.

Ronnie had asked her question without ever actually contemplating a grave for Willi. Tears ran down her face. She made an effort to ask: "When?"

Ainslie said, expressionlessly: "There will be some formalities. It's not up to the local authority. The War Graves Commission will handle everything. But leave it with me. I'll let you know, if you like."

Ronnie managed a smile of thanks. She knew she should be anxious but could only feel numb. "Are you going to press charges against me?"

"Not I. Some might think differently. But it's unlikely, I think." Very neutrally he added: "But you may be in for some unwelcome publicity. If you could leave London . . ."

She went to the door with him. "You've been very kind," she said. "Why? You can't approve of me much."

She had the impression that Ainslie surprised himself as much as her when he turned and touched her cheek gently. "Don't tell me people haven't been kind to you all your life," he said. "A beautiful girl like you." He put his hand on the latch. "You've been very foolish. But for the most part prosecution is about criminal intent, not foolishness."

52

Harvey was back on the night desk. McNair, sympathetic and chauvinistically indignant on his behalf, had suggested it as an interim therapy, but it didn't seem to be working out very well. Twice in one week he had slipped up badly on matters of timing and news treatment. Unruffled, McNair had advised him to see the week's schedule out and then take a holiday until the War Office unscrambled a new movement order for him. Harvey was both contrite and grateful, yet remained unable to find the cutting edge the job required. He repeatedly found himself, as now, staring stupidly at a carbon book while the room receded, darkly distant and seemingly none of his concern. The clock raced, but the words and their purpose remained elusive, bereft of meaning.

To protect the agency he adopted the Ron Bass method of running the news desk: he gave the work to juniors, subbed it apathetically and hoped to God he wasn't doing anything too awful.

The war was hotting up again everywhere. It was the wrong time to be even temporarily out of action. In less than ten days British airborne troops had landed in and liberated Greece; the Dumbarton Oaks Conference had proposed, and all but agreed, the formation of a United Nations Organisation; Churchill and Eden had been in Moscow for a third summit conference; Rommel had committed suicide—his obit had at last disappeared from the hook under the bridge of the news desk; the Germans had fallen back across the lower Rhine; and a final offensive had begun to drive the Japanese out of Burma.

Once or twice he looked up to find one or other of his re-write men looking at him speculatively. He checked the clock now, trying desperately to focus on a fresh batch of cable flimsies. Rival political factions were squabbling in Athens over who was going to run the new Greece. He signalled Berry, a promising recruit from Reuter—PA. "See what you can make out of this. No more than a page unless there's more blood in there somewhere. Stupid sods; not content with killing Germans or being killed, they're doing it to each other now. Dateline it Athens, Monday. I know it's Sunday. But only for another hour and it will look a lot fresher." Berry had his carbon book in his machine before Harvey could light his eighteenth cigarette in four hours.

"Tea!" he shouted. He settled himself in his chair, pulled his Royal close and snatched up a flimsy. "Why isn't there any fucking heating on?" he grumbled. He was embarrassed to find McNair at his elbow suddenly.

"There's a war on," McNair said amiably. "Can you give me a minute?" He indicated his small, frosted-glass cubicle.

"Sure." Harvey looked round. The Desk could never be left, not even for ten seconds. "Bob! Take the Desk a minute, will you?" He was aware that the senior was Berry, but knew it was the right move when Tickner, a 22-year-old, wounded at Dunkirk, flushed with pleasure.

McNair smiled, closing the door. "Nice," he said. "Tickner's a good lad. That's better than a raise for him."

"Scrooge," Harvey said. "You'll be taking schoolboys off their paper rounds next."

McNair adopted a serious expression. McNair hardly ever

sat in his office. It was only a place to keep things. He put both legs up on his desk. A litter of old copies of *Saturday Evening Post* slid off the other side of the desk, overturning a rack of used, wax Dictograph coils. "I'll make this quick and painless." He paused, eyebrows raised. "You don't know what's happened? Okay. Fine. Here it is. War Office have gone coy. They don't want to confirm your accreditation. Or, put it another way ... *What* accreditation?" He looked briefly at Harvey and then fixedly at his toecaps. "Okay," he said. "Let's have a few tears or four-letter words. Then I'll tell you what we're going to do. It's a blow. But they don't own the news world. It isn't a tragedy."

Harvey said nothing. He was trying himself out with the news. He spelled it out to his feelings, quietly. Take the uniform back? So what? Frank wouldn't know now. No big, no nice logical step forward in experience and status. So what? There was no Ronnie to impress, either. No anyone. And he was unimpressed with himself already. He had to remember to register dismay because it was polite and appropriate. He pursed his lips, drew breath and stimulated iron control.

"Yes," McNair said. "It's tough. But I'll tell you what I've done. I've had a word with New York. We have a Canadian there, Byers, who will be more than adequate here. You're going to New York to take his place for a year or so." He beamed, clearly expecting pleasure and relief.

"What as?" Harvey simulated concern overlaying pleasure.

"You'll take your turn as Night News Editor," McNair said. "Just as here. When you come back—who knows—Berlin? Paris?"

"Great!" Harvey said. "Mac, you know I'm grateful. You won't hear of any cock-up there." He forced a huge grin.

"Too right I won't. Or you'll end up in Rangoon for Reuter of Delhi for UPI." McNair put his feet down and stood up. "Okay?"

"Marvellous!" Harvey said. He gripped McNair's hand with a late rush of genuine feeling. "Want some tea? I just called for a brew."

53

Himmler was in a ferment of indecision. No sooner had he
arrived back in Berlin from Wolf's Lair, after a protracted
stay at the court of his idol, than he heard rumours that
Hitler's health had declined suddenly. It became a matter of
priority to return at once to offer help and sympathy. But
return where?

Goebbels had suggested that the Führer-train might be
used to take him to Munich and that the Swiss specialist he
had consulted earlier would be flown to him there. Was
Hitler aboard his train now? And was Munich definitely his
destination? Goebbels was vague. He got nothing much from
Bormann, either, at first. Instead, Bormann had wanted to
talk about the Hitler decree officially establishing the
Volkssturm—under Party control, of course, but with training
and equipment being supplied by Himmler as Commander of
the Replacement Army.

Himmler knew better than to be evasive. Anything of that
nature would be swiftly reported to Hitler. And at the moment the *Volkssturm* was the one ray of light and hope in
Hitler's life. Hastily, Himmler promised to meet with all
concerned within a day or two and personally undertake the
supervision of whatever was agreed. Meanwhile, where was
Hitler? Bormann admitted that the Führer had not finally
made up his mind to travel to Munich. He might divert to
Berlin. Even more irritated and anxious—what if he flew to
Munich only to find that the Führer had arrived in Berlin?
—Himmler pressed harder. Where was he now? Aboard the
Führer-train outside Prenzlau, while he made up his mind.

Himmler left for Prenzlau at once.

On arrival he found to his great annoyance that Goering's
personal train was drawn up in the same siding.

After a long and humiliating wait, which was never explained to him, Himmler was admitted to the Führer's pan-
elled study, where he found Goering sipping mint tea. Gritting
his teeth, Himmler expressed at length his concern over the
Führer's health and urged him to go on to Munich while the

specialist was being summoned by air. Goering agreed, but went on to dominate the conversation. Himmler wished he would go. Hitler, withdrawn and glazed, seemed to have shrunk. He had a convulsive tick in the side of his face. His complexion was poor and his hands shook. He said little and for once seemed content to have company for its own sake.

Goering seemed in particularly good form. Again and again he struck just the right note of optimism and calm. It irritated Himmler so much that he found himself bumbling insipid agreement. After an hour, Hitler indicated that he was tired and wanted to rest.

As he left the train, Himmler, in a mood to be spiteful, said nastily: "You have probably had time to study the English newspapers?"

Goering admitted he hadn't. Genially, he clapped a hand on Himmler's shoulder and guided him towards his own train. It would have been more satisfying if Goering had shown some guilty premonition about what he wanted to say, Himmler felt. Then he wouldn't have to submit to the humiliation of accepting Goering's hospitality in order to gain time to get his point in.

As it was, he had to wait while seemingly innumerable aides relayed messages, delivered despatches and acted for all the world as if Goering had taken over direction of the war himself.

When at last they were alone, Himmler said testily: "If you had read the English papers you would have seen that the man Reiter, who disappeared at the same time as his brother, of the SS, turned up in England. Dead."

He watched closely, but Goering did not appear concerned. "I know," he said blandly. "We have been asked to furnish details of his rank and so on to the War Graves people." He beamed at Himmler and then, toning down a little, added: "I even thought of telling the Führer about it. But I didn't want to rub the old Hess sore. And he isn't well enough to cope with any new riddles." He stared Himmler down.

"You no doubt know, too, what he was doing there and how he got there," Himmler persisted.

Goering shook his head. "Would you care for some more tea? I think I'd like something a bit more convincing than that mint stuff." Himmler brushed the offer aside with a curt gesture. Goering pressed a bell by his chair. "I haven't the least idea what he was doing," he said cheerfully. "Or how he got there. What is your man doing there?"

Himmler was shaken. "The brother?" His voice had risen to a squeak. "In England? Can you prove it?"

Goering laughed aloud. "No. But can you prove he isn't?" He broke off to give the order for his tea. He swivelled his bulk around in his chair and, folding his arms, gazed reflectively out on the autumn shades of the countryside. "I'm inclined to the view that they went together—somehow." He blinked at Himmler sardonically. "Your man was fairly high-ranking, wasn't he? Would he have had contacts, perhaps, able to help them both get away?"

For perhaps a minute Himmler wrestled with the knowledge that he had been outwitted. He would digest that later, and if the opportunity presented itself he would ensure that Goering paid for it. Meanwhile, it was obviously better to retire in good order. He forced himself to relax a little. He yawned—just to show he wasn't on edge. "I sometimes wonder," he said, simulating reflection, "whether we'll ever know the truth of half of what's happening around us." He let that sink home, and when Goering grunted an easy assent, said on a rising note: "You aren't returning to Berlin by any chance?" He looked around him. "You do yourself well aboard this thing."

54

Thelma Franks had been delighted when her brother Jerome had announced, without any prior intentions, that he was going to give up his shop and his flat. Not only that, but he was going to do it immediately.

She had been speechless with pleasure when he added that he had thought over her suggestion that they should join forces at Herne Hill—and was now prepared to do that, too. She had wanted that for so long that it was some days before the pure pleasure of it gave way to speculation about Jerome's motives. Even then she kept her thoughts very much to herself. It was so nice to be together. Even if it had been all a little sudden.

The speed with which he had closed both the shop and the flat and put the furniture from both into store had astounded her. Of course Jerome was a very positive man. He always knew exactly what he wanted. He hadn't cut business itself off just like that. He evidently had some business still in progress. There were calls from time to time. The man Hands, evidently a trader of some kind from quite a different end of the market, was still in touch by telephone. People like that were very useful, too. Over the matter of the furniture, for example. Jerome had explained that many firms these days were short of transport and storage space. That was why Hands had been commissioned to undertake the moving.

At one time she had, perhaps, been a little short with Hands. He had interrupted so many nice moments. And he had such a common way of speaking. But he had been helpful. And she noticed that Jerome himself never, never fobbed him off with a message—through her, for instance, but always took the calls himself, or returned the calls as soon as he was available, no matter how tired he was or how inconvenient it might be. It was clearly in Jerome's interests to give the man these courtesies.

So here they were, just the two of them. The garden was not at its best now. But Jerome would enjoy it so much in the spring. Meanwhile, Thelma was discovering all over again the pleasures of cooking for an appreciative eater. Even with rations the way they were, marvellous things could be done if you were inventive. Jerome seemed to marvel at what she achieved with very little. He was lavish with his praise, as always.

Today, she was poaching some white fish. There was plenty of that, thank goodness. With a little sauce and a tiny drop of white wine, the potatoes creamed and piped, and with fresh spinach, she would produce a masterpiece.

It gave her enormous satisfaction to feed Jerome. Poor Norman, now, had been one of those unrewarding eaters, gobbling everything down in a few minutes, hardly pausing for breath. Jerome savoured his food, just as he savoured his books.

Thelma smiled to herself as she creamed a generous number of potatoes so finely that she could pipe them like icing. Another pleasure she had these days was sitting at ease with her brother. These autumn nights, Jerome on one side of the fire with his current book and she on her side with her mending . . . Jerome got so lost in his reading that he didn't mind, or even notice, if she switched on the radio. She might do that this evening—after they'd done the dishes together.

Sandy McPherson was on for half an hour on the General Forces programme. A cinema organ was lovely; reminding her vividly of her early years with Poor Norman. They had been great cinema-goers then, she and Norman. The organ had often been the best part of those cinema visits: the way it came up like that, glowing all colours and the organist already playing . . .

All at once she couldn't quite see the creamed potato because her eyes were filling with near-tears. How silly! After all these years! It must be because she was so happy again. Living with Jerome, having a man about the house, was almost like being married again. There was companionship, friendship, everything really—except of course for all that other business you had to endure when you were married.

She sniffed and put the pan back on the stove, away from the flame. Dinner would be ready all too soon. She hurried into the drawing-room to warn Jerome.

"In that case, my dear," Fairbrother said, "I'll just wash my hands and be down in a few moments." He beamed at her and went up to the bathroom.

The doorbell rang.

Thelma was trotting through the hall on her way to the kitchen. What a nuisance! She changed course, switching on the porch light from the switch just before the door.

Two men stood in the porch. Rather insignificant-looking men, she thought them; wearing bowler hats and standing one in front of the other. The nearest was small and thin, the other rather large and fat. She thought at once they looked rather like Laurel and Hardy as they stood there so seriously.

"Mr Jerome Fairbrother?" the small one asked. Or was it a question at all?

Thelma opened her mouth to say that it was a very inconvenient moment, that they would be sitting down to dinner very soon. But she remembered Hands, and that Jerome did have some very common-looking business acquaintances. All the wrong sort of people were apt to get hold of quite important antique items, she supposed. Jerome had said as much sometime.

"Won't you come in?" she said. "Mr Fairbrother will be down in a moment." She tried to smile as she thought of her creamed potato stiffening, perhaps becoming unworkable. It would ruin it if she had to add milk and whip it again before piping it into the right shapes. "Perhaps you would like to wait in here." She opened the door to the morning room because she didn't like the room very much at all and felt that would somehow serve them right for coming at a time like this. She couldn't quite invite them to be seated.

Jerome appeared at the top of the stairs. He had heard the voices. He smiled down genially. "Two gentlemen to see you," she said. He frowned and descended to the hall. Thelma put a hand on his shoulder and whispered: "If you could make it quick, Jerome dear. Dinner is only about ten minutes away."

"I'll try," he said. He went through to the morning room. His two visitors stood up, very formally.

"Jerome Fairbrother?" the small one asked.

"Yes, that's right." Fairbrother frowned, sensing an official manner.

"A few words . . ." the larger man said. "Perhaps I should introduce myself. I am Superintendent Tilman, Special Branch. And this is Mr Bernard Cobb, Ministry of Defense."

Fairbrother did not offer a hand. He sensed that it would not be taken. He motioned for them to sit. At once Tilman retired to the back of the room and sat down in an armchair, the one Thelma didn't like but hesitated to throw out because it had such a nice cover. Cobb, though, walked to the fireplace and stood with his back to the empty grate. He was a man of Fairbrother's own build; spare, but with a wintry manner.

Fairbrother took an upright chair by the window, with his back to the window. He felt a chill settle into his abdomen. He reassured himself that they could know very little, if anything, for sure. He forced himself to smile his very special smile. It was probably no more, he thought, than that they had somehow found a thread, a tiny thread of his activities somehow interlaced with those of the Flax and Marsh affair. That was it. In which case he would be polite, helpful and bluff it out. The police, he knew, very rarely acquired as much evidence on their own account as they did immediately they began to interview a suspect. Most people, in fact, convicted themselves. Well, he was fairly smart, too. He dismissed Tilman. He was here, obviously, as the authority for the questions of the Ministry of Defence man, Cobb. And that, in turn, meant that whatever they had was more an intelligence matter than one for the police. He turned to Cobb, genially.

"How can I help?" he said.

Cobb stared at him. "You have friends in Ireland, Mr Fairbrother?"

Fairbrother pursed his lips. "Friends? Not so much friends, perhaps, as business acquaintances. Do you mind my asking why you're asking?"

"I do," Cobb said coldly. "Many business acquaintances, or just a few, or just one or two?"

"Over the years . . ." Fairbrother said judiciously, "quite a few. Some I perhaps wouldn't recognise in the street, though it's been so long since I've seen many of them."

Cobb looked at him a long time. "Your business with these acquaintances would be what?"

"I don't mind your asking," Fairbrother said. "Nothing to hide, of course. Antiques, mostly. Not large antiques. Small things. Jewellery. Pendants, brooches, watch fobs, a watch now and then if it is something of a speciality. That kind of thing."

Cobb gestured impatiently. "And among your acquaintances . . . you would number a man called O'Neill? Aidan O'Neill?"

Fairbrother smirked. He knew of no-one by that name and said so.

"What if his name were not O'Neill," said Cobb. "But something else? Like McCarton? Or Malone?"

A nerve quivered in the corner of Fairbrother's eye, but he was sure it wasn't seen. He managed to look both mystified and bored. "Not even then," he said confidently. But the area of cold in his gut grew and the back of his neck began to feel rigid with the effort of maintaining his poise.

"Mr Fairbrother," Tilman said suddenly, looking out of the window, "have you ever been to Eastcote? You know where it is, of course?"

"I'm sure I have," Fairbrother said at once. "Of course! I move about a great deal in and around London." Without pausing he added: "Look, I really must insist that you tell me what this is all about. I do have some rights, I imagine? I don't really mind very much—if anything I am able to tell you helps in any enquiry you may have in hand, but I do think you might take me into your confidence. If on the other hand, you feel that I have broken some law or regulation, perhaps you will tell me. If you will give me an outline of what case you are pursuing I might even be better equipped to help." He looked from one to the other agreeably. He hoped either to bluff them out of their suspicions or to gain time in which to decide exactly what to admit and what to deny.

Tilman looked at Cobb enquiringly. Cobb, for the moment

arrested by Fairbrother's little speech, looked thoughtful. He cleared his throat and opened his mouth to speak.

The door opened. Thelma put her head into the room, smiled dazzlingly at the two men and whispered to Fairbrother.

"I'm so sorry to interrupt, Jerome dear," she said. "But could you perhaps give me some idea of how long you will be? The dinner—" She shrugged her anxiety about the fish.

"Come in, my dear," Jerome said. He stood up. "I'm afraid that you will have to go ahead without me."

Thelma made a small sound which was very like a wail.

Fairbrother addressed himself to the two men. "I can see, gentlemen, that this is going to take some time. May I suggest that I come with you now, to somewhere we can talk quietly and without interruption?" His expression pleaded forgiveness for his sister. "I'm not sure quite what you have in mind, but I am anxious to satisfy you in every way possible."

"I'm so sorry," Thelma flushed. She turned to Cobb. "I had no idea this was going to be a long thing. I wouldn't for the world have interrupted." They smiled back, Tilman rising from his armchair with difficulty.

Fairbrother was in command again. "I take it you would like me to come with you?"

It was Cobb who nodded.

"Very well. I'll get my hat and coat. Thelma, dear, would you offer these gentlemen something?"

He stepped smartly to the door and, leaving it wide open, bounded upstairs. He turned into the small back bedroom on the first floor which he had lately begun to occupy, opened the wardrobe on the far side of the room and reached into the back.

He brought Stella out.

Without pausing he went into the bathroom next door, closed the door and bolted it.

They knew! They knew about Malone, or whatever his name was. And they knew about Eastcote. Proving it would be no trouble. There was always someone with a good memory who would have seen him. If they could place him there . . . They evidently had both ends of the story. How, he couldn't imagine. From here on they would worry until they had the middle and all the links. And while they did that they would watch him and he would have to sit, like a rat caught, but not killed, in a trap; waiting for the *coup de grâce*. Did it matter how they had managed it? Perhaps they had taken Malone. That alone might not be much—but perhaps Malone had other 'agents'. He had never thought about that. Only about his own security. Perhaps there were many others like himself.

Either way, he knew with certainty that this was it. It was all over. He pushed away the idea that he could struggle against it for a while. It was not dignified. If he had been found, there was only one course open to him. Why else was he standing here—with Stella?

He thought he heard voices in the hall. He took off his jacket and put it neatly over the edge of the bath. Oddly, he felt slightly hungry. Thelma's fish, perhaps. With piped potato. She would be upset, of course. But not so upset as she would be if he stood trial for months. There was a great deal they might uncover. He shrugged.

He measured the distance between himself and the door by balancing Stella between his rib cage and a groove in the moulding. By leaning his weight against it he held the stick in position. Now he reached forward. His arms were too short. He couldn't reach the knob satisfactorily.

Frustrated, he looked round anxiously. The bathbrush? Again he settled the stick between himself and the door, leaned hard and reached forward with the brush. There were two sets of leaves, but they were sprung together. Pressure on one side also lifted the other. It was possible. He tilted the stick down a little to get the right angle of thrust for the blade. It looked just right.

He was very calm. Stella was perfection. Any other way was unthinkable. He didn't bear pain well. There would be no pain with Stella.

There were footsteps on the stairs . . .

Now! He pressed gently with the brush, as if taking the first tension of a trigger. It was a little awkward. He knew a moment of panic that it wouldn't work this way, but dismissed the idea. He tightened his hold on the stick to prevent wobble, took a gentle breath and pressed harder—and at the last moment flinched.

Pain engulfed him. He hadn't allowed for his own fear. He knew Stella to be reliable and instant. But he had flinched just the same. And in that fractional movement had wrecked everything.

For what seemed five seconds he stood almost upright, his body weight leaning on the stick. Someone knocked urgently at the door. His knees gave way slowly and he sat down, suddenly but tidily, his back against the pedestal of the washbasin.

Mistily he knew he should have felt nothing. He had bungled it. Fairbrother the cool, the competent, the perfectionist, had botched the most important death of all. The gall of it and the terror of knowing that he would, after all, survive, were submerged in waves of pain before he fainted and fell over sideways.

55

Ainslie had been right. Willi was to be buried at Fulham. Ronnie had time, during the wait for Air Ministry action, not only to walk the cemetery and find the small section reserved for German servicemen but also to endure again and again in her imagination the moment of burial itself. She had cried a little, lain awake a good deal. With her usual honesty she rejected self-pity. She had, after all, only had Willi very briefly and the full promise of his survival had never been explored. Her pity was for Willi alone, and it endured, fuelling her contempt for Harvey.

When the day arrived she was up at six and ready an hour too early. Composed, even eager, because Willi was to receive one final honour in which all hostility would be set aside, she set out to walk from Queen's Club.

A fine rain, swept about by a south-westerly gusting strongly downriver, had been falling since first light. It was a cheerless, wet-knee day, and unnaturally quiet, as if all London had somehow overslept. In the short distance she saw no more than half a dozen people.

She was relieved to find the Munster Road gate open. She had no status and had worried that she might be excluded. Near the middle of the cemetery three RAF trucks in drab camouflage were drawn up at the side of the main driveway. The drivers, uninvolved, dozed in misted cabs. When she reached the chapel it was still only eight-twenty.

Her arrival startled the young Flying Officer in charge. Nothing had been said about a girl during his sketchy briefing. He found her a most mysterious and tragic figure. Who was she and what had she been to Reiter? At twenty-three he lacked the savoir-faire simply to ask.

Plucked by bureaucratic chance from a seven-day preposting leave for this duty, he had at first protested incompetence, pointing out that he had never commanded anything in his life. The elderly Squadron-Leader had smiled knowingly. "One junior officer, one sergeant, four men for the coffin, six more for the firing party, six rifles, six rounds of .303 blanks and one Jerry flag. We assume the chap was an officer and a gentleman and we bury him with honour. There's a drill for it, of course. Only thing is, we want an early start. No spectators. Otherwise nothing to it. You'll walk it, old lad." Now, too late, he realised he wasn't sure what commands to utter. He looked anxiously around for the sergeant.

At eight forty-five, an old man halted by the tall, ornamental gates, attracted by a rare sight.

Just inside, a young RAF officer and a sergeant stood stiffly at attention as four bare-headed airmen, frowning against the rain, shouldered a flag-draped coffin from the chapel to a position ahead of six more airmen with rifles. After a few moments an RAF chaplain went to the front, and on the sergeant's order the party moved off. The old man shuffled on, disappointed. There were no other spectators.

Ronnie knew her way, and she walked ahead of the slow-moving procession, her umbrella slanted forward, her head down. Tree-bordered and pleasant enough, the cemetery was open to the wind and perhaps a little featureless, without the style and drama of the famous Brompton only a mile away. When she drew level with the RAF trucks she turned back along a minor path. Only then did she see her father standing near the grave with another man, and not until quite close did she realise that the other man was Ainslie. She very much wanted to smile her thanks but her confidence was waning already and she feared that if she unclenched her teeth her composure would dissolve entirely.

Instead she stood well back from the grave with its neat, green tarpaulin border. The RAF party approached.

One moment Ronnie was watching them steadily and the next unreality took her. Her mind buzzed. This coffin—did it really contain Willi? The Willi who had come to her for comfort, slept at her side, and believed that he might survive with her help? It didn't seem at all likely. She wanted to cry now but could not. It was all happening too quickly. She parted her lips, squeezed her eyes shut, willed herself to cry. Nothing happened.

The RAF chaplain began the prayers at the graveside. She heard only a few phrases. Her mind switched on and off. Harvey. It was Harvey who had smashed Willi's hope. How could she have been so wrong about Harvey? Not that the judgements of the old Ronnie mattered now. *She* was dead, too, and a very different Ronnie Croft stood in her place. At last, without any effort at all, tears began to blur her vision.

The chaplain stepped back. On the sergeant's low-voiced order the six airmen took a pace forward, worked their bolts, aimed high, fired their salute and came back to attention.

Under the frugal shelter of some small trees a discreet distance away, two gravediggers shuffled among the sodden leaves. One coughed explosively, the sound like a late echo of the salute.

The young officer stepped forward. (The sergeant will get the rifles and flag back to the stores. You can get off on your leave as soon as it's over.) As the coffin dipped away beneath it, he took one corner of the flag. He folded it, tucked it under his arm and turned smartly.

Ronnie stepped forward in turn and took up a handful of earth. She heard it rattle on the lid of the coffin.

It was over. The chaplain came to speak to her. Again she heard nothing, but they smiled at each other and touched hands as if they were guests introducing themselves at a party. The airmen marched away to their trucks. Only the young Flying Officer lingered.

David Croft took Ronnie's arm and after a suitable wait tried to turn her gently towards the main path, but she resisted strongly. At once he was impatient again. Her liaison with a German had jolted him badly. He could not understand how a girl so essentially English could have loved a German at all, however briefly. To have loved one now, in wartime, seemed not only thoughtless but perverse and undisciplined. Only a deep anxiety about the future of their relationship had prevented Croft from saying so. In these past few days, unable to say anything of comfort or understanding, he had said nothing at all. They had had only short telephone conversations in which each had asked after the health of the other.

Brooding alone at Mount Street, Croft raged at what he

317

saw as his misfortune and even wondered about the effects of the affair on his career. Promptly shamed by that, he later considered that his own unlucky experience with love had disabled him, somehow put him beyond sympathy with what Ronnie, until now a sensible and normal girl, so clearly felt. He had hurried to Fulham only at the last minute, spurred by the conviction that if he was not there he would certainly one day regret it. Cautiously glad that he had come, he remained unresolved about anything else.

"Come home to Mount Street," he urged.

Ronnie smiled vaguely. "Not this week . . ."

"Or we could go to Lammas?"

"If you want . . ." she looked about for Ainslie. "I won't go into a decline," she assured her father. "I'll think of something I want to do. It's too late to get into the war."

"Too late?" Croft was wistful.

"Well, the war is nearly over anyway." She looked at him closely, perceptively. She pressed his arm. "People forget very quickly," she said, meaning it kindly.

Croft was stricken. His eyes filled and he turned away. He took a few awkward steps and stopped. When Ronnie put her arm round him he hugged her close.

He drew a deep breath and stood back, holding on to her hand. He said shakily: "Whatever you decide to do, let's have a few days at Lammas. Call me when you can."

Ronnie watched him walk away. Then Ainslie touched her shoulder. "You have a smudge on your cheek," he said. His smile and manner were those of an old friend. Ronnie rubbed at her face.

"You were very kind to come. Why did you?"

"When I've explained it to myself I'll explain it to you," he said. "Maybe I thought that . . . someone else would make a difference." He looked embarrassed. "To represent, oh, all the rest of us." He studied her seriously and then, seeming satisfied with what he saw, added: "Anyway, if you want a friendly word any time."

Ronnie like Ainslie a good deal. She hoped they would meet again. Now she was the last person left. The two men emerged from under the trees and were loitering nearby. She felt harassed by having to leave, and leave at once. Then she remembered that she could come again, and as often as she needed. As she walked north the gravediggers began work.

The young Flying Officer watched her go. She had not even

noticed him. When she was out of sight he saw her in his mind's eye as she had stood for one hesitant moment outside the chapel: electrifyingly beautiful, her dark hair, pale skin and sad eyes hauntingly appealing. Within the hour he was on his way to his home in Scotland, but for the rest of his life she remained imprinted that way on his mind, enshrined as his unreachable, unknowable ideal.

CLASSIC BESTSELLERS
from FAWCETT BOOKS

☐ ARUNDEL	24456	$2.95
by Kenneth Roberts		
☐ THE LAST ENCHANTMENT	24207	$2.95
by Mary Stewart		
☐ SELECTED SHORT STORIES OF		
NATHANIEL HAWTHORNE	30846	$2.25
Edited by Alfred Kazin		
☐ MAGGIE: A GIRL OF THE STREETS	30854	$2.25
by Stephen Crane		
☐ SATAN IN GORAY	24326	$2.50
by Isaac Bashevis Singer		
☐ THE RISE AND FALL OF THE		
THIRD REICH	23442	$3.95
by William Shirer		
☐ ALL QUIET ON THE WESTERN FRONT	23808	$2.50
by Erich Maria Remarque		
☐ TO KILL A MOCKINGBIRD	08376	$2.75
by Harper Lee		
☐ THE FLOUNDER	24180	$2.95
by Gunter Grass		
☐ THE CHOSEN	24200	$2.95
by Chaim Potok		
☐ THE SOURCE	23859	$3.95
by James A. Michener		

Buy them at your local bookstore or use this handy coupon for ordering.

COLUMBIA BOOK SERVICE
32275 Mally Road, P.O. Box FB, Madison Heights, MI 48071

Please send me the books I have checked above. Orders for less than 5 books must include 75¢ for the first book and 25¢ for each additional book to cover postage and handling. Orders for 5 books or more postage is FREE. Send check or money order only. Allow 3-4 weeks for delivery.

Cost $_____ Name_____

Sales tax*_____ Address_____

Postage _____ City_____

Total $_____ State_____ Zip_____

*The government requires us to collect sales tax in all states except AK, DE, MT, NH and OR.

Prices and availability subject to change without notice.   8211